SUMMER OF PEARLS

PEARLS

· AND ·

SPANISH

BLOOD

MIKE BLAKELY

FORGE®

A TOM DOHERTY ASSOCIATES BOOK
NEW YORK

NOTE: If you purchased this book without a cover, you should be aware that this book is stolen property. It was reported as "unsold and destroyed" to the publisher, and neither the author nor the publisher has received any payment for this "stripped book."

This is a work of fiction. All of the characters, organizations, and events portrayed in these novels are either products of the author's imagination or are used fictitiously.

SUMMER OF PEARLS AND SPANISH BLOOD

Summer of Pearls copyright © 2000 by Mike Blakely

Spanish Blood copyright © 1996 by Mike Blakely

All rights reserved.

A Forge Book
Published by Tom Doherty Associates, LLC
175 Fifth Avenue
New York, NY 10010

www.tor-forge.com

Forge® is a registered trademark of Tom Doherty Associates, LLC.

ISBN 978-0-7653-8361-7

Our books may be purchased in bulk for promotional, educational, or business use. Please contact your local bookseller or the Macmillan Corporate and Premium Sales Department at (800) 221-7945, extension 5442, or by e-mail at MacmillanSpecialMarkets@macmillan.com.

First Edition: January 2016

Printed in the United States of America

0 9 8 7 6 5 4 3 2 1

Praise for *Summer of Pearls*

"The well-developed and carefully defined characters, the detailed setting, and the humor and adventure make this . . . totally satisfying."   —*School Library Journal*

Praise for *Spanish Blood*

"A fine spinner of tales."   —Elmer Kelton,
eight-time Spur Award winner

"Blakely writes with a beauty that rivals the Big Bend country."   —Terry C. Johnston,
author of the Plainsmen series

"Grabs the reader from the first page. [Blakely's] characters are interesting, real, and believable."

—Don Coldsmith,
author of the Spanish Bit saga

Praise for Mike Blakely

"A gifted storyteller."   —*Texas Books in Review*

"Mike Blakely writes with authority and empathy about a people superbly suited to the land they roamed."
—Lucia St. Clair Robson,
Spur Award–winning author of
Last Train from Cuernavaca

"Mike Blakely turns the horses loose in all our souls."
—W. Michael Gear and Kathleen O'Neal Gear,
New York Times bestselling authors of
People of the Songtrail

By Mike Blakely
from Tom Doherty Associates

CONTENTS

SUMMER OF PEARLS

Dedicated to the memory of my
grandfather, Jim B. Blakely,
1906–2000

AUTHOR'S NOTE

Between 1850 and 1910, a series of "pearl rushes" occurred from New Jersey to Texas and from Florida to Wisconsin. In some isolated areas, for mysterious reasons, freshwater mussels produced unusually high numbers of pearls. These local discoveries led to small-scale economic booms for some rural communities as working families enjoyed the treasure-hunting aspects of opening mussels in search of pearls. Most pearl rushes lasted for a year or two at best, as local mussel populations were depleted.

One of the last pearl rushes occurred in 1910 at Caddo Lake, on the Texas-Louisiana border. For this novel, however, I have created a fictitious pearl boom set in 1874 in the dying riverboat town of Port Caddo, Texas, on Caddo Lake. Port Caddo, now a ghost town, was a viable community until railroads preempted the riverboat trade in East Texas.

The Great Caddo Lake Pearl Rush did not occur in 1874, as this novel suggests. All characters in this story are fictitious, and none is based on any particular historical figure. I have, however, attempted historical accuracy in all else, including the riverboat trade, the freshwater pearl industry, life in Port Caddo, and the clearing of the Great Raft by government snag boats. If the Caddo Lake pearl boom had started in 1874 instead of 1910, it might have happened this way. . . .

PROLOGUE

Goose Prairie Cove
Caddo Lake, Texas
1944

To understand the summer of pearls, you must hold the tears of angels in your hand, and know what made those angels cry. You must realize that for every ten thousand moons, only one reveals itself through a rainbow.

I talk crazy when folks ask me about that summer, but if you'll listen long enough, it'll all make sense. It's like the murky floodwaters of this lake, or the morning shade of a cypress brake up some twisted bayou. It's dark and confusing until you stay with it long enough; then it comes clear.

It has taken me a lifetime to absorb everything that happened here in the summer of 1874. I was a youngster of fourteen then. I am a youngster of eighty-four now. You've probably heard there was a lot of killing that summer—the summer of pearls. But there was a lot of living, too. The boilers blew on the *Glory of Caddo Lake*. Gold and silver and pearls circulated like schooling fish. A Pinkerton man shot two outlaws aboard the *Slough Hopper*, and I kissed my first girl.

Some folks say I killed Judd Kelso that year. They say I stabbed him in the chest with a butcher knife. I let folks believe what they will. I am the only one who knows the truth anymore. All the others are dead and gone.

At the time, nobody really cared who killed Kelso anyway. By the end of that summer, just about everybody in Port Caddo *wanted* him dead. Nobody cared to find the killer, except maybe to give him a medal, or a key to the city or something. Of course, a key to the city wouldn't have been worth much, seeing as how Port Caddo barely rated as a village, much less as a city, and would soon be nothing more than a ghost town.

Port Caddo was a riverboat town at the dawn of the age of iron horses. Marshall, the county seat, already had a rail line that went to Louisiana. The Texas & Pacific had plans to build on to that road and make Marshall a major eastern terminal. Railroads could move stuff faster and cheaper than riverboats could, and Port Caddo was not situated well for a railroad, perched as it was at the edge of Big Cypress Bayou, just above Caddo Lake. The railroads were going to be the death of her, and everybody in town knew it.

My pop pretended not to know. That was his job. As editor of the *Port Caddo Steam Whistle,* he was the town's most active booster. In his editorials he kept coming up with schemes designed to keep Port Caddo alive after the railroads took away the riverboat trade.

"We must hold a county bond election to fund a narrow-gauge line from Port Caddo to Marshall," I heard him say one day in the barbershop. "It will link us with the main rail lines."

But few county residents cared to pay to keep our town alive.

Pop also suggested Port Caddo promote itself as a resort town, with duck-hunting clubs, fishing camps, and steamboat excursions on Caddo Lake. "Just think of the folks coming here to line our pockets with money from as far away as Memphis and Little Rock," he told the butcher once in church.

But not many folks had money to burn at resorts that soon after the fall of the Old South and the ruination of the plantation economy. Oh, Pop came up with a lot of wild ideas for the town, and people humored him for doing his job, but we all knew the town was doomed.

I was a boy then, and couldn't stand to think of Port Caddo dying. I still remember the sounds of the steamboat whistles and all those valves and engines hissing hot vapor. I could hear them from the Caddo Academy where I took my lessons. Our teacher, Mr. Diehl, would have fits trying to hold us boys in class when a boat was calling at our stretch of bayou.

Port Caddo was heaven on earth for boys. The steamers would whistle at us when we were out on the lake fishing or fixing up our duck blinds. In summer, all the boys in town turned amphibious and could swim like alligators. On the farms and timber lots, which started just outside of town, we could hunt squirrels, rabbits, hogs, and deer in any patch of woods without even having to ask the owners. All the land was private, but the woodlands were treated as free range then and people just let hogs and boys run wild in them. I knew a thousand secret places in the uplands, and about a million more out in the cypress brakes of Caddo Lake.

Looking back on it after all these years, I forget about the mosquitoes, the water moccasins, the odor of dead fish, and the suffocating summer heat. I can only remember the aroma of pines on the hills, the flat-bottomed hull of my bateau bumping against the cypress knees, and the cool waters of Caddo Lake always at my feet.

Just because the place was heaven for us boys, it doesn't mean it was exactly hell for anybody else, either. Even womenfolk liked it. It was tolerably civilized. A stretch of the main street leading up from the wharf was paved with bricks. We had churches for Methodists, Baptists, Episcopalians, and Presbyterians. Old Jim Snyder ran a store, well-stocked, and Widow Humphry kept a first-rate inn for a town as small as ours. We didn't have a doctor, but as my pop used to say, "We have the healthiest climate in the world. Why the devil would we need a doctor?" We numbered about four hundred souls and everybody knew everybody else's business. Ours was just a podunk backwater bayou town, but we could get anything in the world. The riverboats linked us to New Orleans.

I couldn't tell you how many steamers plied Caddo Lake back then. I never took the time to count them. They came up the Mississippi from New Orleans, entered the mouth of the Red River and steamed past Alexandria to Shreveport.

There they had to find a channel around the Great Raft—the huge logjam that held back the waters of the bayous. The government snag boats worked for years trying to clear the Raft, but every time they carved a channel through the tangle of driftwood, a flood would come along and plug the channel again with trees washed down from upstream.

"Those snag boats are a sin and a waste of taxpayers' money!" my father would rail. "God put the Great Raft there, and when He wants it gone, He'll wash it away. The government has no business playing God!"

To get around the Raft, some steamer pilots came up Cross Bayou, through Cross Lake. Others took the Twelve Mile Bayou route. It depended on where they could find the deepest water. The channels shifted constantly.

Once around the Great Raft and across Albany Flats, the riverboats entered that ancient enigma called Caddo Lake. I have lived by her waters my whole life, and she still hasn't let me in on all of her secrets. She hides things in her muddy waters. Her murky bed swallows all kinds of property. Boats sink and leave no trace. People disappear in her mossy cypress brakes and never come back. Snakes and alligators populate her bayous and sloughs, but they represent little danger. The real killer is the lake herself. You must respect her and suspicion her every little ripple and undercurrent. The moment you trust her, she'll rise up and suck you under like a twig.

Caddo Lake sprawls across the Texas–Louisiana border, like a crazy ink blot, and backs up into a thousand sluggish bayous and still-water coves. She has a lot of open water in her middle, but thickets fringe her shores, islands, and shallow swamps. Huge cypress trees, taller than Roman columns of stone, stand in the water and grip the lake bed. Their roots come up as if for air, bulbous nodules called cypress knees. The branches overhead intertwine and grow bundles of Spanish moss like beards and mustaches. They shut out the sun, channel the wind, and lead the innocent explorers astray with a dark and mesmerizing beauty.

If you want to come home from the cypress brakes, you have to use the wind, the water currents, and the sun. You have to know which sides of the trees the moss grows on in each thicket. You have to know which way the birds fly to feed, and where the snapping turtles go to sun. If you know all that, you might still get lost. If you don't know any of it, the lake owns your corpse as soon as you stray from open water.

But the old steamboats stuck to the open channels, and the pilots knew them well. The water ran shallow in some places, and during the driest months of late summer, the steamers couldn't get into Caddo Lake at all. The trade usually lasted eight months out of the year. From July until some time in October, we didn't see many steamers at Port Caddo. But when the fall rains came and the lake rose again, our little town emerged out of the dog days like a blooming rain lily.

"Spruce up!" my pop would write in his editorial. "The steamers are coming! Pull the weeds and paint the privy!"

Our steamers were small, shallow-draft workhorses for the most part. We didn't have the huge floating palaces like those that plied the Mississippi. Most of ours were stern-wheelers built to handle freight. Side-wheelers were built for wide waters. Our bayous and channels were narrow. Our stern-wheelers carried out a lot of cotton and corn, burned plenty of pinewood, and brought back boxes and barrels of all sorts of things from New Orleans. They also took passengers, of course. We were just two weeks from New Orleans by steamer.

Port Caddo had a favorite riverboat, and her name was the *Glory of Caddo Lake*. Captain Arnold Gentry—as big a local hero as ever walked the streets of Port Caddo—was her owner, builder, captain, and pilot. I can still call his long, spare frame and his gangling gait to mind. He grew pointed mustaches and had a narrow strip of beard on his chin.

Captain Gentry had designed the *Glory* specifically for the Caddo Lake trade. She was the fastest, cleanest, fanciest boat that ever moored in Big Cypress Bayou. She measured a hundred feet and was in the hundred-and-fifty-ton class.

Whenever she steamed into Port Caddo, the *Glory* reminded me of a four-tiered wedding cake, frosted with white paint and trimmed with so much gingerbread work that her carpenters must have worn out a hundred jigsaw blades putting her together. She drew only eighteen inches light, and could get out of the lake, fully loaded, in less than four feet of water. Her five-note steam whistle used to shiver me from the backbone out, and pump adrenaline through my legs like steam through a boiler pipe as I ran to the docks to meet her.

Captain Gentry maintained the *Glory* as a smaller version of the finest Mississippi packets ever to run between

New Orleans and St. Louis. The tops of her tall black chimneys were notched and splayed to resemble huge crowns. The smokestacks had hinges. They could fold down to rest along the hurricane deck so the boat could get up under the cypress boughs in the tight places. Captain Gentry could call at almost any plantation or wood camp on the lake.

For a figurehead, the *Glory* used a beer keg, tapped with a silver spigot extending over the bow. "She draws so light," I once heard Captain Gentry boast in his classic Southern riverboat drawl, "that I can get over the driest sandbar by opening that beer spout and floating on the suds!"

I remember like it was yesterday the last call the *Glory of Caddo Lake* made to our little bayou town. It was the day her boilers blew. The day Captain Gentry died. The same day the stranger, Billy Treat, became our new town hero. That was in June of 1874, and all anybody could talk about were the railroads and the sure fate of Port Caddo. Then Billy Treat came and gave us one last stab at splendor before the town died.

That was the fabulous summer of pearls—a time of great wonder, joy, and hope; of deep tragedy and ruin. When it was all over, Captain Gentry and Judd Kelso weren't the only ones dead. I will tell you about it. The parts I lived I will tell from my own experience. The other parts, the pieces I have put together over the decades, I will tell to you as a story. I have studied over it and thought about it—and even dreamed of that summer—for a lifetime. Even the parts I didn't witness with my own eyes, I can tell with true conviction, for I know what happened.

I guess the mystery over who killed Kelso that night in 1874 will live on forever with some folks, regardless of the truths I am about to unfold. As I said, I'm the only one who knows the truth for sure. I'm the only soul left around here who even remembers the summer of pearls, seventy years ago. I know what happened. I remember it well.

ONE

Port Caddo, Texas
1874

Judd Kelso felt as if he had June bugs in his stomach. He stood at the stern of the *Glory of Caddo Lake,* staring into the muddy waters.

The bayou lay dark and flat as ink in a well. Strange silhouettes of moss and cypress towered around its fringes, raking the dying stars. A pale yellow light reached into the sky from the east, defining the dark, angular shapes of Port Caddo squatting among the pines.

Kelso set his jaw, his facial muscles writhing like animals under his beard stubble. He listened to the sounds of men throwing wood into the furnace, the boat creaking under her load of cotton bales, the cook clanging his skillet down onto his wood-burning stove. He smelled bacon and coffee he knew no one would have a chance to eat or drink. The June bugs crawled in his stomach, and he turned around to study the riverboat.

The *Glory of Caddo Lake* sat low in the water, her first two decks encased in bales of cotton. A buyer in Jefferson had held the cotton in a warehouse for almost a year, waiting for prices to climb at the cotton exchange in New Orleans. Each bale was worth a few pennies more now, and was on its way to market. Captain Arnold Gentry had taken on as much as the *Glory* could handle, careful not to swamp her. She was drawing four feet, but the lake was high and the *Glory* would skim the shoals and plow through the sandbars that lay between her and deep water.

The rousters had stacked bales all the way to the ceiling on the main deck, leaving labyrinth-like passages to the engine room. Then they had stacked more bales on the boiler deck. Cotton completely filled the promenade around the staterooms, blocking the doorways, shutting out the light. The passengers could only enter their rooms now from the doors inside the passenger cabin.

Up the bayou, in Jefferson, Kelso had mused over all the work the rousters put into loading and stacking those bales—bales he knew would never reach New Orleans. He had felt a dark power. Now all he felt were the legs of bugs crawling in his guts.

As the first light of dawn struck the high tops of the cypress trees, the whistle blew. Four notes stepped off harmony as they climbed the scale, then a fifth shook windows as it struck an octave below. Roosters croaked feeble replies. Twin columns of smoke boiled from the chimneys and merged high in the morning air. Cords of pine stood on the foredeck, in front of the furnace. Captain Gentry rang the bell, signaling the engineer to throw open the valves and set the big paddle wheel to work.

Judd Kelso felt the nervous flutter in his stomach surge as he walked forward through the narrow passages left between the cotton bales. "You heard the bell," he said to his apprentice as he reached the engine controls. "Back her into the channel."

The apprentice, seventeen-year-old Reggie Swearengen, cracked the valves and fed steam to the twin engines. The riverboat shuddered as the blades of the paddle wheel dipped into Big Cypress Bayou. The *Glory* backed slowly away from the Port Caddo wharf to the pop and hiss of exhaust valves, rippling the inky bayou.

"Listen for the bells," Kelso ordered as he left the engine room at the stern. "I'm goin' forward."

"Yes, sir," Reggie replied.

Kelso was engineer and mate on the *Glory*. As engineer, he was barely competent, and he knew it. He had little experience with steam machinery. His apprentice had a much better knack for it than he did. He knew just enough about mechanics to keep the steam engines stroking. His real value came in his capacity as mate.

At bossing rousters, Kelso knew he had few equals. The deckhands were muscled-up black men whose scowls alone might wither a timid man. It was Kelso's job to work them as long and as hard as he could without killing them. He gave them no rest when there was work to do taking on freight or fuel, stoking the furnace, or winching the boat over shoals. This was his real job, and he liked it. He thought of the men as little better than animals, and treated them as such.

Kelso stood stump-like in build, shorter than six feet, but weighing over two hundred pounds. His jaws rippled constantly with ridges of muscle as he ground his teeth smooth. The rousters said he had gator eyes—mean little beads set at a slant under the ledges of his bony brow. No one on board liked him, but Captain Gentry knew his worth as a driver of men.

Kelso's father had worked as overseer at a big Caddo Lake plantation before the war. Judd had grown up learning where to poke a man to hurt him without ruining him. He remembered watching his father taunt black slaves with a whip. He remembered that same whip stinging him at times. It had made him tough. That's what he told himself. He took pride in meanness, considered it a strength. When rousters fought on his boat, he thought nothing of splitting their scalps with four-foot-long wedges of cordwood. He was worse than his old man in that respect. In his father's time, black men had held value as property. As far as Judd Kelso knew, they were worthless now.

He grabbed the iron capstan bar as he left the engine

room and walked forward along the dark corridors formed by the bales of cotton. The majestic old boat creaked and moaned as she backed slowly into the bayou under him. In spite of the June bugs that continued to crawl, Kelso wore a smile on his face. He was going to have a little fun with the stokers.

He found the firemen standing back from the furnace, four-foot lengths of pinewood in their hands.

"Give me fire, damn it! Don't just stand there!"

The black men looked at each other. "She's hot, Mister Judd," one of them said.

"Oh, she is?" Kelso waited until the man turned his face away, then jabbed him hard with the capstan bar, between his rib cage and hip. The black man buckled, and the others reluctantly threw their billets of wood into the furnace.

"Get up, boy!" Kelso said to the injured man. "Stoke the fire! Damn you to tell me she's hot. You ever heard of a nigger engineer? I'm the engineer on this boat, and I want steam."

The stokers chucked in more fuel as the roar of the fire grew. Kelso knew they were hoping he would just go away.

"If you don't want to do your job, I can boot your black asses over the guards right now. I guess it wouldn't make much difference. Your jobs are all goin' to shit anyway."

The stokers glanced at each other and scowled at Kelso without looking him in the eyes. "What you mean, Mister Judd?" one of them asked.

"Haven't you boys heard about the railroads comin'? There's a new one gonna build in from Louisiana, through Marshall and Jefferson. They call it the Shreveport, Houston, and Indian Territory. The S.H. and I.T.!"

Kelso laughed like a rasp, but the stokers just looked at one another, puzzled.

"If you boys could spell," Kelso said, "you'd know S.H. and I.T. makes *shit*. Like I said, your jobs are all goin' to shit!"

"Yours too, ain't it, Mister Judd?" said the stoker who had been stuck with the capstan bar, now pulling himself back to his feet and grabbing a chunk of wood.

Kelso brandished the iron rod again, but only grinned at the man without using it. "I'm a mite smarter than you. I already got it planned to make my fortune."

"How you gonna do that?" another stoker asked.

"You'll be the first to know, boy. Now, stoke that fire good. The captain wants to show this town some speed. Good for trade."

Four hogsheads of spoiled bacon stood among the cords of firewood. The bacon had gone bad in a Jefferson warehouse. Captain Gentry had bought it cheap to use for quick heat when the *Glory* needed speed. Kelso pried a lid off one of the barrels and grabbed a hunk of bacon. "Come on, boys. Pour it on!" He threw a few pieces of bacon into the furnace, then brandished his bar at the black men. "We'll need the steam to move all this cotton. Come on, damn it, hurry up!"

The stokers plunged their powerful hands into the stench of putrid bacon. They fought the blistering heat to get near enough the furnace door to throw the fuel in. The bacon fat crackled fiercely as it hit the wood coals and flared.

"Use that whole barrel up," Kelso ordered. "I'll be back directly and it better be empty!" He waved the capstan bar at the stokers. "And sing one of them damn coonjine songs loud enough for the captain to hear. You know he likes to hear you boys sing."

The stokers scowled, but one of them lit into song, hoping Kelso would leave if they started singing. He sang low as a foghorn, and the others grudgingly joined in.

Oh, shovel up the furnace,
Till the smoke put out the stars.
We's gwine along the river
Like we's bound to beat the cars. . . .

They continued singing as Kelso disappeared behind the boilers, heading aft. But he paused to listen and make sure the men continued to feed the fire. He could barely hear two of them talking over the singing and the roar of the flames.

"That fool's gonna blow us to hell," one of them said to the other.

"Just listen for them safety valves," the other replied. "They won't let out steam fast enough to keep her from blowin', but if they start talkin', you know it's time to jump."

Judd Kelso grinned, the nervous crawl in his stomach increasing. He passed quickly by the heat of the boilers, until he got aft of them. Then he stopped, the warmth still reaching his back down one of the corridors of cotton bales. He turned slowly and watched the boilers as he listened to the stokers sing. Poor bastards. They would never know what hit them.

Then he heard it. Above the shuddering of the boat, the hissing of the steam engines, the singing of the firemen, and the crackling of the pork fat, he heard the faint ticking of boiler plates. They were expanding, pulling against their rivets. He eyed the edge of the starboard boiler. Maybe it was his imagination, but he swore he could see it swelling, heaving like a living thing taking in breath. He turned quickly back toward the engine room.

Ellen Crowell rolled out of her berth in her stateroom on the boiler deck. The movement of the boat had wakened her. Feeling her way across the tiny six-by-six room to the window, she pulled the curtains back and saw only shreds of light seeping past the bales of cotton. She had forgotten in her sleep how cotton-imprisoned she was, denied escape to the outer deck in case of an emergency. Her only way out of her stateroom was by the door that led into the saloon. Boats made her nervous. She couldn't swim.

Her son could swim. That gave her some ease. Ben could shame otters. She felt her way back across the tiny room and put her hand on him as he slept in the upper berth. She was taking him to New Orleans to visit family. They had boarded in the night at Port Caddo and waited for hours as the rousters took on wood and the engineer made repairs and adjustments. Now, at last, they were under way.

Ellen knew she couldn't sleep through the vibrations of the steamboat. She put on her robe and opened the door into the saloon. She didn't understand steamboat nomenclature. She was on the boiler deck, but there was no boiler on it. The boilers were below, on the main deck. And this saloon wasn't a saloon at all, but a long, broad hallway running between the two rows of staterooms.

The saloon's piano stood right outside her room. It was a grand piano—too big for a small steamboat, but Captain Gentry did things in a big way where the *Glory* was concerned. Her door almost hit the piano bench as she opened it. She didn't know if she liked the piano being there. She could imagine drunken revelers keeping her awake with wild song, every night, all the way to New Orleans. The thin stateroom walls insulated against sound little better than mosquito bars did.

The so-called saloon was quiet, except for the rattle of pots and pans in the galley, where the cook was fixing breakfast. Ellen passed polished hardwood tables and walked a few doors down to the ladies' washroom. She found a community towel on a rack, and even a common toothbrush tied to the washstand by a string. She was glad she and Ben had brought their own towels and toothbrushes.

She tried to calm herself. She had chosen the finest

steamer on the lake for their trip. Nothing bad would happen. She looked for something to ease her worries. Tin washbasins were nailed down to the wooden washstand. In them, she found fresh spring water. Now, see there. Most steamers used common bayou water. Yes, she had chosen well.

Billy Treat opened his galley door out onto the promenade and threw a bowl of eggshells over the guardrail, into the bayou. The rousters had left him a gap in the cotton bales on the boiler deck so he could throw refuse overboard. The rousters took good care of Billy Treat. He always cooked double what the passengers could eat. Rousters ate leftovers, and the deckhands of the *Glory* fed as well as any on the bayou, thanks to Billy.

He lingered at the rail. It was a beautiful morning. Summer coming on. The boat was still backing into the bayou, getting in position to steam down the channel toward Caddo Lake. He listened to the stokers sing the coonjine as his pale blue eyes swept the sky over the cypress tops.

Billy was a stranger to every man in the crew, though he had cooked for them now for a year and a half. They knew him as a courteous fellow, but one who avoided long conversation. Nobody knew where he had come from. He didn't talk about his past. And, though he didn't frown, he rarely smiled, and never laughed. He was young—maybe thirty. He moved with strength and grace. He had more than his share of good looks. But he was suffering something powerful.

Just as he was about to go back to cooking breakfast, Billy saw the young apprentice engineer, Reggie Swearengen, climbing the guardrails and jigsaw work up to the boiler deck. He enjoyed watching the boy climb recklessly about the boat.

"Good morning, Reggie Swear-engineer," Billy said.

Reggie Swearengen grinned. "Mornin', Billy!" he shouted as he climbed around the cotton bales.

"What are you doing?"

"Kelso told me to lower the yawl."

Billy smirked. "The yawl? What for?"

"Said he wants me to tow him behind the paddle wheel when we get underway so he can look at something."

"Look at what?"

"I don't know," Reggie said, throwing one hand into the air as he clung to the hog chains with the other.

Billy shook his head. "It would be a shame if you should loose your hold on the rope when you were towing him."

Reggie laughed at the suggestion and climbed onto the hurricane deck to lower the yawl.

The *Glory* continued to back slowly up the bayou as Billy turned back into his kitchen. He tested the heat of the griddle, flicking some water onto it with his fingertips. He heard Captain Gentry ring the bell, giving the signal to stop the engines. He felt the vibrations cease, and heard the coonjine, louder now that the exhaust valves were silenced. The pulleys squeaked as Reggie lowered the yawl to the water.

Billy heard the splash of the yawl as he whipped a wooden spoon through a huge bowl of pancake batter. Now the captain would align the boat with the channel, ring the bell for full speed ahead, and blow the whistle as the *Glory of Caddo Lake* steamed down Big Cypress Bayou.

The bell rang. Billy waited for the engine-room vibrations. They didn't come. The captain repeated the bell signal. Something was wrong. Putting his pancake batter aside, Billy stepped back out onto the promenade and looked toward the engine room. He saw Reggie climbing down from the boiler deck and Judd Kelso stepping into the yawl. One of them should have been in the engine room, following the captain's signals. It was Kelso's fault.

Reggie was just following orders. Kelso had no business being an engineer.

The entire boat suddenly came alive under him. It felt as if he were trying to stand on a monster gator twisting its prey to death underwater. The air shook with a sound so loud that he heard it with the marrow of his bones, and something hit him in the back with incredible force.

Now the waters of the bayou were all around him, morning-cold. He felt disoriented, couldn't find his way to the top. As he held his breath and waited, hopefully to surface, he realized that he had heard a double blast, absorbed a tremendous percussion. It seemed long ago, but his senses were coming back to him now, and he knew it had just happened. He found the morning glow of the surface above him and swam upward.

TWO

The world seemed out of control. The sky rained bales of cotton. One splashed ten yards away from Billy Treat, covering him momentarily with spray. Screams and shouts accompanied a vicious hiss of steam. Something ripped into a cypress tree behind him. He treaded water with some difficulty in his long pants and waterlogged shoes. He shook his head to clear his thoughts. Pieces of wood were splashing all around him now, and clattering down on the hurricane deck of the *Glory*. His right shoulder and the back of his head were smarting from whatever it was that had struck him.

His eyes focused. The steamboat was listing severely to port, vomiting hysterical people, shooting a geyser of steam. He began to think clearly. Two of the boilers had exploded and blown bales of cotton away from the starboard side of the boat, throwing her off balance. The pilothouse was gone. There was probably a hole in the hull, because the boat was sinking steadily, tilting ever farther to port.

People floundered around him in the water. He went under and yanked his shoes off. When he came back up, he heard someone moaning. He saw a black man, face burned horribly, clinging to a splintered mass of wood. He swam to the man, helped him pull farther up on the floating lumber.

"Kelso!" he shouted. The son of a bitch was rowing the yawl toward the Port Caddo wharf! "We need the boat!" He saw the apprentice engineer treading water, dazed. "Reggie, get the yawl from the wharf! Swim, Reggie!"

The young apprentice squinted and saw the yawl. He waved at Billy and started swimming with powerful strokes. Billy knew he would make it. The lad was strong, and obviously uninjured.

A deckhand was floundering, screaming, frothing the water with his blood. He went down in a swirl. "Just hold on," Billy said to the burned man he had helped onto the floating lumber. To his surprise, the black man nodded and pushed him away.

Billy marked the spot where the rouster had gone down. He took long, steady breaths as he swam easily to the place. Filling his lungs, he jackknifed his body and plunged downward, headfirst.

The horrible sounds of the world above ended and he could barely see his own hands, outstretched, through the murky water. He descended, pinching his nose and forcing air into his ears to equalize the pressure. He felt for the drowning man with his arms and legs. An air bubble passed between his fingers. More met him in the face. He had plenty of oxygen left. He knew how to conserve it underwater. He plunged until he crashed into the thrashing body of the deckhand.

The black man grabbed him with desperate force. Lord, he was powerful! Billy used all his strength to turn the man around. He pinned one huge, muscled arm back and locked his own elbow under the man's chin. He started kicking for the surface, the drowning man clawing at him with his free hand.

When they finally broke into the air again, the black man was exhausted, holding Billy's hair in his fist, coughing water from his lungs. The man's forearm was ripped open and pumping blood. Maybe the cool water would slow the flow, Billy thought. He kicked toward the floating mass of lumber, which he now recognized as a big piece of the hurricane deck. It was just starting to really dawn on him what had happened. The boilers had blown. People were drowning.

As he fought the bleeding deckhand to reach the floating wood, he looked toward the town and saw Reggie coming with the yawl. That worthless Kelso was lying on the wharf as if he were hurt or something. He had looked healthy enough rowing away.

Above the hiss of steam, Treat heard a bell ringing in town. The Port Caddoans were coming down to the bayou, manning boats. Some of them were in their nightclothes, or in long underwear. They dragged skiffs, pirogues, bateaux, all manner of vessels into the water.

Suddenly five horsemen came galloping down the brick pavement. They plunged across the flood bank to low ground, passed the log jailhouse, and leaped their barebacked mounts from the wharf. They splashed into the bayou, the horses grunting as they started to swim. The riders slipped from the backs of their mounts and held onto the manes. They would tow people to shore, one or two at a time. It would help.

The bayou writhed with screaming people. Billy saw a few sensible men and women doing good work, pulling others onto floating debris. A woman was holding calmly to a bobbing bale of cotton with one arm while she clutched two crying children with the other.

The *Glory* was tilting harder to port, sinking, still spewing steam. The main deck went under and water boiled instantly around the furnace, sending up a cloud of hot vapor.

Billy pulled the bleeding man onto the floating section of hurricane deck and told him to hold pressure on his own arm to stop the flow of blood. The man was starting to recover from the sheer percussion of the explosion, and he nodded vacantly as Billy spoke to him. The other man, the one who had been so badly scalded, was still there, unconscious but grasping the wood.

Without taking time to rest, Billy stroked back toward the throng. He was not even winded. A woman was becoming hysterical, clinging to a piece of wood too small to keep her afloat. She would go under before he reached her, but she would be easier to save than the big deckhand had been. The boats would be there soon.

One at a time, he told himself. You can't save everybody yourself. God knows, even that wouldn't set your life right, even if you could, but you can't.

Ellen Crowell woke up on the floor of the washroom. She smelled her own blood in her nostrils. She had been bending over the washbasin when, suddenly, it had risen to smash her in the face. What was happening? What had gone wrong?

The sounds came to her gradually—the screaming, the hissing of steam. She remembered only now having heard and felt the explosion. She tried to stand up, but seemed too dizzy to keep her feet under her. Then she felt herself sliding across the washroom floor and knew it was a tilt in the boat that prevented her from standing. Ben was in the stateroom, and the steamboat was sinking.

Clawing across the slanting floor, Ellen reached the door frame and pulled herself up into the saloon. The saloon floor was gone forward of the washroom. She could see water coming up in the hole. Morning light streamed in from another hole above. Now she understood what had happened. The boilers had exploded, tearing through the thin planking of the boiler deck, the hurricane deck, the texas, and even the pilothouse.

Luckily, her stateroom was aft of the gaping hole and she didn't have to cross it to rescue Ben. A few passengers were still floundering toward the end of the slanted saloon, but most had already gotten out. Ellen realized that she must have been unconscious for a minute or two. She had lost valuable seconds, but she was sure she still had time to get out with Ben. After that, she would probably drown, but that didn't concern her yet. Ben wouldn't drown. Thank God that the boy could swim.

She scrambled on all fours toward her stateroom. Why wasn't Ben coming out? Was he all right? Relax, Ellen. He can't reach the doorknob the way the floor is slanted. He's waiting for you. She heard his voice:

"Mama!" He sounded more confused than terrified.

She had almost reached the door when the boat settled suddenly to port and the grand piano slid against her stateroom door, blocking it.

She screamed.

"Mama?"

"Ben!" she cried, trying to move the piano.

"I'm all right, Mama. There's water in here."

"Help!" she yelled. "For God's sake, somebody come help me!"

A man appeared at the back end of the saloon. "Come on, lady! This way!"

"The piano!" she yelled. "My son's in there! Help me move the piano!"

"Forget about the damned piano, woman! Get out this way!" The man was gone.

She whimpered in terror. Water was coming up through the hole in the saloon floor.

"Mama! I can't reach the door!" she heard Ben say.

She clawed at the door until her fingernails were bloody. She beat against it with her fists, then kicked it, trying to break it in, but she wasn't a very large woman and the door was solid wood. "Ben?" she cried again, trying to preserve some chord of normalcy in her voice.

"Mama, it's getting deeper!" he yelled through the door.

"Swim, son!" she shouted, tears gushing down her face. "And if the room fills up, you hold your breath!"

Ben didn't answer.

"Do you hear me, Ben?"

"Yes," Ben said.

"I have to get help, son. I'll come back as quick as I can."

"Don't go, Mama!" her son's voice said.

She had to tear herself away from the door and the piano and her son. "Swim, son!" she yelled, so he would hear her going away. "Keep swimming!" She wanted to crawl back to him, but there was no time. She was thinking rationally now. She was trying to save him. But she felt as if she were deserting him, leaving him to drown alone.

Billy Treat had gone under six times for drowning people, bringing most of them up to Reggie, who was strong enough to pull them into the yawl. Other boats were arriving now, and he could no longer see anyone floundering in the water. The five horses had people clinging to their tails as they stroked toward the wharf. The horses had made several trips, and they were exhausted. People were settling down, helping each other. Then a woman emerged from the passenger cabin of the sinking steamboat and began screaming bloody murder.

"My son! Ben is in there! The piano!"

Billy swam to her and climbed onto the tilting boiler deck. "Where is he? Where's your son?"

The woman gripped him with hysteria, but spoke quite plainly. "The piano slid against the door, and I can't open it. Ben is in there. He can't get out!" She virtually shoved him into the flooding cabin.

Billy Treat waded to the door with the piano before it. "Hey!" he yelled. "You in there?"

"Help!" the voice said. "The water's getting deeper. I can't get out."

Billy put all the strength he had into moving the piano, but he couldn't lift it or slide it away from the door. "Can you swim?"

"Yes!"

"I'm coming right back for you! Keep swimming!"

The water was knee-deep in the saloon now, and deeper in Ben's room, which was on the sinking side of the boat. Billy waded to the aft end of the passenger cabin.

"Where's Ben?" Ellen cried when she saw Billy come out alone. "Where's my boy?" Some of the men had forced her into a boat.

"Ellen!" cried a man from another boat. "Where's Ben?"

Billy knew it had to be the boy's father. He didn't answer the mother's questions, or the father's. He just dove into the water and disappeared. He felt his way under the boiler deck, around a few bales of cotton lodged there, and to the submerged engine room on the main deck. He found the door handle and swam into the darkness. Feeling around, he soon located Judd Kelso's iron capstan bar. He knew where Kelso kept it, because he had considered many times throwing it overboard. Of course that wouldn't have solved anything. Kelso could always find something else to hit the rousters with.

He noticed, just before he broke the surface, that his lungs were aching. The swimming underwater was begin-

ning to take its toll on him. Once he had been among the
best in the world, but he hadn't done it in a long time.

The woman screamed wildly when he came up. He only
waved the bar at her, taking no time to explain. The men
held her in the boat. Otherwise, she would have rushed
back in to try to save her son.

Billy knew the old *Glory of Caddo Lake* well. He was
thinking about how she was put together as he made his
way through the water in the saloon, now deep enough to
swim through. The cheapest, thinnest wood was between
the staterooms. The paneling that formed the walls between staterooms and saloon was pretty thick. The doors
were solid. There wasn't much time. Ben's room was almost completely under water now. He decided to tear
through the thin wood partitioning the rooms.

"Keep swimming, Ben," he said when he got to the
piano. "I'm coming through the wall of the next room to
get you!"

"I'm swimming!" the boy cried.

He admired this boy who was being brave, trapped in
that dark room as the bayou squeezed his air out. He forced
himself to relax for ten seconds and took long, deep
breaths. Then he slid through the open door of the room
next to Ben's and disappeared underwater.

It took a full minute of hard work to punch a small hole
in the wall with the capstan bar, but Billy could not see
wasting the seconds it would take to go up for air again.
The boy might not have seconds. He didn't know how far
the boat had sunk as he worked. Maybe the boy was
drowning now. Billy had stayed under longer than this before. No need to go back now. Go forward! In the dark, he
tore at the boards he had loosened until he had two of them
broken away. There was enough room to squeeze through
now.

Every little moment became an eternity. His lungs ached
for air. They racked him all the way up to his eyeballs. But

he had already decided to swim into Ben's room, hoping he would find an air pocket left there. It was a big gamble, but he was not going to take a chance on letting that boy drown. He couldn't take the guilt of leaving someone to die while he lived. Not again. He would rather drown with Ben, a boy he didn't even know.

He bumped his head in the very uppermost corner of the room and felt air on his face. His lungs had already started sucking. If there had been no air, he would have drowned. Then the hands of the boy pulled him under, and he thought he would drown anyway.

"Hey!" he said, coming up again, gasping. "Take it easy!"

They treaded water together, the tops of their heads jammed against the upper corner of the stateroom. They didn't speak, as Billy was gasping for air. They could hear a couple of men grunting through the wall, trying to move the piano above them.

"You holding out all right?" Billy finally asked, having caught some wind.

"Yes, sir," Ben said. "Who are you?"

"Name's Billy Treat. Here, get on my back. Now, listen to me and take long breaths. Stop swimming, just relax. I'll keep you up. Listen while you breathe deep and I'll tell you what we're going to do."

"Yes, sir."

"Shut up, I said. Just listen. Now, when the water gets to our chins, you're going to take in as much air as your chest can hold. We'll go under together. Don't swim. Let me pull you. You just relax and hold your breath. I made a hole in the wall down there. I'll help you through it, then come through after you and we'll swim out through the door of the next room. Easy."

"How long will it take?"

"Shut up, I told you. Breathe deep. Don't worry. You can hold your breath that long. Just relax and let me swim for you."

Someone was beating on the door above them, shout-ing, "Ben! Ben!"

"Don't answer," Billy said. "Save your breath. It's time now. Ready?" They breathed deeply together. "Go!"

Ellen was standing in the yawl, weeping, wringing her hands. Her husband and another man had gone in after the stranger with the iron bar, but no one had come out. She could tell that Ben's room was all the way under water now. She was trying to hold on to some hope, but it was grow-ing thin. She prayed aloud, though no one understood her words, muffled by the sobs.

Then, through the blur of her tears, she saw a movement down the half-hooded saloon. A man emerged. Not her husband, and not the stranger with the iron bar. Then, there was John. John Crowell, her husband! Was he smiling or crying? He reached back into the saloon and pulled some-one else into the morning light. It was the stranger, and the stranger had ahold of Ben! Merciful God!

THREE

I guess I should get as much credit as anybody for making Billy Treat an instant hero in Port Caddo. I was the boy he rescued from the sinking *Glory of Caddo Lake* the day her boilers blew. I'm Ben Crowell. I've told the story a thousand times since then, and people always think I'm spinning yarn when I do. But I won't water it down just to make it more believable. I've been known to branch out a little, mind you, but never when I talk about that summer.

Anyway, saving me made Billy a hero overnight, be-cause by the next day, my father had printed a special extra-edition of the *Port Caddo Steam Whistle*. Pop was wise enough not to celebrate my rescue until the third page. The event was a catastrophe, after all, and a terrible blow to the town's spirit and economy. Seven men were killed, a lot of property destroyed, and our favorite steamboat sunk. The first two pages of the paper quite properly lamented the whole thing as a horrible tragedy.

But my pop was an unquenchable booster and knew he had to keep the spirit of the town going. On page three, he started listing acts of heroism. A woman from Jefferson had taken off her dress and stuffed it with floating pieces of firewood to make a raft for some children to float on. One of the big, strong deckhands had held up a collapsed portion of the forward passenger cabin with his back so people could crawl out under it. The people of Port Caddo, in general, had done all they could to ease the plight of the victims.

There was a big mystery concerning the five horsemen who had jumped their mounts into the bayou. Nobody in town knew who they were. They simply disappeared after the last of the passengers had been rescued. My pop didn't say so in the paper, because he didn't print rumors, but most folks believed they belonged to Christmas Nelson's outlaw gang, which was supposed to be hiding out in the woods around Caddo Lake.

The stranger, Billy Treat, got a whole column all to himself. He had gone under seven times to pull near-drowning people to the surface. Everybody in Port Caddo was talking about how long he could hold his breath. A minute, two minutes, five minutes. Who was this Billy Treat? Was he part turtle, or what?

My rescue was the most detailed account in the special edition, which only made sense, seeing as how the editor was my pop. So I figure I had as much to do as anybody in making Billy the new Port Caddo hero. He was already my own personal hero. I knew that the moment he stood me safely on the wharf.

I remember collapsing beside Judd Kelso and looking back over the bayou. The *Glory of Caddo Lake* had settled crooked on the bottom, only her texas sticking out. The pilothouse was gone. I wondered what had become of Captain Gentry. Then I saw him, hung in a fork of a cypress tree, bent backward, his head almost cut clean off. A huge section of boiler plate was in another tree near him.

Embedded in the wharf, not far from me, was a cotton bale, dry as a candlewick. The explosion had thrown it all the way there from the boat. My mother was clinging to me, sobbing. People were helping others out of boats, onto the wharf. Many were crying and all were drenched and shivering. Some people were hurt bad. I saw more blood than I had ever seen before, and I had experienced a lot of fishhooked fingers, skinned knees, and bloody noses.

That's when I really got scared, after the danger was all over for me. I might have stayed shook up for a long time if it hadn't been for Billy.

"Ben!" he said. "Get up and grab this corner!"

Billy and my pop were lifting one of the deckhands to the wharf, using a blanket as a stretcher. I stared at Billy in disbelief. I thought I was a victim and didn't have to do anything. My mother thought so, too, and she held me back and probably gave Billy some kind of fierce look.

"Come on," Billy said. "You're all right. Help these hurt people."

He was right. There was nothing wrong with me. I had just been treading water for a few minutes, that's all. I had a knot on my head where the explosion had thrown me against a bedpost or something in my sleep and knocked me silly for a minute or two until the water seeped into my room and got my attention. But I wasn't really hurt.

I pulled away from my mother's arms and grabbed the corner of the blanket, which had a knot tied in it, making it easier to hold on to. The man in the blanket was the poor scalded deckhand Billy had saved. His skin looked blistered and horrible. He was unconscious, but moaning. I never learned his name, but I knew him from the *Glory*'s frequent visits to our town. He was the one who sang the low notes of the coonjines.

Billy jumped onto the wharf. "Kelso! Get up and help," he ordered.

Judd Kelso was lying there on his back with his hands over his face. "I can't," he said.

"Why not? You hurt?"

"No."

"Then what's wrong?"

"I don't know."

Billy sneered with disgust and gave me a signal with his eyes to lift my corner of the blanket. I watched his every move and followed his directions. He was helping people, and I wanted to be just like him.

I don't know how things got organized so quickly that morning, but by the time Billy and I and my pop carried the scalded deckhand past the constable's one-cell log jailhouse and up to high ground where the cobblestones started, old Jim Snyder had already turned his general store into sort of a makeshift hospital. There was a bed there where we lay the deckhand down.

Billy motioned at me to make another run with him down to the wharf and we started out, me right on his heels. Suddenly, I bumped into his back, for Billy had stopped dead in his tracks. I followed his eyes and found his stare locked on Pearl Cobb, who was wrapping a man's foot in bandages.

Some people believe in love at first sight. I think it's rare, but it happens. What I saw in Billy's face was love at first sight, only I didn't know it at the time, because just about every man alive looked at Pearl the same way, unless his wife happened to be with him. I was probably the most unabashed Pearl-gazer in Port Caddo. I had a crush on her something fierce.

Nobody appreciates the beauty of a full-grown woman more than a fourteen-year-old boy. He has no point of reference. He doesn't have enough experience with women to know how to judge one from the other. He doesn't even know what to look for. He just looks up one day and sees beauty, and it is absolute. Later, he grows up, gets particular, and starts ranking women and giving scores and silly things like that. But that first beauty a boy sees when his loins go to surprising him is flawless. All of a sudden he feels like as big an aching idiot as ever lived, and he loves it.

That was how Pearl Cobb made me feel. She was a little darker-skinned than your typical white gal, as if tanned by the sun, though I rarely saw her out in the daylight. Women envied her hair, long and dark and full. It possessed a sculpted quality, yet bounced and floated as free as clouds when she moved.

That's when Pearl got to you, when she moved. I don't think women can learn moves like that. Some things you're simply born with. I don't think she could help it. Just the way she was put together made her turn heads when she walked, and even when she just brushed her hair back from her face.

And as faces go, you can take your Mona Lisas and your moving-picture stars. Pearl had them all beat. I guess now I would have to say her features were perfectly proportionate, or something like that—her cheeks round, her lips full, her nose small and cute, her jaw straight and delicate. I might try to tell you about her eyes, how they melted you, embraced you too briefly, shamed you. But when I was fourteen, all I knew was the sheer truth of their large, shining beauty.

Don't think I didn't notice more than her eyes. Pearl had other attractions. A scribe couldn't copy her curves. They defied duplication. No mere line or graduated plane could render likeness to any part of her. You could cast her in gold and not capture the living, breathing loveliness of her. You could stare at her like a fool for fifteen seconds, soaking in her beauty, then turn away and not trust your own recent memory of her perfection, so you would have to look again to be sure.

And I don't know if she made her own dresses or bought them, but how she got them to cling to her—as I wanted to do—is something I haven't figured out to this day.

Pearl worked in old man Snyder's store and lived alone in a little room upstairs. She was a hard worker, kept the place real clean and organized, made perfect change, and balanced the books. About the time I turned fourteen, I started loitering around the store quite a bit. I didn't have any money to buy anything, and Pearl probably knew it. I think she took pity on my innocence, but maybe she just took advantage of it.

She got me to run all kinds of errands for her, taking groceries to old folks who couldn't get around and things like that. There wasn't any money in it for me, just a nice word from Pearl every now and then, maybe a smile. Once in a while she would stroke my sweaty mop of boy's hair with her sensuous fingers. I guess she was just scruffing up my hair a little bit, but it felt like the embrace of pure tingling passion to me.

I was only vaguely aware back then of Pearl's reputation. I had heard some old biddies refer to her as "white trash." I figured they were jealous. Then one day Cecil Peavy, my friend and fishing partner, called her a slut, and we had a knock-around fight over it. Us boys from proper families grew up sort of innocent back then. I wasn't even real sure I knew what a slut was, but the way Cecil said it made me mad.

Slowly it began to dawn on me as I caught morsels of men's talk about her, and listened to some new instinct of my own, what the secret was about Pearl. It took some thinking to sort it all out, and some time to verify it—and even then, I was still a little fuzzy on the details—but the truth was that Pearl could be bought, if a fellow was lucky enough to come by her fee.

Learning the secret about Pearl didn't lower my opinion of her. In fact, it made her all the more fascinating. You have to remember, a fourteen-year-old boy doesn't decide his own morals. His glands do it for him. What preachers and church choir sopranos regard as scandalous, a fourteen-year-old boy might consider cause for sainthood. So, when I finally found out why everybody called Pearl "Pearl"—her real name was Carol Anne— her beauty in my eyes doubled, if it's possible to double an absolute.

If I could see, today, the same Pearl I knew back then, I wonder if I would find her as beautiful. Probably not. I'm more suspicious and critical of women now, as I am of people in general. I haven't seen pure beauty since Pearl, and that may only be because I remember her as she was that summer. Or more correctly, because I remember her with the memories of who I was then. When the summer was over, that Pearl was gone forever.

Anyway, my new hero, Billy Treat, had a lot more self-control than I did, and he only ogled Pearl for a second or two before heading back down to the wharf with me in tow. We brought all the people injured in the explosion to Snyder's store and took care of them as best we could until the doctor could arrive from Marshall.

That's when things started confusing me. I guess that's when my simple boy's life became complicated, and it's been getting more complicated since that day. I was given the job of carrying cold well water in by the bucketful so it could be used to ease the suffering of burns. Every time I entered the store, I couldn't keep my eyes off of Pearl for very long, of course, but the thing was that she couldn't keep her eyes off of Billy Treat. And Billy Treat was not exactly avoiding the occasional glance at her, either.

It was odd, because I had never been jealous before, and men gawked at Pearl all the time. But now it was Pearl doing most of the gawking—at my newfound hero. I caught them actually looking at each other once, for a mere second. Their eyes shared some common brand of remorse that I wouldn't understand for years. Suddenly, it wasn't such fun having a hero.

The first man Billy saved died before the doctor could arrive. Four of the firemen who had been stoking the furnace when the boilers blew also died. Two of them were never found. Caddo Lake took what was left of them and buried them somewhere. The other two casualties were Captain Gentry and a young man from Dallas who happened to have been walking down the saloon, directly above the boilers, when they blew. We all figured he had been heading for the toilets that hung over the stern.

It would take me years to prove that Judd Kelso murdered all seven of the victims for his own personal gain. When the scalded black man died quietly in the store, Kelso was still down on the wharf, his hands covering his face. I guess even Judd Kelso possessed something resembling a conscience.

FOUR

The *Glory of Caddo Lake* disaster left several men unemployed. Most of them boarded the next steamer and went to find work. But Billy Treat stayed. Widow Humphry said she was too old to be cooking for her guests and boarders, and since Billy was a cook, she would provide him with room and board plus a small salary to fix meals at her inn. Billy said it would do until he found something else.

This all made me a little nervous at first, because Widow

Humphry's inn was just across the way from Snyder's store. But after about a week went by, I began to relax. I didn't notice anything out of the ordinary going on between Billy and Pearl. I saw him go to the store once for supplies, and I followed him in there to spy on him, but he hardly spoke three words to Pearl.

"Thank you," she said to him when she gave him his change. That was something, because I had never heard Pearl thank anybody other than me. But Billy only nodded at her before he left. He was my hero, but I thought he must have been a little crazy. When Pearl Cobb came right out and spoke to you, you were supposed to try to speak back. This Billy Treat was a funny character.

One day right after lunch when Cecil Peavy, Adam Owens, and I were chucking rocks at a squirrel in a tree out behind Widow Humphry's inn, Billy came out the back door and called my name.

"Ben, bring your friends over here," he said in that detached voice of his.

They looked at me with their eyes popping out. I had been bragging on how chummy I was with the new local hero, but they didn't believe me till then. To tell the truth, I didn't believe myself till then. I wasn't sure if Billy even remembered who I was. I trotted happily to the back porch with Cecil and Adam behind me, to see what Billy wanted.

"Hi, Mr. Treat," I said.

He waved off the formalities. "Call me Billy. Listen, how would you men like to make a little money?" He was sitting on the porch steps, his sleeves rolled up over his rippling forearms as he adjusted a smart little straw hat on his head.

Us boys just looked at each other with our mouths open for a moment or two. None of us had ever owned more than a nickel at a time. "I guess so," I said. "How?"

"I need some fresh catfish. The fellows down at the fish camp have been selling me day-old fish, and it just doesn't taste as good as it should." He spoke to us in a very professional tone, as if we were negotiating the biggest deal in history. "If you boys could catch some catfish and keep them alive in a holding tank somewhere until I need them, I'd pay you a penny a pound."

I looked at Adam Owens in astonishment. "Sure!" I said, speaking for all of us.

But Cecil Peavy was a cynic, even at fourteen. "Is that live weight, or cleaned?" he asked. Cecil made good in life. Last time I saw him alive, down in Nacogdoches, he owned a whole city block.

"Live weight," Billy answered.

"Sure!" I repeated.

"Wait a minute," Cecil said. "Where are we gonna keep them? How are we gonna catch them?"

"My daddy has a trotline in the barn," Adam said. "Never been used. Got new hooks and everything."

"Do you think he'd miss it?" Billy asked.

Adam grinned and shook his head.

"Where are we gonna keep them alive?" Cecil repeated.

We thought in silence for a moment, then it struck me. "The old horse trough at the Packer place!" It was perfect—a big, round cypress trough, full of spring water, on an abandoned farmstead only a mile from the lake.

"That's a lot of work for a penny a pound," Cecil said.

"Take it or leave it," Billy replied sternly, smirking at him.

Adam and I looked anxiously at Cecil.

"Well, all right," he finally said. "We'll give it a trial to see how it works."

"Good," Billy said. When he shook our hands, we were bound.

"Go get that trotline," I said to Adam, all excited. "We can use old Esau's skiff to run the line."

"What are we gonna use for bait?" Cecil asked.

"We'll wade for some mussels."

Suddenly Billy perked up, and I saw a new light flash

in his eyes for a second. "Mussels?" he said. "Do these waters bear a lot of mussels?"

"They're all over the dang place," Cecil said.

Billy glanced at a watch he pulled out of his pocket. "I think I'll come with you," he said. "I'd like to see these mussels."

Adam snuck his pop's trotline out of the barn along with a couple of cork floats and a good supply of hooks. Billy walked with us the two miles between Port Caddo and old Esau's saloon located on an inlet of Caddo Lake known as Goose Prairie Cove.

Esau was a friendly old man who drank whiskey all day, but never seemed to get drunk. He was dark-skinned and claimed five-sevenths Choctaw blood. I asked him one time how he figured that, and he said, "I've got seven ancestors, and five of them was Choctaw." I think he was really pure Indian and just liked to pull my leg. He kept his hair cut and dressed like a regular civilized man. With his saloon and fishing camp down at Goose Prairie Cove, he managed to make a living that he supplemented by hunting wild game and running a few hogs in the woods. He had several old leaky boats at his camp and never refused them to us boys.

Esau always ran us off after dark, though, because sometimes fights broke out between drunks at his place. But there were a few knotholes in the walls, and we often snuck back and looked through the knotholes to see what barroom life was like. One night when we were peering through the knotholes, Esau walked casually over to a chair by the wall, sat down in it, and sprayed a mouthful of whiskey in Adam Owens' eye through a knothole. I never did figure out how he knew we were out there.

Anyway, when we got to the fishing camp, we found Esau and Judd Kelso sitting in the shade of a big mulberry, sipping whiskey. Judd Kelso had been hanging around Port Caddo ever since the disaster. I didn't think anything of it at the time, but he should have been looking for work somewhere. Kelso was not independently wealthy. However, his family lived over at Long Point, not too far away, so it didn't seem unnatural to me for him to stay in the area after the boiler explosion.

Esau stood up to greet us when we got there. We introduced Billy and they shook hands. Esau offered Billy a whiskey flask.

"I never drink," Billy said.

Esau didn't bat an eye, just put the flask in his pocket. We asked him if we could use a skiff to throw mussels in and run a trotline, and he told us we were welcome to, as long as we brought the skiff back.

"Howdy, Treat," Kelso said, waving glassy-eyed, sprawled across a wooden chair in the shade.

Billy just flat ignored him and went with us boys to the lakeshore. My friends and I waded barefoot into the shallows, towing a skiff behind us. I had worked up a sweat on the walk from Port Caddo, and the water felt good. Billy kicked off his shoes, put his pocket watch in one of them, and followed us in.

It didn't take long for me to find the first mussel. I was probing through the mud with my toes when I felt it, a hard ridge in the muck. I dug it out with my toenail, then used my foot like a shovel to lift it up to where I could grab it in my hand.

It was a pretty good-sized one, but nothing extraordinary—about as wide as the palm of my hand—a dark brown, clamlike shell plastered with mud. I threw it into the skiff Adam was holding by the rope and went on hunting with my toes. Billy sloshed over to the skiff, grabbed the mussel, washed it off, and studied it. I saw that light in his eyes again. He seemed fascinated.

"How many catfish do you expect us to catch?" Cecil asked, throwing a small mussel shell into the skiff.

Billy dropped the mussel he had been looking at and started feeling around with his feet as us boys were doing. "Enough where I can fry a catfish dinner twice a week or so."

We hunted for almost an hour, joking and taunting each other, as boys will. Billy hardly said a word to us. He just searched silently for mussel shells, finding a few, studying them, comparing them. I still idolized him, but I was beginning to think he was a little peculiar. "How many varieties of mussels live in this lake?" he asked us at one point. We didn't know.

When we had waded out to our chins, and Billy to his chest, we finally had enough mussels to bait our trotline. We towed the skiff back to shallower water and sat on an old pier that stuck up just above the water level. We decided to go ahead and open the mussels there, so we could bait our line quicker when we set it out.

There's a trick to opening mussels. Between those two shells they're almost nothing but solid muscle, and they don't open easy. It's a little dangerous. You're likely to slip and cut your hand if you don't watch yourself.

The way Billy had been studying the mussels we found, I was of the opinion that he had never seen one before that day. So, when we got our pocket knives out, I thought I'd show him how to open mussels. I didn't want my hero sticking himself. And, to tell the truth, I wanted to show off a little.

"Hold it like this, Billy," I said, "and stick your knife in right here, then twist it open." I wrestled with the mud-slick mussel shell for some time, poking clumsily at it with the knife, until I finally pried it open. I pulled out the shapeless little animal, threw it in a bait bucket holding a little water, and handed Billy one to try on his own.

His knife moved so quickly that I couldn't follow it. In less than a second, the shell was open in his hand. He pulled out the mussel and felt it between his fingers, as if looking for something hidden in it. He dropped it in the bait bucket, then ran his finger along the pretty purple inside of the shell. He angled it in the sun to catch the iridescent rainbow sheen of the shell lining. He had that look on his face again. His eyes darted and sparkled, and he almost smiled. Then he grunted, tossed the shell in the water, and grabbed another mussel.

He looked at me and found me staring. "What are you looking at?" he said.

"Nothin'," I answered.

Cecil and Adam hadn't noticed anything unusual. They were arguing about where to put the trotline.

"The best place is over on the edge of Mossy Brake, right across from Taylor Island," Cecil said. "That's where all them big opelousas cats live."

"You've got to have live bait to catch an opelousas cat," Adam argued. He didn't know too much, but there wasn't a thing about hunting and fishing he didn't know. "We won't catch anything but willow cats on these mussels."

"Maybe some humpback blues," Cecil suggested.

"Not in Mossy Brake. You have to go out in the Big Water to catch them."

They went on arguing and shelling mussels until only a few were left. I was listening to them yammer and trying to figure out how Billy could get those mussels open so quickly, when I realized he was just sitting there on the pier with his feet in the water, staring at an open mussel shell in his hand.

It was a big washboard mussel—the kind old Esau scraped his dead pigs down with when he was slipping the hair from them at butchering time. The inside of the shell glistened a kind of pink rainbow color. I didn't see what had Billy so captivated until he nudged the mussel with his finger. Then I saw him uncovering a perfectly spherical bead of translucence perched on the rim of the shell. Billy Treat had found a pearl.

"Wow," I said, before I could consider all the ramifications of the find. "Hey, y'all, Billy found a pearl!"

Cecil and Adam stopped arguing and looked. They jumped to their feet and hung over Billy's shoulders to see. Billy had that faraway look in his eyes again, as if he was thinking of someplace else. It almost seemed like he was afraid of that pearl.

"Hey, Esau!" Cecil shouted.

"Esau!" Adam repeated.

"Billy Treat found a pearl!" they yelled together, as if they had rehearsed it.

Esau rose slowly, but Judd Kelso floundered as if wasp-stung getting out of his chair.

I envied Billy something terrible at that moment, and resented him a little, too. What was he going to do with that pearl? I knew what I would have done with it, if I could have found the nerve. But I didn't have the pearl. Billy did. And in my eyes, he had nerve enough for ten men.

I had heard about Caddo Lake pearls all my life, and had seen several girls wearing lopsided ones given to them by their beaux who had been lucky enough to find one. But this was the most beautiful one I could imagine. It was fairly large—bigger than a raindrop. It had an overall white color, but little windows of blue and green and red and purple kept appearing within it, blurred and indefinable. A prismatic haze seemed to cling to its surface like a fog.

I smelled whiskey over the stench of the mussels when Esau and Kelso arrived.

"Well, I'll be damned," Kelso said.

"That's one of the best I ever seen, and I've lived on this lake forty years," Esau said.

Billy looked up at the old Indian. "Pearls are common to this lake?"

Kelso was squinting his gator eyes, scheming.

"Maybe not common," Esau said, measuring his words. "But they turn up. I've found a couple myself over the years. Nothing as pretty as that one, though."

"What do people do with them?"

"Well," Esau said, glancing at Kelso. "A young man might give it to his sweetheart, if he's got one. A daddy might give it to his daughter to play with."

"Nobody ever sold them?" Billy asked.

Esau wrinkled his old dark face. "They ain't worth nothin'."

"They's worth somethin' to me," Kelso blurted. He pulled a large roll of bills out of his pocket and peeled one off. "Here, I'll give you five dollars for it."

"Where did you get all that money?" Billy asked, his voice flat and emotionless as ever.

"None of your business. Here's five. Now, give me that shell slug."

"For five dollars?" Billy said.

"All right, ten!" Kelso peeled off another bill and shook it in Billy's face.

"Don't sell it, Billy," Cecil said. "Use it yourself."

I pushed Cecil and he looked at me as if I was crazy, but the whole incident was making me mad. I didn't want Billy using the pearl the way Cecil was suggesting.

"Use it?" Billy said. "Use it for what?"

Kelso laughed. "I'll use it. I'll take it over to Pearl Cobb and get my piston stroked." He peeled another bill from his roll. "Fifteen. That's as high as I'll go, Treat."

Billy looked up at Kelso. "What do you mean by 'getting your piston stroked'?" he asked.

Now, even I knew what he meant, and I was only fourteen years old, but I guess Billy wanted to be certain.

"Pearl's a whore!" Cecil said. He was so red in the face, you would have thought he had found the pearl.

I shoved him hard in the chest. "She is not!" I shouted. I was getting really mad now, and so frustrated I thought I would cry.

"She'll be a whore tonight!" Kelso said, grinning idiotically.

Billy looked up at Esau.

The old Indian took a sip from his whiskey flask. "She ain't a regular whore for a man who just wants to spend some money," he said in his slow, careful voice. "But if you have a pearl—"

"And I just bought me one!" Kelso shoved the three fivers into Billy's shirt pocket and reached for the pearl.

Quick as he had opened the mussel, Billy slammed it shut in his left hand, the pearl clamped safely inside. With his right hand, he grabbed Kelso by the back of the collar. The speed and strength he moved with shocked me out of my anger and frustration. I saw Kelso fly headfirst from the pier into the water, but Billy did not let go of him. He held Kelso under, facedown. Kelso thrashed like a snared gator. That Kelso was a bundle of muscles and it took some power to hold him down. Billy did it with one hand. His left hand still clutched the pearl mussel.

"What's this about Pearl Cobb?" Billy asked, speaking as smoothly as if he were sitting in someone's parlor. Kelso continued to claw at him ineffectually.

"Her real name's Carol Anne," Esau answered. "She likes pearls, I guess. Does a man favors for 'em. That's how she got her nickname."

Billy shoved Kelso deeper. The man's face must have been in the mud. His feet came up and splashed muddy water everywhere with their flailing.

"What does she do with them?"

Esau reached for the flask again. "I don't know. Keeps them in her room, I think. A fellow told me one time he took her a pearl and she had him put it in a tobacco tin with a bunch of other ones, then—" He looked toward us boys and decided against giving further details. "You gonna let him up for air?"

"A man can hold his breath a long time when he has to. Isn't that right, Ben?"

I was speechless. I didn't know who or what Billy was anymore. Was he a murderer who drowned his enemies? A hero who saved drowning men? Was he my friend, or my rival for Pearl's attention? I didn't stand a chance of impressing her with Billy waving pearls under her nose. Of course, I wouldn't have stood a chance anyway, but I was fourteen and too infatuated to figure my chances realistically. All I knew was that I should have found that pearl. It was meant for me, and Billy had stolen it from me.

It was funny, because I had known for some time who Pearl Cobb was and what she did. It didn't bother me that she had had all those men who brought her pearls. I figured she was just generous. And if she could be generous with them, why not with me? But this Billy Treat was dangerous. I don't know how I knew, but I sensed he might take all of Pearl's generosity for himself.

"He stopped kickin', Billy," Adam said, staring fearfully at Kelso's legs.

Billy pulled the man up. Kelso sucked in some mud and water with his first breath. He coughed and gasped with horrible sounds as Billy shoved him toward the shore. While Kelso caught his breath, Billy opened the mussel shell and removed the pearl. He pulled the mussel out, too, and threw it into our bait bucket.

"Goddam you, son of a bitch!" Kelso wheezed, scooping mud away from his eyes.

Billy took the three bills from his shirt pocket, wadded them up, and threw them at him. "Don't cuss me, Kelso."

Kelso got up and staggered toward Esau's saloon. "You better watch over your shoulder, Treat," he said.

When Kelso was out of the way, Adam asked, "Can I see the pearl, Billy?"

Billy let him look at it as he stepped back up onto the pier. Adam handed it to Cecil to look at, then Cecil gave it to me. I wanted to rear up and throw that pearl back out into the lake, but I didn't know if maybe Billy might hold me under, too. I just stood there, looking at it in my open palm, nudging it around a little with my finger. It was almost as beautiful as Carol Anne Cobb.

"What are you going to do with it?" I asked Billy.

He looked at me, those pale blue eyes drilling me like skewers. "What would you do with it if you were me?" he said.

I swallowed and felt a red flood of anger and embarrassment engulf my face.

Billy smirked at me. "That's what I thought," he said.

"Is that what you're going to do with it?"

With a sudden upward flick of his palm, Billy tapped the back of my hand, propelling the pearl into the air. He snatched it right in front of my eyes, quick as a frog's tongue. "Learn to mind your own business, Ben," he said.

He stared at me, knowing everything I was thinking. His eyes were inscrutable and mysterious, like sky-blue pearls, flecked with shafts of danger, bored with big dark holes. Oh, that Billy Treat could see your naked soul with those eyes.

FIVE

Pearl locked the front door of Snyder's store and found her way by starlight to the stairs around back that led to her room. Her entire life consisted of the store by day and her room by night. She rarely went anywhere else. Not to church, for no congregation had embraced her. Nor to visit friends, for she had none—with the possible exception of old man Snyder and young Ben Crowell. Hattie Hayes, the constable's wife, was civil to her, but she couldn't really count her as a friend.

She entertained an occasional guest.

Where would she go when the town died and the store closed? She had nothing else. The job she did was the only thing she took pride in, though it paid little. She was not proud of her beauty. Her looks were a curse.

She had a can of beef stew in her hand as she climbed the stairs. She would have the stew for supper, if she found an appetite. She opened the door and entered her dark room. She felt for the matches and lit the tallow candle. No need to light the lantern. It was better to save the coal oil.

When the candlelight filled the room, her eyes went immediately to the tobacco tin on the shelf above her bed. The pearls lay within like pebbles of shame . . . her only links to the social fabric of the town.

Carol Anne had come to Port Caddo years before with her mother, a notorious Creole quadroon from New Orleans, renowned for her beauty and wiles. Her father was a gambler named Cobb, whom she never met. When she was six, her mother became the mistress of a rich planter on the Louisiana side of Caddo Lake. For four years, she and her mother lived well in a white frame house at Mooringsport. Carol Anne dressed primly and went to school.

Then the Civil War came on. Her mother's keeper became a lieutenant and died in one of the first battles. When the money ran out, they drifted across to the Texas side of the lake and landed in Port Caddo. Carol Anne's mother rented a small house on the edge of town where she established a practice among the riverboat men, sawmill hands, farm boys, and fishermen.

Carol Anne didn't go to school anymore. There was no public education system, and none of the girls' academies would enroll the daughter of a known prostitute. No white girl of proper family was allowed to befriend her. She played some with the black girls whose mothers washed laundry on Gum Slough, but Negro society was as suspicious of her as whites were righteous above her.

Malaria ruined her mother's health and trade, and eventually left Carol Anne alone in the world. She was fifteen. Kindly old Jim Snyder gave her a job at his store in exchange for room and board. In a couple of years, she was running the store on her own, earning a salary, and giving Jim Snyder more time to look after other business concerns.

She was getting prettier, and growing out of awkward girlishness into womanhood. She had contact with many townspeople through the store, and some of them began to let the memory of her mother fade. She might have had a respectable future in Port Caddo if not for the pearls.

A few of the proper girls who came into the store wore freshwater pearls their beaux had found and given to them. They wore them around their necks on simple silken threads or on slender chains of gold. They flaunted them, rolling them between their fingers as they shopped for white silk. Some wore their pearls mounted in golden ring settings, or on the ends of silver hairpins. A pearl from Caddo Lake was a proposal for marriage when given to a girl. Carol Anne wished she could have one.

A promising young man from a South Shore plantation came to Carol Anne's door one night and asked if he might come in. He held her wrist and pressed a pearl into her palm. It was a fine teardrop of blue smoke and luster. He was in love with her, he said, but he couldn't let anybody know. Their love had to remain a secret until he turned twenty-one. His family already had his bride chosen for him, and might deny him his trust fund if he married the wrong girl. He told her this, then kissed her and went away.

She lay awake that night with the blue pearl in her hand

and dreamed of wearing it someday—a pendant set in gold. She dreamed of the boy, too, and their plantation home, their children, her flower garden.

He returned two nights later and kissed her as he came in the door. He said he had been thinking of nothing but her. He snuffed out the candle and led her to the bed. She found little reason to resist. She was ready.

For weeks, they guarded their secret with care. Carol Anne would fondle the teardrop pearl after he left and dream of their wedding and their life together. Then he stopped coming. She read in the *Port Caddo Steam Whistle* that the boy had been accepted at West Point and had a promising military career ahead of him.

It didn't take long for Carol Anne to realize that before he left, he had boasted to his friends about how he had seduced her, the daughter of the dead town whore, with a worthless shell slug.

Not long after that, someone else knocked on her door. She found a farm boy standing at the top of the stairs. He said he had found a pearl that he would give her if she would let him come in. She almost pushed him down the stairs, but then the farm boy opened his hand to show her, and in the candlelight, she saw the mystical glow of the yellow oval. In its pearlescence she saw the same kind of visions she had seen in the smoky-blue teardrop. She saw family, home, and happiness. The ghostly colors swam in darting schools around the gem.

She let him in, took his pearl. He never came back.

After that, she forgot their faces, but remembered their pearls. Each held for her its own fantasy images of hearth and kin. She pretended they were men they could never be. In her room at night, she lived multiple lives—perfect lives encrusted safely in nacre. She became a collector of pearls. She became Pearl.

Pearl put her can of beef stew on the table and lay down on her bed. She arched the stiffness from her back and

stretched her arms toward the ceiling. She reached the tobacco tin, lowered it to her stomach, and opened it. She
probed the folds of the velvet cloth that cradled the pearls.
With her fingers, she felt the keepers of her fantasy lives.
She knew most of them by touch alone. She closed her
eyes and let the visions swarm.

She had almost fallen asleep when she heard footsteps
on her stairs. It was probably Jim Snyder, the grandfatherly
old man she loved. He came to talk to her occasionally on
her stairs, but would never enter her room.

When the knock came, she opened the door and found
Billy Treat standing at the top of the stairs. He held his
straw hat in his hand; he smelled faintly of kitchen smoke.
She wished she had taken the time to look in the mirror
and straighten her hair.

"Are you Carol Anne Cobb?" he asked.

She nodded.

"I've heard you collect pearls."

She felt confused, and maybe a little ashamed, though
she had learned to hide her shame. Since the day she
first saw him; she had dreamed of him climbing the stairs
to her room. But in her dreams, he never spoke of pearls.
"So what?" she said, rather defensively.

"Well, if you don't mind, I'd like to see them."

"What for?" she asked, suspiciously.

He crumpled the hat brim in his hand. "You might say
I used to collect pearls, too. Saltwater pearls, mostly. I'd
like to see yours, if you don't mind."

She looked in his eyes. It was like looking into a mirror.
His stare couldn't meet hers. He diverted his line of sight.
He was trying to get by some shame of his own.

"All right," she said, stepping aside to let him in. "I
wasn't expecting anybody." She put the can of beef stew
behind the curtain on the windowsill, fluffed her hair a
little, and pulled the bedspread tight where she had been
lying on it.

Billy stood uncomfortably in the candlelight. "Mind if I light the lantern? I can grade the pearls better in lantern light."

"Grade them?" she said, handing him the lantern from her bedside. "What do you mean by 'grade' them?"

Billy held the burning candlewick under the globe and lit the lantern. "See how much they're worth. I'm not up on today's prices, but I can give you an idea of what they'd sell for."

Pearl wrinkled her pretty nose. "Pearls from that old muddy lake aren't worth anything."

"A pearl is a pearl, Miss Cobb. It doesn't matter if it comes from a Caddo Lake mussel or a South Seas oyster. They're all graded the same way."

She stared across the room at him. He was an unusual man to know so much about pearls. Who was he? What had he come here for?

Billy shuffled nervously. "Well, where are they? If you don't mind . . ."

"They're in here." She picked up the tobacco tin from her bed.

They sat across from each other at her table and he opened the container. He angled the box to catch the light, then reached in with his fingertips and nudged apart the square of velvet bundled around the pearls, to get a glimpse of them. "You've got a lot of them," he said.

Pearl shrank into her chair with shame, and Billy looked as if he regretted commenting on the extent of her acquisitions. Perhaps he hadn't meant anything by it. He removed the piece of velvet from the tobacco tin and spread it across the tabletop, letting the light strike and dance upon the pearls.

There were more than twenty pearls of many shapes and colors. About half of them were white. The others varied from blue to purple to pink to yellow to gold. Only a few were perfect spheres. Some were flat, others long and thin like spikes; still others were shaped like flower petals or angels' wings. Then there were the smoky-blue teardrop and the yellow oval.

"You like pearls?" he asked as he pushed them into groups, studying them.

"All girls like pearls." She looked at him blankly, coolly. "I like the white ones best." She felt compelled to speak something she had never said to anyone else. "The colored ones are pretty, but the white ones look like the moon through a rainbow."

He glanced appreciatively into her eyes. "In the South Sea islands," he said, turning back to the pearls, "there's a legend of a god called Oro who rides to Earth on a rainbow." He held a round white pearl up to the light. "And he leaves a little of that rainbow color on the pearls wherever he goes."

She felt her heartbeat quicken. "How do you know things like that?" she asked, fascinated by his manners and his talk.

"Like I said, I used to collect pearls. And I've read everything ever written on them, I guess." He spoke as if pacing his words while he herded the gems into piles, comparing them, moving them from group to group. "The Greeks thought they were caused by lightning striking the water. And the Romans . . . well, the Romans thought they were the tears of angels. Christopher Columbus theorized that they were caused by dewdrops falling into the water from mangrove plants. . . ."

She felt as if she were in a dream. No one had ever spoken to her of such fanciful ideas. That was not bayou talk. "Whatever got you so interested in pearls?"

He shrugged. "My father was a jeweler."

"So? My father was a gambler. You don't hear me going on about cards and dice."

Billy glanced up at her and smiled. "Well, we had a summer home in the country in New Jersey. A stream nearby had mussels in it that my mother liked to fry. She'd send me out to collect them."

"And you found a pearl in one of them?"

"Only after it was cooked and on my plate. The cooking had ruined it. My father said it would have been worth five hundred dollars. It was a big round one. Anyway, that's what got me interested in pearls. I'm out of the business now, though. I had some bad luck with it."

She watched in silence for some time as Billy studied the pearls with a serious look on his face.

"See," she said, mistaking his expression for one of disappointment. "I told you they weren't worth anything."

He looked up at her and squinted his eyes. He smiled slightly. "This blue teardrop is your best one, by my judgment. It'll fetch seven hundred. All together, Miss Cobb, I'd say you have between three and four thousand dollars' worth of pearls here."

Pearl looked back and forth between Billy's face and the collection of Caddo Lake pearls. This Billy Treat was out of his mind! "That doesn't make sense. How come nobody ever sold them before?"

"Probably because nobody knew they were worth anything. The South Sea islanders used to play marbles with theirs, until they found out they could sell them."

That was the third time he had mentioned the South Sea to her. "Have you been there? To the South Sea?"

He looked away from her and nodded. "Yes. Years ago. Listen, Miss Cobb, I know a pearl-buyer who works out of New York City who would probably be interested in buying these from you. If you want me to, I'll contact him for you and have him come take a look."

Pearl got up from her chair to stand beside the table. "I never wanted to sell them," she said, wringing her hands.

"Why not?"

"They're mine. I like them."

Billy sighed. "Look, Miss Cobb," he said, "I know how

you came by these pearls. I don't understand why you'd want to keep them. But if you sell them, you can use the money to get out of this town. You can make a new start. You know how to run a business. You could buy one of your own."

Pearl's anger flared. She put her hands on her hips and scowled at him. "Well, you've got gall to talk to me like that. Anyway, since you know how I came by these pearls, I guess you also know that if I sell them for money, it makes me a whore . . . an expensive one, to hear you talk." She didn't raise her voice, but charged it with deep indignation.

"Whether you do it for pearls or for money," he said, "it seems about the same to me. What I'm telling you is that you've got a chance to turn your adversity into something valuable. That's how pearls are made."

"What's that supposed to mean?"

"A pearl starts out as something that galls the shellfish—whether it's an oyster or a mussel. It could be a grain of sand the creature can't get rid of. Could be that some pearls start as parasites living off of the shellfish. Anyway, the animal takes this thing that frets it, and covers it with the same stuff it coats the inside of its shell with. Covers it and covers it until it's not a problem anymore, but a thing of beauty."

She turned her mouth into a voluptuous smirk. "What about the tears of angels?"

"There may be some truth to that, too. Don't you believe in angels?"

"Yes."

"Don't you believe they cry?"

She paused, thinking. "Yes." She spoke now with less bitterness. "I even know why."

Billy nodded. "Sell the pearls and use the money to your advantage. That's my advice."

She folded her arms in front of her. "I don't need your

advice. They're *my* pearls. I won't agree to sell them just because you come in here with a bunch of stories and put a high price on them." She scoffed. "What makes you think I believe you? What do you care about me?"

He shrugged. "Well, if you change your mind, I'll contact the pearl-buyer." He stood, pulling a handkerchief from his pocket. "I found something today. I want you to have it." He came around the table as he untied a knot in the handkerchief. He turned the corners back and revealed the white pearl from Goose Prairie Cove. He picked it up and placed it in her hand. "This one's worth another hundred and fifty or so."

Carol Anne was seething. Now she had him figured out. He knew what she was, and she knew what he wanted. In spite of his fancy talk and his good looks and his heroism, he was just another riverboat man. She suddenly doubted that he had ever read about pearls at all, or had ever been to the South Sea. He was just making it all up to exaggerate the value of the gift, hoping she would respond in kind.

Still, she was ready to earn that pearl. He didn't know about her power. She could snuff the lantern and turn him into someone else. He would never even realize it. She would keep the pearl, and under its rainbow luster, imprison a million visions of bliss. She didn't need him. She only needed his pearl. She closed her palm around it and began deciding who he would be when he crawled into her bed.

"Like I said, I've had some bad luck with pearls. I'd just as soon somebody else had it who appreciates it." He went to the door and put on his hat. "Like the moon through a rainbow." He smiled. "I'll remember that." Then he was gone.

Carol Anne opened her hand and looked at Billy's gift. She angled her palm and let the perfect sphere roll down her fingertips, onto the velvet. It bumped against another pearl and quenched, in an instant, all the silly images associated with it. Like a ripple from a stone thrown in the water, the power of the new white pearl spread outward and rinsed the fragile fantasies from each of the others, leaving them quiet and dead. Now only Billy's pearl remained animated with hopes and desires.

She burst through the door and ran down the steps. She sprinted around the corner of the store and saw him crossing the street toward Widow Humphry's inn.

"Mr. Treat!" she cried.

He turned.

"Contact the pearl-buyer."

He nodded and waved. "Call me Billy."

SIX

There is no such thing as a fourteen-year-old gentleman. If you think you've found one, he's got you fooled. I don't care how often he says please, thank you, and yes ma'am—in his private mind, he's another person.

Take me, for example. I was well-liked by adults in Port Caddo. They thought of me as a fine boy. Of course, a few of the men who could remember being fourteen were on to me, but the ladies had no clue. My mother, I am sure, thought never a lecherous idea crossed my mind. She would have been horrified had she known the truth.

Cecil Peavy's old man, Joe Peavy, was a horse trader in Port Caddo. He was an expert judge of horseflesh. He could look at horses' legs and tell you how it would feel to ride them. He would comment on the muscling of the thighs, the curvature of the hips. He liked horses spare in the flank and round in the loin. He knew them from throatlatch to tail, from hock to knee. He could even look at a mare and tell you whether or not she would ever "fall apart," meaning to break down and lose her fine conformation at a certain age.

Well, that summer I started applying Joe Peavy's principles to females of the human species. There was nothing gentlemanly about the way I ogled girls and young women, sizing them up like horseflesh. I too liked them spare in the flank and curved in the hips. And I could give you my opinion as to whether or not they would fall apart before the age of twenty-seven.

I knew every vantage in town that facilitated a regular look at girls, and many of them were situated around Snyder's store, for Pearl Cobb was the ideal against which all other specimens were judged.

Behind the store there was a large oak tree with a comfortable fork about twenty feet up that afforded a perfect view of the stairs leading to Pearl's room. I often perched there after dark, hoping to see her ascend. Then I would watch the window and wonder what she was doing. Occasionally I would see her through the curtains. I wasn't exactly a Peeping Tom, for I had no real malicious intent. I was just a fourteen-year-old boy with raging curiosities.

I was there in the oak tree when Billy Treat went up to Pearl's room, and I hated him. I thought I knew what he was going to do with the pearl that should have belonged to me. That's why I was so surprised to see the lantern come on. I saw them sit together at the table. They talked. Then they stood. Then he left.

I didn't know what to make of Billy. I was at first relieved. He hadn't used his pearl as others had used theirs before him. He wasn't trying to trade it in for the vague pleasures of Pearl in the dark. Then, somehow, I knew that that was what made him dangerous. He was a gentleman and I was not.

I saw Pearl run from her room, down the stairs, around the store. I heard her call out to him. She came home alone.

It confused me. Was he going to ruin everything Pearl Cobb was, or was he going to rescue her as he had rescued me from the sinking riverboat? I feared and respected him, admired and hated him. He wasn't a particularly nice fellow to be around, but I liked him. I feared he would find work elsewhere and leave town, and at the same time, I couldn't wait for him to go.

Thankfully, something happened in Port Caddo that took my mind off of Pearl Cobb and Billy Treat for a while. Some workmen came up from Shreveport in a government snag boat to remove the remnants of the *Glory of Caddo Lake* from the bayou channel. The snag boat had been built to winch stumps and dead trees up from the waters and cut them into harmless pieces. Those snags, as they were called, had ripped open the thin wooden hulls of many a riverboat.

Every snag boat I ever saw floated on two hulls that would straddle a snag. A steam winch between the two hulls would lift that snag out of the water where the steam-powered saws could cut it up. The snag boat was invented by Henry Shreve, the old riverboat genius and founder of Shreveport. For years, the government employed him and his snag boats to clear the Great Raft from the Red River, so steamers could navigate above it. Shreve had been dead more than twenty years that summer, but his inventions were still whittling away at that immense logjam on the Red.

This snag boat that was pulling the old *Glory* apart usually worked at removing the Great Raft, but had come up through Caddo Lake to clear the wreck from our channel for us.

Between baiting our trotline and checking it for fish, Cecil Peavy and Adam Owens and I spent a lot of time on the Port Caddo wharf watching the snag boat work. Billy Treat also came out to watch when he wasn't cooking or cleaning up the kitchen in Widow Humphry's inn. He seemed very interested. Every evening when the snag-boat men quit work, he asked them what they had found.

One day a steamer came up Big Cypress Bayou and instead of tying up at the Port Caddo wharf, it anchored first beside the snag boat in the channel. The rousters put a gangplank between the two boats and we saw a fellow in alligator shoes and a silk tie cross the gangplank to the snag boat. He poked around for a long time, asking questions and writing things down. Then he had one of the snag-boat men bring him to the wharf in a rowboat.

"That's him," the snag-boat worker said, pointing at Billy, who was standing on the wharf at the time.

"Are you Billy Treat?" the man asked, stepping up on the wharf. He was a chubby fellow of about forty, dressed in slick New Orleans styles, stained with sweat. He grew little-bitty mustaches that looked like they had been drawn on with a pencil.

"Yes," Billy said.

"You were the cook on the *Glory of Caddo Lake?*"

"Who are *you?*" Billy asked.

The man stuck out his hand. "Joshua Lagarde, Delta State Insurance Company, New Orleans. We hold the policy on the *Glory of Caddo Lake*. The owners have put in a claim."

"The owners?" Billy said. "Captain Gentry was the only owner I knew of."

Lagarde mopped his neck with a handkerchief and shook with a chuckle. "Gentry didn't own the boat, Mr. Treat. He sold it six months ago to pay off some gambling debts. The new owners simply insisted that he continue to pose as captain and owner so as not to damage trade. At least that's the story they give."

"Who are these new owners?" Billy asked.

"I'm not at liberty to say. I would appreciate your cooperation, Mr. Treat, but you'll have to let me ask the questions."

I nudged Adam Owens. "Run to my pop's office and tell him there's a story on the wharf," I said. Adam wasn't listening to what was going on anyway. As long as I knew him, he never cared much for gossip and intrigue. He died a simple working man. He took off at a run toward my pop's newspaper office, delighted to have something to do.

"Now, Mr. Treat," Lagarde said, "the fellows on the snag boat have brought up the steam engines and all their fittings—the throttle, the valves, etcetera. I've found something quite curious about them. All the valves were closed at the time of the explosion. Do you have any idea why?"

"Yes, I do," Billy said. "There was nobody in the engine room when the boat blew up. . . ." He went on to tell how the explosion had occurred, and he told it in such detail that it gave my pop time to arrive. Pop walked up real casual and pretended to be watching the snag-boat work. But he was in easy listening distance of the insurance man. Billy was just finishing up by explaining how the *Glory*'s engineer had climbed into the yawl only minutes before the boilers blew.

"Why would he do that?" Lagarde asked.

"His story was that he wanted to check something on the paddle wheel as the boat got underway."

Lagarde scribbled something down in a notebook. "How much do you know about steamboats, Mr. Treat?"

"I worked on the *Glory* for a year and a half. I knew her pretty well."

"Do you know what this is?" He motioned to the man in the rowboat, who handed up a large iron cylinder, pretty badly mangled.

Billy took it in one hand. "Used to be a safety valve."

"Notice anything unusual about it?"

"Yes. The valve lever has been loaded down with extra weight."

"What does that mean?"

"I think you know what it means, Lagarde. It defeats

the purpose of having a safety valve in the first place, doesn't it?"

Lagarde chuckled again and took the valve back. "The men couldn't find the other two safety valves. This one came from the only boiler that didn't explode. Who do you suppose might have loaded the lever down?"

"You'd have to ask the engineer."

"I have a Mr. Judd Kelso listed as the engineer."

"That's right."

"Any idea where I might find him?"

"Right now," Billy said, "he's probably over at old Esau's saloon."

Lagarde's eyes widened. "He's still here? He hasn't left town?"

"No. I hear he's got family around here."

"Have you noticed him spending money freely, making any large purchases?"

Billy Treat glanced at me. "He's been flashing a big roll of bills."

"That's right," I said. "I've seen it."

Cecil stepped up. "Me, too. That big around." He made a circle with his fingers.

Joshua Lagarde mopped his face and smiled. "Where is this saloon?"

"A couple of miles from town," Billy said. "I'll walk over there with you, if you'd like."

"Why not drive?" Pop said, turning suddenly and stepping up to the men. "I was thinking about taking a buggy over there and having a little drink this afternoon anyway." He nudged Lagarde.

The insurance man smiled and licked his lips.

I don't know how my pop did it, but he could tell you half a man's life just by looking at him. That's what made him such a good newspaper man. He had Joshua Lagarde pegged as a drinker the instant he saw him. Pop wasn't normally a drinker himself, but he'd swallow a few to get in on a good story.

"Ben, you and your friends go hitch the buggy," he said, even before Lagarde accepted his offer.

Well, we didn't own a buggy, but I just sang out "Yessir" and ran to Cecil's daddy's livery stable with Cecil and Adam, and we led a horse and buggy back down to the wharf. My pop often used us boys as his special agents to run errands and ferret out good newspaper stories, and we loved it.

"What kind of business are you in, Mr. Crowell?" asked Lagarde as he and Pop and Billy Treat got into the buggy.

"I own a print shop," Pop said, never mentioning the newspaper. It was true. He did a lot of printing on the side.

Us boys didn't get to ride to the saloon with the men, but I found out later what happened. I asked Pop about it, and read his report when it came out in the paper. Years later, I came across the notes he had made after the meeting at the saloon. He had amazing recall for details and could repeat a conversation almost to the word after the fact. In his *Port Caddo Steam Whistle* article, he didn't use much of the conversation that took place at Esau's saloon, because it didn't prove anything conclusively, and Pop didn't print rumor or speculation. But his notes say the meeting went like this:

Lagarde: Mr. Kelso, were you the engineer on the
  Glory of Caddo Lake the morning she blew up?
Kelso: I damn sure was.
Lagarde: Were you on the boat when she blew?
Kelso: Of course.
Lagarde: Mr. Treat says you were in the yawl.
Kelso: Well, I was, but I was right beside the boat. I
  was going to have my apprentice tow me behind
  the boat so I could listen to a thumping sound I

heard in the paddle wheel and try to figure out what was making it. (Kelso very indignant toward Treat.)

Lagarde: Why wasn't anyone in the engine room when the captain gave the signal to steam ahead?

Kelso: I told my apprentice to let the yawl down and get back into the engine room. He was slow, I guess.

Lagarde: Where is your apprentice now?

Kelso: I don't know. He went off looking for work.

Treat: He rode the *Sarah Stevens* down to New Orleans to find a job. His name is Reggie Swearengen. (Kelso glowering at Treat. Lagarde writing notes.)

Lagarde: Mr. Kelso, in your opinion, what caused the boilers to explode on the *Glory of Caddo Lake?*

Kelso: They were old, and the niggers threw too much wood under them.

Lagarde: As far as you know, were the safety valves on the boilers in good working order?

Kelso: Yes.

Lagarde: How do you know?

Kelso: I set them myself.

Lagarde: Did you hear them releasing steam at any time before the explosion?

Kelso: I didn't notice. I guess they did.

Lagarde: Mr. Kelso, we have recovered a safety valve from the wreck. It was loaded down with extra weight. Can you explain that? (Kelso nervous. Goes outside to relieve himself. Gone two minutes.)

Lagarde: About the safety valves, Mr. Kelso.

Kelso: Yes, I just remembered. Captain Gentry checked the valves the night before the blowup. I saw him.

Lagarde: What are you saying?

Kelso: I'm saying he checked them.

Lagarde: Why didn't you mention that before?

Kelso: It didn't seem worth it. He was always going behind me and checking things.

Treat: He never checked my work.

Kelso: (Angry.) You're just a goddamn cook, Treat!

Lagarde: Mr. Kelso, are you suggesting that Captain Gentry may have intentionally blown the boat up?

Kelso: If the safety valves were loaded down, he must have done it. I know I didn't.

Lagarde: Why would Captain Gentry want to blow up the *Glory of Caddo Lake?*

Kelso: You're the investigator. You tell me.

Lagarde: Captain Gentry had nothing to gain. He didn't have the policy on the boat. He didn't own it.

Kelso: (Doesn't seem surprised.) Maybe he did it for whoever it was that did own it. The son of a bitch! He could have blown us all to hell, but just ended up killing himself! (Laughs.)

My pop's notes also mention that Billy didn't drink, that Kelso insisted on paying for Lagarde's drinks from a large roll of cash he carried in his pocket, and that after a few rounds, Lagarde let it slip that the owners of the *Glory of Caddo Lake* were suspected in a number of other insurance-fraud cases.

In his article, Pop only mentioned that insurance fraud was suspected and that the explosion might have been intentional. He didn't even print Kelso's name, but word got around town that Kelso was a prime suspect. Before long, it was plain that everybody in Port Caddo considered him a murderer. But Kelso was hardheaded and stayed around. He avoided nobody. It seemed he wanted to taunt us. He was an idiot. The days of vigilante lynch mobs were not that far behind us. I guess he figured he was protected because he came from a big family of ruffians, all of them living over at Long Point.

Joshua Lagarde didn't stay in town long. He took the mangled safety valve from the *Glory of Caddo Lake* back to New Orleans as physical evidence. His investigation would eventually prove that Kelso had blown up the *Glory* for a price.

I didn't find out about that until years later, and by that time, the proof was worthless, seeing as how Kelso was already dead. He was knifed to death in Carol Anne Cobb's room and nobody to this day can prove who did it. But I'm getting ahead of myself, because Kelso wasn't killed until September—after the rise and fall of that wondrous event called the Great Caddo Lake Pearl Rush.

SEVEN

The gangplank bent and sprang under the weight of Trevor Brigginshaw as he bounded down it to the Port Caddo wharf. He carried a large leather satchel, buffed with age around the corners, etched everywhere with hairline cracks, and stuffed to bulging with unknown contents. In spite of the July heat and humidity, he wore a white cotton jacket that strained at the seams around his bulk, like an overfilled grain sack.

He looked like a huge animated hero from a romantic painting, his neck rigid, beard full and jutting, chest barreled, legs consuming ground in great, powerful strides. He hummed an Australian marching song as he strode up the bayou bank to the cobblestones, where the business district of Port Caddo began.

People stopped to watch him pass. His size alone made

him conspicuous. He stood six-foot-five and carried two hundred fifty pounds as if chiseled from a great trunk of oak. Despite his size, he did not appear fearsome. In fact, there was something engaging about his energy and lively swagger.

"You there!" he shouted to Robert Timmons, the tinsmith, as he reached high ground. "You, mate! A word, please." His deep Australian brogue pinned Timmons in his tracks. Brigginshaw swept his panama hat from his head as he descended on the local informant. "I'm looking for a Miss Carol Anne Cobb. Where can I find her?"

Timmons pointed up the street as he tried to take in all of Trevor Brigginshaw and make some kind of sense out of what such a character would be doing in Port Caddo, Texas. "Snyder's store," he said. "The building with the red brick front, up the street. She works there."

"Good man!" Brigginshaw said through a toothy smile. He slapped the panama back onto his curly head and hiked up the street on swinging cassowary legs.

The brass bell on the door of Snyder's store jingled in alarm as the huge Australian burst in. His size in the doorway brought the darkness of storm clouds into the building. Pearl stepped back from the counter in surprise and three wives looked up from their shopping lists.

Brigginshaw's eyes fell on the exquisite form of Pearl. "Miss Cobb?" he said.

She nodded.

The worn leather satchel blew dust from the cracks as it hit the hardwood floor. Brigginshaw dragged his panama from his head and onto his gigantic heart. He strode as if entranced to the counter between himself and Pearl. "Billy Treat is a bloody fool to have understated your beauty." He reached for her fingers, bowed over the counter, and kissed the back of her hand.

Pearl pulled her hand away. The three customers were agog, watching from the aisles between the store shelves.

"Who are you?" Pearl said.

"Captain Trevor Price Brigginshaw—Sydney, London, and New York."

"Well. . . . What do you want?"

"I've come to purchase your pearls."

"You're the pearl-buyer?"

"The pearl-buyer?" Brigginshaw bellowed. "Is that how the wretch refers to me? The pearl-buyer? Doesn't he have the common decency to name me? He that saved Billy Treat from pirates among the Pearl Islands of the Southern Seas? I'll thrash the lout when I see him again!" He laughed to keep from shocking her.

"I don't think he meant anything by it," Pearl said.

"You think not? Billy's a calculating bloke, Miss Cobb. He doesn't do anything without purpose. Now, where do you keep this collection of exquisite pearls? If they are as beautiful as you, I promise I cannot afford to buy them."

"Now? I'm working right now," she said. But when she thought of ridding herself of all those angel tears, as Billy had said the Romans called them, she couldn't wait. "Oh, all right, I'll get them." She turned to the customers. "You ladies make your own change," she said, and swept past Trevor Brigginshaw to the door.

When she came back from her room with the tobacco tin, she found the pearl buyer opening his satchel on the store counter. "Not in here," she said. "Over at Widow Humphry's inn. Billy works there."

"I insist on business before pleasure, Miss Cobb. Let's have-a-look at the pearls and strike a deal, then we'll see Billy."

"Let's see Billy first," Pearl said, sternly. "I don't know anything about grading pearls. You might swindle me."

"I? A cheat?" Brigginshaw roared.

Pearl looked away, as if bored.

The big Australian began to laugh. He laughed so loud that one of the customers covered her ears. "Has Billy mentioned only my vilest characteristics, Miss Cobb? I'd brain another man for less, but with a skull as thick as Billy's, it would benefit him no more than it would a hammerhead shark." He buckled the leather satchel. "Is the Widow Humphry as beautiful as you?"

Pearl Cobb and Trevor Brigginshaw caused a sensation crossing the main street of Port Caddo together. Robert Timmons had already alerted the town to the arrival of the big Australian. When Pearl and Trevor reached the inn, the women in Snyder's store dispersed without buying anything or making any change, and went to spread the news.

The buyer and the seller found Billy in the kitchen, cleaning up the dinner mess.

"My God, can it be?" Brigginshaw said. "The king of Mangareva's become a lowly galley rat!"

Billy wheeled. His eyes fell on Pearl first, momentarily. Then he shifted his pale gaze to the Australian. "Trev," he said.

Pearl saw a new Billy. Life leaped into his eyes and molded his face with a smile. He wrung his greasy hands on an apron as he marched forward and fell into the crushing embrace of Trevor Brigginshaw. They shook the whole inn, hopping in each other's arms like boys, each slapping the other's back as if trying to put out a fire.

A couple of the most avid gossips in town happened to come visiting at Widow Humphry's just as Pearl and the two men retired to Billy's room. It was scandalous. The two men went down the hall laughing and talking, and Pearl followed them into the room with her tobacco tin.

When Captain Trevor Brigginshaw took off his white jacket, Pearl almost gasped at the revolver stuck under his belt, its handle inlaid with mother-of-pearl.

"Nothing to fear," he said, sensing her apprehension. "The weapon is intended strictly for security of the company's property. I rarely have to use it."

"The company?" Billy said. "What company?"

"International bloody Gemstones," Trevor said with a snarl.

"I thought you were independent."

"The company's only a temporary inconvenience, mate. Until I can afford another boat and get back among the Pearl Islands."

"What happened to the *Wicked Whistler?*"

"Hurricane, last year on Jamaica. Now, let's not take up any more of Miss Cobb's valuable time with our personal business. I'll tell you all about it later." Captain Brigginshaw opened his satchel, took out a rolled piece of black velvet, and spread it across Billy's table. "The pearls, if you please, Miss Cobb."

She gave him the tobacco tin. He opened it, poker-faced, and shrugged as he poured the pearls onto the black velvet. He began sorting them, as Billy Treat had done in her room. He hummed as he made piles, his rich baritone voicing an occasional phrase. Pearl looked at Billy. He smiled at her.

"They pale in comparison to your loveliness, Miss Cobb," Trevor said after several minutes of sorting. "I'm afraid they disappoint me."

Billy scoffed and chuckled.

"Let's start with these small ones. They're little better than seed pearls. I can pay no more than thirty-five dollars for each."

Billy laughed. "Seed pearls! There's not a pearl there smaller than ten grains! Even the baroques are worth eighty dollars each."

"You've been out of the business too long, Billy. These dogtooth and wing pearls are virtually worthless on today's market. . . ."

They haggled for fifteen minutes and finally arrived at a figure of seventy-five dollars apiece for the first batch of ten pearls. Trevor removed a ledger book from his satchel and mumbled as he penciled in the first purchase:

"A clutch of ten *seed* pearls . . . seventy-five dollars each . . . Miss Carol Anne Cobb."

His thick fingers picked up the ten pearls one by one and put them in a case with velvet folds in it to keep the gems from rolling around. "Now, for this group of seven, I'll pay eighty dollars each. They're hardly superior to the first clutch."

Billy laughed again. "You see what he's done, Carol Anne? He's separated your best pairs. See these two pear-shaped specimens? They're perfectly matched, and worth more when sold together, for making earrings. But Trev here has put them in different batches! Same with these two egg-shaped pearls."

The haggling commenced again, and went on for half an hour. The men regrouped the pearls several times and finally agreed on a clutch of five that would sell for one hundred twenty dollars each. Billy looked at Pearl. She nodded. Trevor made the notations in the ledger book.

The eight finest pearls remained on the black velvet. In an hour, Billy and Trevor had agreed to put six of them in a batch to sell for two hundred each. Billy looked at Pearl for approval.

"Not that one," she said, indicating the pearl of living visions that Billy had given her. "It's not for sale." She removed it from the group and held it in her hand.

Billy's face revealed nothing to Trevor Brigginshaw.

Only two pearls remained unsold. Brigginshaw tried to group them together, but Billy insisted on bargaining for each separately. He graded the yellow oval at nineteen grains. Trevor said it was only fifteen. He took the pieces of a small scale from his satchel, put it together, and weighed the pearl at almost exactly nineteen grains. Billy mentioned its superior shape, luster, and overtone. He would settle for no less than three hundred dollars. Pearl agreed. Trevor relented after forty-five minutes.

They spent a full hour dickering over the smoky-blue teardrop that had begun Pearl's collection six years before. Thirty grains, Billy said. Trevor shook the inn with laughter. But the scale and the pearl's shape, color, and orient ultimately demanded seven hundred and fifty dollars, despite the Australian's fiercest negotiations.

Brigginshaw sighed as he made the final entry in his ledger. "Miss Cobb, my trip to Port Caddo has hardly been worth my time at these high prices. What little gratitude Billy has shown me for saving his life from pirates in the South Pacific."

"Don't let your conscience bother you, Carol Anne," Billy said. "This man's a pirate himself when it comes to pearls. Those big hands have held more pearls than all the royalty in the world put together ever did."

Brigginshaw chuckled. "Now, about that last pearl," he said. "May I have another look at it?"

Carol Anne opened her hand and put the pearl on the black velvet. The buyer picked up a pearl case and probed through a few of the folds. "No, not that one," he mumbled. "No, too small. Wrong color. Ah! Here it is. A perfect match." He removed a white sphere, identical to the one on the velvet cloth. "This one came from Pennsylvania. Since it matches yours, I can offer an extra fifty. Two hundred fifty dollars, Miss Cobb. What?"

Carol Anne took her pearl back into her hand. "This one's not for sale," she said.

"Three hundred?"

"No. It was a gift." She folded her fingers around it protectively.

Billy remained silent.

Carol Anne was about to ask how International Gemstones would pay for the pearls when the Australian lifted a stack of bills from his satchel. He slowly and methodically counted out thirty-four one-hundred-dollar bills.

Before handing them to her, he said, "I insist on one stipulation before making this deal complete."

"What now?" Billy asked.

"Both of you must keep your mouth shut about these ridiculous prices. I won't be taken this badly again if there are any other pearls to be purchased about here. Agreed?"

"I'll agree," Billy replied.

"Yes, that's fine," Carol Anne said.

After the money changed hands, Trevor wanted to celebrate. But Carol Anne said she had to get back to the store. Mr. Snyder was probably furious at her for taking the entire afternoon off. And Billy had to prepare supper for the boarders.

"Just as well," Trevor said, covering his weapon as he put on his jacket. "That will give me just enough time before supper to do a little business in town. Set an extra plate, Billy. I hope you're a better cook than friend."

The inn's parlor had seldom seen as much socializing. When Carol Anne and the two men left Billy's room, a hush enveloped a dozen or more town gossips, men and women. Carol Anne went out first, ignoring the eyes that followed her.

"Who's your friend, Mr. Treat?" someone asked, before Billy could turn into the kitchen.

"Captain Trevor Price Brigginshaw," the big Australian said, letting Billy go with a wave.

"Staying with us tonight, Mr. Brigginshaw?" Widow Humphry asked.

"I would be pleased to, Madam. I was hoping you would have accommodations available."

"Oh, yes. We haven't filled up since before the war. Shall I have the boy take your suitcase up?"

"No, thank you, my good woman. It never leaves my side. It's because of this bloody case that I have never married. It's a terrible burden in bed."

Some of the men laughed, a couple of ladies giggled, and the others gasped. Widow Humphry urged the owner of the case in question to sign the register.

"Whatever you've got in there, it must be important for you to take it to bed with you," said Robert Timmons.

"It is filled with things of great value and beauty," Brigginshaw said. "Things that I am bound to protect with my life."

"Your accent is delightful," said an infatuated young woman. "Do you mind our asking . . . ?"

"Not at all. I've heard that you Texans are a great deal like us Australians—never pass up an opportunity to boast whence you hail. Sydney, Australia, is my home, though I keep residences in New York and London as well."

"Put the name of your firm here, if you wish," Widow Humphry said. She made knowing faces at the locals over the big man's back as he bent to write in the space she had indicated. "Your room will be upstairs. First on the left. Supper at six."

"Thank you, my good woman. Now, if someone will direct me to the local newspaper office . . ."

Several volunteers rendered the directions and the pearl-buyer left, tipping his panama as he stepped out. There was a general rush to read the register when he was gone.

In two minutes, Trevor Brigginshaw had found the offices of the *Port Caddo Steam Whistle*. John Crowell knew about him already, and had been receiving reports from news-gathering spies all afternoon. He was busy setting type, however, and couldn't get out of the office to do any snooping on his own. He was happy to see the news come to him for a change.

"It's my pleasure to meet you," Crowell said, shaking the stranger's powerful hand. "I've been saving a place for you at the bottom of page one. My instincts tell me some import accompanies your visit."

"God bless a bloke who follows his instincts. Mine have kept me alive for many years. Getting an issue together soon, are you?"

"Going to press tonight, as a matter of fact. Your timing is very good."

"Between my timing and your instincts, we may just benefit each other, Mr. Crowell. We very well may." He sat down in front of the editor's desk, holding his satchel in his lap. "I'm here to buy pearls. I've already made one confidential purchase this afternoon, and I'd like to advertise for more in your paper. What are you laughing at, mate?"

"I'm sorry," Crowell said, wiping his inky hands on his apron. "It's just that everybody in town already knows about your 'confidential' purchase."

"That I gathered. But the details will have to remain confidential. I can say only that the local collector had many pearls valued at about ten thousand dollars."

The smile slid from John Crowell's face. "Did you say ten thousand?"

"Roughly. Don't press for details, Mr. Crowell. I can't tell you any more than that. The collector insisted."

"Ten thousand dollars! How many pearls did she have? She couldn't have had more than twenty or twenty-five."

"I'm not at liberty to say."

"Ten thousand dollars!" The editor got up to look at the hole in his front-page plate. "I had no idea those pearls would bring such high prices."

"I wish I could give you more details of the sale for your front-page story, Mr. Crowell, but the collector wants to avoid publicity. I, on the other hand, want to feed it. I wonder if a quarter-page advertisement might make a good start."

"It might," Crowell said. "But a half-page—and a story at the top of page one instead of the bottom—might attract a good deal more publicity. Yes, a good deal more."

Trevor Brigginshaw smiled as he opened his money case. "A sensible newspaper man is more difficult to come by than the finest paragon of pearls. You, mate, are a gem!"

EIGHT

You know when I got religion? When I found out Jesus was a fisherman.

I have lived within casting distance of water all my life, and I guess I've caught fish every which way known to man. I've sailed the Gulf of Mexico and hooked tarpon bigger than calves. I've climbed the Rocky Mountains to fly-cast for rainbow trout in waters barely ankle-deep. I've waded the mouths of big rivers and speared flounder by lantern light with a pointed stick.

But the best fishing waters I know of in the world are right here at Caddo Lake. If you could take all the fish I've caught here in my life and put them together at one time, they would fill up the lake they came from. I'm mainly a sport fisherman now, and just plug some for bass around the lily pads. Bass are good fighting fish and not bad eating. I also enjoy fishing with live minnows on cane poles for white perch. And I once made pretty good money catching those spoonbill catfish around spawning time to pass their eggs off as caviar.

But back in my younger days is when I really caught fish. I would load them in barrels to ship to Marshall, Jefferson, or Dallas. That and duck-hunting and hogs and boat-building have gotten me through some lean years when the sawmills and railroads weren't hiring.

I used to set gill nets and trammel nets in the Big Water and up Jeem's Bayou to catch carp and buffalo by the hundreds every night. Old Esau showed me how to shoot them with a bow and arrow, tying a stout cord to the arrow. I once shot a hundred-and-twenty-pound alligator gar that fought for over an hour before I clubbed it senseless with an oar.

After Billy Treat taught us how to hold our breath for a good long time, Adam Owens and I became famous around here for hand-grabbling those big opelousas cats out of hollow logs and out from under washed-out banks.

But of all the fishing I have ever done, trotlining gives me the biggest thrill. I like it even better than hooking those huge tarpon in salt water or catching those rising trout from the mountain streams. People who consider themselves sport fishermen scoff at the trotline, but I know of no finer tool for recreation or livelihood, and it all started for me that summer back in 1874, when me and Cecil Peavy and Adam Owens were catching cats for Billy Treat's kitchen.

We were on the lake at sunrise the day the Great Caddo Lake Pearl Rush began. It looked like any other summer day to us as we launched old Esau's skiff and started paddling toward our trotline over near Mossy Brake. We were talking about Captain Trevor Price Brigginshaw, who had come to town the day before.

"He's big as ol' Colored Bob over at the sawmill," Adam claimed.

"He's not that big," Cecil argued. "Colored Bob has to duck to go under doors."

"Well, he talks funnier than Colored Bob." Adam had his own strange way of winning arguments.

As they paddled and contradicted each other, I opened mussels to bait the trotline with, and of course I checked them all for pearls.

"Ben," Cecil said, "what are you gonna do if you really find a shell berry in there? Are you gonna trade it in for ten thousand dollars, or a hump with Pearl Cobb?"

"One pearl ain't worth ten thousand dollars," I said, avoiding the more interesting half of the question.

"I thought you said today's paper was gonna talk about Pearl Cobb selling a pearl for ten thousand dollars."

"It doesn't say it was Carol Anne, and it doesn't say it was just one pearl. Don't you ever listen?"

"I guess she probably sold that Captain Brigginshaw a couple of hundred pearls to get that much money. Lord knows, she's got a thousand of 'em."

"Shut up, Cecil," I said.

"You like her, don't you?" Adam asked.

Before I could think of an answer, Cecil said, "Like her? He's in love with her, boy, can't you tell? If Ben found a ten-thousand-dollar shell berry right now, he'd give it to Pearl Cobb for one hump, when he could get a couple of thousand humps for it over at the nigger whorehouse."

"How would you know, Cecil?"

We aggravated one another like that until we saw our trotline floats bobbing. The second-biggest thrill in trot-lining is seeing those floats bob. When you see that, you know you've caught something. We had good-sized cork floats on our trotline, and we hadn't yet caught anything big enough to pull one all the way under. But that morning, as we approached, we saw the cork stay under for five seconds, and we knew we had hooked a monster.

Cecil was businesslike, as usual. While Adam and I were almost falling overboard with excitement, he said, "Take it easy! We'll run it from the north end, like we always do. Whatever it is that's on there, it won't go anywhere. Probably just a big snappin' turtle or an alligator gar, anyway."

We had been using mussels to bait the line and had been catching mostly willow cats, because they don't mind eating dead bait. Billy had been very pleased with our catches.

They were mainly in the three-and four-pound class. A fresh willow cat of that size—skinned, filleted, and fried—is the best-eating fish in the world. The biggest we had caught was maybe ten pounds. We all knew that if we wanted to catch a huge opelousas catfish, we needed to put something live on the hook.

We had also caught a few carp, which we gave to some colored folks we knew, but I didn't think a carp would get big enough to hold the cork float down that long.

Figuring Cecil was probably right, I got a little nervous. An alligator gar big enough to pull that cork under like that would have a snout a foot long, lined with razor teeth. A snapping turtle of the same size could take your fingers off with one snap, quicker than you could blink.

But whatever it was, it wouldn't get *my* fingers. It was Adam's job to take the critters off the hooks. He had a knack for handling thrashing catfish without getting barbed, and I figured he could handle a gar or a snapper, too. Maybe he would just cut the line and let the monster go, the hook still in its mouth.

I figured it was a gar. We hadn't yet taken any turtles off the line on the morning runs. Turtles usually won't bother a trotline at night. Yes, I was pretty sure it was a gar, but that was part of the lure of trotlining. When you see those floats bobbing, you never really know what you've got until you hoist it up from the deep.

We paddled to a big cypress standing in the water at the edge of Mossy Brake. We had one end of our line tied to a cypress knee next to the tree. From there it ran down into a channel where those willow cats liked to prowl. Some people, as a matter of fact, call them channel cats for just that reason.

Adam sat in the front of the skiff. He would grab the line, pull the boat along, and take the fish off the hooks. I was in the back of the boat. I kept the boat straight, helped pull on the line, and put fresh bait on the hooks. Cecil was useless except as a counterweight. With Adam and me hanging over the right side of the skiff, it was helpful to have Cecil sit on the left side, to keep the boat as level as possible. As long as I knew Cecil, he always preferred to let other people do the work for him while he sat back and counted money.

The sun and the rich, rotten smell of the lake were hitting us when Adam began working the line. We pulled the skiff along, passing the rock we had tied on to pull the line to the right depth and keep it tight. Along the main line were lighter cords, about a foot and a half long, tied at six-foot intervals, and on these lighter cords were our hooks. The first few were empty. I untangled the twisted cords and baited their hooks with fresh mussels. Then I felt the first tug, despite Adam's hold on the line.

The biggest thrill in trotlining is feeling the fish tug from down deep. Even a little catfish can pull the line pretty hard. As we approached the next hook, I saw the flash of gray down in the brown, muddy water. Adam was smiling. He lived for simple pleasures like that. He pulled a three-pound willow cat to the surface. It splashed us pretty good before he got it unhooked and into the boat.

Catfish have bony barbs on their pectoral fins, and one on their dorsal fin, too. If they stick you, it aches something fierce for a long time. The skin has some kind of poison in it, I've heard. But Adam Owens wasn't afraid of anything you could pull out of the water, and he knew how to grab a catfish around those bony barbs where it couldn't jab him. He knew how to grab alligators, water moccasins, wild hogs, and snapping turtles, too.

He carried a pair of pliers in his pocket and had the hook out of the fish's mouth in no time. He threw it between the bulkheads at Cecil's bare feet.

"Hey, watch it!" Cecil said as the cat flipped and flopped around. "That thing will stick me!"

"Oh, shut up, Cecil," I said, still put out over what he had said about Carol Anne. "Just keep the boat steady."

We worked down the line, me and Adam feeling anxiously for the tug of every fish we had hooked, and getting more excited as we came closer to the place where something big was pulling the cork float under.

"All right, here it comes!" Adam said. We were only a couple of hooks away. "Hold the line tight, Ben. Don't let it pull a hook through your finger."

"Can you see it yet?"

"No, not yet. But, by gosh, I can sure feel it!"

The plunges of the creature on our line were rocking the boat like crazy.

"Just cut it loose as soon as you can," Cecil said, calmly. "Don't let it tear up our whole line. Hey, maybe it's a little gator. Watch your hand, Adam!"

"I'm watchin'! Gosh, it pulls hard!"

We worked the skiff forward and Adam grit his teeth lifting the catch. Then I saw it. A huge, flat head rose in the muddy water, then turned for the deep as if the light hurt its beady eyes. A broad tail flipped and splashed a wall of water toward me, even though the fish was still completely submerged.

"What is it?" Cecil demanded.

"It's the biggest damn opelousas cat I ever seen!" Adam's muscles were popping from his thin arms like twisted steel cables as he fought to pull the fish up. The line was all but cutting through his hand.

"Hold on tight, Adam!" I said.

He gave a loud grunt and hoisted the monster from the deep. It looked like a dinosaur coming up from Caddo Lake. Its broad, flat head told us it was an opelousas cat. Its mouth looked like the opening to Captain Brigginshaw's money satchel, with a jutting lower lip.

When it broke the surface, I saw its three bayonet-sized

barbs, then lost them behind a spray of brown froth. The boat almost pitched Cecil off of the high side. Adam hollered for joy as he reached into the gill under the monster's head and took a firm hold.

"It must weigh seventy-five pounds!"

"Get it in here, then!" Cecil said. "It's worth two bits to each of us!"

The catfish lunged, beat its head against the boat, and splashed bucketfuls all over the place, but Adam hung on. He didn't fool with the hook. He just cut the line that the hook was tied to. He almost fell over backward pulling the fish into the boat, and still wouldn't turn loose of the gills for fear the biggest fish he had ever seen would jump out of the skiff. The thing was fat and grotesque out of the water, beating itself stupidly against the bottom of the skiff and slapping the smaller fish with its tail.

"I guess you were wrong!" Cecil said triumphantly to Adam. "I guess you *can* catch an opelousas cat using dead mussels for bait!"

"No, I was right all along!" Adam said, panting. "Look!"

He pulled the lower jaw of that monster catfish open and we saw a smaller fish in the big one's mouth. About a seven-pound willow cat had taken our mussel bait and hooked itself. Then that giant opelousas cat had risen from its dark hole somewhere to eat the willow cat that had eaten the mussel. The hook alone probably wouldn't have held a fish that big. It probably could have bent it straight getting away. But when it swallowed that willow cat, the smaller fish set its barbs in the big cat's throat, and died holding it on our trotline for us.

Cecil had to take Adam's place running the rest of the line because Adam didn't trust him to hold onto the big fish. We baited as quick as we could, collected a few more normal-sized fish, and paddled back toward old Esau's saloon.

On the way, the *Lizzie Hopkins II* steamed within forty

yards of us, en route to Port Caddo. The pilot rang his bell and blew his steam whistle when we showed him the fish. The passengers all crowded the rail to see. We felt like decorated heroes. Lucky ones, at that. We hadn't expected any steamers. The lake was getting almost too low to handle them. The *Lizzie* would be the last one of the summer, until the rains came back.

When we came around Pine Island and caught sight of Esau's place, we saw a big crowd of people standing on the shore, others wading, and some floating in boats. It was as if the news of our tremendous catch had preceded us and people had come out to see it. We didn't know what was going on, but we were thrilled.

"Too bad Pop already printed the paper," I said. "Now we won't be in it till next week."

"He ought to print an extra for a fish like this," Cecil said. "I wonder what all those people are doing at Esau's. Wait a minute. I know what they're doing. Look! They're hunting for pearls!" He laughed so hard that he had to quit paddling. "That's Captain Brigginshaw on the shore with his suitcase."

Cecil was right. Everybody in town had seen Brigginshaw's half-page ad and read about the big pearl sale of the previous day. Half the population of Port Caddo had come to hunt up a fortune in Goose Prairie Cove, where Billy had recently found his pearl. Nobody had found anything yet, but a few disenchanted wives had brought old specimens their husbands had given them years before. Brigginshaw was dealing for them in the shade of a big mulberry.

"There's Billy standing beside that Brigginshaw fellow," I said.

"Good," Cecil replied. "He can pay us on the spot for this fish."

When we got closer, we started hollering to attract attention. We paddled in among the pearl-waders and let them look over the edge of the boat at our fish. Esau met us at the bank with Billy and Captain Brigginshaw. They made us feel good, bragging on us for bringing in such a monster whisker fish. Pop was there, too, taking notes on the pearl-hunt, and he promised he would write us up on the front page next week. When Billy said he would pay a penny a pound, as promised, Esau doubled the stakes.

"Might as well fry up some fish to feed these hungry pearl hunters," he said.

Most of the pearlers had come out of the water to view our fish and hear our story. They took turns looking into the big cat's mouth, to see the smaller one lodged in its throat. I was bulging with pride. For the first time in my life, I was earning money and getting recognition for something besides being my parents' son. Even Billy was amazed at what I had done. I wondered what Carol Anne would think when she heard.

What had started out as a pearl-hunt was quickly turning into nothing more than a big fish fry. The novelty of opening mussels in search of riches wore off fast. Most of the men were content to stand around our huge opelousas cat and tell fish stories. As whiskey sales increased, Esau decided to buy every fish we had in the boat. And he hired us to skin and gut them.

A couple of men volunteered to carry our big fish up under a tree where we could hang it, whack it on the head to make sure it was dead, and go to work on it. We felt like local heroes as two dozen whiskey-sipping ex-pearl-hunters followed us up under the boughs of the shade tree. It was shaping up to be the most glorious day of my life.

Then it happened. A shout came from Goose Prairie Cove. At first, nobody paid any attention. Slowly, though, I realized that somebody was yelling his lungs out. I heard a body splashing madly through the water, and turned to see Everett Diehl floundering to dry ground, all wet and muddy.

"Pearl!" he hollered. "I found a pearl!"

NINE

I was accustomed to Everett Diehl spoiling my fun, because he taught school at the Caddo Academy where I took my lessons. But school had been out for weeks now and he still wasn't satisfied. He was trying to upstage my catfish with a measly shell slug. As soon as he hollered "Pearl!" every man standing around the big ugly fish hanging in the tree turned and stampeded to the lakeshore to see what he had found.

"I was just about to give up!" Diehl claimed as the crowd gathered around him. "I thought I'd open one more. I almost threw it back in before I saw the pearl stuck to the rim of the shell. Look!"

Captain Brigginshaw pushed through the crowd of men, his money case like a battering ram. He took one glance and said, "Button pearl. I'll give you seventy-five dollars for it."

Diehl's enthusiasm wilted a little. "Seventy-five? But the paper said they were worth thousands."

"Those were excellent specimens, and many of them."

"Still . . ." Diehl lamented. "Just seventy-five dollars . . ."

"No small wage for two hours of work," the captain said, opening his money case. "Seventy-five dollars, take it or leave it."

As Diehl groused, Billy took the mussel shell from him to examine the pearl. "I'd take it," he advised. "This pearl isn't worth fifty. Captain Brigginshaw sometimes inflates the prices in the early going to promote interest."

The big pearl-buyer sighed and frowned at Billy for revealing his tactics. Diehl decided to sell immediately. When his soft, pale fingers closed around the seventy-five dollars, all the men in sight—except for Brigginshaw, Billy, and Esau—turned and ran into Goose Prairie Cove like boys. It was then that the Great Caddo Lake Pearl Rush truly began. My friends and I didn't get to take part in that first stampede. We had to gut and skin catfish.

The hunting went on fruitlessly until about sundown, when Allen Byers, the sawmill owner, came up with a hundred-dollar pearl. Brigginshaw's luck had held out. The pearl fever would carry over to the next day.

By the second day of the pearl rush, I had established a daily routine. At dawn, I rode in the skiff and opened the mussels we had gathered the day before, while Cecil and Adam paddled to our trotline.

After running the line, we took the fish we had caught to our holding tank on the old Packer place. Like Billy Treat, those catfish could hold their breath a long time. The Packer place was a mile from the lake, but the fish could survive out of water until we got them to the big cypress trough.

By that time in the morning, it was hot, so Cecil and Adam and I were happy to go splash around in the water. Port Caddo must have been almost abandoned that second day of the pearl rush. It seemed every man in town was looking for mussels in Goose Prairie Cove. Some ladies had come, too. They didn't wade in like the men did because it wasn't considered ladylike for them to get their clothes all wet and sticking to them, but some of them opened the shells the men brought to the shore.

Cecil and Adam and I threw the mussels we found into one of Esau's skiffs. We would open them that afternoon, on our evening run to the trotline. First, though, we ate some lunch we had brought from home, and found some kind of useless way to occupy ourselves for a couple of hours along the lakeshore, or up in the woods.

By the time we shoved the skiff into Goose Prairie Cove that afternoon, Captain Brigginshaw had purchased three new pearls. As we were paddling away, someone came rowing into the cove, shouting. It was Junior Martin.

He had found a two-hundred-dollar pearl somewhere on the North Shore. A new surge of excitement fluttered through the pathering of pearl-hunters.

"Where 'bouts did you find it, Junior?" somebody asked.

"The same old mussel beds I've been gittin' my trotline bait from for years. The best mussel beds on the North Shore."

"Where's that?"

"None of your damn business!" he said with a big grin.

Two men vowed to follow him all over the lake all night long to trail him to his lode. He was a good-natured fellow and challenged them to do just that. Junior was a lake rat and knew how to hide out in the brakes and swamps.

When we left to run our line, spirits were running high at Goose Prairie Cove, and folks were talking about scouting new mussel beds all over the lake.

On the third day of the rush, a couple of farm wagons showed up near Esau's place. The news had spread into the hills and fields. The crops were in the ground and wouldn't require much cultivation, except after a rain. A farmer could leave a couple of his older sons to take care of the fields and bring the rest of the family to the lake to hunt pearls.

On the fourth day, Goose Prairie began to look like a camp meeting. More wagons and tents appeared. Trevor Brigginshaw bought five pearls that day. People waded, napped in the shade, drank whiskey at Esau's, cooked, talked, laughed, and played.

Billy walked over to the cove between dinner and supper, and found me and Cecil and Adam watching a wrestling match between two farm boys.

"Ben, we have a problem," he said.

"We do?" Cecil asked.

"Esau can't keep fresh drinking water for all these pearl-hunters. I told him I'd talk to you men about it." He was always calling us "men" when he was trying to get us to do something productive.

"What are we supposed to do about it?" I said.

"Yeah, what are we supposed to do? Make it rain?" Cecil added.

Billy ignored him and talked to me. "Esau will provide the boats and water kegs if you men will row across the lake to Ames Springs every day and bring back water. He'll buy it from you."

Cecil ran to Esau's place and haggled over the price for a while before making the deal. Everybody in camp agreed to use lake water for washing, reserving the spring water for drinking and cooking. After we made our first water haul across the lake that day, we barely had time to run our trotline. My summer was getting busier than I had planned, but now I was making money off of spring water and catfish, and starting to think of things I would like to buy.

My pop's business was booming, too. He became Trevor Brigginshaw's most avid promoter. He was thinking more of Port Caddo than he was of the Australian, of course, but what was good for Brigginshaw was good for the town. International Gemstones continued to run a half-page ad in every issue, so Pop went biweekly.

A regular pearl column appeared on the front page. Pop told where the best pearls had come from, what kind of mussels had yielded them, what they looked like, and what they sold for. By surveying pearl-hunters and analyzing the industry, he concluded that the average man would make a dollar a day in the pearl-hunt. But some lucky hunters would earn small fortunes.

Pop's editorials heralded the Caddo Lake pearl boom as the salvation for our town. Pearl money would replace the dying riverboat trade. He urged everyone in town to spread the news of the pearl rush. People would come from surrounding towns and farms. The stores would sell more goods, the inns would fill with weekend pearl-hunters. Everyone would benefit.

At his own expense, Pop printed fliers announcing a pearl rush of unprecedented magnitude on Caddo Lake, centered at our town. He sent them to surrounding towns. Local business people began to spruce up for a pearl boom.

Summer was supposed to be a slack time for trade. The lake had gotten too low for steamers to ply. But something new had come to Port Caddo. A glimmer of hope. People started talking about making the town a "pearl resort." Pop may have been a visionary, but he sure sold the town on his pearl vision.

The *Steam Whistle* carried regular stories of unusual pearl finds: A fellow came from Marshall and found a pearl in the first mussel he opened. A farmer found one lying loose on the shore—probably dropped accidentally by some careless mussel-opener. A camper gutted a fish and found a pearl in its stomach. A boy found a pearl caked in bird dung under a heron rookery.

Of course there were other news stories to report besides the pearl rush, and one article that caused a sensation around the middle of July dealt with the riverboat trade. After decades of work, the government snag boats were finally getting close to removing the Great Raft from the Red River.

I don't know if I've explained exactly why it took so long to get rid of the Great Raft. It was a huge tangle of driftwood, hundreds of years old, that fed itself constantly with trees washed down from upstream. At one time it blocked over a hundred miles of the Red River channel above Shreveport. It was a concern to Port Caddo, because to get into Caddo Lake, steamers had to skirt the edges of the Raft and find a bayou channel deep enough to navigate. The channels shifted constantly as they got choked with new drift logs.

The government contractors were now claiming, however, that the removal of the Raft and the clearing of a channel would make year-round steamboat traffic possible on Caddo Lake for the first time ever. It seemed that the U.S. Government wanted to keep our steamboat industry afloat, even promising to mark channels to help pilots navigate. Port Caddoans began to talk about a new era of prosperity and a sustainable economy, based on pearls and riverboats.

George Blank, the blacksmith, was one of the first to take advantage of the new prosperity. He started building mussel rakes to sell to the pearl-hunters. He invented two models. One looked like an overgrown garden rake. The other resembled a huge pair of tongs, with two long handles. Both were designed to be used from a boat to get at mussels in water too deep for wading. They sold as fast as he could make them, for a while.

Charlie Ashenback, the best boat-builder on the lake, started taking back-orders. I regarded Charlie as a sort of artist. His skiffs and bateaux were the most graceful things in the water. He used only the best red cypress, and his hands were living tools. He could saw exactly three-eighths of an inch off of a board without even measuring. The boats he built would glide over the water like greased ice. If a fellow had to row all over the lake to find a pearl, he wanted an Ashenback under him.

Trevor Brigginshaw had Ashenback build a rowboat especially designed to carry his great weight, his money satchel, and an oarsman. He hired a young black man named Giff Newton to row the boat for him, while Brigginshaw himself sat in the bow with one hand on his satchel and the other on his pistol, watching for pirates. They made the rounds among all the best pearling spots, black and white.

Colored folks were in on the pearl boom, too. They generally kept to themselves, and hunted mussels where they were harder to get at. Us white folks got all the best mussel beds to ourselves.

Blacks and whites didn't mix much, of course. Around Caddo Lake, the colored population was double that of white folks in those days. Some whites were scared the coloreds would take over if they got education and the vote, both of which they were supposed to have, but didn't. There was a lot of severe harassing of any black person who tried to horn in on what the whites considered theirs.

But nature didn't discriminate against black folks, and they found their share of pearls. In fact, Captain Brigginshaw probably bought as many pearls from black folks as from white. Pop was careful not to print too many stories in the *Steam Whistle* about blacks finding a lot of pearls. He didn't want a bunch of high-handed nigger-haters attacking the black pearling camps and ruining the boom.

Anyway, about the only people in town who disapproved of the pearl rush at first were the preachers. The Reverend Bartlett Towne almost threw a hissy fit when half his congregation failed to show up the first Sunday of the boom. They were all out pearl-hunting. On Sunday! He preached against the evils of mammon for two weeks running, until he realized that not enough of that evil mammon was winding up in his collection plate. The third Sunday, he held services outside of Esau's saloon and asked God to bring luck to all good Methodist pearl-hunters.

And the luck came. Not just for the Methodists, but for all denominations. Most of the pearls found were just small things called seed pearls, or even smaller ones known as dust pearls. They sold for about twenty-five dollars an ounce, but it took a handful of them to make an ounce. Some people got in the habit of paying Esau with seed pearls for whiskey or drinking water. Cecil and Adam and I traded catfish for seed pearls sometimes. The seed and dust pearls enabled just about everybody to at least break even in the pearl-hunting business.

Several times a day, however, we would hear of something bigger than a seed pearl being found. Maybe it would be worth twenty-five dollars all by itself. Maybe it would fetch fifty, seventy-five, even a hundred. Those were tough times in the bayou country, and a hundred dollars could pay a pearl-hunter's expenses for the whole summer and still leave a profit.

Then there were the rare specimens everybody wanted to find: the pearls of fifteen grains or more, about the size of a garden pea, or bigger. Such a gem would sell for at least a hundred dollars. Edgar Burnett, who lived on the North Shore, found a metallic-green pearl that sold for five hundred. Wiley Jones, a woodchopper who came over from the Louisiana side of the lake, sold two matching egg-shaped pearls for three hundred apiece.

The pearl-hunters at Goose Prairie picked up a whole new vocabulary from Trevor Brigginshaw and Billy Treat. It was funny to hear the farmers, who usually sat around talking about bugs and the weather, saying things like "It had good overtone, but the luster was too low" when they talked about certain pearls.

After a couple of weeks, everybody in town knew the difference between a haystack and a turtleback. We could judge size, shape, and orient as well as any jeweler. Even Adam Owens could look at a pearl and tell you whether it was a wing pearl, a dogtooth pearl, a nugget, a ring-around, or a bird's-eye.

Camps of merry pearl-hunters sprang up all over the lake, and everybody made money. We owed it all to the stranger, Billy Treat. It was peculiar how the town idolized him, yet knew so little about him. He didn't hunt for pearls himself. He just continued to cook at Widow

Humphry's place and wander over to Goose Prairie in the afternoons to see what was going on. He taught some hunters the finer points of judging pearls, so Brigginshaw wouldn't take them too badly, but other than that, he mostly stayed out of the pearl business.

He almost always seemed to be sulking over something, like there was a sadness in him he couldn't shake. At times, however, Billy would get to talking real poetic about pearls, and his mood would brighten. I heard him more than once quote a line from Shakespeare's *Othello:* "Speak of me as I am . . . of one whose hand, like the base Indian, threw a pearl away richer than all his tribe. . . ."

One day I came down from the catfish-holding tank and found Billy standing under Esau's mulberry tree with a crowd around him. "The Chinese," he was saying as I got close enough to hear, "believed in magical pearls that glowed and could be seen a thousand yards away. They believed the light of such a pearl would cook rice."

On another day, I was toting a water keg up to Esau's place and heard Billy telling how all the different ancient civilizations explained the formation of pearls. Angel tears, and things like that. "Some reasoned that a white pearl was formed during fair weather, and a dark pearl was formed during cloudy weather."

"What about our pink pearls?" someone asked. Caddo Lake produced quite a few pink ones.

"Maybe dawn or dusk, if you believe in that sort of thing," Billy answered.

He loved pearl legends and folklore, and I loved to hear him talk about them. It added an air of ancient romance to the muddy pursuits of us lake rats.

It was a wonderful summer. I will never forget it. I felt rich and free. It was a time like no other in my life. A time when I knew both the sterling excellence of innocence and the bewitching siren of temptation.

Pearls were my temptation. Mussel pearls and Pearl Cobb. I dreamed of finding the paragon of angels' tears. I dreamed of giving it to Carol Anne. It was the fabulous summer of pearls. I guess I thought it would last forever.

TEN

No, thanks," Billy said, his back to the Australian as he finished drying the pots and pans.

Trevor Brigginshaw held his satchel in his hand." "Come on, Billy," he urged. "Just a drop. It won't hurt you."

"You know I don't drink," Billy said as he hung a heavy iron skillet over the stove. He turned to face his friend. "It's a waste of time and money."

"I'll give you the money."

"Who will give me the time?"

"For God's sake, mate, don't be such a stick-in-the-mud. You don't have to drink if you don't want to. Just come along for the fun!"

Billy took off his apron and hung it on a brass hook. "I like you when you're sober, Trev, but you're a mean drunk. There are happy drunks and sad, slobbering drunks and mean drunks, and you're the meanest of the mean if something rubs you wrong."

"So that's it? That time in Valparaiso?"

"And La Paz, and San Francisco, and Lahaina."

"Lahaina? Oh, now, that was different. The bloke kicked my dog, Billy. I was provoked."

"The *dog* bit the *bloke* first, and it wasn't even your dog."

"Well, I couldn't help that. I like dogs, I do. I've got a mind to get another one."

"What do you mean, 'another one'? You've never had a dog."

"I would have kept that one in Lahaina if you had bailed me out of the stinkin' brig before dawn!"

"And watch you tear another saloon apart? The brig's the best place for you when you're drunk, Trev. No, you go on to Esau's by yourself. I don't want to be there when the place falls in."

Trevor sighed and shook his head. "You've become a cautious soul, Billy. When are you going to stop blaming yourself for what happened on Mangareva and have some fun like you used to? You won't even hunt pearls with these Texans, and I know you want to."

Billy felt the guilt well up like an ocean tide. "I'm out of the pearl business. For good. You go on over to Esau's saloon. I have better things to do."

He stalked out of the kitchen, leaving Trevor there alone. He went to his room, washed his face, put on a clean shirt, and combed his hair. When he was sure the Australian had gone, he left his room, walked through the parlor, and went out the front door of Widow Humphry's place, into the dark. He crossed the street, nodding to a couple of locals who greeted him, and turned the corner of Snyder's store.

There was a light on in Carol Anne's room. He climbed the stairs and knocked on the door.

When Carol Anne saw him standing at the top of the stairs, her breath caught in her throat. She had been wondering if he would ever come to see her again. Billy had been spending so much time with Trevor that she was actually getting a little jealous of the big Australian. "Hi, Billy," she said.

"Are you busy?"

"No, not at all. Would you like to come in?"

"Yes, thank you."

They sat at the table and made conversation for a while, until Billy got around to telling her the reason for his visit.

"I have a business proposition in mind that you may be interested in," he said.

"Business?" she asked.

"Yes. I've gotten to like some of the people around here, and I'm thinking about staying. I'm thinking about going into business, but I don't have the money to get started. I need some investors."

"Just a few weeks ago, people were talking about this town dying," Carol Anne said.

"That was before you started the pearl rush," he said with a grin. His smile was handsome and it made wrinkles line his eyes with character. "I believe that with a little organization, the pearl business could last here indefinitely. Trevor has already started talking to John Crowell about ways to protect the mussel beds. Crowell is going to try to drum up some interest through his paper."

"So, you're going back into the pearl business?"

"No, I'm through with pearls. I have another idea. The inn has been full now for two weeks straight. Widow Humphry says she hasn't had as much business in years. Those out-of-town pearl-hunters have taken every available room, and people are sleeping out on the open ground."

"You're going to build another inn?"

"Yes. And a store, too. And I'm going to buy a big wagon to take supplies out to the pearl-hunting camps so they won't have to come into town to shop. Maybe next year I'll buy a little steam-powered boat so I can reach the North Shore camps as well."

Carol Anne sat back in her chair and beamed at Billy. She loved his big ideas and his poetic talk of pearls. She was glad he was planning to stay in town. He had brought hope to Port Caddo, and he gave no one greater hope than he gave her. "How much do you need?" she asked.

"I have some money in the bank in New Orleans, but it's not enough. I'll need a couple of thousand more. I didn't know if you had any plans for your pearl money yet, so I thought I'd tell you first. I thought you might want to invest some of it."

She didn't want to appear overanxious. She wasn't going to throw herself or her money at Billy. She didn't think he'd respect that. He wanted a woman who could behave with a measure of self-restraint. He would admire her more if she thought it over for a while. "Thank you," she said. "Thank you for telling me before anybody else. I'll have to think about it, though. How soon do you need to know?"

"As soon as possible. I don't want somebody else getting the idea and beating me to it."

"I'll let you know tomorrow," she said. "I'm very interested."

Billy smiled. "Good." He got up. "Well, good night."

"Wait, Billy," she said before he could open the door. "I want to show you something."

She went to her old tobacco tin on the shelf above her bed. She put one knee on the bed to reach it. "I took the pearl you gave me to Marshall and found a jeweler there who could mount it," she said, opening the tin. She removed a gossamer chain of gold, adorned with a tiny pendant—a delicate crown of gold embracing the white orb. She draped it across her fingers so he could see.

Billy touched her hand as he examined the piece. "Nice job," he said. "Will you put it on?"

She shook her hair over her shoulders and reached behind her neck to fasten the chain. She had worn it only a few times, and only in her room. She started to get embarrassed when she couldn't hook the clasp.

"Let me help you," Billy said.

When she turned, he found the chain in her hands under her veil of shining black hair. She pulled her hair to one side so he could see the clasp.

"There," he said, turning her by the shoulders. He

admired her for a moment. "It looks beautiful on you. I hope you'll wear it."

"I will," she said.

He studied her for a long moment. Then he smiled, turned away, and stepped toward the door. "I'll see you tomorrow. Think about my proposition."

"I will." She stood at the door to watch him walk down the stairs, along the back of the building, and into the dark. There was nothing to think about. Of course she would invest in his business ventures. Anything to root him to Port Caddo. The money meant nothing to her. There was nothing at all to think about.

But she did think, and by morning, Carol Anne was glad she had waited. She had come up with a wonderful idea. It was bold, but ingenious. She was going to tell Billy that she wanted to do more than just invest. She wanted an equal partnership.

When Carol Anne told Billy of her decision that afternoon, he accepted immediately. He would invest everything he had, and she would match it. They would split all profits down the middle. She would run the store and the inn, he would man the kitchen and drive the wagon to the pearl camps between meals.

Billy told Widow Humphry that afternoon that she would have to find another cook. Carol Anne broke the news to old man Snyder. She was afraid he would be angry, but he was delighted. She was like a granddaughter to him, and it elated him that Billy had taken an interest in her, even if it meant competition for his store.

The new partners spent the afternoon walking around town together, causing a stir. They looked at several likely sites for their business. A few buildings and lots were for sale, but they were located poorly, off the main street.

There were a couple of lots available just above the wharf, but they were on low ground, only a few feet above the level of the bayou.

Billy asked around. Nobody in town could remember the water getting that high. He went to Goose Prairie Cove to ask Esau.

"I've lived on the lake for forty years," the old Choctaw said, "and I seen the water go that high just once, back in thirty-eight. That was a freak storm that year. I never hope to see the likes of it again. Big Cypress Bayou ran like a river for two days."

"But you don't think it will happen again?"

"It happened once. I guess it could happen again. There would be a risk building there. But if your place flooded there, so would my saloon. I'm no higher here than you would be there."

"It's a good location otherwise," Billy said. "Right next to the wharf."

"And just across the street from the jailhouse," Esau said. "You could visit your friend, Captain Brigginshaw. He almost landed there last night."

"Did Trev cause trouble?"

"Some, but me and the constable got him settled down. He's one of those mean drunks, Billy."

"I know."

Billy and Carol Anne agreed that afternoon to risk high water and construct a new building for their store and inn on the low ground just above the wharf. Theirs would be the first business the steamboat passengers saw when they disembarked.

They dined together that evening at Rose Turner's eatery. Billy had ham steaks and potatoes. Carol Anne ate broiled chicken and greens. She wore her pearl pendant. Rayford

Hayes, the local constable, and his wife, Hattie, stopped by their table to congratulate them on their partnership. The news was all over town.

"I threatened to put your friend, Captain Brigginshaw, in the jailhouse last night," Rayford said. "He was picking fights out at Esau's place."

"I heard. Did he hurt anybody?" Billy asked.

"No, Esau got him settled down. He likes that old Indian for some reason. Did you know Brigginshaw carries a gun?"

"He's licensed to carry it. He provides his own security for the pearls he buys and the money he carries. He didn't pull a gun on anybody last night, did he?"

"No, but he pulled his jacket back where I could see it."

"He likes to fight a little when he gets drunk, but he won't draw a weapon unless somebody pulls one on him first, or goes for his satchel."

"He ought to leave that satchel locked up somewhere instead of carrying it around all the time," Rayford said. "Anyway, he apologized to me this morning and said he'd try to behave himself."

"I hope he does," Carol Anne said. She knew Constable Hayes as an old Confederate hero and the surest man in town with a handgun.

"That's a lovely necklace," Hattie suddenly said. "Is that a local pearl?"

Carol Anne was stunned to have one of the prominent local wives speaking to her in public. Hattie had always been civil to her in the store, but this was quite different. She figured she owed the honor to the fact that she was dining with the famous Billy Treat. "Yes, ma'am," she explained. "Billy found it at Goose Prairie Cove and gave it to me as a gift."

Hattie gasped joyfully and made all sorts of eyes at Billy. "So this is the famous Treat Pearl that started the pearl boom. It certainly is a beautiful one."

"Thank you," Carol Anne replied.

When Rayford and Hattie left, Billy asked, "What was all that about?"

Carol Anne rolled the pearl between her fingers. "Oh, she probably got the wrong idea. Used to be, around here, that when a fellow found a pearl, he would give it to the girl he wanted to marry. I guess I should have straightened her out."

Billy shrugged. "Let them think what they want to think. I gave you a gift. You shouldn't have to explain it to anybody."

The next day, the gossip hounds spread the word that Carol Anne was wearing the Treat Pearl. People stopped her on the street to look at it. She was amazed at the warmth they extended to her. It was as if she had never owned another pearl.

Billy bought lumber, paint, hardware, shingles. He hired carpenters and worked beside them. The happy cadence of hammers rang from sunup to sundown. The frame building was plain, but there would be time to add gingerbread later. The Treat Inn opened a month after the partnership was formed. The partners were seen together regularly around town.

Their inn offered three levels of accommodations. A large back porch enclosed in mosquito netting provided twenty cots where low-budget pearl-hunters could sleep for two bits a night and eat common fare for another two bits a day.

The first floor of the inn consisted of small rooms patterned after riverboat staterooms, six-by-six, with double berths. Common washrooms, one for men and one for women, stood at the end of the hall.

Upstairs, half a dozen suites had brass bedsteads, private washstands, mirrors, and armoires. Trevor Brigginshaw left Widow Humphry's place and took a suite in the Treat Inn. The good widow was actually a little relieved. The captain came home drunk once or twice a week, sang loudly in the middle of the night, and generally disturbed her other guests.

Billy's room adjoined the kitchen, behind the store. Carol Anne's room was above his. They were in debt by the time they opened, but immediately began catching up. The pearl rush was still building. Farmers, woodchoppers, and roustabouts rented cots. Clerks and professional men filled the staterooms. A few big planters and rich business-men peopled the suites upstairs. Pearl-hunting appealed to all classes.

Carol Anne ordered stock for the store with pearl-hunters in mind. She sold knives suited to opening mussels, and all kinds of camp gear. She couldn't keep mosquito bars in stock.

"Keep some sandalwood oil on hand, if you can," Billy suggested. "It keeps the pearls from drying out and im-proves their luster."

Between cooking meals at the inn, Billy drove a well-stocked supply wagon to the South Shore pearling camps, which now extended from Annie Glade Bluff, past Taylor Island, to old Esau's place on Goose Prairie Cove. He sold almost everything in the wagon on each trip and took or-ders for more goods.

He often crossed paths with the open-topped coach from Joe Peavy's livery barn. It made a constant circuit through the camps and past the mussel beds, shuttling pearl-hunters to and from town. Passengers commonly paid their fees in seed pearls.

Peavy had also established a twice-weekly stagecoach service that ran south to Marshall, where he would pick up pearl-hunters who had ridden the rails in from Louisi-ana. The stagecoach stopped right in front of the Treat Inn, and turned around at the wharf, swinging past the jail-house.

In his kitchen at night, Billy made projections based on the gross profits the inn and the store had made so far. He estimated that he and Carol Anne would be out of debt by the time the lake level rose and the riverboats came back. Then they would start recouping their investments.

Pearling would drop off severely when the water got too cool to make wading comfortable. Some pearlers would try to use George Blank's mussel rakes through the winter, but Billy knew few of them would stick with it. That kind of pearl-hunting was hard work, compared to the pleasures of summer wading. The pearl rush would lie virtually dormant until next spring, but the riverboats would be running, and that would sustain some measure of prosperity until the waters warmed.

He was being conservative when he judged that he and his partner would turn their first profit about July, next summer. Then he would ask her to marry him. They would have known each other over a year by then. He would have gotten around to kissing her by then, too, probably around Christmastime. Maybe under some mistletoe. He would marry her, and then it wouldn't matter if the Caddo Lake pearl industry went belly-up like a dead fish, or if the railroads forced riverboats into obsolescence, or if Port Caddo died and sank into the bayou. He would have Carol Anne for life. They could go somewhere else and start over.

For the first time in years, he was planning his future. He had once been an inordinate planner, but he was going to try to control that now that he was finally through grieving over his catastrophe in the South Pacific. Maybe what had happened there was his fault, and maybe it wasn't, but he couldn't punish himself forever.

Don't try to plan the lives of everyone in town, he thought. Just mind your own business, and give your advice when asked. That way, if something goes wrong, you won't have to blame yourself. You don't have to save this town for these people. Let them do it themselves.

It was strange that he had found the pearl here. He of all people. There was more to it than just chance. It was as if the weeping angels and the gods who rode the rainbows were trying to tell him something. He had suffered enough. It was time to live again. He was in love with Carol Anne.

ELEVEN

Trevor Brigginshaw held a glass of whiskey in one hand, a cigar in the other. His satchel full of pearls and money rested between his feet. He was on a Saturday-night tear at Esau's pearl camp and saloon. Someone had started him talking about pearling in the South Sea islands.

"I had my own vessel then. A sloop I called the *Wicked Whistler*. Just forty feet she was, but full-rigged and quick as a hungry shark." The more he drank, the thicker his Aussie brogue became.

Esau's saloon was just a shack with some tables and chairs scattered around inside and out. At night, the men liked to come inside and smoke the place up with cigars and pipes to keep the mosquitoes out. There was no bar to lean against, but there was whiskey—some of it store-bought and labeled, some of it cooked in Esau's moonshine still that was hidden in the swamps.

"I had a four-pounder swivel gun mounted on the fore-deck to discourage pirates," Trevor continued, "and my pearl-handled pistol." He pulled back his white cotton jacket to reveal his weapon.

"Pirates?" Judd Kelso spouted. He had been matching

the pearl-buyer drink for drink for about two hours. His bankroll had been shrinking all summer. He had lost most of it in card games with pearl-hunters. Now he was down to a few thin bills and was watching them go quickly into Esau's till. "I don't believe in no damn pirates!"

"Then you're either ignorant or a fool. There are thieves on the high seas as sure as you have them on land. What's the name of that outlaw gang about here, Esau?"

"Christmas Nelson's gang?" the old Indian said.

"Right! Bloody idiotic name, isn't it!"

"They say he was born on Christmas Day," Esau said.

Kelso shifted in a creaking chair. "Christmas Nelson's just a good ol' rebel Southern boy who don't know the war's over yet. He ain't no damn pirate."

"Of course he's not a pirate!" Trevor shouted. "He doesn't even have a boat! But there are pirates in the Southern Seas as sure as life. Common criminals is all. Ask Billy Treat. He narrowly escaped from them, he did."

"What about that Billy Treat?" a backwoods farmer drawled. "He 'pears to know a hell of a lot about pearls. Where'd he come from to know so much?"

"I found him in New York City. Looked me up, he did. Said he wanted to go pearling. He had found a freshwater pearl in a stream in New Jersey and all he talked about was pearls. The Romans, the Greeks, what all the ancient civilizations thought about them. He was a strapping Yankee lad, so I took him where he might find some pearls."

"You mean *damn* Yankee, don't you?" Kelso said.

The Australian's angry glare sliced toward the gator-eyed man.

"Where was it you took Billy to find pearls?" Esau asked, before Trevor's ire could reach its boiling point.

"Where? Bloody where did I not take him, mate! I was an independent buyer then. I fetched the best pearling waters of the Pacific every year, then sold my pearls in New York and London. Billy went 'round the Horn with me—this was sixty-one, I recall, because the war had started here—and he made a fair sailor. He had a look at Venezuela, Panama, Mexico. Didn't like what he saw until we got into the Pearl Islands of the South Seas. That's where he became king of Mangareva, in the Gambier Islands."

"Where?" Judd Kelso said, laughing disparagingly as if the place didn't exist.

Trevor set the cigar between his teeth. "Mangareva, I say, man! In the Gambiers. Volcanic islands they are, and Mangareva's the best pearl island among them. Bloody beautiful tropical spot that is, gentlemen. Green mountains rising from the sea. The water there is so clear you can see pearl oysters on the reef five fathoms deep. And the women! Dark-skinned as Esau here, fair as angels, and bare as babes above the hips, every one!"

"You mean naked?" a pearl-hunter asked.

"And willing! That's where Billy Treat jumped the *Wicked Whistler*. He made Mangareva the richest pearl island in the South Seas. Wasn't easy, either. The natives don't like work there. They like to catch fish, chop coconuts, lay about under the palm trees, swim a bit, and make little natives, but they don't like work."

"How did Billy get them to work?" Esau asked, reaching for his flask.

"Not by my methods. I suggested he trade them rum for pearls. They like rum, they do. But he's against drink. You all know that. He wouldn't hear of it. So here's what he did. He became one of them! He bloody well did! He lived in a hut thatched with palm leaves, just like they did. He fished with them, chopped coconuts, learned everything they knew till he had their confidence.

"I left him there, and sailed to Sydney. When I came back to Mangareva several months later, he had the men, women, and children diving two hours a day, every one. And the pearls he had to trade looked like billiard balls compared to your little mussel pearls here.

"They loved Billy Treat on Mangareva. He had his pick from the whole lot of naked girls there, he did. I think he liked it there. Wouldn't you?"

"Damn right!" an old married pearl-hunter said, and laughter filled the smoky saloon.

"But wait!" Trevor said, after draining his glass and signaling Esau for more. "The most peculiar thing about Billy in Mangareva was that he would dive with them every day. Maybe that's the way he got them to do it in the first place—by example. He could hold his breath almost three minutes, he could. I clocked him one day. He would dive four fathoms and come up with oysters broad as my hat!" He flourished his panama at his listeners.

"By God, that's how he done it!" Junior Martin said. "I've heard how he saved seven drownin' men when the *Glory of Caddo Lake* went down. They say he stayed under three or four minutes getting John Crowell's boy out."

"I was there," said George Blank, the blacksmith. "I swear I had given him up for dead a full three minutes when he finally came up for air."

Some of the pearl-hunters looked sideways at Judd Kelso when talk of the *Glory* started, but Kelso just sat remorselessly in his chair. He even snorted a little to show his disregard.

"That's how he learned pearls," Trevor said. "He used to tell me his plans for preserving the oyster beds. He had everything scheduled to the year and month. He would protect the oysters in certain localities about Mangareva during certain years, to make sure the natives didn't harvest them all. He wasn't happy just to dive for them, either. He wanted to become the world's expert on pearls. He was going to spend five years diving for them, the next five buying them, like me, and the rest of his life acquiring and collecting them. I believe he would have done it, too, if the bloody pirates hadn't come to Mangareva."

"Oh, hell," Kelso groaned. "Here come the pirates again."

"What about those pirates?" George Blank asked. "What happened?"

"Bloody pirates they were," the captain said, putting out his cigar and sipping at his whiskey jar. "Outcasts from France, Spain, the East Indies, and South America. Cutthroats. No other name for them. They told Billy they wanted half the pearls the natives harvested or they would kill everyone in the village. Billy got mad then, he did. He had a pistol I had given him, and he put it against that pirate captain's head. He went with them to their schooner, holding that gun on the captain. Made them throw their cannon off the bloody deck. Two six-pounders! He told them never to come back and threaten him again or he would have the natives boil them alive!"

"But they came back anyway, I guess," Esau said.

"Aye, they came back, mate, and Billy knew they would. He was ready for them. He and his pearl-divers had brought those two six-pounders up from the harbor. He had learned how to shoot them, too, and borrowed some powder from the *Wicked Whistler*. They kept a watch up day and night, and when those pirate bastards sailed into the harbor with new cannon and fired on the village, he crippled them good. Blew the mizzen mast away and sent them limping for Tahiti!"

"So, he whipped 'em!" Junior Martin said.

Trevor shook his head sadly and nudged his satchel with his foot to make sure it was still there. "They came back yet again, they did. I was there at Mangareva in sixty-seven when it happened. The guards were posted about the harbor, and Billy was ready for another attack by sea. But the bloody cutthroats had anchored out of sight, around the coast, and they sneaked into the mountains above the village. At dawn, they came down. Every one of them had a revolver and the best rifle available. Billy had only a few old muskets and the pistol I had given him.

"We fought at first, we did. But it was suicide to stay. I

used all my ammunition and jumped in my launch to reach the *Wicked Whistler*. I told Billy to come, but he wouldn't. He tried to organize the natives, but they were scattering all over the place running like scared dogs. The bloody pirates were killing them everywhere. My God, what a mess that was. Young children killed, women violated. Billy stood on the beach and shouted, trying to pull the villagers together, but they didn't know much about fighting pirates. He wouldn't leave, so I knocked him on the head with my pistol butt, threw him in the launch, and took him away by force."

"And you got away?" Junior Martin asked.

"Hell, he's here, ain't he?" George Jameson said, and the saloon shook with laughter.

"The pirates were shooting at the *Wicked Whistler,* but we were well out in the harbor. Once we got out around the reef, they had no chance of catching us."

"What happened to the village?" Esau asked.

"Destroyed. The whole thing burned. Billy went well-nigh crazy with guilt. He swore he had brought death and ruin to those simple natives. He said I should have let him stay on the beach and allowed the pirates to kill him, too. Bloody stupid move that would have been. It wouldn't have helped anything, but Billy tortured himself.

"I had saved the Mangareva pearls in my launch when the Frenchmen attacked. When Billy found those pearls aboard the *Wicked Whistler,* he went screaming about the deck, throwing them in the ocean like a madman. I put him ashore in San Francisco. Never thought I'd see him again."

The saloon fell silent, and Captain Brigginshaw took a swallow of Esau's moonshine.

"Well, I lost the *Wicked Whistler* last year in a bloody, wretched hurricane on Jamaica, so I've been buying pearls for International Gemstones to earn enough in commission to buy a new vessel." He sneered a little when he

mentioned his company's name. "I was in New York when
Billy's letter came from here. He's not the same old Billy
yet, gentlemen. Coming around a bit, but he's still got
Mangareva on his conscience. Won't bother with pearls,
either. Says they brought evil last time he fooled with them.

"Anyway, that's the story of Billy Treat. He knows
pearls, he does. And a few other things as well." He drained
his jar and handed it to Esau for a refill.

Kelso had finished his drink, too, and got up to buy another. He smirked and shifted his ugly gator eyes as he
crossed the smoky room. "So that's the story of Billy Treat.
Hell, it all makes sense now. I see why he gets on so good
with Pearl Cobb." He stood beside Brigginshaw and held
his glass up to Esau. "They belong together. Him a coward
and her a whore."

The blow came without the slightest warning. Kelso's
eyes stood level with the big Australian's shoulder, so the
fist angled down on him, backhanding him to the floor.
Esau moved gracefully aside. The saloon customers
gasped, then sat still and quiet.

Kelso jumped up but, dizzied by the sudden stroke,
stumbled back against a table whose legs rattled across the
wooden floor like the hooves of a startled horse. He shook
his head, touched his brow to check for blood, gathered
himself, and rushed the pearl-buyer with grunts and grit-
ting teeth.

Trevor doubled over and latched one big hand around the
handle of his money satchel. Kelso's fist against his temple
staggered him a single step, but he slung the smaller man
aside with his free arm, sprawling him across a cracker
barrel.

Some of the men left the saloon quickly, others merely
stood and moved out of the way. A few smiled with excited eyes, and one shouted, "Get him, Captain!"

Trevor drew himself to his full height, holding the
satchel in his left hand. He waved Kelso in with his right

hand, then made a fist of it. "Come ahead, mate," he said, his teeth showing a smile in the middle of his beard. "You're a little man, so I'll just use my one fist. I fight fair, you know." He cocked his arm like a pugilist, elbow down, slightly bent, his fingers curling up and in toward himself.

Kelso stood and got both fists up. His eyes narrowed with anger. He moved in cautiously, staying out of reach, circling to the Australian's right. The moment he made his move, Trevor came around with the heavy satchel, catching Kelso in the head and bowling him into a shelf filled with jars and glasses.

The roaring laughter of the pearl-buyer followed the tinkling of shattered glass. He dropped his guard and looked around at the men in the saloon. "Never trust a drunken sailor to fight fair, mates! It isn't in him!"

Kelso chose the moment to spring from the shattered glass and throw a wild blow at Brigginshaw's head. The captain's beard absorbed the punch as his knee came up and caught Kelso in the ribs. He made playful jabs at Kelso's nose and ears, backing him up until he knocked him over the stove. There was no fire, but the stovepipe fell out and a black cloud of soot dropped into the saloon.

When Kelso got to his feet, the leather satchel swung again, knocking him all the way through the door and into the woodpile outside. Trevor began shaking with laughter, and the customers remaining in the saloon joined him. Even Esau smiled, though he was shaking his head and surveying the devastation around him.

"Not to worry," Brigginshaw said. "International bloody Gemstones pays all my expenses." He put the leather satchel on a table and began unbuckling it. "Including damages incurred in protecting my pearls."

As he peered into his leather case, Trevor sensed a sudden change in the mood of the crowd. He pulled back the tail of his jacket, found the grip of his revolver, and drew it. As he turned, he cocked it, and found Judd Kelso in the sights as the burly little man came through the door, an ax above his head.

Kelso stopped so suddenly that his shoes slid across the dirty wooden floor. He was still quivering with rage, but he knew better than to rush the big man now. He stood as if in leg irons, the ax handle at his shoulder, the broad steel blade above his head.

"Drop that weapon," Trevor said.

Kelso's face writhed with flexing muscles.

Trevor raised his aim a few inches and sent a bullet glancing off the ax head, humming through the wall, and sailing out over the lake. The weapon jerked in Kelso's hand. A couple of customers bolted for the door, and others dove under tables or behind barrels.

"Drop it!" Brigginshaw repeated.

Kelso threw the ax aside.

The big Australian laughed again, but in a distinctly devious tone. "You'll wish you hadn't raised a weapon to Trevor Brigginshaw when I'm finished with you, mate."

Esau shuffled through the broken glass. "Captain, let him go," he said. "There's been enough trouble. The constable may have heard you shoot."

"Not until we finish our fight," Trevor said, easing the hammer down on the pistol and returning it to his belt.

"I ain't fightin' you with that gun on!" Kelso said.

"Then you will be shot," Trevor said, bringing both fists up and assuming his boxing pose. "The choice is yours."

"There's been enough damage done, Captain," Esau said.

"There's been too much bloody damage done," Trevor answered. "And no one will leave this room until some of it's been accounted for." He bent his head forward and moved toward Kelso.

"I don't want to fight no more," Kelso said, taking a step back. "I give."

"Run, and a bullet will stop you, mate. Put your fists up and fight like a man!"

Reluctantly, Kelso put his fists in front of his face and circled away, backing around chairs and tables clumsily. "Goddam, Esau! Stop the crazy son of a bitch!"

Esau did nothing.

Trevor continued to stalk the retreating man until he got him trapped in a corner. When Kelso crossed his arms in front of his face, a flurry of crushing blows arrived, coming with incredible rapidity from a man of such size. Kelso doubled over until a punch to his chin stood him straight. Another snapped his head against the wall. His knees buckled and he slid unconscious to the floor.

Trevor, as if he had failed to see his opponent fall, continued to belabor the wall until a board came loose, letting all the lake's animal croaks and chirps into the saloon.

Still fuming, he turned to glower at the men left inside the saloon. He saw his leather satchel open on a table. He saw the ax on the floor. He stalked across the room, picked them both up, and went outside.

Esau breathed a sigh of relief when he heard the ax splitting wood. He motioned to a couple of customers. "Drag Kelso out through the back," he said. "Don't let the captain see him." He mopped his sleeve across his forehead and reached for the flask in his pocket. "That Australian sure gets mean when he drinks."

TWELVE

I got soot in my eye when the stovepipe fell out of the ceiling. Adam Owens and I had sneaked down to Esau's place after dark to watch through the knotholes in the wall. We were hoping to see a fight, but hadn't bargained on guns and axes. Adam ran for home as soon as the pistol slug glanced off the ax and ripped through the wall.

I was more curious and less cautious. I stayed until the bloody end, and even watched Captain Brigginshaw chop wood until he was so tired he could hardly stand up. I watched from a distance, because it was frightening to listen to him heave and grunt, and to look at his crazed face. He must have split enough wood to last a week.

While Brigginshaw was chopping, I was wrestling with my conscience. It wasn't the fight that was on my mind, but the story the pearl-buyer had told of Billy on the island of Mangareva. It had given me an unforgivably wicked idea. I knew it was wrong, but I couldn't help myself from thinking about it. I was fourteen and in love with the most seductive woman in creation.

Before Billy Treat, there had been a far-fetched hope that Carol Anne would share her body, if not her heart and soul, with me someday. But since they had gone into business together, and started socializing around town, arm in arm, there was no hope of anything. Billy would have her all—heart, soul, and body.

Billy had saved me from the sinking riverboat. He was the first adult to treat me as a man. He had started me in the lucrative catfish and drinking-water enterprises. He was my hero, and a hero of the entire town. I idolized him. It was difficult to think of stabbing him in the back, but I was a desperate whirlwind of surging confusion.

My crush on Carol Anne had become an obsession. She was everything to me. Visions of her consumed me, day and night, only to be intruded upon by visions of Billy Treat.

Until that night at Esau's place, I had thought Billy invincible. There had been no chance of weakening his hold on Carol Anne. I was doomed to watch him take her. Then I heard the story of Mangareva. I knew why Billy seldom smiled. I knew why he suffered. There was no greater shame for a man than to be labeled a coward, and Billy had so labeled himself for not dying with his island friends. I saw a weakness in the invincible Billy Treat.

It was wrong to even think of it. I knew very well it was wrong. I personally didn't think of him as a coward, even if he thought of himself that way. I knew what kind of mettle he was made of. I owed the man my life.

But I was fourteen and driven by motives I could not control. I couldn't win. Either I would lose my slim chance with Carol Anne, or I would lose the respect and friendship of Billy. According to the stuff that was coursing through me, there was no choice to make. I could do without Billy.

I waited until the next morning after breakfast, when Billy drove the store wagon to the pearling camps. I sauntered into Carol Anne's store, already ashamed of what I had not even done yet, and waited until she and I were the only ones in the room.

She looked at me and smiled. She had taken to smiling more since she and Billy had started their business. She was wearing the Treat Pearl, the one I should have found. Lord, she was a sight to make a boy yearn. I knew then that I would betray a hundred Billy Treats for a thousand-to-one chance at knowing the pleasures of her flesh.

"Hi, Ben," she said. She was dusting the tops of some canned goods and she couldn't prevent herself from moving provocatively all over, though she was only using a feather duster. She didn't do it on purpose. She was just put together that way.

"Mornin'," I replied. "Have you heard?"

"Heard what?" she asked.

"Captain Brigginshaw got drunk last night at old Esau's place."

"Oh, yes. I think I even heard the gunshot last night. I know I heard something."

"I was there."

"Ben!" She propped her fists on her hips and stared at me, half amused and half concerned. "What's a boy like you doing around there? You should have been home in bed!"

That hurt, but I only shrugged. "You know what the fight was about?"

"From what Billy says, Captain Brigginshaw doesn't need much of a reason to fight when he gets drunk." She was not really very interested.

"Judd Kelso said Billy was a coward."

She stopped in a shaft of morning light that was streaming through the store window. Tiny particles of dust swarmed around her like the fancies of a young boy, wanting to be near, but afraid to touch her. She suddenly seemed to realize that I had come to tell her something important. "That was a stupid thing for him to say. Why would he even think such a thing?"

"Captain Brigginshaw told everybody at Esau's a story about Billy, and Judd Kelso said it made Billy a coward." I didn't tell her that Kelso had also called her a whore. I wasn't trying to destroy her image of herself, just her image of Billy. It was a sneaky, cowardly thing for me to do, but I was beyond honor. I was fourteen.

She asked me to sit down with her behind the counter, and I repeated the story as Captain Brigginshaw had told it, trying to remember his every word, wishing I could borrow his accent. In my version, Billy put up a little less of a fight as Captain Brigginshaw thumped him on the head, deserted the island village a little easier, and went a little crazier with shame aboard the *Wicked Whistler*.

It was sad to watch Carol Anne's face as I talked. The story hurt her. I thought it might be breaking her heart. By the end of the tale, her fingers had fallen from the Treat Pearl and lay clasped in her lap. She wasn't smiling now.

"So that's it," she said. "I knew there was something. I

could tell." She got up and walked aimlessly out into the middle of the store, holding her fingers to her lips. "That's why he never talks about the South Seas. I knew something had happened there."

I barely enjoyed ogling her. The story had taken the luster off her smile. "Well, I thought I'd better tell you," I said.

She turned and looked at me. Her eyes were glistening with tears that wouldn't quite roll down her cheeks. Suddenly she came toward me. I jumped from the stool I had been sitting on just as she reached me. She put a warm hand on each side of my face. I felt electricity in her touch.

"Thank you, Ben. I'm so glad I heard it from you instead of from some gossip."

She leaned toward me and kissed me square on the forehead. I went almost as blank as Judd Kelso had the night before. Fire started on the spot where her lips had touched me, and sent a wave of crimson across the rest of my face. It was happening fast. Too fast for me to handle.

I pulled her hands away from my face and took a step back. "I gotta go now," I said. I tried to regain some semblance of composure. "I have to haul some water to the pearl camps. Those folks won't have any water if I don't." I figured that while I was tearing Billy down, I might as well build myself up. I must have been cardinal-red when I left.

I walked to Esau's camp in a trance. She had kissed me. My betrayal of Billy had worked quicker than I could have imagined. It was only a kiss on the forehead, but I never expected her to kiss me on the lips the first time.

I was virtually worthless hauling water with Cecil and Adam that afternoon. Cecil kept trying to get me to tell him about the fight at Esau's the night before because Adam had a poor memory for details, and had left before it was over, but I was so wrapped up in Carol Anne's lips that I couldn't concentrate on anything.

"Well, Ben?" Cecil said. "Ben!"

"Huh?"

"Well, what happened then? What's wrong with you? Didn't you hear me? What happened after Judd Kelso came in with the ax? When did Captain Brigginshaw shoot?"

Poor Billy Treat. I had ruined him. It was a sorry reward for his saving my life. It hadn't been fun destroying him, only necessary. Anyway, I didn't have a lot of room left in me for pity. I was too full of wonder. My skin still tingled where she had kissed me.

"Ben. Ben!" Cecil shouted.

"What?"

"Why haven't you got the danged mussels opened yet? We're almost to the trotline, boy. Hurry up. Haven't you been listening to me? You must be sick or something."

"He don't look too good," Adam said. "I think he's feelin' peaked."

I avoided my usual haunts that evening after supper. I didn't want Cecil or Adam intruding on my thoughts of Carol Anne. I had plans to make. Tonight was the night Carol Anne was going to tell Billy she didn't want to wear his pearl any longer. It was a vicious thing, but I wanted to see Billy get rejected. Not because I would get any pleasure from it, but because I wanted to make sure he was really out of my way.

Well, maybe I would get a little pleasure from it, and that was the disturbing part. Until that moment, I truly believed that I wasn't doing anything to spite Billy. I could have sworn that I was only filling my own instinctive needs. It was primal, like a coyote howling for a mate. But I had to admit I was going to get some kind of kick out of knocking Billy down a peg, and that vicious feeling gave me no pride. My shame began to build, but there still wasn't much room for it next to the hope I had been breathing in all day.

I was naive beyond imagination. I truly believed that just because Judd Kelso had called Billy a coward and I had repeated it to Carol Anne, she would think of him in that way. That little peck she had given me on the forehead must have soaked through my skull and addled my brain. Can you believe that I actually had some kind of hope that she was going to shun Billy and take up with me?

Of course my plan backfired. I'll tell you how I found out. I wandered around to the Treat Inn that evening to flirt with Carol Anne. I was approaching the building when I saw Billy knocking on the door to Carol Anne's room. Unseen, I stepped into the shadows to watch. Carol Anne came to the door. I couldn't see her face, but I figured she was telling Billy to get lost because word was all over town that he was a coward, and she didn't want to be seen with him anymore.

Poor Billy Treat, I thought. He had taken some hard knocks. First Mangareva, now this. He would never kiss Carol Anne. She wouldn't want to wear the pearl of a coward. He would probably leave town. It would be a relief to see him go, but it would make me a little sad, too. I was going to miss him. I admired him and I knew he was no coward, but he was standing between me and Carol Anne, and that was justification enough for my treachery.

"Sorry, Billy," I whispered as I watched from a distance. "But I was here before you."

Then it happened. I saw Carol Anne step from her room. Her hand reached behind Billy's neck, and she kissed him. I don't mean on the forehead like that little smack she had given me earlier that day. She kissed him full on the mouth, and pressed herself against him in the most aggravating way. I turned and walked away then, because I couldn't take it anymore.

The hope that had been filling me all day fled. I felt sick and helpless. My heart was tender and it fell into halves, as if some pearl-hunter had pried it open with his mussel

knife and, finding no gem there—for my treacherous heart
was destitute of anything that worthy—had thrown it back
into the murky waters.

My pain and shame deepened. Confusion mounted. Anger surged. The hollow where my heart had been froze. It
was awful.

It took me years to understand, but one morning I woke
up thinking about the summer of pearls and realized what
had happened. No honorable man wants to be a coward.
He can think of nothing worse. Billy Treat was a brave
man, but he blamed himself for what had happened on
Mangareva. The fact that he had not stood and fought to
the death made him feel like a coward, whether he was or
not. It wasn't as if he had had a choice in the matter. Trevor
Brigginshaw had knocked him on the head and dragged
him away. Still, Billy blamed himself.

No honorable woman wants to be a whore. She can con-
ceive of nothing lower. Carol Anne wasn't a whore, but
she had thought of herself that way. She had allowed herself no excuses. It didn't matter that she had grown up
watching her mother take strange men into her bedroom.
The fact that Carol Anne had been seduced with a pearl
excused her from nothing. She had punished herself by
secretly, privately, calling herself a whore of the lowest
order—that is, until Billy convinced her otherwise.

Billy had given her honor, and she was only too happy
to return the favor. A woman can restore a man's self-
respect even if he has given up finding it himself. I'm sure
Carol Anne knew ways I will never fathom. She knew how
Billy suffered under the weight of his own useless shame.
She knew how to relieve him, renew him, replenish his
dignity, his honor. A good woman can do that. Those two
needed each other more desperately than the earth needs
the sun.

Of course none of that occurred to me as I walked away
from the Treat Inn that night. All I knew then was that I

had betrayed Billy and lost Carol Anne in the same day. I was shamefaced, guilt-ridden, and heartbroken. I knew how Billy Treat must have felt after Mangareva. I deserved it. I had gone behind his back—like a coward.

I made up my mind about one thing right then and there. Maybe I would never have Carol Anne, but I was going to earn my self-respect back somehow, because I felt too terrible to live. I was through passing gossip. I was not cut out for intrigue. Never again would I attempt to hurt someone else to better my own lot.

Strange it is that often from the worst of burdens, a person's character can find the way to its greatest worth. Such is the way of the pearl. It begins as something that galls and hurts. It results in something fine and beautiful to behold. But no pearl emerges overnight. It takes time. It takes a long, long time.

THIRTEEN

I was useless for days. Adam and Cecil might as well have run the trotline and hauled the water without me. I didn't care about making money anymore. All I knew was an empty void. I stayed at home and sulked at night, instead of prowling around spying on girls.

"What's that boy been so crotchety about?" my pop asked my mother one night when they thought I was asleep.

"Leave him alone, John," she said. "He's in love."

Women are peculiar creatures. Especially mothers. I don't know how Mama knew, but it actually helped a little to hear someone acknowledge it. Yes, I was in love. I would always be in love with Carol Anne Cobb.

Luckily for me, always doesn't last too long when you're fourteen. The summer wore on and I got bored silly feeling sorry for myself. The pearl boom was attracting more

fortune-hunters all the time. Families were coming down
from the hills and crowding the lakeshore all the way to
Harrison Bayou. Some of them brought daughters, of
course, and I hated to admit it to myself, but more than a
few of them made my eyes swivel in their sockets.

I stuck my hand into my pocket one day and discovered
a lot of money there. I hadn't spent a dime since my heart
got broke, but all of a sudden I figured that maybe what I
needed to get over Carol Anne once and for all was to buy
something. Something big. Something that had beautiful
curves and was fun to ride. I wanted an Ashenback bateau.

The bateau was sort of the official boat of Caddo Lake
back then. It's something like a canoe, but wider and flat-
ter across the bottom, and it pitches up more in the front
and back, and has prettier flares all around. It's made for
paddling sluggish bayou waters.

Charlie Ashenback made the finest bateaux ever to float
the lake. I set my mind to saving enough money to buy one
of his works, with mulberry stems, red cypress planking,
a live well in the middle, and a minnow box within easy
reach of the seat. I learned a trick that summer that still
works for me: If you want to get your mind off of women,
think of money and boats.

We had picked up the game of baseball from somewhere
that summer. Cecil Peavy and I wound a bunch of old trotline cord into a ball and Adam Owens found a pine limb
that made a pretty good bat. We would get some farm
boys together on the lakeshore at Goose Prairie and teach
them the rules and we would have some pretty good games
and arguments and fistfights. The girls stood around,
watched, and giggled at us.

Well, one day I was playing third base when I saw Billy
approaching. He had been stepping a lot livelier since shar-
ing Carol Anne's dark room with her. I guess I would
have, too. Trevor Brigginshaw had been heard to remark
that Carol Anne had uncovered the old Billy Treat. Billy

smiled and joked more than he had since coming to Port Caddo. When he drove his supply wagon down to the pearling camps, he attracted a regular crowd.

I still hadn't spoken to him since that night. Half out of shame, and half out of anger. I really didn't want to have anything to do with him, but as he approached our baseball field, he headed straight for third base.

"Morning, Ben," he said. "Who's winning?"

"Who's keepin' score?" I said. "We just play till the fight breaks out."

He laughed. I couldn't believe it. I made Billy laugh.

"Well, when the game is over, I have an idea for you and your partners. That is, if you want to make some more money."

I would have said I wasn't interested, but he had engaged my interest with talk of profits, and I got a sudden vision of the Ashenback I was going to buy. Maybe Billy could take Carol Anne away from me, but he would never take my bateau once I had saved the money to buy it.

"What kind of idea?" I asked, concentrating harder than usual on the batter, so I wouldn't have to look into Billy's eyes.

"I've been thinking about all these dead mussels the pearl-hunters have been throwing in piles around here. It's not sanitary."

"They stink somethin' fierce," I said.

"Yes, they do. And that's the problem. Some of them are regular maggot ranches."

"So where's the money in it?" I asked.

He paused for a moment while the batter swung at a wild pitch. "You're starting to sound like your friend, the Peavy kid. I'm talking about doing something that will benefit the whole camp, and all you can think of is money."

I smirked at him pretty severely. "You're the one got me started makin' money this summer. What's wrong with that?"

"Nothing, as long as you do a good job and enjoy the work. But when somebody offers you a deal, find out what's involved first. Then, if you're still interested, ask about the pay. Otherwise, you'll end up in some kind of job you don't like just to make money."

"What's involved?" I asked.

"It was Esau's idea. He said that if somebody would build a hog pen near the camp, the hogs could fatten on the mussels and keep this place smelling better."

The kid who had been batting either struck out or got tired of swinging and threw the bat down.

"I don't have any hogs," I said.

"Esau has some wild ones running back in the woods along Harrison Bayou that he doesn't want to fool with anymore. He said that if you and your partners can trap them, you can have them, and fatten them on mussels. Then you can sell them in the fall at pure profit."

"What do hogs sell for?"

"Read your father's paper. He prints farm and stock prices twice a week." He turned and walked back toward his supply wagon.

"If you know, why don't you just tell me?" I shouted.

He stopped and flashed a smile at me. "When I was your age, nobody told me about pearls. I learned about them on my own. If you want to know what hogs sell for, find out yourself."

I stared at the back of his head as he walked away. Just then a thump came from home base and that ball of trot-line sang right past me like a cannon shot. Some kid at second base told me to keep my mind on the game. I told him to shut up, and the fight commenced.

Cecil carried Esau's ax, Adam hauled a sack of shelled corn he had snuck out of his daddy's barn, and I brought a black eye from the ball game. We paddled a skiff back into

Harrison Bayou and found a place not far from the water where hogs had been rooting for bugs and worms.

Cecil got me and Adam to do most of the chopping and dragging of logs while he chose the site for the trap. We knew as well as he did there was no trick to choosing a site, but he pretended to be busy at it long enough for us to do most of the hard work. Cecil was like that. He was always afraid hard work was going to sap strength from his brain.

"I hear some of these old pine-rooters get big tushes on them," he said as he marked off a square in the forest litter with his bare toe.

Adam laughed. "You're scared! Ain't you never caught a hog before?"

"I'm not scared. I just said they had big tushes."

"Well, don't worry," Adam said. "I'll bring old Buttermilk. He'll get 'em by the ear so we can gather their back legs and tie 'em up."

"I'm *not* worried," Cecil replied.

No, he wasn't any more worried than I was. Cecil and I had both heard wild hogs pop their tushes together before, and knew they meant business. We were both wondering how we would move those trapped hogs out of our pen without getting a couple of fingers snapped off. Adam mentioning old Buttermilk made me feel a little better. According to Adam, Buttermilk was the best hog-rasslin' dog on the South Shore.

We built our trap by laying up limbs sort of like a log cabin. We had brought some rope to tie the limbs together at the corners so the hogs wouldn't push the walls down. On one side of the square trap, we left a hole for a door that we had already built out of some old planks Esau let us have. We rigged that door to slide up and down in the hole.

That's when Cecil surprised me. It seemed he really had chosen the trap site for a good reason. There was a pine limb growing right over the sliding door. We tied a rope to the door and ran the rope over the limb. Adam cut a stake and drove it into the ground at an angle in the middle of the trap. Then we tied a loop in the end of the rope and hooked it over the stake. That held the sliding door up so the hogs could get in.

We fooled around with the stake and the rope for a while, adjusting them so a nudge would make the rope slip off the stake, letting the door fall shut. Finally we tied an ear of corn to the rope and hooked it over the stake, setting our trap. The hogs would come in, yank on that free ear of corn and pull the loop off the stake, letting the sliding door fall. Before we left, Adam made a few trails of shelled corn on the ground, all of them leading to the trapdoor.

Adam and I stood back for a moment and admired the ugly little log pen. He took as much pride in building it as I did. Both of us liked to do things with our hands, unlike Cecil.

"Well, come on. We better run the trotline before it gets dark."

"Yassuh, Marse Cecil!" Adam sang.

I almost hurt myself laughing. Adam didn't come up with many jokes, but when he did, they usually tickled me something fierce with their suddenness. It felt good to laugh after sulking for so many days about Carol Anne. Maybe I was going to get over her after all.

They say dogs sometimes get to looking and acting like the people who own them, and Buttermilk was a good argument for it. He was a canine Adam Owens-lean, strong, not too bright, and utterly unafraid of any wild animal. He was the color of buttermilk, medium-sized, with perky ears, and a crooked tail he always carried high.

"Why doesn't he ever let his tail down and cover his asshole?" Cecil asked as we paddled back up Harrison Bayou to check our hog trap the next day.

"He's daring you to sniff it," I said.

Buttermilk had been jumping all around the skiff, looking for critters in the water and getting in Cecil's way. As we got closer to the trap, he started quivering with excitement, as if Adam had told him he would get to tackle a hog this morning.

We could see from the skiff that the door had fallen on the trap. When we pulled the boat up on the muddy bank, the trapped hog heard us and tried to knock the pen down, but the log walls held. I thought Buttermilk was going to bust with hysterics, but Adam had trained him well and he didn't dare take off after anything without permission.

I was nervous about meeting Mr. Pig, but Adam looked like he was taking a Sunday stroll. He sauntered up to the trap and watched the hog smack its snout a couple of times on the log walls. From his pocket he removed a length of cord that had a loop in it like a snare. "You ready, Buttermilk?" he said, and the dog crouched. "Git him!"

Buttermilk skipped off the top of the log wall and leaped blindly into the pen with the wild pig. Now, this pine-rooter wasn't like any barnyard slop-eater you ever saw. When pigs go wild, they get long-legged and lean, and grow teeth that can cut like scissors. They get so strong that they can root up pine saplings with their snouts, looking for worms and stuff to eat. When Buttermilk lit alongside the two-year-old boar in our trap, he had a fight in front of him.

The hog jumped to one side with a grunt and backed into a corner to get a look at Buttermilk. The dog barked a couple of times and the pig lunged backward against the logs until it figured out it had nowhere to go but forward. Then it put its head down and ran at Buttermilk like a cow protecting her calf. The scissor teeth snapped at air as Buttermilk sprang on all fours, humped his back, and bit down on the end of the boar's right ear.

Grunts, squeals, and growls filled the woods for several seconds, and our little log trap shook like a boxcar on a downhill run. Buttermilk tried to get a better bite, lost his hold and went flying against the inside of the pen. When the boar rushed him, he leaped out of the pen, nimble as a cat, but I think he started jumping back in even before he hit the ground between me and Cecil. He must have been taking lessons from the fleas he hosted, because he looked like one of them springing back into the pen.

He came down on the hog like an eagle and this time got a firm bite on the base of the ear. The piercing squeal lasted about two seconds, then the pig went to its knees.

Adam bounded over the log partition in a blink and jerked the hind hooves off the ground as Buttermilk clenched the ear to the dirt. Adam tied the hind legs together first, then produced another length of cord from his pocket to lash the front ones. He tied them quick as a rodeo cowboy. "Git out!" he said to his dog, and Buttermilk sprang over the logs like a deer. When he lit, he went prancing around the pen, wagging his tail.

The pig soon stopped squealing and trembled as if it had taken the palsy. We ran a long green limb in between its legs where they had been tied together, and carried it out of the pen to the skiff. We set the trap again and spread more corn before we left, having gotten off to a good start in the hog business.

Buttermilk perched in the bow and wagged his tail in broad, proud sweeps as we paddled back to Goose Prairie Cove. We grinned over our success and poked a lot of fun at each other. The sticky swelter of the bayou summer caressed us and made us carefree as we wove among the cypress knees. The hog lay between the bulkheads and rolled its eyes in fear. It looked dumb as a boated catfish tied up there.

The moss in the cypress limbs strained the sunlight like lace as we paddled through air pockets of different temperatures; here as moist and warm as a woman's breath, and there as cool as the draft she leaves when she's gone in the night. Caddo Lake was mysterious like a woman. Like life.

I had been lost in Harrison Bayou before, but I knew where I was going this morning. I wished I could say the same about my future. My heart still hurt a little when I thought of Carol Anne, but I knew I would get over her. Then what? Pigs and catfish the rest of my days? I wasn't worried about it, just curious for the first time. It was a mystery and it intrigued me.

That was the summer of pearls. Mystery and discovery. Love and heartbreak. Wealth and poverty. Pigs and catfish. I was a boy, learning. I stabbed my paddle deep into the inky waters and stroked with undaunted strength. I had things to do.

FOURTEEN

I gave Charlie Ashenback every penny I owned and told him I would have the rest of the money by the time he finished building my bateau. It would take him a week or so to get around to it, but only a day or two to build. Charlie could slap a boat together in his sleep, but he had a lot of orders from pearl-hunters ahead of me.

I fell into a daily routine again after I swore off thinking of Carol Anne. All the desire I had once held for her I now directed toward my bateau, my work, and my earnings. I took the risk of becoming like Cecil Peavy, always thinking of money, but it eased my heartache to have my brain occupied.

I rose at dawn every day and met my friends at Goose Prairie. We took Buttermilk with us everywhere now, and he loved watching Adam pull big catfish up on the trotline.

He would bark at them as they splashed in the water. After selling the fish, or throwing them in the holding tank, we would paddle to our hog trap and let Buttermilk do his job. We had barely enough time before lunch to make the morning water run to Ames Spring, across the lake.

In the afternoons, we shoveled dead mussels into a wheelbarrow and hauled them to our hog pen. The pearl-hunters helped us by throwing the mussels in designated piles. They didn't mind, because we kept the lakeshore clean and smelling tolerable. They also threw garbage in with the mussels—any kind of refuse a hog would eat, and that covers about everything that will rot and stink.

We built the hog pen of rails about halfway between the lake and our catfish holding tank. Once they had gorged on mussels for a couple of days, our hogs calmed down pretty well and started acting domestic. After catching eight hogs in ten days, we abandoned the trap on Harrison Bayou.

After slopping the hogs, we would take it easy for an hour or so and wade for mussels. I had given up on finding a pearl, and just sold any mussels we didn't need for the trotline to rich tourist pearl-hunters who didn't want to get in the water.

On some days we would go out on the islands and cut hay to sell. Grass grew eight feet high on some of the islands where no stock ever grazed. With all the horses and mules in camp, we had little trouble selling hay, or trading it for seed pearls. A few campers had even brought milk cows with them, and they needed hay, too.

Toward late afternoon, we would paddle to Ames Spring on the second daily water run. That left us just enough time before sundown to make the evening run to the trotline.

My arms became hard as hickory from paddling all over the lake. My pockets began to fill back up with money earmarked for the Ashenback bateau. My parents glowed with pride.

"You've earned that Ashenback," my pop said to me one evening. "Billy Treat told me yesterday what a fine job you and your friends have done keeping the camp clean and supplied with hay and water. I'm proud of you, son."

Things seemed to be getting simple again, and I was hoping that my love affair that never happened with Carol Anne was just an aberration in life that would never recur. Once again I could look into an uncomplicated future. I saw myself working, making money, buying boats, and spending time with my friends. Only one thing could have plunged me back into wonderful chaos, and when it happened, it was like this.

One day Adam was shoveling mussels into the wheelbarrow I had been pushing along the lakeshore, when Cecil, who hadn't bent his back to do a lick of work all afternoon, said, "Hey, look, Ben, that girl over there's smiling at me."

I glanced toward a neatly kept camp and saw a blonde-haired farm girl sitting under a wagon-sheet shade cloth. What surprised me was not only how pretty she was, but that she was smiling at me instead of at Cecil. Cecil's eyes never did see the truth very well where women were concerned. He went through three wives before he finally just gave up, hired a housekeeper, and patronized the whorehouse twice a week. He was always much happier with the women he paid than he was with the ones he married.

But anyway, when I saw that blonde country girl smiling at me, I felt the hot flush and got the same silly quivering feeling Carol Anne used to give me. I would have groaned in disgust if it hadn't felt so good. I should have realized then that the world was too full of women for things to remain uncomplicated for long.

"She's not smilin' at you, Cecil," Adam Owens said. "She's smilin' at me." Adam was even less realistic about women than Cecil was. Maybe that's why he died a bachelor.

Cecil went after her like a business deal, but Adam and I didn't have the nerve to enter her camp. We just continued collecting garbage and dead mussels. While we were slopping the pigs, Cecil came trudging up to the hog pen, looking dejected.

"What's wrong with you?" I asked.

"She said she wasn't smiling at me," Cecil grumbled.

"I told you it was me!" Adam shouted so loud that he scared the pigs.

"Oh, hell, why would she be smiling at you, Adam? It was Ben she wanted to know about."

They looked at me as if they would throw me to the hogs.

"Me?"

"Yes, you. Her name's Cindy. Said her old man brought the family all the way from Longview to hunt pearls. If you want to know anything else about her, you can find it out yourself." He stalked away, obviously mad at me for getting smiled at in his stead.

"Dang, what's he so mad at?" I said.

Adam frowned and shoveled some more slop to the hogs. He wasn't feeling real friendly toward me, either. This was a new experience. My friends and I harassed each other daily, and often got mad enough to fight. But this was a silent anger I was feeling from them now. It was the same treatment I had given Billy after that night the lantern went out in Carol Anne's room.

I had to admit that Cecil and Adam were the last of my worries. What concerned me was how to approach that pretty blonde girl named Cindy. In the next few days I suffered brief moments of rationality during which I told myself it would be better to leave her alone than to risk getting my heart wrenched out of my chest again. Then I would see her smiling at me as I carried a load of catfish or a barrel of water, and knew I would have to find the nerve to speak to her.

As it turned out, she came to me one afternoon as I ate my lunch under the mulberry tree at Esau's place. She snuck up behind me and said, "Are you the boy with the hogs?"

I turned like a startled deer and almost choked on a biscuit when I looked into her blue eyes. My mama had taught me better than to talk with my mouth full, so I just had to nod and turn red while I chewed.

She smiled. "My daddy wants to see you." She had such a beautiful, twangy, piney-woods voice that I knew she had to be exaggerating it some for my sake. "Come on," she said tossing her head toward her camp.

I was afraid her daddy might want to fill my britches with rock salt for being there for his daughter to smile at, but I wasn't about to refuse to follow her. "What's he want?" I managed to say, wiping crumbs from my face with my sleeve.

"He wants to buy a couple of them hogs of yours."

"What for?"

"He found a pearl. Got a hundred and sixty-five dollars for it. We're gonna celebrate tonight."

"You inviting the hogs?" I said, trying to be clever.

"No, silly. We're gonna cook 'em."

"Oh."

We walked on in excruciating silence for seconds that seemed like hours. I couldn't think of anything to talk about but catfish, and I knew she wasn't interested in that. She smiled at me a couple of times as we headed toward her camp. The silence didn't seem to bother her, but then, she didn't need to talk, and she probably knew it, as females know things.

"I'm gonna buy a boat," I blurted at last.

She seemed impressed. "What kind?"

"An Ashenback bateau."

She wrinkled her pretty little freckled nose. "I don't know much about boats."

"That's the best kind there is." We were approaching her camp.

"When you gonna buy it?"

"I guess after your pop buys those hogs from me. I should have enough money then."

"Maybe . . ." she said, glancing toward her camp and lowering her voice. "Maybe you can take me for a ride in it."

A light of pure joy filled the air around me until the shadow of Cindy's father blocked it out. I almost ran into him as he came around the back of the wagon. "Cindy!" he shouted, making me flinch. "Oh, there you are. Is this the boy?"

"Yes, sir," Cindy said.

"What's your name, boy?" He looked big to me, but was probably average-sized, made of good solid country stock. He had stubble on his face, a battered straw hat on his head. "I say, what's your name?"

"B-B-Ben Crowell," I answered.

"You the boy owns them hogs?"

"Yes, sir."

"Want to sell a couple?"

I glanced at Cindy. "Sure, I guess."

He offered me a price on two head of swine and I took it without attempting to negotiate or confer with my partners. I figured my third of the sale price quickly in my head, and it was enough to pay Charlie Ashenback the rest of what I owed him for the bateau. And Cindy wanted a ride! I was happy as a drunken possum when her pop put the money in my hand.

"We'll come up to the pen and get them hogs this evenin'," he said.

"Just pick whatever pair you want."

He nodded and shook my hand, then disappeared behind the wagon.

Cindy walked me to the edge of her camp. "Don't forget about that boat ride, Ben," she said.

It was over two miles to Charlie Ashenback's boatyard in Port Caddo, but I ran every step without stopping to rest. He had my bateau on a pair of sawhorses. "Sure, you can take it now," he said. He was a friendly old man with sawdust in his white hair. "Paint's dry."

It was so beautiful I was nearly afraid to touch it. It almost looked alive, arching its back as if diving into the water. It wanted a bayou under it. "Will you help me carry it to the water?" I asked.

"Sure." He picked up the bow and we lifted the boat and headed for the bank of Big Cypress Bayou. "Don't fret if she leaks a little at first. Just leave her in the water and those planks will swell and close the cracks. Then she'll be tight as a virgin with her legs crossed." He turned his face up and laughed as he waddled along with his end of my boat.

When we put the bateau in the dark bayou water, I swore I felt her trying to swim. It was at that moment I realized I didn't own a paddle. Old Charlie had some for sale, but they were above my means. The bateau had just about cleaned me out.

However, I had Cecil and Adam's share of the hog money in my pocket. I knew one of them would lend me enough to buy a paddle, so I went ahead and paid Charlie for one of his. I was dying to get that boat between me and water.

Bayou water is flat, but the Ashenback seemed to go downhill everywhere it went. It was like flying compared to the way Esau's cumbersome skiffs plowed through the water. I wasn't sure if maybe I hadn't wasted my money, as well as Cecil and Adam's, on the paddle. It seemed my bateau would go all the way across the lake with one push.

I had never known a happier moment. I had earned that

boat. As I slipped effortlessly past the mouth of Pine Island Slough, I thought of how Cindy would look in the bow. I imagined Carol Anne there, too, but only briefly. Cindy was my age. She belonged in my bateau. Carol Anne belonged to Billy Treat.

I took a shortcut through Mossy Brake, to see how my vessel would handle among the trees. She went like a snake, twining her way around the cypress knees. The air was dark and still back in the brake, but my bateau brought me through to Taylor Island before I could even worry about getting turned around. I passed right by our trotline, but didn't even glance at it. I was having too much fun to think of work.

I used all my strength on the last stretch to Goose Prairie Cove. I wished the steamboats were running, so I could have showed off to the passengers. I passed the first of the pearl camps and noticed some of the waders admiring my speed, which gave me strength to stroke even harder. I was dying to show Adam and Cecil. I could give them their share of the hog money, then we could celebrate with Cindy's family. It was going to be a great day.

When I slipped into Goose Prairie Cove, I didn't see my friends anywhere. I raced past Captain Brigginshaw in his Ashenback rowboat so fast that he said to his oarsman, "Giff, why don't you row as fast as Billy Treat's young friend, there?" Wading pearl-hunters turned their heads to watch me streak by.

Esau greeted me as I beached my bateau near his saloon. "That yours?" he asked.

"Yep. Just bought it."

He slipped his flask into his back pocket. "That's an Ashenback, ain't it? I can tell by the way he angles the planks on the bottom."

"Yep. Where's Cecil and Adam? I want to show them."

"They were here looking for you a while ago. They said they would wait for you at the hog pen."

"Thanks, Esau." I started up the lakeshore.

"That's a good boat," he said, stopping me. "You work hard, and stay away from whiskey, and you earn a lot of good things like that."

I paused before continuing up the shore. Esau had never lectured me or given me advice before.

"Ben," he said, stopping me again. He grinned. "They looked mad."

"Who?"

"Your friends."

"Mad? About what?"

Esau shrugged. "Somethin' about the hogs." He reached for his flask again as I turned away.

FIFTEEN

I saw them sitting on the rails of the hog pen, scowling and fuming. They had been a little edgy toward me lately, because of the way Cindy flirted with me all the time instead of with them. But I couldn't think of what I had done to make them this mad. I reasoned it was probably Cecil's doing for the most part. Adam usually didn't get mad unless somebody told him to.

Cecil jumped down from the fence when I got close, and Adam quickly followed. Buttermilk stood between them, wagging his tail. They ground their teeth and glowered at me until I was near enough for them to holler at.

"What the hell's going on?" Cecil demanded.

"That's what I want to know!" Adam added.

"What are you talking about?" I said.

"Your girlfriend's daddy came up here and took two of our hogs. Said you told him he could do it."

"She's not my girlfriend."

"Well, whoever the hell she is, her daddy came up here

and took our hogs. What did you do, trade him a couple of hogs to feel on her or something?"

I was still in good spirits from buying my bateau, but that sort of talk was going to make me mad quick. "I sold him those hogs," I said.

Cecil took off his hat and threw it on the ground. "You what?" Buttermilk grabbed the hat, thinking Cecil wanted to play. "Who gives you the right to sell our hogs without asking us? I thought we decided to fatten those hogs till fall. Now you've sold them cheap and run off with the money without even asking us."

"Yeah!" Adam said.

"I didn't run off with the money. I just went to buy my new bateau from Charlie Ashenback. Come on down to the lake and look at it."

Both of them fumed. Adam threw his hat on the ground.

"You used our money to buy your bateau?" Cecil shouted.

"No! I just used my own money for the bateau. I've got your money in my pocket."

"Well, let's have it. I want to see what you sold those hogs for. And I'm going to ask that little bitch from Longview what her daddy paid, too, so don't try to short me."

Now we were all about equally mad. "You don't have to talk about her like that, Cecil. She hasn't done anything to you."

"I'll bet she hasn't done anything to you, either, and if she did, you wouldn't know how to do it, anyway. Now, give us our money!"

I looked at Adam as I scooped the money out of my pocket. "Here's your cut," I said, getting ready to count out his share. "Oh," I added, after putting the first coin in his hand, "would you loan me enough to buy a paddle?"

"Hell, no, he's not going to loan you any money!" Cecil shouted.

"Hell, no, I'm not going to loan you any money!" Adam echoed.

He probably would have if Cecil hadn't said anything. There wasn't a greedy bone in Adam's body. I counted the rest of his share into his palm as Cecil watched.

"Is that all you sold those hogs for? Is that our whole share? Damn, Ben, that farmer took your shirt!" He held his hand open.

"Cecil," I said, before giving him his share, "I don't suppose you would loan me the money for the paddle?"

He answered by thrusting his open palm at me. I put the money in his hand in one lump sum, but I knew he was going to count it.

"Wait a minute," he said. "Wait just a damn minute. How come Adam got more than me?"

"Well," I said, "the truth is I already bought that paddle. I thought one of you would be my friend enough to loan me the money."

"That does it!" Cecil said. He kicked his hat toward the hog pen, and Buttermilk went after it again. "I'm about to kick your ass, Ben!"

"Oh, settle down," I said. Then Cecil's fist hit me right in the forehead and knocked me to the ground. When I looked up, he was standing over me with his fists waving in front of him. Buttermilk was jumping around with excitement, wagging his tail.

"All right, Cecil," I said. "If that's the way you want it."

He rushed me when I got up, but I ducked his wild punch and hit him in the lip with the top of my head. I pushed him away and got my fists up. His lip was bleeding.

"Damn you, Ben, I'm really gonna kick your ass now!"

"That's right, Cecil," Adam said. "You show him!" Adam loved a good fight, even if he wasn't in it.

Cecil rushed me and I slipped in a quick punch to his nose that buckled his knees and landed him on his rear end.

"Cecil!" Adam yelled. "What are you doin', boy? Git off your ass and *git him!*"

Now, old Buttermilk didn't know too much English, but *git him* was his favorite phrase. He took two springs toward the pen and landed among the hogs before Adam even realized what he had said. A great surge of pork crashed against one side of the fence, and logs flew as if they had been blasted. I tried to jump in the way of the last two hogs *left* in the pen, but with Buttermilk behind them, they thought little of running over me, their scissor-like teeth gnashing in my face.

"Damn it, Adam!" Cecil yelled as he got up. "Don't ever say *git him* when Buttermilk's around!"

The dog had caught one of the pigs by the ear and had it almost immobilized.

"Ben, fix the hog pen! Adam, go catch that hog!"

Adam sprinted for the pig Buttermilk had caught and I started stacking the logs back. By the time we got the single hog back in the pen, the mayhem had started down at the pearling camps. All five remaining pine-rooters had stampeded the tent city. We could hear pots and pans clanging, women screaming with terror, children shrieking with joy, men swearing, dogs barking.

If not for Buttermilk, we never would have recaptured any of them. The steady diet of mussels and garbage had slowed the hogs down a little and made them easy for the dog to catch. People tried to herd them, shoo them, and tackle them, but Buttermilk was the only successful hog-rassler. With his help, we managed to catch three, but two escaped to the woods.

There was a big panic for the first few minutes of the hog scramble, then everyone in camp pulled together to catch the strays. Many grown men ran from popping tushes while their wives stood their ground with shovels or frying pans. Nobody blamed us boys. I guess we and our hogs had done the camp more good than harm over the long haul.

When all the hogs had been tied or run into the woods, a group of men helped us carry the caught ones back up to the pen. Billy Treat was among them. He had pulled his supply wagon up at the pearling camp about the time the stampede broke out.

"Hey, no hard feelings," I said to Cecil when we got the last tush hog in. "I'll pay you back for the paddle."

He had dried blood all over his mouth and chin. He smirked and waved at me in a peculiar way as he walked off.

"What was all that about?" Billy asked, coming up behind me.

"Nothin'," I said.

"I thought you two were friends."

"I thought so, too."

Billy grunted. "What was the fight over? Girls or money?"

The men were returning to their camps, leaving Billy and me alone at the pens. When I looked at him, I couldn't help grinning a little. He was sharp, that Billy Treat. You had to like a guy like that. "A little of both," I said.

He grimaced. "Well, don't worry, he'll get over it."

We stood there together for a few quiet seconds, looking out over the camps and the boats and the lake.

"I heard you bought an Ashenback."

I nodded,

"Well, where is it? Let's see it."

I felt better almost instantly. I was dying to show off my bateau. "Come on, I'll show you," I said. I forgot all my troubles as I walked with Billy toward Esau's place. My partners and I had lost two hogs, but they hadn't cost us anything but time and a little sweat. Now that I had the Ashenback, I wasn't worried much about money. I had my mind on my bateau, and that girl, Cindy, from Longview.

To make conversation, I asked Billy how the business was going, and he told me all about it. He mentioned Carol Anne's name several times, but it barely fazed me. It seemed as if I hadn't been in love with her in a long time.

"I bet she moves like a skipping stone," Billy said, examining my bateau.

"Yeah, you want to try her?" I asked.

But before he could answer, I heard a voice as sweet and smooth as wild honey call my name.

"Hi, Ben," Cindy said, strolling by on the lakeshore.

I felt myself blush. "Oh, hi," I replied.

"That your boat?"

I nodded.

"I still want that ride." She stopped and flipped one side of a mussel shell over with her bare toe. "See you at our party tonight."

I watched her walk down the shoreline until I heard Billy whistle quietly.

"That's who the fight was over?"

"Yeah," I said, groaning with embarrassment.

"I'd fight you for her myself if I was fifteen years younger."

I scoffed, because I knew Cindy had nothing on Carol Anne.

"My God, Ben, why are you turning so red?"

"I don't know." I cringed and waded into the water next to my bateau. "Shoot, I don't know anything about girls," I said.

"Yeah, neither do I. I guess that's what gets us so all-fired interested in them. They're a mystery, and no man can resist that."

I glanced up at him and caught that sparkle in his eye, like when he talked about pearls. "You must know something about them," I said, a little accusingly. "You sure got you one."

He was looking at the sky. "All I know is to behave like a gentleman. That's all there is to it, Ben." He smiled, still looking skyward. "That throws them. They don't encounter much of that."

I looked to the north to see what he was staring at, but found nothing in the sky where his eyes led.

"It's a rare thing, Ben."

"What is?"

"True love. Rare as a pearl."

I felt awkward listening to him philosophize. Fourteen-year-old bayou boys don't have much use for that kind of talk. But nobody was listening, and he had complimented my bateau, and besides, I idolized Billy. I decided to humor him a little. "How rare is that?" I said.

He looked at me suddenly, as if stunned to think he might have gotten through to me or something. Then he stroked his chin and dredged deep into his reservoir of philosophies. "Have you ever seen the moon through a rainbow?"

I wrinkled my face. He was looking at that place in the sky again.

"Rainbows don't come out at night," I said.

"No, but sometimes you'll see the moon in the daytime."

"But if there's a rainbow, that means it's been raining, so there are probably some clouds in the sky. They would cover up the moon." It was a strange conversation, because I didn't really even know what we were talking about.

"True. But a rainbow also means there's some sun shining. That means clouds are clearing. Conditions would have to be just right, Ben, but it could happen." His gaze fell from the sky and landed on me. "It might happen one day out of ten thousand. That's how rare a pearl is. That's how rare true love is. It's one in ten thousand. Like the moon through a rainbow."

Suddenly I wasn't embarrassed anymore. I was thinking higher thoughts with Billy Treat. I was imagining the
full moon through a rainbow. It was like a pearl! I turned
to that place in the sky over the lake. I could almost see it
there, perfectly round and shimmering through the bands
of light-borne color. When I looked back at Billy, he was
walking toward his wagon.

"Just remember you're a gentleman," he said, looking
over his shoulder and shaking a warning finger at me.

But Billy had misjudged me. I was no gentleman.

The party drew almost everybody in the tent city to the
camp of Cindy's parents. The hogs were roasted and carved
on spits over banks of orange coals. Catfish fried in huge
iron kettles. The fiddlers and banjo-pluckers circled the
campfires. Pots of brewing coffee filled the air with a
fine, rich aroma. With all the campfire and tobacco smoke,
the mosquitoes found few opportunities to probe for blood,
preying mainly on the men who went to sip whiskey in
the dark.

Cecil and Adam avoided me, still mad about the hogs,
envious of my bateau, and jealous over Cindy. Most of the
other Port Caddo kids went home after dark, so I was left
to shift for myself. After I ate some pork and cornbread, I
didn't have much to do, but I kept wandering around, hoping to bump into Cindy, and yet avoiding her wagon for
fear I would bump into her. I was about ready to give up
and go home when it finally happened.

When I saw her coming, I fought an urge to turn and
run. I could face Cecil Peavy in a fistfight every day of the
week, but I was sure scared of girls.

"Hi, Ben," she said in her cheerful, self-assured drawl.

I returned the greeting and looked away, nervously only
risking glances at her. Our conversation consisted mainly

of her asking me questions and me grunting affirmative or negative.

"Daddy said to tell you those hogs was good eatin'."

I shrugged modestly. "A little tough. We should have fattened them longer." I was wondering when she wanted her boat ride, but I wasn't about to just come out and ask her. That seemed so forward I was afraid she might slap me.

"When are you going to give me that ride in your boat?" she asked, as if reading my mind.

"How about tomorrow?"

"Why not right now?"

Now? In the dark? Alone on the lake with Cindy? I was dumbfounded. It wasn't a bad idea, though. It was a very dark night. I wouldn't have to worry about looking stupid if she couldn't see me. Not a bad idea at all.

"Well?"

"All right," I said. "Come on."

That Cindy was a natural talker, which was lucky for me because my brain could hardly form a single word. She talked about everything from pearls to watermelons as we walked to my bateau on the lakeshore. She waded in ankle-deep and got in the bow, holding my arm to steady herself as she stepped in. I waded deeper and climbed over the gunnel to my seat in the stern.

"Where do you want to go?" I asked.

"Oh, I don't care. Just paddle around."

I slid my bateau out onto the lake with a powerful stroke of the paddle. Cindy's voice flowed like running water—a strange and beautiful sound to a boy from the bayou. The lights from the party came at us like skipping stones, leaving long trails as they clipped the wave tops. The sounds of the people droned with the singing bullfrogs. Out on the water, a warm breeze blew just stiff enough to keep the mosquitoes off of us. I didn't know how much Cindy knew about boats, so I stayed in water shallow enough to wade in. I didn't want her falling out and drowning.

"Do you like me, Ben?" she asked suddenly, in the middle of a soliloquy on something unrelated.

"Yeah," I said.

"Do you think I talk too much?"

"No."

"My brother says I talk too much. Sometimes my daddy says I talk too much, too. I like you, too."

I made a big circle in Goose Prairie Cove and let Cindy talk all she wanted. When I figured she had had enough of a ride, I took her back to the shore near Esau's place and helped her out.

"That was fun," she said. "You can take me again some time, if you want to. Do you want to?"

"Sure," I said, pushing the bateau onto the shore.

She held my hand as we waded to dry land and I felt a delirium I had never experienced. I wanted to grab her right there and put my hands all over her just to see what she was made of, but I remembered what Billy had said.

We stopped together a few steps from the water and turned toward each other. "Do you want to kiss me?" she asked, smooth as honey. I didn't get to answer, because the next thing I knew, her lips were on mine.

I never have put much stock in beginner's luck. That Cindy from Longview had done some kissing before. I know girls come by some seductions naturally, but she had practiced on somebody else before me.

I remember thinking how foolish I had been to misinterpret that peck Carol Anne had given me on the forehead weeks before. That was nothing compared to what Cindy was doing to me now. Even when I closed my eyes, I saw stars. But like everything else in the summer of pearls, it was too good to last long.

"Ciiindyyy!"

I heard her mother's long, siren call from the camp

party. Cindy's lips broke from mine. She had both hands on my face, but my arms were paralyzed against my sides. I was afraid to move them, thinking that if I went to grabbing at her, I might not be able to stop.

"I have to go," she said. "Mama's callin'." She turned and ran like a sprite toward the camp lights. "See you tomorrow!"

It was all very overwhelming. She wanted to see me again. Tomorrow. I hadn't done anything stupid. I hadn't scared her off or made her mad. Maybe Billy had something. Maybe I really could learn to be a gentleman after all.

I left a good portion of who and what I was right there on the lakeshore that night. I can still show you the spot where it happened, and I can almost recall the feeling that numbed me for days and nights afterward.

There are moments you anticipate in life. Many of them disappoint you when they finally come. Others exceed your most fanciful expectations. That first kiss of mine at Goose Prairie Cove changed me. It confused and enlightened me. It fulfilled me, yet left me desperately longing.

Life was going to get complicated again, but I knew one thing for certain after that night. Ben Crowell was going to become a gentleman. He wouldn't be fourteen forever.

SIXTEEN

Henry Colton got his first look at the Goose Prairie pearl camps from Port Caddo Road. It was midmorning and getting hot. He stopped in the shade of a pine and mopped his neck with a handkerchief as a few hopeful tourist pearl-hunters walked past. He thought Chicago had been hot when he left, but this place was suffocating.

He suddenly understood more clearly the lure of a hunt that drew its participants into the water.

He sat at the base of the tall loblolly pine to observe the activities down at the lake. He knew virtually nothing about pearl-hunting. Dozens of wagons and scores of tents dotted the lakeshore for as many miles as he could see. Hundreds of campers milled about on the shore, and hundreds more appeared as heads bobbing on the lake surface.

The coach from town rattled by him. It made a constant circuit of the pearl camps for those who didn't want to walk to or from Port Caddo. He shook his head in amazement. He had seen people get this excited over gold and silver, but never over pearls. He checked his pocket, as he had done a hundred times each day since leaving Chicago, to make sure the little coin purse was still there. It was.

After watching for a while, he figured out that no one mode of pearl-hunting predominated. There were almost as many methods as pearl-hunters. That was a relief. It would be easy to fit in. This job was going to be a regular holiday.

Colton finally got up and sauntered down to the lake. He sat down on a drifted log and continued his observations. The men and boys who came out of the water had mud between their toes and under their toenails, so he knew the waders were feeling for the mussels with their feet. A pair of men about fifty yards out in the cove were throwing their mussels into a skiff. Another fellow, without a boat, opened his with a knife as he found them.

Colton caught some familiar motion in the corner of his eye. Looking to his right, he saw a dark-skinned man—the man whose movements had attracted his attention—loafing in the shade of a mulberry with a couple of companions. The man looked to be Indian, but had short hair. There was a shack there. Something familiar about it, too. No, he had never been to Caddo Lake before, but that shack represented something he knew well. What was it?

Turning back to the cove, he observed a man lying on his stomach in a skiff. To keep the sun from scorching, the skiff had a wagon sheet fixed to it on bows, like a prairie schooner. The man propelled himself through the shallow water with his hands. Occasionally he scooped a mussel shell from the mud and threw it over his shoulder into the covered skiff.

Colton shook his head. These pearl-hunters were a strange bunch of—

There was that distinct motion again! This time he glanced quick enough to see the old Indian reaching for the flask in his pocket. Ah, now he recognized the shack. Saloon. He had enjoyed better from Denver to San Francisco, but he had survived far worse in a hundred cow towns and mining camps.

A right handy saloon would make this vacation all the more endurable. Besides, he had to blend in. If the pearl-hunters were drinkers, well, he had better take an occasional snort, too. His bosses had told him to curb his vices or find other employment, but they didn't understand how it was in the field.

He licked his lips. True, it was early. If he started now, he'd stay drunk all day. The old Indian reached for the pocket flask again, as if to goad him. Better watch that muscular fellow next to the Indian. Those beady little squint-eyes meant trouble. Seen that look before. Pure meanness.

A trio of boys beached a skiff and began lugging kegs up to the saloon. Whiskey? No, drinking water. The kegs were heavy, but the boys handled them well. It was routine to them. He remembered being adrift at their age— Illinois to California. It was a wonder he had survived those years.

He found himself surveying the saloon again. After all, there was no hurry. The pearl-buyer wasn't even around. He had a description of Brigginshaw. A man that size would be hard to miss. Get acquainted with the drinkers first. Might learn something. He got up and sauntered casually toward the shack.

By noon, Henry Colton was somewhat drunk and very hungry. "Where's a man eat around here?" he asked.

"We'll fry some fish directly," Esau said. He heard Billy's buckboard rattling down Port Caddo Road. "Or you can buy some cold meats and stuff from the wagon." He pointed his thumb over his shoulder without looking.

"That sounds good," Colton said. He checked the purse in his pocket as he rose. He noticed the beady-eyed man sneering at the approaching wagon.

The wagon drew a crowd when it pulled up. Colton thought he recognized the driver from the Treat Inn. Popular fellow. Everybody had a smile for him, and a kind word or two.

"Aren't you the cook at the Treat inn?" he asked as he paid Billy for his lunch.

"I am."

Colton congratulated himself. Drink, he believed, actually sharpened his mind for observations, even if it did slow his reflexes a little, and skew his judgments. Nothing to worry about on this job, though. Strictly routine. He retired to the shade of the mulberry with his food.

While eating his lunch, Colton saw a rowboat enter the cove from the main part of the lake. A black man pulled the oars, dwarfed by a huge bearded fellow who stood in the bow like George Washington crossing the Delaware. He had one hand on a pistol butt and the other wrapped around the handle of a satchel. That's where the money is, Colton thought. And the pearls.

The trace chains jerked on the supply wagon. Colton turned in time to see the driver wave. He followed the man's gaze out onto the lake. Brigginshaw removed the hand from his pistol grip and returned the salutation to the wagon driver. Friends. Interesting.

You're good, Colton. You don't miss anything.

"Pearl!" The cry came from the cove. "Over here, Captain!"

Brigginshaw's oarsman dipped the blades and wheeled the rowboat, propelling it easily toward the pearl-hunter in the water. As he chewed his cold ham and biscuits, Colton pulled his hat low over his eyes and watched the man in the white suit and panama. The oarsman held the boat beside the pearl-hunter, who handed Brigginshaw something over the gunnel. The buyer inspected the specimen and spoke to the hunter. Making an offer, Colton surmised. The hunter groused for a while, but finally nodded.

Colton narrowed his eyes against the glare and watched carefully. The Australian opened the satchel. He removed a small black case in which he placed the new pearl. Now the glint of a gold coin came from the satchel. Brigginshaw pressed it in the pearl-hunter's hand, inside the gunnels, so the hunter couldn't blame him if it fell into the water. Then the big man reached into the satchel again. He pulled out the notebook. Colton watched closely as the Australian made an entry with a pencil drawn from his jacket.

There it is, he thought. The entire procedure. This was going to be easy. Just figure out a way to separate Captain Brigginshaw from his satchel. Even for thirty seconds. How difficult could that be?

He finished his lunch and had Esau fill his jar with whiskey again. He watched as the buyer made two more purchases out in the cove. Same routine. The pearl, the money, the entry in the ledger book. Finally the captain had his oarsman pull for the shore.

The muscular, beady-eyed man got up. "See you later, Esau," he said.

"Where you goin', Kelso?" the old Indian replied, smirking a little.

"To take a shit and name it Brigginshaw."

The Indian smiled and winked at Colton.

It was the slowest wink Colton had ever seen. "What was that all about?" he asked when Kelso got far enough away.

"Fight a few weeks ago. Captain Brigginshaw hurt him pretty bad."

Colton nodded and watched the big Australian consume the lakeshore in huge strides. He lifted his panama and smiled warmly as he approached the mulberry.

"Good day, my Choctaw friend. Gentlemen."

"Hello, Captain," Esau said.

"Mr. Kelso's not feeling sociable today?" The Australian's laughter shook the mulberry leaves.

Colton was thinking: Let's see how much this big man will stand for. "He said he was going to take a shit and name it after you."

"Did he, now? And who are you, mate?"

"Henry Colton. Just drifted down from Indian Territory. Heard about the pearl rush." He stood and offered Brigginshaw his hand. The Australian shook it and smiled. He was big and strong, with a heart to match. Good-natured, but be careful. As the Indian said, he hurt that Kelso fellow pretty bad. He hadn't loosed his hold on the satchel yet.

"Captain Trevor Price Brigginshaw. Pleased to meet you, Mr. Colton."

"Oh, don't 'mister' me. It's Henry to my friends."

"Thinking of doing some pearl-hunting, Henry?"

"I don't know. What are my chances of finding a pearl here?"

"In the bottom of a whiskey jar? Not good, mate." His laughter boomed into the pines. "Not good at all!"

Colton slapped his knee and laughed along. "Well, how much do you give for a pearl?"

"That depends on many things. Could be anywhere from twenty-five dollars an ounce for dust pearls to eight hundred dollars for a single specimen. I bought a fine drop pearl for three hundred this morning on the North Shore. Isn't that right, Giff?"

Brigginshaw's black oarsman had come up beside him after tending to the boat. "Whatever you say, Captain."

"How many have you bought in all?" Colton asked.

"Today?"

"No, I mean since the rush started."

"Good God! Thousands!"

"My goodness. How do you keep track of them all?"

The captain patted his satchel. "I carry my office everywhere I go. Pearls, money, and records." He hitched his coattail behind his pistol grip. "And security, as well."

"Mind if I look at your record book? See what pearls are selling for? Might help me make up my mind whether or not I want to hunt for 'em."

The Australian shook his head. "Sorry, Mr. Colton," he said firmly. "All sales must remain confidential."

"Now, don't 'mister' me, I told you. It's Henry to you, Captain."

"And Trevor to you, Henry. You might as well try your luck for a few days. You'll earn drinking money even if you don't get rich." He looked at his oarsman. "Take a rest, Giff. I'm going to walk through the camps."

"Yes, sir," Giff said, sitting on the ground against the trunk of the mulberry.

When Brigginshaw had walked beyond earshot, Colton looked at the black man and said, "Hey, boy. How about that fellow out there in the water? The one the captain bought the pearl from when you first rowed him into the cove. How much did he get?"

"Captain said that's nobody's business," Giff replied. "He said keep my mouth shut. He don't tell nobody what them pearls sell for."

"But you know."

Giff shrugged. "Sometimes I hear. Other times he don't even say out loud. Just write it down on paper and show the pearl-hunters and they say deal or no deal."

"But you can see the book when he writes in it."

"Can't read noways," Giff said.

Colton took a long draw from the whiskey jar and watched Brigginshaw deal for pearls at a camp a hundred yards away. "Does he really keep all those pearls in that leather case?"

"Safest place he knows," Esau said.

Colton whistled. "Is he crazy? I heard in the Indian Territory that some outlaw gang was hiding out down here: Christmas so-and-so."

"Christmas Nelson," Esau said. "The captain ain't scared of them. He sleeps with them pearls in his bed, he says. I'd hate to try to steal 'em from him."

"I'd hate it, too," Colton said, grinning. "I'd hate the hell out of it!"

He wandered through the pearling camps that afternoon, asking pearl-hunters how much they had received for their finds. Their claims varied widely. He couldn't rely on them. The information would be of little use. He needed specifics. Checking the coin purse in his pocket, he drifted back to Esau's saloon to enjoy a few more drinks before returning to the Treat Inn for supper.

Near sundown, the mosquitoes began their forays, and Colton, now quite intoxicated, strode uncertainly back toward Port Caddo. As the afternoon wore on, he had thought more and more of the woman he had seen at the Treat Inn when he registered the night before. A real bayou belle. Maybe he would look her up tonight. He had thought it useless to approach her last night, sober. But now he had the cocksureness of a drunk. How could she resist him?

He arrived just as supper was being served, found an empty table in the corner, and sat down. Billy came out of the kitchen carrying four plates, which he delivered to another table. Colton caught his eye and waved.

"Be right with you," Billy said.

"No hurry," the guest replied, smiling. Then he saw her. The woman from last night had grown even more provocative. To Colton, it seemed she flirted a great deal with the male diners as she leaned over their shoulders to fill their glasses with water. He was sure he saw her pressing herself against them. Now he had her figured. She wanted company tonight, and he was just the man.

Billy came through the kitchen door with a plate of steaming food for the new diner. "Here you are, sir. Enjoy it." He smelled whiskey on the man's breath and remembered seeing him at Esau's place earlier. "Any luck pearling today?"

"Huh?" Colton said, tucking a napkin into the front of his shirt. "Oh! Hell, I didn't even get my feet wet. Maybe tomorrow."

Billy could read drunkenness in a man's eyes the way he could grade the luster of a pearl. But, unlike Trevor Brigginshaw, Colton didn't seem to be a mean drunk. He would probably go to bed after supper without causing any trouble. "Carol Anne will bring you some water in a minute," he said, heading back to the kitchen.

"How about something stronger?" Colton said, with his mouth full.

Billy stopped. "That'll be coffee," he replied, and left the man to his meal.

"Hello, darlin'," Colton said when Carol Anne came with the water pitcher. He mistook her suspicion for a look of interest.

"Good evening, Mr. . . ."

"Call me Henry, darlin'. Henry Colton. You remember me. You signed me in last night. Room number five."

"Oh, yes. Mr. Colton." She poured the water calmly.

"Now, don't 'mister' me. That's Henry to you, darlin'."

He grabbed her wrist as she finished filling his glass. "That's room number five." He winked, now doubly drunk with desire on top of the whiskey. When he looked at her, he was sure he saw her wink back.

Carol Anne twisted her wrist from his grasp and turned for the kitchen. When she did, he reached for the roundest, softest part of her he could find and pinched it smartly between his thumb and forefinger.

The customers heard Carol Anne yelp, and looked up in time to see her empty her water pitcher in Colton's face.

"Goddamn, woman!" he said.

Billy was out of the kitchen in seconds and caught Carol Anne as she tried to rush by him. "What's going on?"

Her features were twisted in anger when she pointed. "He grabbed me!"

Billy marched to the table. "Get out!" he said to Colton.

"What? Are you gonna take the word of a water girl over a guest?"

"She's half-owner of this inn, mister, and I'm the other half. Get out before I throw you out."

"But, my dinner."

Billy yanked the wet napkin from Colton's collar, clenched a handful of his shirt, and lifted him to his wobbly legs. The chair fell over and slapped against the floor. The dishes rattled on the table as Colton kicked in surprise. One of the guests was quick enough to open the front door as Billy dragged the offender there and shoved him out.

"Goddamn!" Colton said as he lifted himself from the dirt. It had happened again. How many places had he been thrown out of now? Always drunk.

He looked up and saw the light of the open inn door wavering above him. He saw something coming. His suitcase and the rest of his belongings landed on top of him, knocking him back down. Reflexes slow. Damned whiskey. And this his last chance.

Where would he go now? He stood and staggered a few steps before he got his balance. Back to the pearl camps. Nowhere else to go. He stuffed his suitcase with his things, unable to keep his balance. He suddenly felt a great deal drunker than he had before.

Finally getting his belongings together, he began weaving toward the pearling camps in the dark. Halfway there, his stomach began to boil. He stumbled into the bushes to vomit.

He tried to stand again, but his stomach hurt. He felt better on the ground. Fumbling with his suitcase, he pulled out a pair of pants to use as a pillow. He squirmed under the pinpricks of thirsty mosquitoes. His head was aching now. He felt a chill, pulled another article of clothing over him.

Maybe he should check his pocket for the coin purse. To hell with it. Who really gave a shit, anyway?

This was a familiar misery. Too familiar. His only consolation was knowing that sleep would soon come—the insensible sleep of a drunk. He would go to sleep curled up on the pine needles like a stray dog. Yes, he would sleep. Just as soon as he got through puking again.

SEVENTEEN

After several days, Henry Colton had Captain Brigginshaw pretty well patterned. The pearl-buyer arrived at the Goose Prairie camps about dinnertime every day and rowed out a couple of hours later for other mussel beds around the lake. Colton knew all he needed to know about the Australian now to put his plan into effect.

He was standing chest-deep in water, as he had done every morning for the past four days. He didn't think it would look good if he found his pearl too easily. But four days would have to suffice. Colton was not accustomed to bathing daily.

The morning after he got thrown out of the Treat Inn, he had sobered up and cleaned up, waited for Billy to take the wagon to the camps, then gone to see Carol Anne in the store. He carried his hat in his hand and kept his eyes on the floor.

"I was drunk and out of line," he said.

"Is that supposed to be an apology?" she asked, wishing Billy were there with her.

"The best I can manage," he admitted.

"All right, you're sorry. Now, get out before Billy finds you here."

He went to find Billy then. Henry Colton was a hard man to shame. He thought Billy might rough him up, but he could take a beating as well as any man. He went through the same routine. Hat in hand, eyes on the ground. "Drunk and out of line."

"That's no excuse."

"It won't happen again."

"Just stay away from our inn. You won't be welcomed there."

"If you say so."

He got drunk with Trevor Brigginshaw two nights later at Esau's place, and told the story of what had happened at the Treat Inn. Laughed about it, in fact. He found out then that the Australian was a mean drunk who didn't like strangers grabbing the lady friends of his old mate, Billy Treat. The fight didn't last long. Colton got in a few punches before the leather satchel laid him out.

When he came to, he thought it was remarkable that the

pearl-buyer would not set his satchel aside even in a fist-fight. It was going to be harder to get a look in there than he had at first thought. The beating had been worth it, though. He had learned quite a lot about Captain Brigginshaw.

Colton was not a man to hold a grudge. Even after the licking Trevor gave him, he became a friend and drinking partner of the pearl-buyer. For every wild tale the Australian told of the high seas, Colton had a match from the western territories. He had been everywhere. New Mexico, Montana, Oregon. Mining, cowboying, drifting, and gambling, he claimed.

He and Trevor both understood the debilitating pleasures of saloon life. Funny how many friendships he had started with fistfights over the years. Of course, the friendships never lasted long. He had to keep drifting in his line of work. He liked Trevor Brigginshaw; he truly did. After the fight and a few nights of drinking together, they got along well. But their friendship wouldn't last.

Now, wading in the murky waters of Goose Prairie Cove, Colton was planning the exact moment the friendship would end. The water he waded in did not feel the least bit cool. The long summer had warmed the shallows. Besides being warm, it was unusually muddy. For nearly three months, hundreds of pearl-hunters had been churning up the mud with their toes in search of mussels. When he came out of the water every day for lunch and drinks, Colton found layers of silt in his pockets, and his fingertips looked as wrinkled as prunes. He had enjoyed as much hunting as he could stand. It was time to find his pearl.

Giff Newton rowed the captain into the cove right on schedule. Colton reached into his right-hand pocket and found the little coin purse he had brought from Chicago. Carefully, he removed it from his pocket and opened it just wide enough to get his fingers in. He probed cautiously so as not to swish out the contents. In the bottom of the purse, the same thumb-and-forefinger grip that had pinched Carol Anne so smartly now delicately grasped the pearl he had been given in Chicago—a fine, round, freshwater gem of twenty-five grains. He let the purse sink and placed the pearl carefully in his left palm, closing his fist around it.

He drew in a breath and shouted "Pearl!" His voice cracked when he said it. He waved at the big Australian and saw the rowboat angle toward him.

"Henry!" The big man's voice came booming across the top of the water. "I have no time for bloody pranks!"

Colton held the fist above the water. "Prank, hell, Trev!" He put on his biggest grin. "You ain't gonna believe what I found."

The surrounding pearl-hunters stopped to watch the boat approach Colton in the water. Henry hooked the gunnel of the rowboat in the bend of his left elbow and slowly, carefully opened his hand. Brigginshaw stroked his beard, pushed his panama back on his forehead. His huge fingers delicately grasped the pearl and lifted it from Colton's lake-softened palm.

"This is what the fuss is all about, Henry? This?" His eyelids sagged disinterestedly. "Fifty dollars."

"Ha! Don't bullshit me, Trev. I didn't go into the pearling business half-cocked. I've talked to every successful hunter in camp, and read all the *Steam Whistle* articles from three weeks back, even before I came here. I know what a pearl is worth, and I won't take less than five hundred for that beauty!" He could feel the nearby pearl-hunters straining to hear.

Trevor rolled his eyes and looked at his oarsman. "Another overnight expert, Giff."

Giff played along, pursing his lips and shaking his head.

"With all due respect to my friend, John Crowell, his newspaper accounts are based on exaggerated hearsay. All pearl sales are confidential. I can offer no more than a hundred and fifty dollars for this slug."

"You're gettin' there," Henry said. "Pretty big jump, Trev, fifty to a hundred and fifty, but you've got a sight more jumpin' to do. That slug, as you call it, will go thirty-five grains, and I can't possibly take less than four-fifty."

The Australian's rich laughter skipped across the water. "What do you know about grading pearls, Henry?"

"When I was in the beef business, I could judge 'em on the hoof. When I was mining, I could assay a ton of ore with my eyes closed. Now I'm in pearls, and I know what's what with 'em. Get your scales out, Trev. I'll bet you four hundred fifty dollars that pearl weighs thirty-five grains."

The big man chuckled as he removed the pieces of his scale and put them together. He placed the pearl in the pan, and added weights to the tune of twenty-five grains.

"Bloody Hell!" Trevor said. "I had judged it at no more than fifteen grains. Its lack of luster makes it look smaller, Henry, but if it's twenty-five grains, I'll go as high as two hundred and fifty."

"Lack of luster, my ass, Trevor! That's the best pearl you've seen on Caddo Lake yet. Don't try hoodwinking Henry Colton!"

The captain smirked at Giff. The oarsman shook his head and looked at the sky.

"Three hundred," Trevor said.

"Four hundred."

"Three twenty-five, and that's the absolute ceiling."

"Three seventy-five."

Trevor looked at his oarsman. "What do you think, Giff?"

Giff shrugged. "Meet him in the middle, Captain."

Henry cupped his hand and splashed the oarsman. "Oh, hell, boy, you don't even know where the middle is!" he shouted.

The surrounding pearlers did not so much as ripple the surface. They were statues in the water, not looking, but listening to the negotiations and wishing they had ears like swamp rabbits.

"What Giff lacks in education, Henry, he makes up for with good common sense. His principle is a sound one, don't you think? If you won't take three-fifty, you might as well throw that pearl back to Goose Prairie Cove. I won't pay more, and I'm the only buyer on the lake. You could peddle it in New York, but your traveling expenses would consume everything over three hundred and fifty, if you could get more than that, and I doubt you could. Three-fifty, take it or leave it, mate."

Henry grinned. "Three-fifty and you buy the drinks tonight," he said.

"Bloody mercy, Henry! You drive a hard bargain. Done! Esau's saloon tonight at dark." He shook the grinning pearl-hunter's hand, pulled a velvet case from the satchel, and inserted the gem. "Now, what will it be? Gold, silver, or government notes?"

"Gold's the heaviest. I guess I ought to take some of that off your hands so's the next man to get hit with that money bag won't hurt so bad when he wakes up."

Trevor rocked the rowboat with his laughter. He counted out the gold coins, put them in Colton's hand, and reached for the ledger book. Opening the book, he held it above Colton's line of sight and flipped to the appropriate page. He reached into his coat pocket for his pencil and began writing in a careful, deliberate hand.

"What are you writing down in there, Trev?" Colton asked.

"White sphere . . ." he said slowly, speaking the words as he pencil spelled them. "Twenty . . . five . . . grains. Three . . . hundred . . . fifty . . . dollars. Henry . . . Colton."

"You sure you know how to spell three hundred fifty?" Colton said. "Ask Giff if you don't."

"I spell it 'three, five, zero,' you bleeding idiot." Brigginshaw laughed, slammed the book shut, and inserted it in the leather satchel. "To the camps, Giff. We've wasted enough time with Mr. Colton."

"Now, don't 'mister' me, Trev! I'll see you tonight at Esau's."

EIGHTEEN

Henry Colton sat in his room reading the latest edition of the *Steam Whistle*. He had booked an upstairs suite on the north side of Widow Humphry's inn. Through the rain-streaked glass of his window, he could watch the movements around the Treat Inn and keep tabs on Trevor Brigginshaw. He still frequented Esau's saloon with the captain, too, and had learned that Trevor intended to take the first steamer to New Orleans, now that the rain had brought an early end to the pearling season.

September had come on wet. Day after day of rain and drizzle had dampened the spirits of the pearl-hunters and sent the farm families packing for their fields. After several days of rain, the Caddo Lake pearling camps had become little more than ash heaps and leftover wood piles.

The tourists left town as fast as Joe Peavy's stagecoach could carry them off. Many of them were concerned about getting back to Marshall before the road got too muddy. Wagons had been known to bog down between Port Caddo and Marshall.

In Port Caddo, however, morale remained high. These early rains would raise the lake level and bring the riverboat traffic back. It looked as if the town's run of luck would hold. The *Steam Whistle* predicted that the steamer season would begin early, supplementing the economic lift the pearls had brought to Caddo Lake during the summer.

That John Crowell is a hell of a booster, Colton thought as he turned a page. Hardly a dreary word to report in the whole newspaper. He glanced through the windowpane, then returned to the article Crowell had written about the steamer traffic.

The government snag boats had virtually finished removing the Great Raft from the Red River. Steamers would find a more navigable channel into Caddo Lake once the giant logjam was gone. True, Marshall was getting a railroad, but Jefferson, upstream on Big Cypress Bayou, had decided against the iron horse, preferring to stick with the familiar riverboat trade. Steamers would ply Caddo Lake for many years yet, according to the *Steam Whistle.*

Sentimental fools, Colton thought. Riverboats couldn't compete with railroads. They were slower, smaller, less reliable, and more expensive. Any town that chose steamboats over trains was signing its own death warrant.

The pearls, though—that was a different matter. Crowell's editorial headlined "Sustainable Pearl-Based Economy Challenge to Port Caddo" seemed to make sense, if the local folks would take it to heart.

"Our mussel beds," Crowell had written, "are more valuable than any deposits of gold or silver found elsewhere upon the continent. Our resource is a living, renewable one that if protected, will continue to produce fine gems for generations to come. . . ."

Crowell quoted extensively the two local pearl experts—Treat and Brigginshaw—and finally arrived at four laws recommended to protect the Caddo Lake mussel beds for future generations:

1. Divide the lake into four sections and allow pearling in just one section each year.
2. Establish limits regarding sizes of mussels to be opened and number of mussels allowed to each pearler.

3. Close the pearling season from January through May.
4. Prohibit destructive apparatus (such as George Blank's mussel rakes and tongs).

Maybe the pearl industry would last, Colton thought. But even if it did, Trevor Brigginshaw wouldn't be a part of it. His days as a pearl-buyer were numbered. If only he could get into the Australian's leather satchel. That was proving to be the toughest part of this assignment. The captain rarely let the thing get out of his grasp, much less his sight. Colton couldn't be sure of success until he got into that case, and the sooner the better.

This was his last chance. He had to see this job through, or find employment elsewhere.

He was about to doze off with the newspaper on his lap and the rain beating against the window, when the faint blast came. A single note from a faraway steam whistle. The pearl season was over and the steamer season had begun.

The boat was an ugly patchwork of unpainted lumber that had reached the age of ten in a rare case of longevity among light-draft steamers. She was called the *Slough Hopper,* and her pilot was an infamous old rake by the name of Emil Pipes, who had no objection to wiles such as price-gouging, smuggling, and graft, though he had never gotten rich off of any of them.

Unlike most Caddo Lake steamers, the *Slough Hopper* was a side-wheeler. Most people considered her unsafe because her paddle wheels were exposed. Huge fenders had once enclosed them, until Pipes decided to strip all unnecessary woodwork from the *Hopper* to lighten her and make more room for cargo. Now there was nothing to keep a man from falling into the churning machinery of the giant wheels that reached from the waterline to the texas. The exposed wheels presented danger to passengers and crew on the main deck, the boiler deck, and the hurricane deck.

If the *Glory of Caddo Lake* had once headed the list of favorite Port Caddo riverboats, the *Slough Hopper* anchored the other end. Her so-called "staterooms" were separated by moldy curtains. Her galley fare was barely edible. Her drab appearance was enough to drive a man to depravity, which was probably why the *Hopper* carried such a large stock of poor whiskey and hosted nightly poker games.

It was a sorry way to start the riverboat season, but it was a start nonetheless, and an early one at that.

The rain had let up some by the time the *Hopper* moored at the Port Caddo wharf. Townspeople started appearing on the street, easing toward the wharf to greet the first steamer of the season and to get the latest news from New Orleans.

Through his window, Henry Colton saw Trevor Brigginshaw and Billy Treat leave the Treat Inn and slog through the mud to the wharf. The captain had his leather case with him, of course. Colton folded his newspaper and left his room to join the throng.

A considerable commotion obscured his approach. People were talking and shouting to crew members on the steamer. Roustabouts sang a coonjine as they carried huge loads of firewood aboard. Colton reached the end of the cobblestones and slid down the muddy flood-bank between the Treat Inn and Constable Hayes' log jailhouse. Reaching the wharf, he eased up behind Billy and Trevor, who were looking at the *Slough Hopper* when he drew close enough to hear them speak.

"Why don't you wait for another boat, Trev? This thing's barely floating."

"The sooner I can get back to New York, the better."

"Why? What's your hurry?"

Trevor lifted his satchel and patted it. "Thanks to your little pearl rush, Billy, I've made enough in commission on this trip to buy a new sloop. The *Wicked Whistler Two*, I'll call her. I'll be back among the Pearl Islands next summer."

"You're not coming back here next year?"

"Afraid not, mate. I belong on the open seas, not in these bloody bayous."

Colton removed himself from the pair of friends and joined several Port Caddoans who were boarding the *Slough Hopper* to talk with the crew members. He had to jump between two wood-toting rousters to climb the mud-slick gangplank, which bounced under the weight of men and cordwood. He climbed the creaking stairs to the boiler deck and entered the saloon from the front of the passenger cabin.

Passing the whiskey bar and the dirty dining table, Colton came to the first of the berths enclosed by curtains. He pulled back the tattered cloth. He imagined Trevor lying in the berth, intoxicated. He might find his chance to open the leather satchel while aboard the *Slough Hopper*. He could reach in through the curtains and have a look-see while the Australian was sleeping off one of his violent drunks.

He left the saloon and climbed the next flight of stairs to the hurricane deck. He saw Emil Pipes smoking a cigar outside the grimy glass pilothouse standing above the texas.

"Afternoon, Captain," he said.

Pipes shook some ashes down on Colton, but didn't return the greeting.

"What's the schedule?" Colton queried.

"Ask the clerk." He turned into his pilothouse to avoid further interrogations.

Colton found the clerk on the bow taking note of some cargo the rousters were off-loading to the wharf. "What's the schedule?" he asked again.

The clerk was all of nineteen. "Take on wood and head upstream for Jefferson. We'll be back here, probably tomorrow night, for the downstream run to New Orleans."

Colton thought for a moment. "Can I take a berth upstream to Jefferson, then hold on to it for the downstream run to New Orleans, too?"

The clerk glanced from his ledger book. "Of course."

"I'll be back directly with my belongings."

Colton trotted back down to the wharf with his suitcase, but stopped before climbing the gangplank and veered toward Trevor and Billy. "It was a pleasure drinking and pearling with you, Captain, but it's time I headed back to my squaw in the Indian Territory."

Trevor was unusually formal because Billy was there, and Billy was still mad at Colton for having groped Carol Anne. "Very well, Mr. Colton."

"I've told you a dozen times, Trevor. Don't 'mister' me. It's Henry to my friends."

The shrill whistle of the *Slough Hopper* blew.

"So long, Captain. You, too, Mr. Treat."

Billy frowned, but tipped his hat.

NINETEEN

Henry Colton stood on the bow of the *Slough Hopper* and watched the dark bayou pass in the night. The rain had stopped while the boat was taking on cargo and a few passengers at Jefferson. Now the *Hopper* was steaming downstream for Port Caddo, New Orleans, and all points in between. The sky had cleared and stars were shining.

He would have seen them more clearly but for the burning pine knots. They flared and popped in a large iron basket that extended over the water from the bow, like a flaming figurehead. Coals fell into the bayou, but occasionally a spark blew back and landed on the deck.

It's a wonder this boat hasn't burned yet, he thought.

He was hurting pretty bad. He had pulled a good drunk in Jefferson. He had made unwise advances toward the girlfriend of a bully in a billiards hall. He could still feel the cue stick breaking over his head. That glorious drunk would have to stave him off until New Orleans. He would have to stay sober on the riverboat if he wanted to get a look into Trevor Brigginshaw's satchel.

He knew the captain was waiting to board at Port Caddo and ride to New Orleans. There was no other way the big Australian could get out of town. The roads were too badly bogged to get to Marshall.

A rouster came forward with a shovelful of fatwood chunks and threw them into the big iron basket to burn. A few sparks flew past the hogshead Colton was sitting on. "Watch it, boy!" he said.

The big black man didn't reply.

The trunks of huge cypress trees flickered strangely in the shadows, very near the boat in the narrow bayou. Emil Pipes rang the bell often. He used his side-wheels well to steer the *Hopper* through the crooked bayou, sometimes shutting down one wheel to take bends, or turning the wheels in opposite directions to make sharp turns in the channel.

"Good evenin', Mr. Colton," someone suddenly said over the pop and hiss of the steam engines.

Colton turned to see the *Hopper's* young clerk smoking a pipe. "Howdy," he said. "Glad you happened along. I want to talk to you."

"What about?"

"When we get to Port Caddo, a big fellow named Brigginshaw is going to board for New Orleans. Wears a beard, talks with an Australian accent. You can't mistake him."

"And?"

"Well, I'd just as soon he didn't know I was on board. Personal matter. You understand."

"No, not really."

Colton took a gold coin from his pocket and flipped it into the air. "Well, if you could refrain from using my name out loud, and see that I get my meals behind the curtain in my berth, I would make it worth your while." He held the double eagle out for the clerk to take.

"I don't see any harm in that, Mr. Colton." The youth slipped the coin in his pocket.

"Now, don't 'mister' me, son. Just call me Henry."

He was watching from the shadows of the hurricane deck when the *Hopper* moored at the Port Caddo wharf. It was the middle of the night. He expected to see no one but Brigginshaw board. But as soon as the gangplank fell on the wharf, a burly man trotted from behind the jailhouse, to the wharf, and sprinted up the gangplank.

Colton got only a glimpse in the dark, but recognized the new passenger as the man with the gator eyes. He had learned at Esau's that Kelso was suspected of blowing up the *Glory of Caddo Lake* three months before. And, he had a grudge against Brigginshaw. Colton sighed. He didn't care for complications at this point. What did Kelso have in mind?

Brigginshaw didn't leave the Treat Inn until the final whistle blew. Billy came out on the front porch and shook the big man's hand. Carol Anne hugged him. They were good friends to see him off past midnight.

As the captain boarded, Colton went quickly to his berth

and pulled the curtain. He strapped on a shoulder holster holding a .44-caliber Smith & Wesson revolver. He pulled a light jacket on over the weapon and lay down on his berth to listen.

There was a card game going on in the forward part of the saloon, but he heard the Australian's long strides tramp across the floor, muting the swearing voices and clinking glasses.

"This will be your stateroom, here, Captain Brigginshaw," the clerk said.

"Stateroom, is it?" The deep laughter filled the long saloon.

Brigginshaw was across the saloon and three berths aft. Colton could lie behind his curtains and keep track of Trevor's comings and goings. He hoped Trevor was in a drinking mood. It had been three nights since the big Australian had tied one on. Colton had him pretty well patterned. Yes, the big pearl-buyer would be thirsty tonight.

But where was Judd Kelso? He hadn't come up to the boiler deck. Probably riding among the cargo on the main deck. The fares were lower down there. Every pearler in the Goose Prairie camps knew Kelso had run out of money two weeks ago. He had tried pearling for two days, then disappeared. Tonight was the first Colton had seen of him since then. What was he up to, sneaking aboard like that?

The *Slough Hopper* was backing into the Big Cypress Bayou channel when Colton heard Brigginshaw's boots pace forward to the whiskey bar. Someone was playing a harmonica, and playing it rather well, Colton thought. The steam engines were barking again. Still, he could hear Trevor's rich voice ordering a drink. The smell of the clerk's pipe tobacco hung in the stagnant air of the passenger cabin.

He found himself wishing for whiskey, though his stomach was still sore from retching this morning. Nothing to do now but wait. Wait for Trevor to get drunk, pick a fight, lay some poor devil out with the satchel, and retire to his berth. It would take till dawn.

He had been listening to Brigginshaw's loud talk and laughter for over an hour when the steam whistle blew.

"What's that about?" Brigginshaw asked.

"Someone wanting to board at Potter's Point, I guess," the clerk answered.

"You bloody guess!" The captain was beginning to feel belligerent. "I suppose I'll have to find out for myself."

Colton peeked through his curtains and saw the captain leave through the forward saloon door. He quickly left his berth and headed aft, climbing the stairs to the hurricane deck as soon as he left the saloon. Once above the passenger cabin, he snuck forward on the starboard side, passing between the texas and the exposed moving members of the huge paddle wheel.

Remaining in the shadows, he looked ahead and saw a lantern on the shore. He saw men and horses in the small circle of light. The bayou was wider here, the cypress trees fewer and farther away from the channel. Stepping momentarily into the light of the burning pine knots, he looked down on the boiler deck and saw Trevor standing directly under him, clutching the satchel, watching the men and horses at Potter's Point.

The *Slough Hopper* made for the lantern light and lowered the gangplank. Five men waited to board, with six saddled horses. Colton didn't think the extra horse unusual, except that it was saddled. Perhaps the men were taking the extra horse and saddle to a friend across the lake.

The clerk went down to the main deck to collect the fees for men and horses. The first four mounts clapped up the gangplank behind their owners as if they boarded riverboats every day. The fifth animal proceeded with much more caution, balking every few steps and craning its neck to see in the glare of the pine knots. The horse took the last step onto the main deck in a leap that knocked one of the horsemen down.

Colton heard Captain Brigginshaw chuckle.

The sixth horse at first refused to negotiate the gangplank. When finally persuaded to climb the narrow ramp, it got halfway up and jumped off, falling into the shallow water. Trevor stomped the boiler deck and roared with laughter.

One of the horsemen mounted the unwilling animal and rode up and down the dark lakeshore for two or three minutes, whipping and spurring the horse relentlessly. When the animal was well spent, it climbed the gangplank almost anxiously. Trevor laughed down on the entire episode from the boiler deck, and Colton looked down on Trevor from the shadows of the hurricane deck.

When the gangplank was raised and the *Hopper* under way again, the five horsemen climbed to the boiler deck where the Australian stood. Colton saw the buckle of a gun belt at one man's waist. Another carried a gunnysack, apparently stuffed with a change of clothes.

"Bloody fine entertainment!" the captain said as the men reached the top of the stairs.

"From up here, I reckon it was," the man with the gunnysack said.

"Come inside and let me buy you a drink for your trouble," Trevor said.

"Hell, partner, we don't want to drink that rotgut this old tub sells." He reached for a bottle in his gunnysack. "But you're welcome to drink some of our good whiskey with us."

Colton could barely hear their voices over the steam engines. The new passengers exchanged introductions, shook hands with Trevor, passed various bottles and flasks, talked and laughed loudly. The *Slough Hopper* was back in the channel, steaming forward, heading for the open water of Caddo Lake.

This might be just the break, Colton thought. These horsemen might be just what it takes to get Trevor drunk. He was thinking about sneaking back into his berth from the rear of the saloon when he heard a voice call from the boiler deck, below and aft:

"Hey, you ugly Australian son of a bitch!"

Colton recognized the voice as that of the gator-eyed man, Judd Kelso. He had almost forgotten Kelso was aboard. Now it looked as if he wouldn't be aboard for long. Brigginshaw was sure to throw him off.

"Who the hell is that?" one of the horsemen said.

"He must be talkin' to you, Captain. We're from Arkansas."

The horsemen laughed.

"Aye, he's talking to me, mates," Trevor said. "And he'll bloody answer to me as well."

The thin voice of the gator-eyed man rose again: "I owe you a ass-whipping Brigginshaw. Come and get it."

From the deck above, Colton followed the footsteps and the jingling spurs aft, wondering what he should do, if anything. He knew Brigginshaw could handle Kelso. Maybe that's what concerned him. Kelso should have known it, too. Ol' Gator Eyes couldn't be stupid enough to think he'd fare any better against the big Aussie this time. Maybe he had a gun. Maybe he had murder on his mind.

"Hot-damn, boys," one of the horsemen said. "Looks like a fight." When Colton came to the churning paddle wheel, the engine and machinery noises drowned out all the talk from the deck below. He strained to hear above the blasts of the exhaust valve and the rotations of the huge wheel. He didn't know for sure if he heard anything un- usual, or if he saw a shadow move in a way it shouldn't have, or if he just plain smelled trouble. But suddenly he sensed that Trevor Brigginshaw needed help bad.

Colton stepped to the rail in front of the paddle wheel, leaned over, and looked below. The man with the gunnysack had put it over Brigginshaw's head from behind. Another man was pulling on the leather satchel in the Australian's right hand. A third held the pearl-buyer's left arm. A fourth had a leg. The man wearing the gun belt had drawn his pistol and was using it to beat Trevor about the head. Firing it would make too much noise, alert too many passengers. Instead, the men were trying to pistol-whip and push the big pearl-buyer headfirst into the turning paddle wheel. They were going to let the *Slough Hopper* do their murdering for them.

Trevor still had one leg free and was kicking heroically with it. With his outstretched arms against the structural members and hog chains, he was preventing the robbers from beheading him with the paddle wheel. But Colton knew that not even Brigginshaw could hold out long against six men. He drew his Smith & Wesson from the shoulder holster. No good. From his position above, he could barely see the bandit with the pistol, and that was the one he needed to shoot first.

He pulled himself back onto the hurricane deck and sprinted as lightly as he could to the forward stairs. He took the steps four or five at a time, leaping down to the boiler deck. He turned the corner of the passenger cabin and ran back toward the fight at the paddle wheel, leading with his Smith & Wesson.

Now he heard Kelso's voice: "Move, Christmas, and let me split his head open." The gator-eyed man wielded the *Hopper's* iron capstan bar over his head.

The bandit with the pistol looked forward. Colton was proud to be sober. His aim was superb when he wasn't drunk.

The Smith & Wesson fired as the capstan bar came down on Brigginshaw's head. The bandit with the pistol fell, and the others scattered, leaving the Australian's body slumped inches from danger on the boiler deck, the sack still on his head. The robber tugging at the leather satchel came away with it and ran aft. Then Trevor's body fell over to one side, and Henry thought the paddle wheel would finish what the outlaws had started. The pearl-buyer's head came so close that the crushing wheel snagged the sack and yanked it off, exposing Trevor's bloody face.

Two of the bandits produced weapons and fired back at Colton. Coolly, he ignored the muzzle blasts and fired at the man carrying the satchel. The bandit fell, dropping the leather bag. Kelso jumped from the boiler deck, into the water. Two others swung over the railing, down to the main deck where the horses stood. The last outlaw ran down the aft stairs.

Colton heard the hooves drumming crazily on the main deck as he trotted aft. He kicked the revolver away from the first robber he had shot, for the man was still moving. He pulled Trevor away from the paddle wheel. He saw blood in the Australian's hair, but the huge chest was still heaving.

He continued aft and put his pistol to the head of the second bandit he had shot, but could tell that the man was dead when he rolled him over. The leather satchel was in the bandit's death grip. Colton grabbed it.

Horses were pounding the deck below, leaping into the lake. Colton looked over the rail and considered letting a few rounds go at a man on a swimming horse. No need. Let them go. Don't draw their fire now.

He looked forward and saw that Trevor Brigginshaw was still out cold. The leather pearl-and-money bag was in his own hand now. He had what he needed, and two outlaws, to boot. He felt his heart racing. He felt more alive than he had in months. Years!

Damn, Henry, he thought. Your luck's comin' back.

TWENTY

When Trevor Brigginshaw came to, he saw several blurry men looking down on him. He heard voices and smelled tobacco smoke. He focused on the ceiling of the riverboat saloon and felt for his satchel with each hand.

"He's coming out of it, Mr. Colton," a voice said. "I mean, Henry." Trevor recognized the voice as that of the young riverboat clerk.

He tried to sit up, but his head hurt terribly, and the exertion made his stomach feel ill. He closed his eyes and remembered the smelly sack over his head and the horrible sounds of the paddle wheel, screeching inches from his ears. He remembered Judd Kelso, and a name: Christmas.

Opening his eyes again, he saw a familiar face. He grabbed Henry Colton by the collar. "My case."

"Easy, Trev. I've got it right here. I looked after it for you while you were out."

Trevor felt the familiar handle in his hand. He tried to sit up again, and succeeded with some help from the passengers. He found himself on the dining table of the *Slough Hopper*. "Henry, what in the bloody hell are you doing here?" He touched his head where the capstan bar had hit him.

"Saving your life, looks like," Colton said.

"The Christmas Nelson gang tried to rob you," the clerk added.

Trevor looked around at the passengers, then back at Colton. "I thought you were going back to the Indian Territory."

"That was just a story, Trev. Sorry I had to lie to you. Comes with the job."

"What bloody job?"

"Mr. Colton's a Pinkerton detective," the clerk said.

"That's right, Trev. I've been after that Christmas Nelson gang. Sorry you had to get between us."

The Australian saw two bloody men stretched out on the saloon floor. "Is that them?"

"Two of them," Colton replied. "One dead, one damn near dead. I don't know if either one of 'em is Christmas Nelson himself."

"Did they get anything?" He fumbled with the latches to his leather case.

"Not a thing, Trev." Colton put his hand on the big man's shoulder. "I stopped them before they could open it. Your goods are safe."

The pearl-buyer breathed a sigh of relief and stood, steadying himself with one hand on the table. "Where the hell are we, Henry? How long have I been out?"

Henry chuckled. "You've only been out a few minutes. That iron bar would have killed any other man on this boat. We're heading back to Port Caddo to put that live one in jail. Captain Pipes didn't hardly want to, but I told him the Pinkerton Agency would pay for the lost time."

Trevor motioned for a glass of whiskey that one of the passengers was holding. "Why are we going back to Port Caddo? They must have a better jail in Shreveport." He poured the contents of the glass over his wounded head, wincing as the whiskey stung him.

"Last thing I want to do is cross a state line with a prisoner. If that wounded one lives, I'll have all that extradition foolishness to deal with to get him back to Texas for trial."

Brigginshaw chuckled a little as he held his glass out for a refill. "You, Henry? A Pinkerton? I never would have guessed it in a million years." He poured the next jigger down his throat instead of over his head.

"That's the idea, Trev."

"How did you know the gang was going to try to rob me?"

"I didn't. If I'd have known that, I'd have warned you. I

got a tip from an informant that they would board this boat tonight somewhere between Jefferson and Shreveport. And it looks like my informant was right."

"That it does," Brigginshaw said. "That it bloody does, and thank God for it. I owe you one, mate." He laughed, in spite of the condition his head was in. "Pinkerton detective!"

Colton went up to the pilothouse and asked Emil Pipes not to blow the whistle when the *Slough Hopper* returned to Port Caddo. "Last thing I need is a bunch of citizens around when I'm trying to put a man in jail."

"The son of a bitch is damn near dead," Pipes growled. "How much trouble could it be to get a near dead son of a bitch in a jailhouse?"

"It's standard procedure, Captain Pipes. I won't risk getting any civilians hurt if I can help it. For all we know, that Christmas Nelson gang might be on the way to Port Caddo to rescue their men. They could beat us there on horseback."

"Aw, the hell," Pipes growled.

"I've worked among outlaws for years, Captain. They'll surprise you."

The pilot growled and dismissed Colton with a wave of his hand. The Pinkerton man went back down to the saloon and pulled the clerk aside. "There's a constable in Port Caddo named Rayford Hayes. He lives three houses uphill from the livery barn. Do you know where that is?"

"Yes, sir."

"Good. As soon as we dock, I want you to run get him. Have him meet me at the jailhouse next to the wharf."

Henry Colton saw the *Slough Hopper's* clerk leap to the wharf with his lantern before the rousters had the mooring lines fast.

He went back into the saloon and found the Aussie nursing his head wound and drinking whiskey. "Trevor, you said you owed me one. Now's your chance to make good."

"Name it, mate."

"You can carry that live one to the jailhouse for me. You're strong enough to do it on your own, and I'd just as soon keep as many people clear of the jail as possible. Never know who you can trust. I'll guard your leather bag while you carry the prisoner."

Trevor rose. "I've never trusted another living soul with this satchel." He smiled. "Until tonight, that is." He handed the leather bag to Colton and stooped over the outlaws laid out on the floor.

"Not that one, Trev," Henry said.

"What?"

"That's the dead one. Pick up the other one."

"By God, Henry! You're right!" The Australian put his hand to his head wound and filled the saloon with laughter.

Trevor was relieved to see Constable Hayes standing at the bottom of the gangplank with the *Hopper's* clerk when he and Henry came down. The weight of the wounded outlaw in his arms burdened him little. It wasn't far to the jailhouse. He would deposit the outlaw there, get his pearls back from Henry, and be on his way at last.

"What's all this about, Captain Brigginshaw?" Hayes asked, yawning. He looked rather ridiculous with his gun belt strapped around his nightshirt, his black boots contrasting with his white legs.

"Ask Henry. He's the detective."

"Huh?" Constable Hayes looked at Colton.

"Give the constable your lantern," Colton said to the clerk, "and keep everybody on the boat."

"Yes, sir."

"Detective?" Hayes said, taking the lantern. "You?"

"Pinkerton Detective Agency," Colton said. "This wounded man is a member of the Christmas Nelson gang. There's a dead one on the boat. They tried to get Captain Brigginshaw's pearls."

"Christmas Nelson! Well, I'll be damned!" The constable trotted ahead of Trevor with the lantern to open the jailhouse door, his boots slipping in the mud as he ran.

Trevor had taken note of the Port Caddo jailhouse, wondering if he would ever land there drunk. It was a one-room log building with a door facing town and a tiny window facing the bayou. Both openings were covered by crossed iron bars, riveted together. The iron door swung on heavy hinges threaded deep into the logs. It was crude, but secure.

Rayford Hayes unlocked the door and opened it for Trevor. The big Australian had to duck to carry the wounded man into the cell. The iron grating of the jailhouse ceiling was barely over six feet high, and he didn't care to bump his already aching head on it.

"Just lay him out on the bunk," the constable said, holding the lantern inside the jailhouse.

When he lay the wounded outlaw in the cell, Trevor heard his satchel drop with a splash into the mud, and turned in time to see Colton shutting the iron door on him. Acting on reflex, he rushed to the door and put his foot in its path to keep it from slamming. Colton's Smith & Wesson appeared out of nowhere and leveled on Trevor.

"Colton, what the hell . . ." Constable Hayes said.

"Don't interfere, Hayes. Just give me the jail key so's I can lock him in. Trevor, back up."

The big Australian looked into the barrel of the revolver, his anger building. "Henry, what in the bloody hell are you doing now?"

"Look here, Colton!" Constable Hayes said, stepping forward with the lantern.

"I said don't interfere, Hayes. I'll explain everything just as soon as I get the good Captain Brigginshaw locked in your jailhouse. Now, give me the key. Trevor, move your foot and back up."

The Australian felt his face grow feverish with rage. He kept his foot against the iron door. He glanced at his leather satchel on the muddy ground outside of the jailhouse. "My pearls!" he said. "He's robbing me, Rayford!"

"Don't move, Hayes!" Colton warned. "I'm not robbing anybody. I'm a Pinkerton agent arresting Captain Trevor Brigginshaw."

"Arresting him for what?" Hayes said.

"Embezzlement."

"Embezzlement!" the Aussie roared. "Rayford, can't you see he's lying? He's after the pearls!"

"I'm tellin' the truth. Constable, pick up the pearl-bag. I'll let you hold on to it to prove I'm not after it. You can cover me with your pistol if you want. The evidence I need is in Trevor's ledger book."

Hayes put the lantern down on the muddy ground to keep his gun hand free. He moved carefully toward the leather bag and picked it up. Then he backed off a few steps. "Colton, put your gun away and we'll sort this out. You must have made some kind of mistake."

"No mistake. After I get Trevor locked behind this door, I'll surrender my weapon to you, Constable, and explain everything."

Trevor eased his right hand toward the mother-of-pearl grip of his Colt revolver.

"Your pistol won't do you any good, Trev. I took all the cartridges out while you were unconscious. Go ahead, check it."

Trevor carefully drew the pearl-handled Colt and spun the cylinder, finding the chambers empty. He was seething so with rancor that he felt on the verge of attacking the

Pinkerton man, in spite of the cocked revolver aiming at him.

"Sorry I lied to you again, Trev, but like I said, it comes with the job. I wasn't after Christmas Nelson. I had no idea his gang would be on that boat tonight. I was after you."

Trevor felt a dark wave of guilt sicken his stomach, but tried to hold on to some kind of hope. "Don't trust him, Rayford. He'll lock me in and shoot us both dead for those pearls."

"Just give me a chance and I'll explain everything," Colton argued. "Like I said, Hayes, you can draw your pistol now and cover me if you want to."

For a moment, the only sounds were those of crickets and bullfrogs along the bayou.

"Let him say his piece, Captain," the constable finally suggested. "He could have shot you already if that's what he wanted to do. Maybe there's been a misunderstanding."

"No misunderstanding," Colton argued. "International Gemstones has suspected Trevor of raking off money for a year now. When he started out working for them, he was the best pearl-bargainer they had ever employed. Then he started losing his ability to get the lowest prices."

"I don't follow you," Hayes said. "No crime in that, is there?"

"Not in itself," the Pinkerton man answered. "But the company trusted his ability more than his honesty. They figured he was padding the prices he got and keeping the extra for himself."

"You're a lying little bandit!" Trevor bellowed. "You're no Pinkerton man! Look at him, Rayford! Does he look like a detective to you?"

Hayes looked as if he didn't know who to trust. "I still don't get it," he said. "You're not making sense to me, Colton."

"All right, listen and I'll explain it so's anybody can

understand. I brought a pearl down here with me from the Chicago Pinkerton offices. International Gemstones sent me the pearl to use. I posed as a pearl-hunter for a couple of days, pretended to find the pearl I had in my pocket all along, and sold it to Trevor. He paid me three hundred and fifty dollars of his company's money for it."

"So what?" Hayes said. "That's the man's job, ain't it?"

"I'm not through yet, Hayes. When Trevor was knocked out cold on the boat tonight, I finally got a chance to look in that ledger book of his. According to the ledger, he paid me four hundred, not three-fifty. Now do you get it? He kept the extra fifty dollars for himself. Fifty dollars of his company's money. That's theft."

"For God's sake, Henry," the pearl-buyer shouted, straightening so quickly that he bumped his head on the jailhouse ceiling. "Did you stop to think I might have made a mistake and written four hundred accidentally?"

"Now, there you go," Hayes said. "That explains it, don't it, Colton?"

"I had you repeat the sum three times, Trev. I even tricked you into spelling it out to me as you were writing it in your ledger book. You couldn't have written four hundred unless you meant to."

"I don't know, Colton. It's just your word against the captain's. I don't feel right about locking him in jail just on your say-so."

"That colored boy, Giff Newton, was a witness. And some pearl-hunters were standing around listening. Besides, I'm sure I wasn't the only one whose price Trev doctored a little in his ledger book. He's probably done the same thing on every purchase he's made on Caddo Lake. Now, if you'll give me the key and let me lock him in overnight, we'll interview some local pearl-hunters tomorrow. See what they got for their pearls, and compare that to what Trevor's ledger book says. Then if you don't think we have enough evidence to prove what I'm sayin', you can let him out of your jailhouse and put me in there."

The jailhouse grew so quiet that Trevor could hear the shallow breathing of the wounded outlaw in the cell with him. He shifted his eyes from the leather satchel in Hayes' hand to the pistol in Colton's. How he longed to be aboard the *Wicked Whistler* now, far out to sea, where he made his own laws. Yes, he had skimmed a little off the top, but he had always planned to pay it back later. It was a loan, not a theft.

"Captain Brigginshaw," Hayes finally said. "I'm sorry, but I'll have to go on his word until we get this straightened out. I'll make sure you're comfortable in here tonight, and we'll sort it out first thing in the morning."

Colton grinned. "You heard him, Trev. Now, back up and let me close the door."

The Australian used every measure of control he possessed to cinch his temper in place. "Don't 'Trev' me, you lying little bastard. It's Captain Brigginshaw to you."

"Whatever. Back up."

Brigginshaw grit his teeth. He cast his eyes downward and sighed, as if in defeat. Slowly, deliberately, he slid his foot back from the doorway and took a half-step backward.

Colton pushed the door closed and aimed at Trevor through one of the squares in the iron grating. "The key," he said to Hayes.

The lone key jingled on its iron ring. Trevor watched Colton's eyes. Colton held his left hand open to take the key from the constable. The key came into view through the grating. Colton's hand closed around it. Trevor stood as if in resignation, but he was ready to explode.

The Pinkerton man's stare merely darted to the keyhole on the door, but it was enough to trigger Brigginshaw's attack. His huge leg kicked toward the iron door in a tremendous burst of angry desperation. Colton jerked his trigger, but the bullet clipped an iron bar and sang into the log wall above the wounded outlaw's body.

The heavy door swung open and caught Colton in the face. His head jerked back. The Pinkerton man flew backward as if blasted in the chest with a load of buckshot. The Smith & Wesson sailed into the darkness.

Trevor exploded from the jailhouse like a bear from its den. He glimpsed the astonishment on the constable's face, saw the lawman reaching for his side arm. He barreled into Hayes, knocking him over backward and wrenching the leather case from his hand at the same time. He struck Hayes in the jaw with his elbow—a blow he thought would surely knock the constable out cold. He began running for the *Slough Hopper,* unsure of what he would do when he reached her. Halfway to the boat, he heard a voice behind him.

"Stop, Captain!"

The words surprised him. The old constable could take a punch. The burning pine knots from the *Slough Hopper* cast a faint light across the muddy ground as he continued to run.

"Stop!" the constable yelled.

Trevor was almost to the riverboat when the bullet caught him in the leg. He fell, then tried to get back up. Another shot echoed across the bayou, and he dove into the mud. He tried to get up again, but the wounded leg slipped. A third shot missed him. He lay still. The shooting stopped. He should get up and run. But where? He was hit once already. The constable was a surprisingly good shot. He was caught. His head was still hurting. He clutched the leather satchel in his hand. Now how long would it be until he saw the high seas again?

There was a sickening silence about Port Caddo. The gunfire had quieted the bullfrogs. Then he heard Rayford Hayes' boots sucking at the mud. The constable moved cautiously in on him and took the leather satchel away.

"Go get in the jailhouse, Captain," he said.

Trevor tried to get up. "You've shot me, Rayford. I can't bloody walk."

"Then crawl, damn it. Get in the jail!"

Trevor saw the crew of the *Slough Hopper* watching him from the bow of the boat. He heard the door of the Treat Inn open. Looking back, he saw a guest peeking into the street. Thank God it wasn't Billy. Don't let Billy see you crawl. He managed to stand on his good leg and started hopping toward the jailhouse. He slipped once, and glanced up at Constable Hayes, the lawman's nightshirt caked with mud, looking so comical that Trevor almost laughed.

He hopped past the lantern on the ground and past Henry Colton, still stretched out motionless on his back. He ducked into the log jailhouse and collapsed on the floor.

Hayes covered the doorway with his pistol and went to get the jailhouse key from the mud beside Colton. When he came to the door, he said, "Back up, Captain. All the way across the floor."

Trevor obeyed and Hayes closed the door, locking the Australian in. Next, the constable went to check on Henry Colton, thinking to rouse him out of the mud. But he sighed as he put his pistol back in the holster.

"You've done it now, Captain. You've really done it good. Henry Colton's skull is split. He's dead."

TWENTY - ONE

I never did have much of a mind for larceny. Worry is work to me, and I get nervous just thinking about criminal activity. That's why I had such a hard time understanding Pop's explanation of what had happened to Trevor Brigginshaw. I could comprehend stealing something like a chicken or a watermelon—actually sneaking in to grab it and run. But to think of a man going to all that trouble with the pearls and the ledger book and his company's money was a little more than I could grasp.

The town was usually pretty quiet when I left for Goose Prairie at dawn each morning. But that day the streets were humming with excitement as soon as I stepped outside. Pop was coming in at about that time, and I could tell he had been up a while.

"What's goin' on?" I asked.

That's when he took me into the house and told me all about the death of Henry Colton and the jailing of Captain Brigginshaw. He had heard the gunshots in the night and had gone out to investigate. Light sleepers make good small-town newspaper reporters.

". . . and the outlaw from the Christmas Nelson gang died half an hour ago," Pop finally concluded. "They just carried him out. Constable Hayes sent a rider to Marshall to fetch the doctor. He let Brigginshaw take some laudanum to kill the pain. His leg is busted and swollen up pretty bad."

"What'll happen to him now?" I asked.

"He'll probably stand trial for stealing his company's money and for killing Colton."

"What'll happen to him then?"

My pop looked at me with a hard set to his eyes. "In this county, aggravated murder is a hanging offense. It just goes to show you, Ben. Even a little crime like shaving some money off the top can drag you deeper and deeper, till you wind up where Captain Brigginshaw is now."

I vowed right then to give up stealing watermelons forever.

The sun was high by the time Pop got finished with the story, so I ran to Esau's place where Adam and Cecil were waiting to run the trotline. They hadn't heard about what had happened overnight, so I got to tell them. It was all we could talk about the whole time we were catching our fish and baiting the line.

"You reckon any pearl-hunters will ever come back?" Adam asked. "Now that Captain Brigginshaw's gonna hang?"

"Yeah, they'll come back," I replied. "As soon as the road to Marshall dries up some. Pop said the pearl company will probably send another buyer once they find out Captain Brigginshaw's in jail."

"You're just hoping that Cindy comes back from Longview," Cecil said. "I saw you two on the lakeshore at night."

That changed the subject for a while, but by the time we put the catfish in the holding tank, Cecil and Adam were wanting to sneak down to the jailhouse and look at Captain Brigginshaw through the iron grating. I wanted to go, too, but couldn't. I had invested in a gill net and was catching fish on my own in my bateau. I hadn't invited Cecil or Adam in on this enterprise with me, and they were still mad about it. Once you get started doing business with friends, it's hard to stop without hurting somebody's feelings.

They ran off for the jailhouse as I shoved off alone in my bateau. I didn't feel so left out once I got onto the lake. After all, I had an Ashenback, and they didn't. Cecil and Adam had squandered about all the money they had made over the summer on trinkets and hard candy.

My net was a small one and didn't take long to run. I caught enough to halfway fill the fish box in my bateau and started paddling for Port Caddo, where I could sell them. I had owned my Ashenback about three weeks by that time, and it was still a thrill to me. It was that summer that I learned the joy of paddling the lake alone in a good boat.

When Port Caddo came into view around the last bend in the bayou, my eyes pulled toward the jailhouse. I knew Trevor Brigginshaw was in there. For the first time, I felt sorry for him. Everybody in town liked him, except maybe when he got drunk. He was part of our pearl rush—almost as big a hero as Billy. When I thought of him lying wounded in that cell, or worse, dangling by the neck from a gallows, I got a sudden pang of remorse. I felt as if I had had a hand in it. I was part of that summer of pearls, after all, and now it had gone wrong. A Pinkerton detective and two outlaws were dead, and a fourth man was doomed.

I could feel the gloom settling over the town, though the sky was clear for the first time in days. People were standing on the cobblestone street talking and looking down toward the jailhouse. The bayou ran muddier and faster than usual, owing to all the runoff.

It was an unnatural day—a dark day for my town. I found myself doubting what I had told Adam earlier, what my pop had told me at dawn. They couldn't send anybody to take the captain's place. How could there be another pearl-buyer after Trevor Brigginshaw? It seemed over. I suddenly got the feeling that I would never experience another summer of pearls.

I pulled my bateau up on the bank as usual, and prepared to hike up to town to see who wanted to buy fish. But when I looked toward town, I realized something I hadn't noticed before. The log jailhouse obscured my view of the cobblestone street. The only doorway I could see was that of the Treat Inn, and nobody was standing there. I was hidden.

I don't know exactly why I wanted so badly to look at the Australian in the jailhouse. Maybe I had to see for myself that it wasn't just rumor, even though I had heard it from my pop, who never repeated rumor. Maybe a morbid fascination for the doomed man had fixed a hold on me. I had never seen a murderer before, with the exception of Judd Kelso, and there was no solid proof against him yet.

Whatever the reason, I couldn't overcome it. The tiny window on the bayou side of the log jailhouse drew me like a magnet. I had to have a look.

The mud oozed between my toes as I sneaked silently

up the slope to the jailhouse. I felt like as much of a thief as Brigginshaw himself, though all I wanted to steal was a peek. I never got the chance.

When I reached the window, I heard a familiar voice:

". . . but why, Trev? Why did you need to *steal* it?"

"I have no excuses, Billy." The Australian's voice was muted in defeat, and slurred a little by the laudanum, I supposed.

"I'm not asking for excuses. It's too late for excuses, anyway. But you must have had a reason."

There was a brief silence, then the captain's voice rose with a touch of the familiar bravado. "I'm an independent, Billy. These bloody freshwater-pearl rushes are like hell to me. I go to sleep feeling the *Wicked Whistler* under my feet. I see the palm trees, and the island divers. The bare, brown breasts of the women. All the beautiful women. And the waters so clear you can see six fathoms. I dream of them at night, Billy. You probably do, too."

"I used to."

"Yes, well, I'll never make it back now any more than you will."

I heard Billy sigh. "If there's any way," he said, "I'll get you out of this. I'll do everything I can."

The jailhouse bench creaked under Brigginshaw's weight. "Leave it alone, Billy. There's no use."

"I felt the same way that morning the pirates came down on Mangareva. I didn't think I deserved to live after that. But you got me out of there, Trev. And I'll do everything I can to get you out of this."

"Mangareva was different. It was the pirates who should have been punished there, not you. In this case, I'm the guilty one. I killed a man. Didn't bloody mean to, but that does him little good. No, Billy, there's nothing you can do for me now. . . ."

A sudden unexpected image drew my attention away from the jailhouse conversation. I saw my Ashenback drifting slowly down Big Cypress Bayou. It took a second for me to make sense of it. I knew I had pulled the boat up on the bank. It had never dislodged itself before. It didn't seem possible. But I knew my bateau, and there it went.

I sprinted from the jailhouse and dove off the wharf, splashing into the muddy water. When I came up and caught the gunnel, I heard some townspeople laughing at me. Everybody knew how I treasured that boat. As I swam back to the wharf, pulling my bateau, I glanced up at the jailhouse window. The huge bearded face filled it, smiling. Captain Brigginshaw had roused himself from the bench to witness the commotion. Any embarrassment I felt was worth it. I had given a doomed man reason to smile. There was nothing more I could have done for him.

I didn't figure out until later why my bateau had taken off on its own. The bayou was rising and had lifted it from the place I had beached it. It was raining hard somewhere upstream.

I sold my catch and went about my daily routine, which seemed sadly empty since the pearl camps had been struck. There were no water barrels to haul, no dead mussels to feed our hogs. My partners and I had been buying corn to feed them, but we didn't have the cash reserves to do that for long. We were thinking about turning them back out into the woods, or selling them, unless the pearlers came back soon. Anyway, lessons would take up at the Caddo Academy in a couple of weeks, and we wouldn't have time to fool with hogs.

I hid my bateau under some pine branches at Goose Prairie Cove and made the evening trotline run with Cecil and Adam. We had no idea that it would be our last run. When the sun set beyond Port Caddo, we had no way of knowing it was setting on the summer of pearls, and even on the town itself.

TWENTY - TWO

A barrage of wind-whipped raindrops against my window woke me that night. I could hear gusts roaring in the trees. I slept in the half-story attic of our house and there was nothing between me and the storm but a few boards and cypress shingles. The first thing I thought of was my bateau filling up with rainwater where I had left it down at Goose Prairie Cove.

I got out of bed and went to the dormer window that looked out over the street. A flash of lightning gave me a glimpse of pines whipping in the wind like stalks of grass. The roof was shaking around me. A light passed below—a lantern that stopped in front of Constable Hayes' house, just up the street from ours. No one would have been out on a night like that unless there was trouble. I stepped into my pants, pulled on my shirt, and scrambled down the narrow stairway to the parlor. My pop was there, lighting a lantern wick.

"What is it?" I asked.

"I don't know," he said. His eyes shot up the staircase and he almost told me to go back to my room. But then he looked at me and put his hand on my shoulder. "Let's go see," he said. "Maybe somebody needs help."

The wind nearly tore our door from the hinges when we went out. The cold rain soaked us to the skin instantly. Water ran down the cobblestones like rapids. I can smell tornado weather now, and that's what I smelled that night, though I didn't realize it at the time. Twister weather charges the air with a fine, rich aroma—almost like the smell of fertile dirt.

The ground was already saturated from the rain we had received in previous days, and the water had nowhere to go but into the bayou. I remembered my bateau lifting mysteriously from the bank that morning. I knew what was happening. The bayou was coming up. It had been coming up all day.

The lantern came back down the street from Rayford Hayes' house. Rayford was in his nightshirt, his gun belt around his hips, his black boots on his pale legs, the key to the jailhouse in his hand. The tinsmith, Robert Timmons, carried the lantern.

"What's wrong?" my father asked as we fell into a trot beside them.

"The bayou's up!" Timmons shouted over the roar of the storm. "The Treat Inn and the jailhouse are flooded! We've got to get Brigginshaw out!"

When we got to the end of the cobblestones, we stopped and stood in shock, along with several other people who had brought lanterns out. The wharf was invisible under the rushing current. I had never seen the bayou go any faster than a crawl, but it was piling up against the cypress trees now. Billy and Carol Anne were helping their guests to high ground. The bayou was into the lower floor of their inn. The jailhouse was already half under. I could see Captain Brigginshaw's fists on the iron grating of the jailhouse door.

"My God!" Timmons shouted to Hayes. "It's come up two feet since I ran to get you!"

Hayes didn't hesitate. He ran upstream about thirty yards and waded in, feeling for footholds.

"Wait, Rayford!" my pop shouted. "You need a rope or something."

"No time!" the constable shouted.

I knew he was right. He had to get the jailhouse door open and help Captain Brigginshaw to the shore before the current grew too swift to cross. Brigginshaw wouldn't be able to swim well with a wounded leg. I made a move toward the water, but my pop held me back.

Constable Hayes was in up to his waist when he slipped.

The water had filled his boots like sea anchors and dragged him down. He floundered helplessly, cartwheeling in the water, clawing at the bayou with the fist that held the key. The current carried him twenty feet away from the jailhouse door.

I tried to go in after him, but my pop held me back again. I saw Brigginshaw's arms reach through the iron grating, almost too thick to fit. "The key!" he shouted. "Throw the key, Rayford!"

The constable lobbed the key on the iron ring as he went under. It arched through the rain and hit the side of the jailhouse, about a foot beyond the Australian's reach. The captain drew his arms back into the jailhouse. I knew he was on his stomach, underwater, feeling for the key through the grating. I also knew he would not be able to reach it.

Without the key in his hand, the constable was able to stay afloat a little better. Then I saw Billy dive into the bayou after him. Carol Anne was helping the last of the inn guests up to the cobblestone street. I saw the expression of terror on her face when she saw Billy dive in.

Her eyes sparked something in me. I tore away violently from my father's grasp and plunged in to help. I heard Pop come in after me. The current carried us swiftly down to where Billy had grabbed Constable Hayes. I swam against the torrent as hard as I could, but still slipped quickly downstream. I passed the flooded Treat Inn as I reached Billy and Rayford, and grabbed the constable's arm. Pop was soon there with me, and the four of us drifted into the shadows. We pulled the constable out of the swift current, into shallow water. We finally found our footing behind the Treat Inn.

When we pulled him out, Hayes was coughing and heaving, but we knew he would survive. His boots and the weight of his gun belt would have killed him if not for Billy, my pop, and me.

"Get higher!" Billy shouted. "I'm going after Trevor."

The constable's hand grabbed Billy by the elbow. Hayes couldn't speak yet, but he shook his head, begging Billy not to go in again.

Billy pulled loose and ran through the water toward the Treat Inn, diving in and swimming up to the back porch.

I found more strength than I had ever known. I could have lifted Constable Hayes myself, but with Pop there to help, he felt light as a feather. We carried Hayes to high ground and came through a neck of brush to Widow Humphry's inn, where I dropped the constable and ran back toward the jailhouse.

Pop shouted for me to wait, but I tore on toward the flood. I saw Carol Anne holding onto Billy beside the rushing bayou. He had a crowbar in his hand that he had taken from his flooded store. She was crying, begging him not to go in after the Australian.

The jailhouse was almost flooded now, and the rain was coming down harder than ever. My pop overtook me and grabbed ahold of me with a permanence I knew I wouldn't break. He all but tackled me. Through the lashing rain and the roaring wind, I could hear the long, horrifying cry of Captain Brigginshaw:

"Biiillyyyy!"

I tried to fight my way closer to the rushing bayou. If Billy was going in, I wanted to help him. But my pop wrestled me down with a physical might I had never before felt him use. We slid down the muddy bank together and stopped near Billy and Carol Anne.

"Please, Billy!" she cried, pleading, clinging to him as my father was to me. "You can't help him!"

"Let me go!" he shouted.

"Billy! Billy! He's going to hang, Billy! Don't risk yourself for him! He's going to hang anyway!"

The big prisoner's desperate cry was nearly lost in the

maelstrom of wind and water. "Biiillyyyy!" It sounded miles away.

Billy tore free of Carol Anne and sprinted up the bank with his crowbar. The lantern light from high ground illuminated her as she sank to her knees at the edge of the rising bayou and buried her face in her hands. My father would not let me go. I tasted tears of helplessness in the streams that ran down my face.

The hero Billy Treat dove into the water well upstream of the jailhouse and let the current carry him to it. The water piling against the upstream side was almost going over the roof. I was wishing the flood would simply lift that roof off or tear it to pieces so Brigginshaw could get out. But I knew the chances of that were slim. The jailhouse had been built to prevent escapes. Iron bars rooted it deep into the ground to keep prisoners from jacking up the logs and crawling under. Trevor's only hope was Billy.

He came against the jailhouse door like an eagle landing on its prey. Brigginshaw had hardly a foot of breathing space left, and the bayou was still rising. I saw Billy's head bobbing, the arms of both men on the pry bar. I could see only the top of the iron door above the water, hoping any second to see it open. But even if it did, the two men would still have to swim to safety, and the Australian with a broken leg.

The current piled higher against the log jailhouse, obliterating hope as it pressed the air out. Maybe it was just my imagination, but the last glimpse I got of the jailhouse door before it went under was by the brief flare of a lightning bolt, and in that fleeting instant, I thought I saw it swinging open, away from the log wall.

A horrible creaking sound came to me from downstream, and I looked in time to see the Treat Inn floating from its foundation blocks. It drifted downstream like a toy and shook as it hit the trees and the abandoned dry dock behind it. The water was inching toward us, so my father pulled me to my feet and forced me up the bank to high ground.

I watched the Treat Inn shake and tilt strangely in the force of the flood, then my eyes turned to Carol Anne. She was backing away from the rising bayou, looking toward the jailhouse, her soaked dress plastered against her like a second skin. When she called his name, it came out as an animal scream:

"Billeee!"

I looked back toward the jail, but the bayou had sucked it completely under. It—like Billy Treat, Trevor Brigginshaw, and the wonderful summer of pearls—was gone.

TWENTY - THREE

When the rain stopped the next day, every boat that had survived the storm was on the lake looking for traces of Treat and Brigginshaw. My bateau was not among the searchers. The lake had sucked it into some deep hole and buried it. After searching all day, the general feeling was that the bayou had done the same to Billy and the Australian.

The water receded amazingly fast. Less than twenty-four hours after the flood, the jailhouse poked back into view and began rising almost as quickly as it had sunk. Some men in a boat examined it before sundown and found that Billy and Trevor had succeeded in prying the jailhouse door open.

It was a relief to me. In the first place, I hated to think of Captain Brigginshaw drowning in there. I knew how he must have felt waiting for Billy to rescue him from the jail as Billy had rescued me from the *Glory of Caddo Lake*. In the second place, I didn't want to see them pull his body out.

Carol Anne remained down at the bayou from dawn to dusk that first day after the flood, waiting hopefully for a miracle. I felt bad enough about Billy, and I figured it probably hurt her twice as bad as it did me. That's why it surprised me so when she spoke to me. I was watching the men in the boat look over the jailhouse when I heard her steady voice touch my ears.

"He's out there, Ben," she said.

I turned and found her standing at my shoulder. "What?" I said, startled.

"Billy's a strong swimmer. He used to dive for pearls in the South Seas. I'm afraid Trevor's dead. He couldn't swim with that leg wound. But Billy's still out there. He'll turn up."

It was sad to hear her hanging on to a hope so slim. But it was also a little infectious. For a moment, I believed. Billy was one heck of a swimmer. "If my boat hadn't got washed away," I said, "I'd be out looking for him right now, myself."

She looked at me and smiled, and briefly I saw the flawless beauty I had once fallen in love with. She put her hand on my shoulder. "I know you would," she said. "Don't worry. He'll come back."

The Treat Inn had settled crookedly, about thirty yards from its original location, and it suddenly occurred to me that Carol Anne's home had been wrecked. "Where are you going to sleep tonight?" I asked.

"I'm staying in my old room above Snyder's store until Billy comes back. Then we're going to leave this town and start over somewhere."

The floodwaters were still subsiding when the town went to bed that night. No one could have guessed that the lake would continue to fall to a level lower than anyone—even Esau—could remember. But when the morning came,

Cypress Bayou and Caddo Lake looked as if they had suffered six months of drought.

My pop was the first to figure it out. Those government snag-boat men who had been clearing the Great Raft from the Red River had made a gross error in their calculations. They had predicted that removal of the Raft would provide a better channel into Caddo Lake, opening our town to steamer traffic more of the year. What they had failed to figure out was that the logjam was actually a natural dam that caused Big Cypress Bayou to back up, deepening Caddo Lake. The flood had washed away the last vestiges of the Great Raft and removed the natural dam, lowering the lake level instead of making it more navigable, leaving tens of thousands of acres of lake bed exposed.

The government, in one ill-planned stroke, had crippled our riverboat trade, drained our mussel beds, and doomed our town. I know it's not a productive thing to hold grudges in life, but I held a dim view of the government for decades because of what happened to Caddo Lake in '74.

The second day after the flood, Cecil and Adam and I walked over to Esau's place to find Goose Prairie Cove nothing more than a mudflat. Esau's shack had been flooded, but it was out of the way of currents and didn't get washed away. Esau was taking things out and setting them in the sun to dry.

"Good mornin', boys," he said, as if it were just another day. "Come to check the trotline? Sorry, but my boats all floated away or sank."

"What trotline?" Cecil said with no small tinge of disgust in his voice. "It probably got torn off into the lake somewhere."

"Probably so," Esau said. "Too bad, ain't it?"

"We just came down to let the hogs loose," I said. "Unless you want them."

The old Choctaw reached for the ever-present flask of

whiskey in his hip pocket. He took a small swig, same as always.

It struck me that I had never seen him empty that flask. I had never even seen it near empty. I wondered if he ever really drank any whiskey at all. He shook his head as he put the flask away. "No," he said, "I don't want them hogs. Let 'em go back to the woods. You boys breakin' up your partnership?"

I hadn't exactly thought of it that way, but it seemed as if that was what we were doing. Adam looked at me and I looked at Cecil. Cecil looked out across the ugly field of mud that had once felt the toes of a thousand pearl-hunters.

"I guess," Cecil said. "Me and Ben have to go back to the Academy in a couple of weeks. Adam's old man will have his ass out in the fields, if the flood left them anything to harvest. We don't have a trotline. We don't have any mussels to feed the hogs. We don't have a boat to haul water in, or any pearl-hunters to sell water to."

"We ain't got a damn nickel for all the work we done all summer," Adam added. "Ben don't even have his Ashenback no more."

Esau stood and looked at us sadly for a moment. He was trying to think of something to say that would cheer us up. I beat him to it.

"But we're still partners," I said. "Always will be." I started to hike up to the hog pens. "Well, come on," I said, looking back. "Don't y'all want to see them run?"

I saw the eyes of Adam and Cecil brighten, and knew I had said the right thing.

We let the logs down on one side of our pigpen and had a great time chasing the hogs into the hills, yelling like wild Indians until we were too winded to run any farther. Then we collapsed in the pine needles and talked for hours about everything that had happened that summer. We had survived fights over girls and money. We had gotten rich and gone broke together. We were better friends than ever.

We made a promise to one another that morning under the pines, and we never forgot that promise. We vowed to remain friends and partners until we died. The three of us turned out different when we grew up, but we never lost our friendship. The last time all three of us were together, we were old men, fishing on Caddo Lake. Now I'm the only partner left.

I wish the summer of pearls had ended right there. In fact, as my partners and I walked back to Esau's shack about noon, with the intention of helping him clean his place up, I was sure it was over. I knew that none of the good things about that summer would ever come back, but I didn't think anything else bad could happen. That's when I looked out over what had once been Goose Prairie Cove and saw a familiar figure slogging through the mudflats.

At the time, nobody had connected Judd Kelso with the Christmas Nelson gang or the attempted pearl robbery. The only two witnesses to the crime—Brigginshaw and Colton—were gone. With Captain Brigginshaw wounded, Constable Hayes hadn't interrogated him thoroughly on the subject. Trevor may have told Billy about Kelso's involvement in the robbery attempt, but Billy was missing, too, and presumed by almost everybody but Carol Anne to be dead. In fact, it wasn't until years later that I was able to prove Kelso had taken part in the crime.

"What the hell is he doing?" Cecil asked the old Choctaw.

Esau sneered as his black eyes angled toward the drained cove. "Lookin' for mussels."

"Pearl-hunting?" I asked.

Esau nodded.

"What for?" I asked.

"He's a fool," the old man said. It was the first time I had ever heard him speak ill of anybody. "You boys come to help me clean up?"

"Yep," Adam said. "What do you want us to do?"

"Just take everything out to dry. Then we'll shovel the mud."

I worked around Esau's place for a couple of hours, until I looked up and saw Kelso sitting in one of Esau's chairs, covered with mud. He was holding a keg of whiskey over his head, letting the liquor trickle into his mouth from the open spigot. He cut his malicious little eyes toward me and caught me staring at him. I was afraid of him. I had seen him rough up the rousters on the old *Glory of Caddo Lake*. It worried me to have him there with no Billy Treat or Trevor Brigginshaw around to handle him.

Cecil, on the other hand, threw a shovelful of mud right past him and went to talking business with him as if he were any other citizen. "Find any pearls?" he asked.

Kelso put the keg on his knee. "Hell, no. Ain't like it's your business anyway, boy."

Cecil leaned on the shovel handle, as he had been doing most of the afternoon. "What are you going to do with one if you do find it? We don't have a pearl-buyer anymore."

The gator eyes squinted as Kelso smiled. "Don't you know?"

"Know what?"

"Boy, how old are you?"

"Fourteen."

"Haven't you ever got your peter wet?"

Cecil straightened. "Maybe I have."

"Maybe!" Kelso put the keg in the mud and laughed.

"That's a sure sign you never have if you have to say maybe. Boy, when I was you age, I had me my own nigger gal. Got her three times a day if I wanted."

Cecil turned red out of anger and embarrassment. "What's that got to do with pearls?"

"Things is back to usual around here, ain't they? That goddam Billy Treat and that big Australian son of a bitch are gator bait. The town's back to what it was before summer. I'm gonna find me a shell slug and go get me a piece of that whore."

I felt a sickness rise in my stomach. "What whore?" I asked.

Kelso picked up the whiskey keg. "Pearl Cobb," he said, pouring the liquor down his throat again.

My fear of him gave way to worry and anger. "Her name's Carol Anne, and she's not a whore."

He spewed whiskey from his mouth as the keg came down to his knee. He coughed and laughed as the cruel gator eyes locked onto me. "She was Treat's whore, wasn't she? Soon as I find me a shell slug, she'll be mine." He put the keg back on the ground. "I'll owe you for the whiskey," he yelled to Esau as he trudged back toward the muddy cove.

I watched him dig for mussels and open them all afternoon, hoping he wouldn't find so much as a dust pearl. If he did, I planned to run ahead of him to warn Carol Anne, and maybe alert Rayford Hayes. I felt as if Billy were counting on me to look after Carol Anne now that he was gone—or until he got back. I was still holding on to the hope I had caught from Carol Anne. The hope that said Billy was still alive and just lost in a cypress brake somewhere, trying to find his way home.

Finally, though, Kelso came up from the cove about sundown without anything to show for his day of hunting. My partners and I left when we saw him coming. He looked to be in a sour mood and we didn't want to hang around if he was going to get drunk.

When we got to town, I said so long to Cecil and Adam and went home for supper. I didn't have much of an appetite. All the way through the meal, I worried about Kelso finding a pearl. Maybe the next day, or the day after. I couldn't talk to my folks about it. Especially not to my mother. They were awful quiet over supper, too. The only thing Pop said was that he was going to have to drop four pages from the paper and go back to a weekly format.

After we ate, I helped clear the table, then started to slip out through the front door.

"Where are you going, Ben?" my father asked.

He caught me off guard. We had a deal that I could go out and prowl at night, as long as I didn't get into any trouble and came home by nine-thirty. I usually ended up looking through a knothole at Esau's, or spying on some girl who had a habit of leaving her curtains open. Now I knew, however, that those ungentlemanly pursuits were behind me.

"I don't know. I guess I'll go over to Cecil's." That was a lie. I knew exactly where I was going, but I didn't feel comfortable telling my pop about it. He would probably have tried to stop me. I was going to tell Constable Hayes that Kelso had been making noise about bothering Carol Anne. Then I was going to watch her room. But this time I wouldn't be trying to peep at her through the curtains. I would be guarding her, in case Kelso showed up.

"All right," Pop said. "Just be back by ten."

I smiled. "Yes, sir." Some kids' folks never let them grow up. When I became a father, years later, I learned how difficult it was to let my kids go out on their own. My pop let me do a lot of growing-up that summer.

Rayford Hayes' wife, Hattie, greeted me at the front door. "Well, hello, Ben. Come in." She shouted at her husband, in another room: "Rayford, your little hero is here to see you."

Constable Hayes came out of the back room, bootless. "Howdy, Ben," he said. "If you've come to check on me, you might as well go home. I'm sound as a horse, thanks to you and your old man. And Billy Treat, God rest his soul."

"I didn't come to check on you, sir," I said. "I wanted to talk to you about something."

Hayes motioned to a chair near the dark fireplace. "Have a seat," he said, "and tell me what's on you mind."

I looked nervously at Hattie. "Well, it's kind of . . . I don't think Mrs. Hayes wants to hear about it."

The constable wrinkled his brow at me for a second, then held back a smile. "Well, you heard the boy, Hattie," he said to his wife. "Excuse yourself."

"Oh, all right," she said.

When she left, I told the constable about what Judd Kelso had said that afternoon at Esau's saloon. I could tell by the expression on Hayes' face that he took me seriously. "So, Kelso's back at Goose Prairie," he said, rubbing his head. "I was hoping he would stay at his place over on Long Point." He leaned back in a creaking wooden chair and asked me a lot of questions, several times making me repeat exactly what Kelso had said about Carol Anne.

"I could keep an eye on her place," I suggested.

"No, Ben, don't do that. That's not your worry. I'll have a talk with her tomorrow and warn her. Delicate subject, though. Maybe I'll send Mrs. Hayes to do it—woman to woman. Anyway, I wouldn't worry about it. Kelso's not likely to bother her unless he finds a pearl, and that's not likely, either. I bet he'll give up and quit town in a day or two, go on back to Long Point, or head to Shreveport to find work on another steamer. Sure won't find any steamers to work on around here." He got up. "Thank you for bringing it to my attention, though. I'll keep an eye out for him."

I rose and shook the constable's hand. Just as I was leaving, Hattie burst into the parlor from the back room, pale as a sheet and out of breath.

"My God, woman!" Rayford said. "What's gotten into you?"

"It's gone!" she said, gasping.

"What's gone?"

She pointed into the back room. "The leather case with the pearls and the money in it!"

"What do you mean, 'gone'?" her husband demanded.

"I just went to check on it again, and it's not there!"

"Are you sure?"

"Yes!"

"When was the last time you saw it?"

"I took it out to look at the pearls just before supper. Then I put it back. Now it's gone!"

"Gone where, woman?"

"The window was open," she said, almost crying. "I think somebody reached in and stole it!"

A terrible notion struck me. "Mr. Hayes," I said, "what if Kelso took it?"

"Now, calm down, everybody," he said. "Just stay put. Let me get my pistol and I'll look into this."

But I could not stay put or wait for Hayes to find his pistol. Kelso could have stolen the pearls an hour ago. He could have been in Carol Anne's room long enough to . . .

I tore out through the front door and barely heard the constable shouting at me to wait. I wondered what I would do if I found Kelso in Carol Anne's room. I didn't have a clue. I just knew I had to get to her room fast.

I knew the hidden passageways of Port Caddo better than anybody. I cut behind houses and leaped picket fences like a deer. I sprinted like a boy with a mean dog on his heels, but felt twice as terrified.

I had seen too many things go wrong already. The *Glory of Caddo Lake* had sunk, almost taking me with it. The pearl beds had been drained. The riverboat channels had run shallow. Billy and Trevor had been swept away by the flood. I could not stand to think of Judd Kelso forcing himself on Carol Anne now. That would be the worst thing of all. Port Caddo had seen enough ruin for one summer.

When I turned the back corner of Jim Snyder's store, I saw no light in Carol Anne's room. I sprinted up the stairs, taking three steps at a time. I have never run faster in my life, but I felt as if I were wading chest-deep in molasses. A thousand thoughts went through my mind before I reached the top of the flight.

I pounded on the door. I heard someone call my name from back toward Hayes' house. I probably didn't wait half a second before bursting into Carol Anne's room.

I spoke to her as I entered, took two steps, and tripped over a bulk on the floor that I knew in an instant was human. I landed on the leather satchel and heard pearls rolling across the wooden flooring. I bounced once, scrambled to the back of the room, and turned to see the vague form of a human torso against the faint moonlight streaming through the door. One pale moonbeam glinted against the metal handle of a knife, jutting straight up from the dead body.

I couldn't tell if it was a man or a woman. The clothes were wadded and wrinkled in such a way that I couldn't even tell if the dead person was lying face-down or face-up. But I could clearly make out the severe lines of the knife handle, its blade buried deep in the corpse.

I heard people coming, but could not move. I thought of every possibility. At best, the body belonged to Judd Kelso. At worst, it was Carol Anne. I might as well have been dead myself for all the good I did huddled on the floor. I suddenly wondered if I was the only living person in the room. Maybe a knife would find my chest next.

I heard footsteps on the stairs and heard my father call my name. The light from a swinging lantern cast strange shadows up the staircase. When it filled the doorway, the light blinded me for a second. Then I identified Judd Kelso, lying dead on the floor between my father and me, and felt a surge of relief. At my feet was the leather satchel, money and pearls spilling from its open mouth.

Pop looked at the dead man as Constable Hayes came to his side, gasping for breath, holding his pistol in his hand.

"Ben," Pop said. "Are you all right?" He hurdled the dead man and helped me up.

"Yes, sir," I said.

"Who?" He pointed at the body and looked at me as if I might have stabbed Kelso myself.

"I don't know. I tripped over him coming in."

Hayes put his hand on Kelso's throat. "Still warm," he said. "Hasn't been long." He looked at me. "What about the woman? Where is she?"

"She wasn't here," I said. "She's gone."

TWENTY - FOUR

Carol Anne Cobb vanished from Port Caddo like a fog, and the mystery over who killed Judd Kelso began. I have heard all sorts of theories. Most people believe Carol Anne killed Kelso, then fled town, fearing Kelso's people over at Long Point would seek revenge.

I never did believe that. If the knife had been in Kelso's back, I could have considered it. But I never saw how Carol Anne, a healthy young woman though she was, could have overpowered Kelso face-to-face.

Some wild imaginations have come to the conclusion that I killed Judd Kelso. They say I caught him trying to force himself on Carol Anne and plunged the kitchen knife into his chest. They say Carol Anne agreed to disappear then, to make everyone think she had killed him, so the Kelso clan wouldn't come after me.

Take my word for it, that theory is hogwash. Even if you won't take my word, consider this: at fourteen, I wasn't strong enough to take on Judd Kelso, either. And as long as they lived, my Pop and Rayford Hayes swore I couldn't have killed Kelso. They had entered Carol Anne's room only a minute behind me. They knew I didn't have time to kill Kelso and help Carol Anne disappear.

Besides, if I had killed Kelso, I would still be bragging about it today instead of denying it.

A third theory says the Christmas Nelson gang killed Kelso for trying to take all the pearls and money for himself. That doesn't make a lick of sense, of course. Trevor Brigginshaw's satchel was left in Carol Anne's room. Those outlaws would have taken it with them if they had killed Kelso. Kelso was killed for reasons other than greed.

The wildest explanation of all says that Billy Treat rose from the swamps and killed Judd Kelso to rescue his true love. I liked this theory, of course, but where was the proof? For four decades, I tried to think of a way Billy could have come out of the flood alive. It wasn't really all that difficult to imagine. Billy could swim like an alligator and hold his breath almost as long. He could have survived the flood that washed him and the Australian out of the Port Caddo jailhouse.

But why did it take him two days to get back to town? Over the years, I came up with a lot of possible reasons. Maybe Brigginshaw survived the flood, too, and Billy had to help him escape to Louisiana before returning to Port Caddo.

Or, if Brigginshaw drowned, which seemed more likely, Billy could have been trapped in a cypress tree anywhere between Carter's Chute and Whangdoodle Pass for a full day before the water went down. A stranger to Caddo

Lake, Billy could have wandered another day in the swamps trying to find his way back to town.

Then what? Perhaps Billy got to Carol Anne's room shortly after Judd Kelso did, or shortly before. Either way, once both men were there, the fight started, and Kelso grabbed a kitchen knife. Billy took it from him and killed him with it. He would have been strong enough, even after spending two exhausting days in the bayous. He had plenty of motive.

And Carol Anne's disappearance? How did I explain that one to myself? She and Billy were wise to quit town after Kelso was killed. The Kelso clan had been thick in the old Regulator-Moderator feud. Violence didn't spook them. They would have sought revenge.

Eventually I found out what happened, but you'll have to take my word for it. There is no solid proof. Only my word. You have to understand that the summer of pearls became a lifelong obsession for me. A few years after it was over, I started investigating all its angles and facets, and continued searching for clues for forty years. I repeatedly questioned everybody involved, from Giff Newton to Emil Pipes. I searched old records and newspaper reports. I turned up a lot of evidence, but the final proof found its own way to me.

After the government accidentally drained Caddo Lake, a few riverboats continued to steam all the way up to Jefferson, but only during the wettest of times. Port Caddo declined steadily.

In just five years, there was not enough of a town left there to support my pop's newspaper, so my folks moved to Mount Pleasant, where they died as honored and respected citizens of that town, after forty-seven years of good news coverage. I was nineteen and mature enough to make my own decisions when the *Steam Whistle* went under. I didn't follow my folks to Mount Pleasant. I stayed in the old family place at Port Caddo. I also talked my pop out of any of his old notes that in any way related to the summer of pearls.

To my surprise, I found Billy Treat's diary among Pop's notes. Pop said he found the diary in the Treat Inn the day after the flood. I'm sure Billy had always kept a diary, but his old one would have been destroyed when the *Glory* went under. The diary Pop found began the day after the boiler explosion, and ended with the night of the flood. Billy made amazingly detailed entries, sometimes even recording conversations he had had with Carol Anne or Brigginshaw. That diary, more than anything, sparked my need to know everything about the summer of pearls.

The year my folks left Port Caddo, I finally took my trip down to New Orleans—by rail—and hunted up Joshua Lagarde, the insurance investigator who had looked into the sinking of the *Glory of Caddo Lake*. He told me that the owners of the *Glory* had been convicted in a number of insurance-fraud cases and multiple claims. One of the owners had confessed after a two-day police interrogation and named Judd Kelso as the man hired to blow up the *Glory*.

When I got back to Port Caddo, I learned that Charlie Ashenback had died while I was gone. I spent my last pennies buying his tools from his heirs, who lived in Dallas. I started building my own boats, but it took me thirty years to learn how to make a bateau that would stand up against an Ashenback.

Cecil Peavy moved down to Nacogdoches shortly after that and went into business. I went down there to see him every winter until he died a few years ago. And he came back to Caddo Lake every summer to go fishing with me and Adam. When it was all over for Cecil, he owned four stores, two cafés, and a hotel—and didn't have to do a lick of manual labor in one of them. He created a lot of jobs in Nacogdoches. His employees hated him, though.

Some time in the eighties, things got hot around here for the Christmas Nelson gang. They went west and tried to rob a bank in Waco. The Texas Rangers were waiting for them. Every member of the gang was killed, except for Christmas himself, and he was shot eight times and captured.

When I heard about the arrest, I spent my entire bankroll getting to Waco. It had occurred to me that if Judd Kelso had stolen the pearl satchel the night of his death, maybe he had been in on the attempted robbery aboard the *Slough Hopper* three nights earlier. I was the first person to even think about linking Kelso to the Christmas Nelson gang.

Posing as a New Orleans newspaper reporter, I wangled an interview with Christmas Nelson in jail. He was the most pleasant and well-mannered man I have ever met, but he was also a cold-blooded killer and didn't mind telling you about it. Among other things, he told me that he and four of his men were in Port Caddo the morning the boilers blew on the *Glory of Caddo Lake*. They were the horsemen who had rescued so many passengers.

I grilled him thoroughly on the attempted pearl robbery, of course. He told me that the Kelso clan over on Long Point often let his gang hide out on their place. He said Judd Kelso had come up with the idea of robbing Trevor Brigginshaw. He also said he kicked Kelso out of the gang for jumping off of the *Slough Hopper* like a coward when the shooting started. He claimed he would have come to Port Caddo to steal the pearls if he had known Captain Brigginshaw was in jail, or presumed drowned. But he didn't know. He also said he would have gladly killed Judd Kelso, but didn't.

When I returned broke to Port Caddo, Adam Owens told me he had fallen in love with a girl from Buzzard's Bay, across the Louisiana line. Eventually he tried to marry her, but she jilted him—actually left him standing at the altar in front of all the wedding guests. It almost destroyed him. He started drinking and lived like a hermit in a filthy shack up Kitchen's Creek, across the lake. He used to shoot at people who came up the creek. He even shot at me once.

I finally got him to give up drinking, but I had to move in with him for a year to do it. We fixed up his house and he stayed there until he died. Never married. I don't think he ever knew the pleasure of having a woman in bed. He was my friend for life, and a wonderfully innocent kind of fellow. He knew things about animals and nature that God shares with only a few chosen mortals.

I went to find that girl Cindy from Longview once, and found out she had gotten married and fat. I went through a lot of girlfriends and finally fell in love with a beautiful thing from Marshall. I married her and moved her to the house in Port Caddo. She became my best friend, most horrific critic, constant debating partner, and the love of my life. We had a wonderfully successful marriage and I have five kids and twelve grandkids to prove it. I lose count of the great-grandkids.

By the turn of the century, the riverboat trade and Port Caddo were dead. My family was the only one living in the deserted city that had once been a port of entry to the Republic of Texas. Our house stood like an oasis of life in the ghost town.

About that time, I got the notion to go to Chicago and look in the Pinkerton Detective Agency records to see what Henry Colton had written in his reports. I had to sneak out in the middle of the night, because my wife didn't want me spending the money on my silly obsession with that summer of '74.

Those Pinkertons were a peculiar bunch, and wouldn't hear of any old bayou rat snooping around in their files. I had to bribe one of the office workers to get Colton's reports for me. They made up some of the most humorous writing I have ever enjoyed.

Colton had led an unbelievably reckless life as a Pinkerton, and was a pretty successful detective, except that he had a habit of shooting people the Pinkertons wanted him to take alive for questioning. He also drank too much, fought too often, and treated all good-looking women like prostitutes. The International Gemstones case was his last chance as a Pinkerton, and he failed in the most permanent kind of way.

His final report was written aboard the *Slough Hopper,* just after his shoot-out with the Christmas Nelson gang. He was sure proud of himself in that report. I guess he died happy.

To keep my wife from divorcing me on grounds of abandonment, I had to swear on the family Bible that I wouldn't go off on any more wild-goose chases. I was out of leads, anyway. I had spent a fortune sending letters of inquiry to every postmaster and newspaper editor in the states of New York and New Jersey, trying to track down Billy Treat's family. The only leads I got turned out to be false ones.

I finally resigned myself to the fact that I would never know who had killed Judd Kelso. I would never find out what had happened to Carol Anne that night. I would never know for sure if Billy was alive or dead. The summer of pearls would have to remain an enigma to me. It had become sort of a tragic legend around Caddo Lake by that time. As I reached my fiftieth year, I became known as the unofficial historian for the Great Caddo Lake Pearl Rush. People would come around to ask me about the stabbing death of Kelso, and we would talk about all the theories. To most folks, it was just a story. To me, it was real—an image I carried with me all day long, every day, then even into sleep. It was only then—when I resigned myself to search no longer—that the proof found its own way to me.

The summer of pearls prepared me for life. It was like a lifetime in itself. It was that summer when I made and lost my first fortune. I have made and lost many more since then. It was that summer when I first got my heart broke. It got broke many more times before I finally found my wife. And it's even been broke a few times *because* of my wife. That summer I forged the friendships that sustained me through life. Friendships that even death cannot end, but only interrupt. Friendships that will resume in the afterlife. It was that summer that I learned life would not always be simple, or fun, or easy. Neither would it always be complicated, or painful, or hard.

It was the summer I learned nothing would stay the same. Change would come, and come again, and destroy things, and strengthen things, and shock, and soothe, and sadden, and fill with rapture. That is why I should not have been surprised by the most astounding change of all, but I was.

The government, after thirty-seven years, finally decided to repair the damage it had done to Caddo Lake in '74. It built a new dam down at Mooringsport, Louisiana, that raised the level of the lake to what it had been in the days of the Great Raft.

As soon as I heard about them building the dam, I bought the piece of land where old Esau had once run his saloon. My wife thought I was crazy, but I knew the lake would fill Goose Prairie Cove again, and make a fine location for a fishing camp, hunting lodge, and boat-building yard.

The lake came up just as the government said it would, believe it or not, and I began to make a pretty tolerable living. My wife and I built a new house where the pearl camps had once stood. If I had told her that I had situated it to overlook the spot where I had once kissed a girl named Cindy who hailed from Longview, she would have done me in like Judd Kelso was done in.

Then it happened. The thing that ended all my torturous questions about Kelso, Carol Anne, Billy, and Trevor Brigginshaw. Proof came to my fishing camp, for only my eyes to see, and my ears to hear.

EPILOGUE

Goose Prairie Cove, 1944

I am an old man now. I alone remember the summer of
pearls. I have told everything I saw with my own eyes
as it happened to me. The parts I didn't witness personally, I have told as a story, but I know those parts as if I
had been there, and I can prove them through documents,
statements, and interviews.

This last part I cannot prove, however, because the proof
came to visit only me. And it is the final, clinching evidence. This incident I am about to tell you happened thirty
years ago. I never told it to anyone else, because I was protecting someone. But those I sought to protect were older
than I was, and so must have died years ago. There is no
longer anyone to protect. You wanted to know about the
summer of pearls, and here is the final chapter.

It happened a couple of years after the government dam
raised the lake level, and exactly forty years after the summer of pearls. It was 1914. One day, a Cadillac automobile drove down to my fishing camp. The sun was just
rising on a summer morning, warm and humid. There was
a thunderhead in the west, and I was hoping we might get
some rain, but the dark cloud didn't take up much of the
sky.

I was trying to decide whether or not I should water the
vegetable garden when I heard the Cadillac coming down
the old Port Caddo Road to my fishing camp.

Thinking a rich sportsman had come to hire me to guide him at hunting and fishing, I walked to the front gate to greet the automobile. The driver's door opened and an old man stepped out. He was a good seventy years at least, but he stood straight as a pine. Instantly, I felt that I recognized him, yet couldn't quite place him.

"Mornin'," I said. "Can I help you?"

He looked me up and down. "Mind if we look around?"

"Not at all. Can I show you a cabin?"

"No, thanks. We just want to look around."

"Feel free," I said.

The moment I saw him walk, I remembered Billy Treat. Some things about people don't change, even with age. It could be him, I thought. But I had made that mistake before. I was always looking for Billy wherever I went, and never finding him.

The door on the passenger side opened, and an old woman got out. The old man met her at the front of the car and they came through the gate. As she walked by me, she looked at me, smiled, and pulled her collar together at her throat, as if against some kind of chill.

I had to wonder if it was Carol Anne. Of course there was no way I could have recognized her, even if it was her. The Carol Anne I remembered was the peerless beauty of my fourteenth year who would never grow old, never wrinkle, never die.

I watched them walk to the lakeshore. They seemed like something from a dream to me. The old man found the place where Esau's shack had once stood. He took the woman's hand and they walked along the shore, pointing at landmarks, talking, even laughing. They spent about fifteen minutes on the shore. Then they walked back to the gate.

I intercepted them at the car. "Sure you don't want to stay?" I asked.

"No, thanks," the old man said. "But we appreciate you letting us look around."

I caught the old woman's eyes and raced to her side of the car to open the door for her. "Come back any time," I told her. "Fishing's been good."

"Thank you," she said. When she bent forward to crouch into the car, a gold chain swung like a pendulum from under her collar. I only got a glimpse of it before she grabbed it and tucked it back in at her throat, but I swore I recognized it. The Treat Pearl. The perfect orb that had launched that wonderful summer, long ago.

Two doors shut me out and the car started. That Cadillac was the first automobile I ever saw that had an electric starter, and it caught me by surprise when it cranked itself up.

"Wait!" I shouted, over the engine noise. The car backed away. "Wait!" I waved like a madman and ran to the driver's side. I banged on the window until the old man stopped. "Let the glass down!" I yelled, making motions with my hand.

The old man lowered the window and looked at me. "Well?" he said, in a demanding tone of voice.

No, I wasn't absolutely sure. It could have been another pearl. But I had to know, even if it meant making a fool out of myself. "I was wondering . . ." I began. "Whatever happened . . ."

The old man swallowed and gripped the steering wheel tighter.

"Whatever happened to Captain Trevor Brigginshaw?"

He tensed in the driver's seat and faked a look of ignorance. "Sir, I don't know what you're talking about."

Then the handsome old woman put her hand on his arm and leaned over him to look at me through the car window. "He died, Ben," she said. "About ten years ago on the island of Mangareva. He went there to live after he sent back all the money he had taken from that gemstone company. He sent us a photograph once of his wife and three beautiful little dark-skinned children. He was dressed like an island native. Can you believe that?"

I stared at her in awe and felt years of sorrow wash away from me. "Yes," I said. "I believe it."

The old man was still staring. "Ben?" he said. "Ben . . . Crowell! My goodness, boy, you're an old man!"

I laughed, and felt tears of gratitude filling my eyes, but I held them back.

"We had to leave, Ben," Carol Anne said. "If they ever found out we helped Trevor escape. . . . Then there was the Kelso clan. . . . We *had* to leave."

I nodded. "I know. I've missed you both, but I understand."

Billy Treat flashed the biggest smile I had ever seen him wear. "I'm glad it's you, Ben. I'm glad you're here."

I smiled back at them until I could no longer keep the tears from coming down my old weathered cheeks.

Carol Anne stroked a few tears away from her eyes as well. "We have to go now, Ben."

I nodded and stepped away from the car. Billy put it in gear. He smiled at me and drove away. I didn't wave as they left. I just watched until the Cadillac disappeared over the hill toward the ghost town of Port Caddo.

I stood in the road for a while, then walked down to the lake. My wife came to the back door of the house. "Who was that, Ben?" she shouted. I waved her off. She wouldn't understand. Nobody would.

I took off my shoes and waded in, feeling for mussels with my toes. I had suffered bouts of nostalgia before, but never one like this. As I found the mussels, I opened them with my pocket knife and probed carefully at the unfortunate little animals. I heard the rumble of thunder again to the west, but didn't even look at the sky.

A couple of my cabin guests rowed out to the lake in

one of my boats to do some fishing. "Going to bait a trot-line, Ben?" one of them asked.

"Nope," I replied. "I'm pearl-hunting."

They laughed and floated over the stumps of cypress trees that had been cut down during the years of low water.

I had left my hat in the garden, and when the morning sun rose over the treetops, I felt it beating down on the bald spot on the back of my head, so I waded out. The summer of pearls was long ago.

About that time, my son, Ben, Jr., drove up in his Model T and dropped his three kids off at the gate. I was expecting them. Junior waved at me, and drove on.

The thunder spoke to me again—a long grumble. This time, I looked. The dark cloud had come closer, but was drifting north. It would not rain on me today. I should water the garden. A light-gray curtain of rain was slanting from the cloud, and the morning sun was striking it. A rainbow was beginning to form.

Just as I looked down for the garden hose on the ground, something white bulged from the side of the dark, drifting thunderhead. I glanced back up to the west and saw a chalky moon, almost perfectly round, peeking out from behind the cloud as it moved north. The moon was falling fast, nothing between it and the horizon but a rainbow. It would be gone in a minute.

"Hi, Pop," Ben the Third yelled. He was seven, and his little sisters were five and four.

"Come here, kids!" I called, waving them toward the garden. They met me at the garden gate. "You kids remember me telling you about the summer of pearls?" I

"Yeah, all the time, Pop," Ben the Third said. "You're not gonna tell us again, are you?"

"No, but remember how I told you that someday I'd show you a pearl?"

The girls got more excited than their brother. "You found a pearl?" Vickie shrieked. "Where is it? Let me see!"

"Let me see!" Connie said, hopping like her older sister.

I glanced to the west. The moon was diving like a kingfisher. And the rainbow—why, it was waiting there, its colors growing deeper and richer. The moon and the rainbow were just about to touch. "I don't have a real pearl," I said, "but I'm going to show you exactly what one looks like."

I lined them up and turned them westward. "See the moon?" I said.

"I see it," Ben the Third answered.

"And a rainbow!" Connie squealed.

"Watch!"

The moon slipped behind that rainbow as a little wind came from somewhere and whipped the shower into a light mist, heightening the hues in the arching bands of color. The moon seemed to slide along inside the curve of that rainbow, all the way to the horizon, like a South Seas god riding to Earth.

The girls clutched at my arms, and Ben the Third bearhugged my waist. Their little gasps told me they knew how rare a moment it was.

Billy Treat was right. It was one in ten thousand. It was just like a pearl.

SPANISH
BLOOD

This book is dedicated to Kim Golden Blakely:
my sister-in-law, my original fan,
and my tireless supporter.

ACKNOWLEDGMENTS

Thanks to Layne Preslar, of the Bug Scuffle Ranch, Cloudcroft, New Mexico, for showing me around the Sacramento Mountains from Wild Boy Springs to Burnt House Canyon.

For their hospitality and love of their land, I thank the people of the great state of New Mexico.

Special thanks to the Mescalero Apache people.

This work of fiction is inspired by, but in no way intended to represent, the exploits of James Addison Reavis, the "Baron of Arizona."

PART ONE

ONE

The label on the package was stamped in ink, as if with an often-used woodcut daubed on a blotter. The postmark came from Santa Fe. The address, hand printed, was to Bartholomew Cedric Young, Tulane University, New Orleans, Louisiana.

Bart slid the small package across the saloon table to his friend, and glanced out through the beveled glass at a passerby on Bourbon Street.

"Rattlesnake eggs?" Randy Hendricks said. "What in the world?"

"I ordered them from a Santa Fe trading company. Those are registered diamondback eggs. Take a look."

Randy regarded the postmark, the address, the authentic ink stamp. It was just like Bart Young to raise venomous reptiles from eggs. "What are you gonna do with rattlesnakes?"

"Pull their fangs out, and you can have all kinds of fun with 'em. You know, leave 'em in peoples' beds and things like that. Mailboxes—whatever. Go on, take a look. Bet you've never seen rattlesnake eggs before."

Randy picked up the box and judged its weight. He donned a skeptical smirk, and opened the cardboard lid.

Even before his eyes could find the source, the noise burst from the package—a loud, aggressive rattling.

Randy's knees banged against the bottom of the table, his warm beer sloshing from the mug. He felt his heart throb in his ears, and looked wild-eyed into the open box as he scrambled in his seat.

Where he expected to find a coiled snake, he saw instead a dismantled alarm clock with thin pieces of wood tied to where the alarm bells would ordinarily go, the tiny hammer still winding down, tapping against the wood with diamondback rapidity.

Across the table, Bart Young was almost choking on his own laughter, his head rolling all around on his shoulders, his eyes moist with gladness, his mouth wide and bellowing.

"Damn you, Bart!"

The prankster took an ink-stained woodcut from his pocket and tossed it on the table in front of Randy. "You can get 'em down at the jetty. The old man there will carve anything you want on 'em. As for the postmark—well, I just mailed the box to the Santa Fe postmaster, and asked him to send it back to me."

"I don't care how you did it." Randy shoved the box back at his grinning friend.

"Notice how I attached the alarm trigger to the lid of the box?"

"Ingenious," Randy said, his sarcasm thickening. "I've been wondering who made off with my alarm clock."

"You can have it back now. I won't need it where I'm going. The roosters wake you up there."

"Where?"

Bart tapped the box labeled RATTLESNAKE EGGS. "New Mexico."

"New Mexico!" Randy Hendricks rubbed the knee he had banged on the bottom of the table. "When?"

Bart shoved two train tickets across the table. "I leave for Dodge City tomorrow afternoon. From Dodge I take the stagecoach to Santa Fe."

"What'll your old man say?"

Bart shrugged. "He's in Houston. He won't know a thing about it until I'm long gone."

Randy fell back in his chair to study Bart's face. It looked sincere this time, but with Bart Young, you could never be certain. "Who's the other ticket for?"

"You."

Randy scoffed, rolling his eyes. "Now I know you're insane. You'd better cash in those tickets and start paying attention to your studies if you ever want to pass the bar."

Bart's grin flashed quickly across his face. He had perfect teeth and flaunted them often. He used the grin to draw attention away from his forehead, which worried him a great deal. He was only twenty, but his hairline was already receding. He planned to grow a beard to make up for the loss, just as soon as he was safely beyond the reach of his father in New Mexico. "That's just it," he said, "I've already passed the bar."

"You couldn't pass the bar examination given free run of the library."

Bart shoved his beer mug aside, opened a manila envelope on the table, and pulled some documents out. "Take a look at these."

Randy's brow wrinkled above his green eyes, and he scratched his curly red hair like a dog with fleas. It was an annoying habit with him. Suddenly, though, his fingernails stopped working his scalp and he sat perfectly still, staring at the papers in his hands. "Where did you get this diploma?" He shuffled the documents. "And this is a certificate from the Texas bar! How did you get these?"

"I found some old diplomas nobody ever claimed in the files of the bursar's office when I worked there last year. I just bleached the old names off and . . ."

"Never mind. I don't want to know." Randy shoved the papers back at Bart as if they were burning his hands.

"As for the bar certificate, my father won't miss it for another—"

"I said, *I don't want to know!* Someday one of these little tricks of yours is going to get you into trouble."

As the redhead put his mug to his lips and tilted it, Bart reached across the table and lifted the bottom of the glass, causing beer to cascade down Randy's chin.

"Dang it, Bart! You're going to chip a tooth doing that!"

Bart slapped the table and laughed. "But seriously, don't you think it would be funny to pull one over on the whole university *and* the bar association?"

Randy glowered as he dried his chin. "When you talked me into leaving the milk cow on the second floor of the library—now, that was funny. Loosening the hubs on Professor Stangle's buggy was funny. But this . . ." He paused to look over his shoulder. "This is *forgery*," he said in a whisper.

"That's not what you called it when I faked your father's handwriting."

Randy squirmed a little in his chair. Once, when he had spent his quarterly allotment on a Bourbon Street harlot, Bart had helped him out by forging his father's signature on a check.

"That was different," Randy said. "That was between me and my old man. But this . . ." He gestured fearfully toward the manila envelope.

"They won't know the difference, or care, out in New Mexico. It's wide open out there."

Randy frowned and shook his head. "Why New Mexico, of all the godforsaken places?"

"Because a good lawyer can make a fortune out there with those old Spanish land grants."

"The only problem is you're not a good lawyer. You're not a lawyer at all. Do you know the first thing about acquiring a Spanish land grant?"

"We'll figure it out. We'll have more money and land than you ever dreamed of."

"So, it's the land thing again. Bart, you wouldn't know what to do with my granddaddy's forty-acre farm. What makes you think you could manage a New Mexico land grant?"

"There's nothing to it. We get some old Spanish grant, make a few improvements, sell it off at a huge profit, then buy a bigger place. You can handle all the legal stuff, and I'll take care of the land."

Randy started to argue but knew it was useless. Bart Young would persist. With exams coming up, he didn't have the time to waste in debate. He simply sighed and looked away.

"My old man fought there during the war, you know. He told me about the mountains. Most beautiful place in the world, he said. It's got to have something if even my old man can rave about it."

Randy looked at Bart straight-faced and threw his arms into the air. "All right." He picked up one of the railroad tickets and rose from the table.

"You mean it?"

"If we're leaving tomorrow. I'd better go pack. And you'd better get to work on my diploma."

Bart's face made a rare reflection of surprise. He had doubted he would succeed in uprooting Randy from his studies even if he talked all night, which he had been prepared to do. But now it appeared the redhead was finally loosening up and deciding to live. "Well, I'll be damned! My good influence is rubbing off on you." He got up to follow his friend out of the saloon.

They squinted against the afternoon sun as they stepped out onto Bourbon Street.

"You won't regret it," Bart said. "This is the best decision you'll ever make." He burst into a sudden and joyful fit of laughter. "Rattlesnake eggs!"

*   *   *

Bartholomew Cedric Young was a flatlander, born and raised in Houston, Texas. He had never even seen a hill that amounted to anything and had begged his father to send him to study law in some mountain state. He went instead to New Orleans.

There had never been any question that Bart would become a lawyer. His father was a lawyer, and Bart was to join the family firm once he passed the Texas bar. He didn't like his father very much. The only fond memories he had of George Young revolved around Sibley's Civil War campaign in New Mexico.

Bart's father had ridden with General Sibley out west to El Paso and engaged Union troops all the way up the Rio Grande, helping to capture the city of Santa Fe. He had been badly wounded at the battle of Glorieta Pass, where the Yankee forces destroyed the Texans' supply lines and ran them all the way back to El Paso. He had spent weeks recuperating at the rancho of a rich native New Mexican near Santa Fe. When he finally recovered, he was granted amnesty by the Yankees and allowed to return to Houston.

When Bart occasionally got his father to talk about New Mexico, the descriptions of the mountains, the high plains, and the deserts engrossed him. His father never spoke of the battles, but Bart wasn't interested in that, anyway. He wanted to see the ground rising five thousand feet above him. He wanted to taste snow. He wanted to find out for himself if adobe walls really made the houses feel that cool, even under the blistering summer sun.

Most of all, he wanted to escape the suffocating Gulf Coast air. Even though he had never lived anywhere else, he knew there was better wind to fill his nostrils with. He smelled it on the winter northers that blew down all too infrequently from the northwest.

Bart didn't have much use for law school. New Orleans was much like Houston, except bigger. He had convinced himself that he should have been the son of a High Plains rancher. He should have inherited a spread instead of a law firm.

After his first year of law school, Bart discovered something about his father that truly angered him. George Young had once owned a league and a labor of land south of Austin. He had never seen it, but he had held the deed on it. The place had been settled by George's grandfather, who had come to Texas when it was still part of Mexico. The claim was part of an old Spanish land grant, and George was the only heir. He had sold it to finance his education.

When Bart found out his father had traded more than four thousand acres for a lousy law school sheepskin, he started planning his escape from New Orleans. He felt his destiny had been denied him by a mere generation. That old Spanish land should have been his.

Then he read an article in a legal magazine about land-grant speculation in New Mexico. He decided he would go to Santa Fe and acquire some huge old Spanish grant for pennies an acre. But instead of parceling it up and selling it off at high profits as most speculators did, he would keep it. He would become a cattle king or a land baron or a mountain lord.

It was a very vague image, however, and that's why he decided to rope his friend, Randy Hendricks, into the plan. Randy was good at fleshing out details. He actually enjoyed wading through statutes and manipulating technicalities. No one had forced *him* into law school.

In fact, Bart was rather surprised that Randy had so readily agreed to quit law school for New Mexico. He assumed the talk of acquiring land grants had done it. If Randy loved thinking law in school, he would doubly enjoy putting his skills to practice in the real arena of a New Mexico land office or courtroom.

When he put the ink on Randy's fake credentials that night, he felt as if he were charting the course for his own glorious future, signing the deed to his own Spanish land grant.

Bart found Randy at the depot the next day, sitting on a bench, scratching his scalp, two suitcases at his feet.

"Where have you been all day?" Bart asked.

"Classes."

"You attended classes *today?* We're heading west, boy. What were you thinking?"

"My father doesn't live in Houston. If I had missed a lecture, some professor might have sent a message across town to the old man, inquiring as to my whereabouts. He's got them all looking after me like watchdogs."

Bart sniffed at his friend's paranoia, but resisted taunting him. "I guess you have a point."

They boarded the train and took their seats. When the locomotive jerked the couplings together, Randy nudged his companion. "Let me see my papers," he said.

Bart grinned with pride as he produced the forgeries from his portmanteau. "I've prepared everything you'll need. Diploma, transcripts, certificates . . . I even wrote you a letter of recommendation from Professor Stangle."

The train was inching out of the station.

Randy thumbed through his false credentials. "Stop looking over my shoulder!" He took a gold piece from his vest pocket and handed it to Bart. "Go back to the smoker and order us a couple of drinks while I check these documents. I'll be along in a minute or two."

"Now you're talking sense." Bart rose, turning the coin between his fingers, and strode down the aisle.

He bought two whiskeys in the smoker and took a seat by the window where he could watch the scenery pass. The train was slowly increasing in speed, and his excitement seemed to build with the pace. He was free of the wretched university. Soon he would smell the high, dry air of the West. Someday he would peer down from a mountaintop he called his own to survey his personal kingdom. His goal was a league and a labor—the inheritance his father had traded away. He didn't even know how much land that was, really, but he envisioned it rolling away under him from one horizon to the next.

As he smelled the whiskey and took his first sip, Bart heard a knuckle rap on the window at his elbow. He turned and found Randy Hendricks's fake law school diploma plastered to the glass. The forged document pulled away from his eyes, and he saw a grinning Randy taking long strides to pace the train, waving the forgeries in his hands.

"Hey!" Bart shouted, oblivious to the other men in the smoker. "What in the hell are you doing out there?"

Randy yelled something that the steam whistle obliterated, and tore his fake diploma in half. He threw his head back and laughed, wild-eyed. He ripped another forgery in two, and let the pieces flutter into the air. He was trotting now to keep up with the train.

"You son of a bitch!" Bart yelled. "I worked all night on that!"

"Hey, boy," the bartender warned. "Mind your language in this car."

Bart ignored the bartender and ran to the door at the end of the car. Bursting out onto the platform, he leaned over the rail and found Randy loping along beside him, still laughing, shredding papers, and throwing them into a cloud of locomotive smoke. "Randy, get your ass back on the train!"

Randy broke into a dead run and pulled his train ticket from his pocket. "Who do I look like? Sancho Panza?" He tore the ticket in two and let the pieces flutter to the ground behind him. "You don't need me to tilt at your New Mexico windmills!"

"Have you lost your mind, boy? Give me your hand! Jump aboard!"

Randy slowed and let the gap widen between himself and Bart. "I got you, Bart! I got you good! Beat you at your own game!" His laughter died as the train rushed away from him.

The reality hit Bart like a wave of steaming New Orleans air. He almost got mad, until he saw the beauty of it. "You son of a bitch!" he yelled, shaking his fist at the shrinking figure trotting beside the cars. "Damned if you didn't!" A smile pulled across his face, and he laughed to the rumble of the steel wheels. Randy had learned something from him after all. His fist opened, and he waved.

TWO

D o you mind?" Lieutenant Delton Semple said, elbowing his fellow passenger in the ribs.

"Huh?" Bart grunted, waking with a start.

"Wake up. You're falling all over me!"

The stagecoach was hot and uncomfortable. The trip from Dodge City had been a long one, and the snotty little lieutenant had made it more miserable than necessary for everyone—complaining constantly, bossing the other passengers, exaggerating his military authority.

"Sorry, Lieutenant," Bart said. "It's just that I've made this trip so many times, the scenery lulls me to sleep." It was, of course, Bart's first day in New Mexico Territory, as it was the lieutenant's, but Semple had been asking for it, and Bart was going to pull one over on him.

"You didn't tell me you were familiar with the territory. What do you do here?"

"Land grant speculator. I've lived here for years."

"Then you know about the Indian problems."

"Know about them? The Red Devils?" A lurch pitched him against the coach door, and he used the sudden commotion to cover a wink he sent to the passengers sitting across from him. "They're worst around . . . Where did you say you were going to be stationed?"

"Fort Union."

"Oh." Bart made his face go pale and looked out under the rolled canvas at the dry New Mexico plains. "Well, think positively, Lieutenant. You can make rank quicker at the more dangerous posts." He smiled sympathetically, then turned back to the scenery.

The other passengers, two hard-bitten miners and a scarfaced gambler, caught on and started telling stories of Indian butchery. Bart grinned out of the far side of his mouth as he listened to the men branch out.

So far, he hadn't been very impressed with New Mexico. The only timber he had seen grew in the form of scrubby piñon and juniper trees. He had left New Orleans during the greenest time of year, and the lack of vegetation here awed him. But there were mountains on the horizon to the west, and Bart suspected there was much more to see.

"Just wait till we get to Maxwell's Ranch tonight at Cimarron," one of the miners said to the lieutenant. "You'll see your first Indians there, sure."

"Maybe we'll see some action, too, it they're on the warpath," the gambler added.

Semple tugged at the almost invisible wisps of his yellow mustache, lifted his campaign hat, and smoothed back his slick blond hair with an immaculate hand. "If you gentlemen are trying to scare me, you'll have to do better than that." His face was smooth and fair, except for the red patches high on his cheeks.

Bart laughed as if he were on Semple's side. "You can't hoodwink this one, boys. He's too smart for you. We could use more like him out here in the territory."

The lieutenant beamed with victory and gazed through

the window, until a bump in the road pitched him almost across the coach. "How much longer to Maxwell's Ranch?" he asked Bart.

"We should make it about nightfall." Bart knew only because he had asked the driver at the last stop.

"I understand Mr. Maxwell exerts quite a lot of influence over the Indians," Semple said.

"You'll want him on your side if you're going to be stationed at Fort Union," the gambler said. "He's the only thing standing between the Indians and war right now. The Utes, the Jicarillas, even the Comanches respect him."

"A *civilian?*" the lieutenant said. "Is he the Indian agent there?"

"Not officially, though the agency is located at his ranch on the Cimarron. No, it's mainly the fact that he's not afraid to fight them on the one hand, and he respects them a great deal on the other hand. He lets them live and hunt on his grant. He owns well over a million acres, you know."

Bart had to restrain himself to keep his eyes from bugging out. A million acres! He had no idea.

"So I've heard," the officer said. "It's criminal that one man should be allowed to take up so much land."

One of the miners laughed. "I'd keep those opinions to myself, if I was you, Lieutenant. Maxwell has some of the best grazing lands, timber, and working gold mines in the territory, and as far as he's concerned he's earned them. He'll treat you with the finest hospitality if you stay on his good side, but don't cross him."

"Maxwell's a fine gentleman," the gambler added.

"But damn near deaf as a post," Bart suddenly said, flashing his eyes at the other civilians. "Make sure you speak up loudly when you talk to him. He gets terribly upset if he can't understand you. Don't be offended when he shouts back at you, either. That's the only way he can hear himself speak."

He turned back to the window and looked across the

dusty plains. He saw a small herd of antelope grazing in the distance. Beyond them, the Sangre de Cristo Mountains rose on the western horizon. They were too far to pass judgment on, but Bart sensed their beauty. Those were the mountains that had moved even his stolid father.

With a resonant thump, an arrow shaft suddenly appeared near the shoulder of the scar-faced gambler sitting across from Bart. The gambler looked at it as he would a pesky fly, snapped the shaft off and quickly studied the markings.

"Comanches," he said, looking at the other passengers.

A blast from the shotgun rider's double-barrel spurred the men to action. Bart clawed at the latches of his portmanteau. As he searched for the Remington revolver he had bought in Dodge City, Lieutenant Semple stepped over him, crawled out through the coach window and climbed onto the roof. Bart could see the canvas-covered boards above him bending with the officer's weight.

"Git up there with him, young fella'," a miner said to Bart, waving the barrel of his single-shot pistol out the window. "You've got a six-shooter. Don't let the son of a bitch show you up!"

Bart stood in the rocking coach and shoved his pistol under his belt. He could hear the war yells of Indians as he swung out through the coach window and searched for handholds that would get him to the top. When an arrow ripped through the canvas top beside him, he all but flew to the roof, uncertain how he had gotten there.

There were two seats facing each other on the roof—one looking forward, one back—where passengers rode on the more crowded runs. Semple was on his knees on the rear seat, holding his Colt revolver with two hands, squeezing off shots. Bart pulled his Remington from his belt as he took in the situation.

About a dozen Indians were chasing the coach, but keeping a safe distance. They were short, paunchy men, much to Bart's surprise, but their horsemanship surpassed everything he had heard about them. They were fanning out far to the right of the coach, slowly gaining on it. It looked as though some of them intended to get in front of the mule team.

Looking past the driver and the shotgun rider, Bart saw that the road ran between the head of a prairie arroyo on the left and the base of a bluff on the right. It seemed the Indians intended to get in front of the stage and meet it at that bottleneck. He saw timber in the arroyo and knew it would serve well as cover.

Semple was firing methodically at the Indians.

"Save your rounds!" the shotgun rider yelled.

"*You* fired!" Semple replied. "Why shouldn't I?"

"I've already reloaded, and you'd better do the same by the time we pass between that arroyo and that bluff. That's where they'll try and turn us!"

Semple looked ahead, speed plastering the front brim of his campaign hat against its crown. "We're not going under that bluff! We're going to run for that timber down there in the gully. We'll make a stand there!"

"Like hell!" the driver yelled, shifting the quid of tobacco in his cheek, and streaming its juices into the wind. He shook the reins and cussed the mules. "That's where they want us to go!"

"I order you to steer for that timber in the gully!" Semple shouted.

"Go to hell!" the shotgun rider replied.

Bart tapped the officer on the shoulder. "We call it an arroyo out here, Lieutenant, not a gully." He had Semple primed for ridicule—assuming the two of them lived beyond the encroaching attack.

The Comanches fired a few long shots as they rode to get in front of the coach. Bart watched the arrows they lobbed, amazed that the Indians could come so near hitting their target while galloping full-out at such a distance.

He put his knees on the seat behind the shotgun rider and got ready to meet the attackers at the bottleneck in the road. Semple came up beside him, obviously flustered at his lack of control over the battle.

"Don't you boys shoot till we git right on 'em," the driver said. "Wait'll Bob shoots his scatter gun; then make every shot tell."

Semple didn't wait for the shotgun. Fifty yards from the waiting Indians, he stood up on the coach seat and fired—a round that completely missed the attackers. The driver swerved his mules, shifting the coach out from under the lieutenant's feet, almost slinging him off the top.

"Damn you, boy! I said wait!" the driver yelled.

By the time Semple crawled back onto the seat, the men in the coach below had already opened fire on the Indians closing in from the right. The shotgun spoke, crippling a warrior's horse. Bart saw the nostrils of the Indian ponies flaring, streaks of war paint almost near enough to touch. He fired but realized he wasn't aiming. He had never shot a handgun before, anyway. He saw muzzle blasts and blurs of arrow shafts, one passing between his shoulder and Semple's.

The shotgun took one Indian. Semple's revolver hit two others. Bart tried to find a target to aim at, but they were now going past him too fast. Then he saw the sinewy arm of a mounted brave reach for the mule harness. The shotgun rider was reloading. Semple was firing behind. Bart aimed for the brave and jerked the trigger. His shot hit the Indian pony in the spine, just in front of the rump. The collapsing horse pitched the unlucky rider under the stagecoach wheels.

"That's smart shootin'!" the shotgun rider yelled, looking over his shoulder for more targets.

Bart was still feeling the unpleasant bump of the coach wheels over the screaming brave as he floundered to the backseat with Semple and emptied his revolver. It was more lucky shooting than smart. He had aimed for the brave's head. He couldn't say he had killed the warrior. Not directly, anyway.

As the coach left the crippled war party behind at the bottleneck, the passengers heard another war whoop, double that of the original. Looking east, they saw scores of braves pouring out of the timbered arroyo Semple had ordered the driver to steer into. The stagecoach men said nothing, but Bart couldn't let it alone.

"See there, Lieutenant," he said. "If we'd have driven in there like you said, we'd all be hairless about now."

The larger war party only feigned giving chase. The driver let the mules slow down a little, then looked over his shoulder, grinning with relief.

Bart nudged the unhappy lieutenant good-naturedly. "Let's go see how the boys down below fared."

As the driver had predicted, the coach neared Maxwell's Ranch just before sundown. Bart was leaning out the window, squinting against the dust and holding his hat to his head, when he caught sight of the ranch headquarters. New Mexico suddenly looked better.

The coach passed a few poor Mexican's coming in from their irrigated fields on the Cimarron, then rumbled by a small collection of tepees near a cottonwood grove. The mules slowed to a trot at a huge stone mill. Across an open plaza, Maxwell's whitewashed adobe mansion rambled among shade trees, surrounded by a low rock wall.

When the coach stopped in the plaza, Bart wasted no time getting out. Smoke rose from several chimneys, and the whole compound smelled like food. He suddenly realized that he had a real Spanish land grant under his shoes. The vague vision of empire became a little clearer. Maybe he would never have a million acres, but someday he would build a mansion like Maxwell's on his own mountainside.

The other passengers tested their legs behind Bart. The two miners got their luggage out of the boot on the back of the coach. They were quitting the stage line at Maxwell's Ranch, and heading west to Elizabethtown— "E Town" as it was called. They were going there to work in Maxwell's Aztec Mine.

The coachmen encountered some difficulty in getting the harnesses off of the mules, so naturally Lieutenant Semple found it necessary to advise them on the problem. The rest of the passengers strolled toward the mansion, where a hot meal waited. Maxwell's Ranch was the finest stage stop on the line.

Just as they came through the gate, Lucien Bonaparte Maxwell appeared on the front gallery of his mansion. He looked about fifty years old—and prosperous. "Welcome, gentlemen," he said, raising his hand. He wore a suit of fine black cloth, well-filled with muscle. He removed his hat, revealing a bald pate that made Bart immediately sympathetic toward him, and strode down a flagstone walk to greet his guests.

The gentlemen exchanged introductions and were telling Maxwell about their scrape with Indians—until they heard the stagecoach driver shout. The driver had been cussing his mules all day, but not with the rancor he was voicing now.

"Goddamn your hide, Lieutenant!" he yelled. "Go to hell and let us handle our own mules!"

"Who's that?" Maxwell asked.

"A new kid for Fort Union," the gambler explained. "His name's Delton Semple."

"He has aggravated the business out of us ever since Dodge City," Bart added.

"How do you mean?" Maxwell asked.

Bart glanced at the coach to see Semple stalking toward him. "Said he had an accident on parade recently. Got too close to the cannon when it went off. Temporary deafness. He can't hear a thing unless you shout at him, and he can't even hear himself unless he yells his lungs out. Most aggravating thing I've ever put up with."

Maxwell turned a skeptical eye toward the fair lieutenant as he came through the gate.

"Lieutenant Semple!" Bart shouted. "Allow me to introduce Lucien B. Maxwell, our host!"

"How do you do, Mr. Maxwell!" Semple shouted back, leaning toward the land baron as he spoke.

"Pleased to meet you, Lieutenant!" Maxwell answered, speaking loudly. "I understand you're to be stationed at Fort Union!"

The coach passengers backed off a few steps from the two yelling men, working hard to stifle their smiles.

"Yes, sir!" Semple said, leaning toward Maxwell again, shouting ever louder. "That is correct!"

Bart turned giddy over the way his prank had played out. He was holding his breath to keep from busting out in laughter. Even the stagecoach employees had turned to see what all the yelling was about.

"We're always in need of good young officers!" Maxwell shouted. "The Indians are a constant menace!"

"So I've seen!" Semple hollered, leaning ever closer to Maxwell.

"Have you any experience with Indians?" the rancher asked loudly.

"Only that skirmish today!" the lieutenant replied. He was about to fall over on his host, yelling almost in Maxwell's ear. "But I graduated near the top of my class at West Point, and—"

Maxwell, wincing at the volume of the officer's voice, put his hand on the uniformed shoulder and pushed Semple away.

"Lieutenant!" he yelled. "Why the devil are you shouting in my ear. *I'm* not deaf! *You* are!"

Semple's astonished face turned pink as his four fellow

passengers exploded in laughter. "But . . . Young told me . . ."

Maxwell's eyes darted among the laughing men, then glared at Bart. Slowly, a sly grin curled his lips. "If you're going to play the trickster in this territory, Mr. Young, you'd better be able to take a joke as well as you played that one."

"I'll consider that fair warning," Bart said, bowing slightly.

"As well you should." He allowed himself to chuckle. "Now, come on in, gentlemen, and let's have supper!"

Five men went laughing toward the mansion, but Semple stood in his tracks, his confusion turning to rage as he realized how gullible he had been. He might have stayed there until the stage left for Fort Union, but he heard the coachmen laughing at him from the plaza, and decided he would just as soon face the men in the house as the two stage line employees.

THREE

After supper, Lieutenant Semple asked where his quarters might be located, then excused himself. The other men repaired to Maxwell's study for brandy and conversation. It was a warm adobe room, with tile floors, a large fireplace, hand-hewn furniture, and a chandelier made of deer antlers. The evening became considerably more enjoyable with the absence of the brash young officer. Bart was even moved to offer a toast to Semple's speedy delivery southward.

"I'll drink to that!" Maxwell said, raising his glass. "I thought that was a rather rank trick you pulled when you all arrived—telling him I was deaf. But I see now how he must have deserved it."

"Rank?" Bart said defensively. He had considered it rather ingenious.

"Well, it was a little amateurish, you must admit," Maxwell said.

"Amateurish?" Bart said.

"I thought it was hilarious," the gambler said. "Bart was so convincing that I almost believed you were deaf myself, and I've known you for years."

Maxwell chuckled. "Well, it was amusing. But who will remember it ten years from now? You've got to think bigger than that, Bart. Not just in pulling pranks, but in everything you do. That's my philosophy. Take Kit Carson, for example. Now, Kit was one to play jokes now and then, but he did them in a big way."

"You knew Kit Carson?" Bart asked.

"Knew him? We were the best of friends for twenty-five years. He pulled jokes on people that will go down in history. In Santa Fe they're still talking about the time he had fake menus printed and switched them with the real ones at the Rico Café: rat-tail soup, roast mule, coyote cutlets . . . He pulled some beauties. Even got me with them sometimes. But not even Kit could beat the joke Daniel Boone played on me back in 'forty-two."

Bart looked quizzically at the rancher. "Daniel Boone wasn't even alive in 'forty-two."

"That was the beauty of the joke," Maxwell said, tapping his temple with his finger. "It was still tricking people twenty-two years after old Daniel died."

"What kind of joke was it?" Bart asked, pulling himself to the edge of his cowhide chair.

"The biggest. The best I've ever seen. Don't know that it will ever be beat."

The scar-faced gambler was interested now. "Well, are you going to tell us about it or not, Lucien?" he asked.

Maxwell sat back in his chair and stared at the ceiling

timbers for a moment while he stroked his chin. "Me and Kit were scouting for Colonel Fremont that summer on his first expedition. Kit wasn't there the day we found the stone. He was leading another party off somewhere else. I was with Fremont on the South Platte when we found it."

"Found what?" Bart asked.

"The Daniel Boone stone."

"What's that?"

"Well, sit back, boy. I'm trying to tell you." He chuckled, and reached back through the decades again. "I was riding ahead on the south bank of the South Platte— somewhere between Plum Creek and where Julesburg is now—looking for a good campground, when I came across a big slab of rock. I glanced at it, and you'll never guess what I saw on the top face of it."

"What?" Bart demanded.

"Writing! Chiseled letters on the flat side of that boulder. Well, I got off my horse, brushed the dirt away and had a look-see. I'll never forget what it said as long as I live. In four lines—big letters that took up most of the smooth face—it said, 'Here passed Daniel Boone in the year of 1816 en route to the Rocky Mountains.' Then, at the bottom, it said, 'Read more information on the other face.'

"Well, I see what the joke was already," Bart said. "Daniel Boone lived in Kentucky. What would he be doing way out on the South Platte?"

"That's what I thought," Maxwell said, pointing his cigar at his guest. "I figured it for a hoax. But it was still a sight, I tell you. A chiseled stone out there in the wilderness! I rode back to tell Fremont, and then I learned a thing or two about Daniel Boone.

"Like you said, everybody knows Boone lived in Kentucky. But in his old age, he moved to Missouri, and when he was eighty-some-odd years old, he made a trip to the Rockies. And that was in 1816. Colonel Fremont knew all this some way or another. That man knew just about everything—and thought he knew what he didn't. Still does, I guess.

"Anyway, Fremont got all interested in reading the bottom face of the stone. I guess I was, too. The year of 1816 was two years before I was born, so the thing was an antique to me. I was pretty excited to think I was exploring the same ground Daniel Boone had, and was reading something he had chiseled, so when Fremont told me to chop a pole to prize that slab up, I went to it like a contest.

"Well, one pole wouldn't prize a rock that big. Hell, four poles wouldn't. We had to hitch a horse. But even a horse and seven men couldn't turn that stone! It was getting on to dark, and we were hungry and hadn't even made camp yet, but Colonel Fremont was determined to read that bottom side. He figured old Daniel had left us some secret map to a mountain pass or some such thing.

"We must have hitched every horse and every strap of leather and every rope we had in the whole party to that damned stone, and finally started it turning over after dark. I was driving a horse when it started to move. It angled up a little, and I turned to whip that horse on and get the boulder turned over so Fremont would let us rest. Then it came over quicker than anybody could have guessed, and I fell down right where it was going to land. And that's the reason I will never know what the Daniel Boone stone said on the other side. . . ." Maxwell hung his head, sighed, and closed his eyes.

Bart was hanging on the very edge of his cowhide chair, about to fall into the fireplace with anticipation. "What do you mean? Why don't you know what it said?"

Maxwell raised tearful eyes to his young guest. "Because," he said, "The damned thing rolled over on me and squashed me dead right there!"

The gambler and the two miners joined Maxwell in a mighty salvo of laughter aimed at Bart Young. They doubled over in their chairs, sloshed their brandy, stomped the tiles, and sent echoes down the labyrinth corridors of Maxwell's mansion.

Bart reeled back at first, but it only took him a moment to realize how badly he had been taken in. He ground his teeth and pursed his lips. "Damn," he said.

But Bart knew how good it felt to execute a clean one, and Maxwell had pulled this one off flawlessly. He would not deny the land baron his fun. He covered his face as if in embarrassment and joined the laughter.

"Bart," Maxwell said, wiping the tears away from his eyes, "you went along so well, I just couldn't resist it. But, now, let me tell you what really happened with Fremont on the South Platte." He stood by the fire with his brandy and turned back to his guests. The memories flooded back again: the Daniel Boone stone, Fremont's first expedition, the days of his youth—a landless, careless vagabond adventurer, friend to the greatest frontiersmen who ever lived.

"Oh, no, you don't," Bart said. "I won't fall for another one."

"Just sit still and listen. I'll explain everything. The stone didn't really kill me, of course, but everything else I told you was true. And, actually, the thing came near crushing my leg when it flipped over. It was dark. I slipped. The boulder came down like a tall timber and landed on my boot heel. We had to unlace my boot to get me loose and dig under it to get it out.

"Anyway, Colonel Fremont jumped up on the stone then, and cleared off all the dirt while I made him a torch to read with. Those of us who knew our letters—and for me, that was just barely—well, we gathered around to have a look-see with Fremont."

Maxwell looked at his young guest, calling the image to mind, and smiled. "It was the damnedest thing, Bart. In four lines—big letters that took up most of the smooth face—it said, 'Here passed Daniel Boone in the year of

1816 en route to the Rocky Mountains.' Then, at the bottom, it said, 'Read more information on the other face.' Right about then I felt like you did a minute ago. I had been roped, tied, blindfolded, and branded gullible by the best joke ever. Old Daniel Boone got me, twenty-two years in the grave."

Bart did not laugh, but he smiled and felt a heartthrob of something—maybe admiration or envy or awe. He sat back and visualized the chiseled boulder. Maxwell was right. It was pure genius. The greatest prank ever. It possessed the lasting quality of stone. Once sprung on one victim, it lay ready for the next. It was large and simple and permanent.

Bart knew then that he would have to start thinking bigger. If he came to New Mexico for a league and a labor, he would probably get no more than he sought. If he satisfied himself with rank tricks, he would enjoy only the laughter of an amateur.

Lucien B. Maxwell had taken nearly two million acres. Daniel Boone had chiseled the world's best prank in stone. How was Bartholomew Cedric Young going to top that?

FOUR

hat was his name again?" Antonio Montoya asked the youth at his gate.

"Young. George Young. He was a captain in Sibley's Brigade."

Don Antonio stroked his black mustache that was turning gray where it met his sideburns. "I am sorry, my friend. There were so many wounded men here. Some from Texas, others from Colorado. Both armies. I cannot remember their names."

Bart stepped deeper into the shadow of the grapevine arbor. "He was wounded bad in the stomach. Said he was one of the last to leave because he took so long to heal."

The old don's eyes widened and met Bart's. *"Un momento.* There was one who stayed here a long time. Yes, I think I remember. He said he lived near the ocean. He told me about the waves, and the green grass everywhere. Houston!"

"Yes!" Bart said. "That was my father. I'm Bartholomew Young!"

"Por Dios!" Antonio said, holding his arms wide. "And now you have come to tell me how my old friend is doing!"

Bart returned the unexpected embrace when it came, slapping the dignified old man heartily on the back.

"You will stay here with us," Antonio said, "until you are completely recovered from your long trip. Tell me, how is your father doing?"

"All right," Bart said, removing the loop handles of his portmanteau from the saddle horn. "His gut still bothers him some, but he's still practicing law and making good money." He obeyed Don Antonio's gesture, urging him to the house. A boy led his horse away.

The invitation to stay came as a welcome relief. It had been a hard trip from Maxwell's Ranch for a young man unaccustomed to the saddle. He had planned to ride the stage all the way to Santa Fe, until Lucien Maxwell invited him to ride over the mountains.

"I have to go to E Town and check on the mines," Maxwell had said. "I'll loan you a horse, and you can ride with me. From there you can ride down to Taos and into Santa Fe. That beats the hell out of taking the stage through Fort Union. If you pass through there, Lieutenant Semple's liable to have some corporal shoot you as a comanchero."

So he had ridden with Maxwell up the Cimarron, into the mountains, among the tall pines and the running streams. This was the New Mexico he had envisioned. He held his horse back on occasion to take in a choice view. He loved to see roll after roll of timber falling away to the valleys.

In E Town, he had asked if Maxwell knew Antonio Montoya.

"Everybody in the territory knows Antonio," Maxwell had answered. "Those land-grant speculators you're going to join have been trying to buy his grant for years, but he won't sell."

After E Town, Bart had gone on alone, with more than a borrowed horse to show for his acquaintance with Maxwell. He also carried a general letter of introduction from Maxwell, and a personal letter to Don Antonio.

He had found Antonio's hacienda looming on the hillside east of Santa Fe, like some medieval castle overlooking the fields of its peasants. It had been built in the old colonial style, with a high adobe wall surrounding it for protection against Indians.

Now he was inside the high wall, strolling with Don Antonio toward the hacienda, looking forward to the cool relief of the adobe walls. A few boys were tending a small herd of sheep in one corner of the compound. A fruit orchard shadowed another. Elsewhere, cottonwoods lent greenery and shade.

Like the wall that surrounded it, the hacienda could be made nearly impregnable. It had only two entrances—the main one facing west, and the other around back on the east. The huge wooden gates stood open, and Bart could see all the way through the shady courtyard to the corrals. But with the two entrances closed, he knew the mansion would stand as solid as a fort. Not one window opened to the outside.

As he entered the mansion, he was telling Antonio what his father had been up to since the Confederate invasion. George Young wasn't Bart's favorite subject, but his father was his only link to Antonio Montoya, and he intended to exploit it. He did not know a soul in Santa Fe. An acquaintance with Don Antonio might prove beneficial.

There was something else, too. Lucien Maxwell had taken him by the sleeve at E Town, and, looking over both shoulders to make sure nobody would hear, had said, "Antonio has two daughters of marriageable age, Bart. It wouldn't hurt to ask him if you could marry one. That would put you in line to inherit some of that community grant he's been buying up over the years. I think it covers fifty thousand acres or so."

Bart had narrowed his eyes suspiciously. "You think I'd marry a girl just to get my hands on her daddy's land?"

"How else are you going to get ahold of land out here? You'll be competing against every speculator in the territory, and you don't know a one of their tricks. Besides, Antonio's daughters are renowned for their looks." Maxwell had then launched an explanation of the old Spanish courtship customs, so Bart would know how to go about getting a Montoya bride.

Now he was searching Antonio's courtyard for a glimpse of the renowned beauties. The courtyard in itself was a thing to behold. It covered almost as much space as a town square. Every room in the hacienda opened out to it, the upper rooms by means of balconies. Tree branches and grape vines shaded the gardens and stone walkways below. A well stood near one corner.

"I am happy to hear that your father is doing well," Antonio said, leading his guest into the courtyard. "And what about your lovely mother?"

"Oh, she died," Bart said. "Yellow fever, the year after my father came back from the war."

"I am very sorry," the don said, removing his sombrero.

Bart saw a young Spanish woman breeze under an archway across the courtyard. Maxwell, it seemed, had been right. She wasn't hard to look at. She was dressed fetchingly but tastefully in a close-fitting white blouse and a long red skirt, a lace rebozo wrapping her shoulders.

"Sebastiana!" Antonio said. "Come here and meet our guest. Bring the gourd with you so that he may have a drink of water."

The young beauty obeyed, dipping the gourd in the well bucket and sweeping across the courtyard toward the *rico* and his guest. She was definitely of marriageable age, Bart thought. Certainly desirable enough. Her eyes searched him without a hint of timidity, and a faint smile made him stand a little taller and strike a more gallant pose.

"Cool your throat, amigo," Don Antonio said as Sebastiana handed the gourd dipper to Bart. "It has been a long, hot journey for you."

Bart ogled the woman between his hat brim and the gourd as he drank. He had expected a teenager. This woman was mature—his own age, if not a year or two older. How long was Antonio going to hold on to her?

"Sebastiana, *querida*," Antonio continued, "this is Bartolome Young, from Texas."

Bart liked the sound of his name in Spanish. He embraced the senorita's hand with a warm grip, not too firm.

"Bartolome . . ." the *rico* said, "my wife, Sebastiana."

Bart's hand went cold as a dead fish. This was the old man's wife! And she wouldn't turn loose of his hand! She wet her lips and raised one eyebrow at him.

"M-m-m-my pleasure," he stammered. Her fingers caressed his palm with something more than the customary welcome. The handshake lingered until Bart was sure the hacendado would grow suspicious. Still, Sebastiana refused to release his hand.

To his relief, a racket that sounded remarkably like a fight between two rabid cats echoed sharply through the courtyard, causing Sebastiana to lose her grip. She rolled her eyes at the shrill voices and turned away with indifference, glancing back at Bart only once before she disappeared in the cool shadows of the adobe walls.

Two awkward girls marched into the courtyard, each

one trying to stand in the way of the other. They snapped at each other like hens, rattling off Spanish with such momentum that Don Antonio could not quiet them from where he stood. The hacendado marched toward them, but just before he reached them, one grabbed the other's hair, and a battle of fingernails and shin kicks began, the likes of which Bart had never seen.

"Tomasa! Gregoria!" Antonio shouted, pulling them apart.

Bart beheld them with awe: two clumsy girls of tangled tresses, large flaring nostrils, snarling lips, clenching fists, and cheeks billowing with the angry breaths they heaved.

"Can you not see that we have a guest here in our courtyard?" Antonio shouted.

The girls glanced around until their wild eyes found Bart. They started pulling hair back from their homely faces and straightening their disheveled clothing. When they smiled, he saw they had crooked teeth.

"Now, that is better," Antonio said. "Bartolome, these are my two beautiful daughters, Tomasa and Gregoria."

Beautiful daughters? Where? These poor things were as fat and ugly as bloodhound pups. Still, Bart had to smile back. Maxwell had pulled a good one on him. Renowned for their looks? Yes, they probably were! He held back a guffaw and smiled at the two Montoya girls until he saw Sebastiana leering at him from the shadows of an archway, where only he could see her. The hacendada allowed her eyes to rake him from the heels of his boots to the crown of his hat and back again. He looked away from her before Antonio could catch him blushing.

And he was going to stay in this hacienda where all the women looked at him as though they had never seen a man before? This was going to be dangerous. Maybe even amusing.

FIVE

Don Antonio Geronimo Montoya de Cordoba y Chaves de Oca was one of the last of the old *ricos,* and one of the few who had learned to profit from the Yanqui invasion. But he had always understood capitalism, even before the Americans came. He had started building his fortune with a string of ox carts that he kept busy on the old road to Chihuahua. Later, he realized even larger profits on the Santa Fe Trail to Missouri. He had established a trading house in Santa Fe, still operated by his two sons, one of whom also served in the territorial legislature.

Years before the Yanquis took over New Mexico, Antonio had organized a group of settlers to petition the Mexican government for a grant of land. In due time, the governor had approved the grant and placed Montoya's people in possession of eleven square leagues, about forty-eight thousand acres, situated on the mountain slopes east of Santa Fe. To earn title, the settlers had to grow crops, become virtually self-sufficient, and weather the occasional assault by Utes or Jicarilla Apaches.

The land did not belong to Antonio Montoya himself. It was a community grant, intended to populate the Northern Frontier with Mexican citizens. Like the other settlers, Antonio claimed only a small piece of land for his hacienda and a small field irrigated by a mountain stream. The vast remainder of the grant belonged to all of the settlers in common. There they grazed their herds of cattle and flocks of sheep, they cut timber, and they hunted.

As trade increased on the Santa Fe Trail, many settlers decided to sell their rights to the grant and move into Santa Fe to work. They found a willing buyer in Antonio Montoya. He paid fair prices for the small houses and fields, and with each he acquired another share in the common lands. It was his aim to someday gain exclusive ownership to all eleven square leagues.

After the United States won New Mexico, the Anglo land speculators came and began trying to buy shares in what had become known as the "Montoya grant." Antonio advised his people against dealing with the Anglos.

"If you want to sell your titles to the grant," he told them at a meeting one night in his hacienda, "sell to me. I will pay more, and I will let you stay in your houses and plow your fields as long as you live. The Anglos will make you leave if you sell to them. They do not care about you. All they want is the land."

Now only a handful of old settlers continued to hold on to their grant rights. Antonio knew that as they grew older or died off, he could buy the rights from them or their heirs and ultimately gain exclusive right and title to the entire Montoya grant—its irrigated fields, pastures, and timber.

But it would have to happen quickly. The Anglo lawyers were getting trickier. They had figured out ways to force Mexican landowners to sell their grants—ways to trick them out of their land—ways even Don Antonio could not prevent. The Anglo legal system differed so markedly from the old Spanish and Mexican courts that Antonio couldn't grasp its complexities.

That was why this Bartolome Young seemed like such a godsend. The son of a lawyer. New to the territory. Befriended already by the likes of Lucien Maxwell, whose horse he had ridden in on. Just the sort of man he could use on his side.

So Antonio showed the visitor to one of his finest guest rooms, on the second floor with a balcony overlooking the east side of the courtyard. Bart found no bedstead in the room. The New Mexicans slept on thick mattresses of wool, which during the day were rolled and placed against a wall. Along with the mattress, Bart found a candle, a washstand, and a small fireplace.

"My sons will arrive soon from Santa Fe," the hacendado said. "Then we will eat. You have time to refresh yourself and relax before they get here."

"Gracias, Señor," Bart said. He dropped his portmanteau on the floor as the *rico* left him. He took off his shirt to get closer to the coolness of the adobe walls. After washing his face and hands, he unrolled the mattress and stretched out on it to take a short siesta. He dozed off staring at the peeled timbers above him. He felt strangely at home with the architecture of New Mexico.

He hadn't been asleep very long when he heard his door latch click. His eyes opened and saw a person moving toward him. Pulling himself up on his elbows, he found Sebastiana descending on him. The young hacendada put her hand on his bare chest and pushed him back down onto his mattress. She let her eyes pass over him as if feasting on his flesh.

Bart smiled nervously.

"You are a very light sleeper," she said.

He could think of no reply.

"Antonio is a very sound sleeper."

"You mean your husband?"

"He never wakes up. I will prove it to you tonight."

"That's not necessary. I believe you."

"After he goes to sleep, I will come to you here."

His eyes shifted. "I think that might be asking too much of Antonio's hospitality."

"You will see. After he goes to sleep, he never wakes up. He is an old man." She searched him with her eyes again. "You are young. Tonight."

Sebastiana parted her lips and leaned over Bart's face. Her hair fell from her shoulders and tickled his neck. He held his breath and shrank as deeply as he could into the mattress as she put her lips very near his. But she didn't kiss him. She smiled wickedly and left the room like a breeze.

He lay there, contemplating Sebastiana, until he heard the hoofbeats. Stepping out on to the balcony as he buttoned his shirt, he saw two paunchy, well-dressed young men alighting from a carriage. Antonio's sons, he presumed. In minutes, Antonio was at his door, inviting him to supper.

The dining hall was filled with rustic New Mexico furnishings, accented with a few Spanish-colonial pieces. Planks comprising the table top had been hand-hewn and smoothed. The chairs around it were small, square specimens. As Bart had learned at Maxwell's Ranch, the men would dine in this room alone, while Antonio's wife and daughters, and the other women in the hacienda, would eat in a dining room of their own.

Bart met the hacendado's sons, Francisco and Vicente. They extended little of the hospitality Antonio had shown. Both around thirty years of age, they behaved with a great deal of arrogance. Vicente was the legislator, but Francisco seemed more apt to lead.

"Bartolome's father was one of the wounded Texans here during the war," Antonio explained.

"Where is the food?" Francisco replied.

"Yes, I am starving," Vicente added.

They seated themselves at the table as two señoritas began bringing in the food. When the brothers started speaking to Antonio in Spanish, Bart let his attention wander to the girls who were serving the meal. They were dressed in neat peasant skirts and blouses. The Montoya men did not so much as glance at them. They were rather plain looking, their eyes lacking energy. They served the men by routine.

Then the third girl came in, carrying goblets and a bottle of wine. Bart knew instantly that she was different. She wore the same peasant dress, but her beauty was striking, though she was only fifteen or sixteen by his estimation. Her bright eyes darted among the men. When they met his, they cut quickly away, but she smiled slightly as she went about her duties. Bart could hardly keep his eyes off of her.

"What?" Antonio said, in a suddenly louder voice, in response to something one of his sons had said. He looked at Bart. "Bartolome, when you stayed with Maxwell, did he tell you he had sold his grant?" The pretty servant girl was at his shoulder, pouring the wine.

"Yes," Bart said. "That reminds me"—he reached into the pocket of his jacket—"Maxwell asked me to carry this letter to you."

When he handed the letter to Don Antonio, Bart caught the servant girl's eyes and held her stare long enough to make her spill the wine on the hacendado. Antonio leaped back from the table and let fly a string of what Bart took for Spanish cuss words. But when he turned his angry eyes on the girl, he became suddenly silent.

"Bitora!" he said, after taking a moment to compose himself. "What are you doing in here?"

"I wanted to meet the guest," she said, glancing at Bart. "Tomasa and Gregoria got to meet him, and I did not."

"How dare you dress like that! And you should be eating with your sisters and your mother."

"That witch is not my mother," Bitora said.

Antonio raised his hand. "Watch your tongue! I will slap you for such talk!"

Bart could tell by the way Bitora smirked that she had never been slapped in her life.

"I want to be introduced to our guest, like everyone else," she demanded.

"Yes, but you are *not* like everyone else!" Antonio roared. "You do not know your place!" He grabbed his youngest daughter by the arm and led her to the door. Her bright eyes settled on Bart for a moment before the door shut her out.

"My apologies, Bartolome," the old man said, his eyes flashing as if he had really enjoyed the confrontation. "That one has always been trouble."

"The prettiest ones always are," he replied.

The hacendado returned to his chair and opened the letter from Lucien Maxwell. "I hope you will not consider me ill mannered if I read this letter in your presence, Bartolome, but I haven't heard from Señor Maxwell in a long time."

"Not at all," Bart said.

Antonio scanned the letter for a few seconds, then raised his eyes to his sons. "It is true," he said. "He has sold his grant to some Englishmen. Ha! He is suggesting that I do the same thing. He says he will find the buyers if I wish."

"Are you trying to sell, too?" Bart asked.

"Never. No price is high enough. I will be buried here."

Instantly, Bart's admiration for the hacendado doubled. He had finally found someone who knew what land was worth. A man could become a part of his land, like a tree taking root.

"Maxwell has bought Fort Sumner from the army," Antonio said, astonished, "and he is going there to live! *Incredíble!* Why would he want to live so far from the mountains? It will kill him!"

The *rico* shook his head as he turned to the second leaf of the letter. Then his worried eyes brightened. "This part is about you, Bartolome. Maxwell says you have come to New Mexico to get some land and become a rancher."

Bart nodded. "As soon as I figure out how the speculators do it," he said. "I want a piece like yours—reaching into the mountains, with timber, pasture lands, and running water."

As Don Antonio came to the bottom of the page, his face went blank. He stared long enough to let Bart know he was reading the last paragraph over and over. Finally he folded the pages, slipped them back into the envelope, and turned his chair to face Bart. "Now I understand why you have come to see me," he said.

"Sir?" Bart said.

"Señor Maxwell has made your proposal for you, as you wished, and he speaks very well of you. You will receive my fairest consideration."

"Thank you," Bart said, wondering what Maxwell had written about him.

"Now, tell me. Which of my daughters do you wish to marry? Or does it matter to you?"

The jaws of the Montoya brothers locked as they turned their dark eyes on Bart for the first time since they had met him. They had no desire to share the family fortune with a new son-in-law.

Bart almost choked on a large bite he had just taken. He remembered Maxwell explaining the Spanish courtship customs. It was common for a friend to recommend a prospective groom in a letter, and it seemed Maxwell had done so. Bart didn't even have to know the customs to realize how deeply he would offend Antonio now by telling him he didn't want to marry any of his daughters.

Thankfully, he had the mouthful of food to chew, which gave him some precious time to think of a way out of this. He couldn't imagine himself standing at the altar with either of the snarling butterballs he had seen scrapping in the courtyard earlier. And Bitora was a mere child.

Even in his panic, he had to admire Maxwell. The land baron had given him fair warning, and Bart still hadn't seen it coming.

He reached for his wine glass, not yet knowing what he would say. But then it came time to speak, and the inspiration seemed to come to him out of pure ether.

"It matters a great deal to me which of your daughters I would marry," he began. "I'll name her if you'll let me explain my circumstances."

Antonio nodded.

"I'm new to the territory. I have no money or land. I don't even have a job yet. Despite what Maxwell says, I am certainly not much of a prospect for your daughters at this time." He found the brothers nodding in agreement with him, and Antonio listening with curiosity.

"However," the Anglo continued, "I intend to have all those situations remedied in four or five years. By that time I should think that I would be a highly favorable prospect."

"Perhaps," Antonio said. "But which daughter will wait that long for you? Tomasa and Gregoria have each received several proposals. I intend to see them married within the year."

"Yes, but my interest is in Bitora."

The old don bristled. "Bitora!"

"She's only a girl now," Bart said, "but in four or five years, she will be of marriageable age."

"You wish to marry my little Bitora?"

"Only if she is in agreement. I insist she be given her choice."

Francisco's eyes sparked, and he nudged Vicente, thinking the guest wouldn't notice. Both brothers realized how easy it would be to turn Bitora against this Anglo over the course of four or five years.

The stern look on Don Antonio's face lost some of its edge as he saw the many ways around the proposal. Bartolome might not get rich enough in five years to warrant serious consideration. He might not even last a year in the territory. On the other hand, if he proved ambitious enough to become wealthy and landed in five years, he might prove to be a valuable son-in-law.

Still, he did not reply. It was better to let the young man sweat. He turned his attention back to his food, and the men ate the remainder of their meal without conversation. When Antonio finally looked up from his plate, it was as if there had never been any talk of marriage.

"Let us retire to the courtyard," the hacendado said, rising. "Sebastiana is going to play the guitar for us. Wait until you hear her sing, Bartolome." He grinned boyishly. "I would kill for that woman."

As they left the dining hall, Bart asked Antonio to wait a moment before proceeding to the courtyard. "I don't mean to sound ungrateful," he began, "but it's about my room."

"What is wrong with your room?"

"Absolutely nothing. It's the finest room I've ever seen, but . . ."

"Please, what is it?" Antonio said.

"Well, I was wondering if I might have a room on the west side of the courtyard. I want to look across it and see the sun rise over your mountains in the morning."

Antonio smiled. "Of course, amigo. I should have thought of it myself." He put his hand on Bart's shoulder and started him walking toward the courtyard.

"But please don't mention to your wife about my changing rooms," Bart added. "I would die of embarrassment if she thought I was in any way ungrateful."

"Of course not," the *rico* said. "I will keep it just between you and me."

SIX

I am not going to marry you," Bitora said.

She had come up behind Bart so silently in the courtyard that her voice startled him, making him slosh coffee from his cup. He rose from his bench, slinging the scalding liquid from his hand. Again he was struck by her youthful beauty.

The rising sun was on her face, lending a fiery light to her eyes, bathing her warm complexion in golden hues. She had lost her peasant skirt and blouse, and now wore a blue organdy dress with ruffles and a matching rebozo. Silver pins held her hair up, and high-heeled leather shoes had replaced her sandals, as if she had risen in wealth and standing overnight.

He smiled. "Can't say that I blame you."

"My father cannot make me marry you. The old customs are ridiculous."

"I agree. Don't worry, Miss Montoya, I didn't come here to marry you or anybody else."

She appeared suddenly insulted, and glanced up and down at him as if she couldn't believe his nerve. "What do you mean? My brothers told me you brought a letter of proposal with you."

Bart chuckled. "A friend of mine tried to trick me into marrying one of your sisters. I didn't like the idea of that, so I used you as an excuse to get out of it. I said it was *you* I wanted to marry, when you got old enough, figuring that would give the whole thing four or five years to simmer down."

She stepped back and glowered at him indignantly. "So, I am just your *excuse?* You should know that there are many handsome young men around here who would like to marry me."

"I'm sure there are, but I'm not one of them."

She put her hands on her hips. "And so now I am not good enough for you? It is because I was dressed like a peasant girl last night, isn't it?"

"What are you getting so riled about? You said you didn't want to marry me, anyway. I had to use you as an excuse to keep from insulting your father. I surely wasn't about to marry one of your sisters."

Her hard stare finally relented, but she held her defiant pose. "And so, you did not come here to marry me?"

"No offense, Miss Montoya, but no. I didn't even know you existed until I saw you last night."

Suddenly Bitora laughed and looked away.

"Now, what's so funny?"

"Francisco and Vicente told some terrible lies about you."

"I don't doubt it. What did they say?"

"That you were addicted to opium, that you cheat at cards, and that your parents never married."

He turned red and trembled, embarrassed and incensed to hear an innocent repeating such lies about him.

Bitora regretted telling him. "I didn't believe them," she said quickly. She was trying to think of a new topic of conversation when she heard Sebastiana's taunting laughter across the courtyard. Her stepmother passed briefly under a shadowy archway, another figure following close behind, reaching for her.

Bart couldn't tell if it was Vicente or Francisco pursuing Sebastiana, but right now one was no different from the other to him. He took a step toward the archway, bent on teaching whichever brother it was what he thought about liars, but Bitora grabbed him by the arm.

"Don't make trouble," she said. "If my father finds out about them, something terrible will happen."

"If he finds out about who?"

"That witch and my brothers."

He looked down at her hand, still clenched tightly around his elbow. "You mean, your brothers . . ."

"That is why they leave their wives in Santa Fe when they come here. But they are so stupid, they don't even know about each other. She is making a fool of every man in this house, and I am the only one who can see it. She will probably try to make a fool of you, too."

"She already has," Bart admitted, "but I threw her off my trail last night."

"How did she do it?" Bitora asked, her eyes flashing.

"She came to my room yesterday afternoon." He was suddenly a bit stunned to think of himself telling such things to a sixteen-year-old girl, but he found her easy to talk to. "Dang near pounced on me right there on the floor."

"She will not stop there. Vicente resisted her for a while, but she finally got him, too. Francisco did not resist at all. Now she sneaks into their rooms in the middle of the night. Or she leaves messages in their beds, telling them to meet her someplace. I know all about it. There is something wrong with her. She is a crazy witch."

"Maybe you should tell your father."

She shook her head and stepped back in dread. "No! I am afraid he might kill them. And her, too. You don't know my father. He believes in the old customs. He would kill you, too, if he caught you with Sebastiana. I am warning you. He doesn't care what the Yanquis would do to him. He would murder someone if he found out."

"There you are!" a voice suddenly called.

Bart flinched, and turned to see Antonio, smiling and approaching him across the courtyard.

"Are you ready to take our ride?" the old don said.

"Yes, sir," Bart replied, composing himself.

"Bitora, what are you doing here?"

"I want to go, too," she said.

"You are not going. Leave us. Go do something else."

"There is nothing else to do. I'm bored!"

"Go away, child. You cannot ride with men."

Bitora glanced at Bart, then stomped away, holding her ruffles above her ankles.

Antonio chuckled. "To tell the truth, Bartolome, she can ride better than either you or I. She hates the sidesaddle I bought for her. She would rather straddle her horse like a boy. She has always been the one to cause trouble!"

Bart spent the rest of the morning touring the Montoya grant with Antonio. Four servants came along to care for the horses, and to serve the food and wine. They ate on a mountain ridge, under tall pines. From their vantage they could see the plaza of Santa Fe, miles distant.

The day was one to fix the vision of empire in Bart's head. There was no other place like this in the world. He was glad he had dropped out of law school and come to New Mexico while there was still a chance of acquiring an old Spanish land grant.

"When I die, this is where I want to be buried," Antonio said to his guest. "This is the highest point on my grant. Here I am close to heaven, and my journey will not be so long."

SEVEN

Vernon Regis sat hunched over a copy of the old papers for the Lopez grant, trying to figure out a way to trick the Lopezes out of it. The Spanish government had made the grant to two Lopez brothers in 1767. Their heirs still lived on the land, grazed it, farmed it. None of them would answer his inquiries, nor come to Santa Fe to talk about selling.

The only piece of land Regis wanted more than the Lopez place was the Montoya grant east of town. He just wanted the Lopez grant to parcel up and sell at a profit. The Montoya grant was different. He would divide most of it, but he wanted to keep the Montoya hacienda as his own weekend retreat. Old Antonio had the finest mansion in the county.

On this day, however, he couldn't figure out a way to get his hands on either grant, and it was frustrating the devil out of him. To make things worse, he had heartburn again. Damn Mexican food tore his stomach up something terrible. He stood and unbuttoned his vest to give his gut some room. He was a large man, poorly built. He had narrow shoulders and hips, a large head, a bulging stomach, and tremendous feet. His hands were soft, pale, and thin-skinned, with fingers like pitch-fork tines.

He paced, then stood at the window to look out at the plaza. The view depressed him. Cottonwoods cast shadows on the dusty streets. Rambling adobes surrounded the square like so many dirt dobber nests. To the left was the Palace of the Governors; it held the archives where he had schooled himself in the particulars of Spanish and Mexican land grants.

A black sombrero passed in front of his window, and Regis turned back to his desk, determined to study the Lopez grant until the answer came to him. He heard the brass bell ring on the door of his outer office. Whoever it was, his office manager would take care of it.

Just as he was delving back into the grant papers, a knock came at his door, and his office manager stuck his head in.

"There's a fella here who says he wants to talk to you about a land grant."

Regis frowned. "Send him in. Do me good to cuss somebody out today." He slipped the Lopez grant papers under some others on his desk and stood ready to greet the visitor. A young Anglo holding a big black sombrero entered, and Regis wondered what self-respecting American would wear such a hat.

"Bart Young," the visitor said, "lately of Texas."

"What can I do for you?"

"I hear you speculate in land grants."

"I'm a lawyer," Regis replied.

"I'd like to work for you."

Regis invited the visitor to sit in the chair facing his desk. "I don't need any help right now."

Bart handed Regis a few leaves of paper. "Here are my credentials."

Unwillingly, the speculator sat down behind his desk

and began perusing the documents. The first appeared to be a letter of recommendation from none other than Lucien B. Maxwell. The next was a Tulane University diploma, then came a certificate from the Texas bar. This wasn't the first time some snot nose had skulked in here to horn in on Vernon Regis's empire.

"Very impressive, Mr. Young, but I really don't have any use for some greenhorn Texas . . ." He was about to hurl a few unabridged profanities when he shuffled to the last document in the stack: a letter of introduction from Antonio Montoya. In midsentence, he smiled and looked up at the fledgling lawyer: ". . . some greenhorn Texas legal genius come here to put me out of business. Tulane's a very good school. Where are you staying?"

"At the hacienda of Don Antonio Montoya. I have a letter from him there."

Regis smirked and tossed the credentials back to Bart's side of the desk. "I know of Montoya. Good fellow. But, like I said, I really have no need for a clerk or what-have-you."

"I'll work strictly on commission," Bart said. "I just want to learn the ropes."

Regis opened a hardwood cigar case and urged his guest to take one. "I don't have time to be anybody's mentor, son, but maybe we can find something appropriate for you in town. What exactly is your relationship with Señor Montoya?"

"He and my father were best friends."

Regis covered a giddy streak he felt coming on. "And what is your interest in Spanish land?"

"I want to own a chunk of it."

"For what purpose?"

"To live on. Start a ranch."

"I see," Regis said. He stroked his chin, leaned back in his chair, and propped his huge feet on his desk. "When do you expect to acquire this cattle empire of yours?"

"I figure it would take a number of years to learn the business of acquiring the land grants—and to find the right piece of property."

Regis's big head nodded on his skinny neck for several long seconds. "I admire your ambition, young man. I think I know just the place for you."

"You do?" Bart said, pulling himself forward in his chair.

"Now, keep this to yourself, because the information is confidential. I happen to know that a position will soon be vacant in the archives division of the territorial government. That's the best place in the territory to study land grants. Do you read Spanish?"

"Not much," Bart admitted.

"Doesn't matter. You'll learn. When can you start?"

"As soon as I can get a room in town."

"Good. I'll arrange the position for you. Come see me after you get yourself situated. The job should open up within the week."

Bart shook the speculator's hand, then strode triumphantly from the office. He couldn't wait to get ahold of pen and ink so he could write Randy back in New Orleans.

After his visitor left, Regis crossed the corner of the plaza to the Palace of the Governors. Passing beneath the flimsy porch roof the Americans had tacked on to the venerable adobe, he marched to the office of Alfred Nichols, secretary of the territorial government's records division.

"Morning, Al," he said, entering the small, windowless room.

"Vernon." The bureaucrat slid a file drawer shut. "What brings you over?"

"I have a favor to ask. I want you to fire that Mexican who handles the Spanish archives for you."

"Gonzales?"

"Whatever his name is."

"But, he knows the archives better than anybody. He

was here when Kearny took the territory from Old Mexico."

"He's also so damned old that he can barely open the files. He's got a pension coming doesn't he?"

"Yes, a small one."

"Then get rid of him."

"What do you care who handles the archives?"

Regis sank into a chair and crossed his legs, swinging one foot like a sledge hammer. "I know somebody who will be perfect for the job."

"Does he know Spanish?"

"He said 'adios' when he left my office."

"What makes him perfect for the job?"

Regis paused and raised one of his skeletal fingers as his dry lips formed a smile. "He's a friend of Antonio Montoya."

Nichols wrung his hands together nervously as his eyes shifted around his tiny office. "You're going to recruit him?"

"Hell, no. Then he'll want a share of the grant, like you and everybody else. I intend to use him without him even knowing it."

"How?"

"That's my worry. All you have to do is get rid of Gonzales and hire this new kid. Bart Young is his name."

"And?" Nichols said.

"I made you a deal years ago, and it still stands. You help me acquire the Montoya grant, I'll see that you get a one-eighth share in the land. All you have to do is hire Young."

EIGHT

H ow are your Spanish lessons coming?" Antonio asked.
"*Bastante bien,*" Bart answered.

They sat alone in the dining hall, sipping their after-dinner drinks: a brandy for Bart, and a rich port for Antonio.

"Are you able to read the documents in the archives?"

"Not as well as I'd like," Bart admitted. "Those old Spanish pen scrolls take some getting used to. But from what I can translate, they tell some great tales. There are stories of Spanish noblemen, bands of peasants—exploring new places, fighting Indians, settling the land grants."

"So you like working there?"

Bart grinned, his eyes sparkling. "I've got documents in there over a hundred years old. Some of them have sailed back and forth across the ocean, and have signatures of dead Spanish kings on them."

Antonio dismissed the servant girls and poked at the fire for a while. It was November, and the flames went well with the port to pierce the cold creeping down from the mountains. "Have you discovered the name of Nepomeceno Montoya on any of the old papers?"

Bart scratched at the beard he had been cultivating in preparation for the winter. "No, but I can look if you want me to. Ancestor of yours?"

The *rico* pulled a chair up to the hearth and asked Bart to join him. "He was my great-grandfather. The first in my family to come to New Spain. It was 1769 when he arrived on the frontier as a captain of dragoons. One hundred and one years ago, Bartolome. I don't know much about him except for the campaign against the Indians in 1775."

"I've seen references to that campaign in the archives."

"It was maybe the biggest war ever fought between the

Spanish Army and the Indians. It made my great-grandfather a famous hero."

"How did it happen?" Bart asked, sliding to the edge of his chair like a boy.

"A man named Hugo O'Conor was the Comandante Inspector then. That was the highest ranking military post on the frontier."

"O'Conor?" Bart snorted. "What kind of name is that for a Spanish officer?"

"I think he was born Irish. Anyway, in 1775 he ordered two thousand men in presidios all across the Northern Frontier to march into the Apache country to punish the Indians for raiding. Nepomeceno Montoya, my great-grandfather, was garrison captain at San Elisario, down the river from where El Paso is now. He was ordered to march north with about a hundred men into the Sacramento Mountains.

"I remember my father and my grandfather telling me about it. They said it was August, and very hot on the desert. But when Nepomeceno got high into the Sacramento Mountains, he found it very cool, with plenty of water running from the mountains in streams. And there were tall trees there, and plenty of rain.

"Nepomeceno found the Mescaleros, but he did not do very much fighting with them at first. He had orders to meet Hugo O'Conor on the Rio Grande, so he had to take his men west. Then he led O'Conor back to the Sacramentos—and that was when the real fighting began.

"The Mescaleros were great warriors. They still live in those mountains, and they are not finished fighting yet. But O'Conor had the best soldiers on the Northern Frontier with him, and they had some bloody battles.

"One morning, when Nepomeceno was leading O'Conor to one of the Indian villages he had discovered, the Mescaleros surprised them and got between O'Conor and my great-grandfather. It was on a steep mountain trail through tall trees, and the soldiers were marching in single file. The Indians attacked the middle of the file to divide the command, and surrounded O'Conor and a few of his men.

"The soldiers scattered all over the place, but Nepomeceno pulled them together and broke through the circle of Mescaleros who had surrounded O'Conor. He led the attack himself, and was shot twice with arrows, but not badly wounded. He fought with his saber and—so the story goes in my family—took the head off a warrior who was trying to kill O'Conor with a knife."

"No wonder he became a hero," Bart said.

"O'Conor recommended Nepomeceno for the Order of Carlos the Third—a very great honor in Spain."

"He should have gotten a land grant in the Sacramentos where he saved O'Conor's life. I've read in the archives where war heros sometimes got big Spanish grants."

"That would have been a fine place for a grant."

Bart poured the last of his brandy down his throat. "You've been there?"

"Once. A long time ago. I had been taking my ox carts to Chihuahua for a few years, and the road along the Rio Grande goes not too far from the Sacramentos, so I decided to take some of my men on horses and see where my great-grandfather saved the life of the Comandante Inspector. We took plenty of powder and bullets, because the Mescaleros were very powerful then."

Antonio smiled, and the firelight flared in his eyes. "We went above the piñons and came to the big timber, and the trees were the tallest I have ever seen. That night we camped and it was very cool, though it was the middle of summer.

"We explored the mountains for seven days. There was water and grass, and deer and elk to hunt. And I heard wolves and lions in the night. We climbed very high, and

I think we could see California from up there. I got the idea that I could build a great ranch there, in the Sacramento Mountains. It was so cool that I didn't want to come down."

"So why didn't you?" Bart asked, rolling a log on the andirons.

"The Mescaleros," Antonio whispered, widening his eyes. "On the seventh day, we were riding on a trail when I saw an Indian brave watching me from the forest. He was so close, a whip could have cut him. I pulled the reins back, and stopped in the trail. One of my men followed my eyes to see what I was looking at. Before I could stop him, he pulled an old horse pistol out of a saddle holster and shot at the Indian."

"Killed him?" Bart asked.

Antonio chuckled. "No, he blasted some bark away from a big tree, and the wood chips got in the Indian's eyes, and made him scream and fall back on the ground. Then the forest came alive with those Apaches. They seemed to spring down from the trees and up from the ground like magic. There were only six of us in my party, and there seemed to be a hundred warriors with bows and arrows that would shoot ten times as fast as our old muskets."

"What did you do?"

"I knew that if we fired, we would be slaughtered, so I told my men to draw their weapons, cock them, aim them, but not to shoot unless the Indians shot their arrows first. They were afraid of our guns. When we aimed at them, they jumped behind trees to hide.

"The Indian who had the wood chips in his eyes finally stopped screaming and sat up on the ground, rubbing his eyes. I told my men to keep their guns pointed at the Indians. I put my rifle in the saddle scabbard and, taking my canteen, got down from my horse."

"Canteen? What were you going to do? Drown them?"

"No, *idiota,* I helped that Indian wash his eyes clear of

the tree bark, and then I drank with him from the same canteen, like brothers."

"And they let you go?"

"A chief named Ojo Blanco came down from the forest. He spoke very good Spanish. He was a young man—maybe not a head chief, but just a leader of that band or something. He told us that if we would give them our weapons, they would let us go."

"Did you?"

"What would you have done, Bartolome?"

Bart paused to pick his teeth with a wood splinter. "I don't believe I'd ever give up my guns to Indians."

"But Ojo Blanco said he would kill us if we didn't give up our guns."

"Well, I hope you told him there would be a lot of widows and orphans back at his camp before he got your guns away from you."

The *rico* smiled and smoothed his mustache into his sideburns. "I didn't say it that way, but Ojo Blanco understood me. We argued for a while and threatened to kill each other a dozen times, until finally the chief told me I could take my men out of the mountains if I promised never to come back. If I did return, he said, he would kill me for certain."

"Did you ever go back?" Bart asked.

"Never. But the memory of that place is always with me. I wish I could go back there." He sighed and shook his head as if to clear the thoughts from his mind. "I will probably never see it again. It is a wild place and I am an old man."

"You mean it's an old place, and you're a wild man," Bart suggested. "If you want to go there again, why don't we just get up an expedition?"

Antonio chuckled. "I have other pleasures to divert me here. I could not stand to spend that much time away from Sebastiana. Not even one night, amigo." His eyes twinkled.

"Afraid you might miss something?"

"I know I would."

"Every night?" Bart asked.

"Each and every night." The hacendado grinned and raised his eyebrows.

Bart shook his head in disbelief. "You amaze me," he said. But he was thinking of the way Bitora so often spoke of her stepmother: That woman was not natural.

NINE

Vernon Regis sucked the match flame into his cigar as he leaned across R. T. Fincher's desk. "It sounds simple, but it took me a long time to think of it," his thin lips said around the stogie. He was bragging to the surveyor general about his recent acquisition of the Lopez grant.

"How did you do it?" Fincher asked, blowing smoke rings over his leaded-glass lamp.

"I just had some associates send letters to various members of the Lopez family until I had half of them convinced that the other half was going to sue for sole possession of the land. After I got them feuding amongst themselves, they couldn't wait to sell their shares, just to keep their own uncles and cousins from taking them."

Fincher chuckled and puffed smoke at the ceiling. "Now, don't gloat, Vernon. It's no great feat to take land from people as ignorant as these Mexicans."

Regis's big head bobbed. "You're right, as usual," he said.

Hobnobbing with the surveyor general was a crucial part of his job. One of Fincher's duties was to recommend approval or denial of Spanish land grants to Congress. He knew more Greek than Spanish and understood little of land grant history, but Congress almost always followed his recommendations. Without congressional approval, the Lopez grant would become public domain, and Regis's title to it would be worthless.

Regis was hoping to get Fincher to invest in the grant. The surveyor general speculated openly in Spanish land and saw no conflict of interest there, though he virtually had the power to confirm or deny the grants he invested in with his congressional recommendations.

"Did you look over the papers?" the speculator asked.

Fincher smirked. "It all looks like gibberish to me. I sent them to one of my title experts." He glanced at the grand-father clock standing against the adobe wall. "He should be here any minute to report to me on it. You might as well stay and hear what he has to say."

"Don't mind if I do," Regis said. "But I know the title is firm. I wouldn't be asking you in on the deal if there was any question about it."

"I trust you," the surveyor general said. "But I have all the grants checked by experts so I'll know what to write in my reports to Congress. Now, we might as well sip some whiskey until the grant papers get here."

"Anything but tequila," Regis said.

They had poured the liquor and drank their first toasts when they heard a knock at the door. Regis burst out laughing when Bart Young came in carrying a box of papers. "This is your so-called expert? He hasn't even been in the territory a year!"

Bart put the box down and brushed the snowflakes from his coat. "I didn't know you would be here, Vernon." He snapped his fingers. "I've got a new riddle for you."

"Bart's partial to riddles," the speculator said.

"So am I," Fincher replied. "Let's hear it."

Bart pulled up a chair. "Let's say you have five eggs in a bowl. How can you divide the five eggs among five men, yet leave one in the bowl?"

Regis scratched his head with a cadaverous finger as if actually contemplating the puzzle. He hated riddles. They were a ridiculous waste of time. But it was important to string the archivist along if he was going to own Montoya's hacienda someday.

R. T. Fincher broke the silence with his voice in a state of near hysteria. "I know! Scramble them! Leave one in the bowl, scramble the other four, and let the five men divide the scrambled eggs!"

"Good try," Bart said, "but that would only be dividing four eggs. How about you, Vernon? Care to try?"

"No, you've stumped me again, Bart. What's the answer?"

"You simply give the fifth man the egg *and* the bowl!"

Regis spread his arms to the ceiling, like a vulture taking sun on his wings. "Now, let's see if you're as clever with land titles as you are with riddles. What did you find out about the Lopez grant?"

Bart put on his professional demeanor and removed the first sheet of parchment from the box. "The earliest document pertaining to the grant is this petition from two Lopez brothers, Juan and Filipe, dated 1765." He put the petition aside and reached for the next document in his box. "Now, here is the governor's report on the petition, dated several months later—you know how slow things move in government."

"Mr. Young," Fincher suddenly said, "I assume all these details are in your report?"

"Of course."

"Then get to the point. Is the title to the Lopez grant valid, or not?"

Bart almost withered. He had rehearsed this presentation document by document. "There's no doubt in my mind that it's a good grant, and Vernon has acquired full possession of it."

"That's all I wanted to know," the surveyor general said.

"However . . ." Bart added. The speculator and the bureaucrat looked at him with wrinkles of concern on their brows, and he felt himself in control again.

"Well?" Regis said.

Bart made furious excavations into the box of old papers. "It doesn't affect the validity of the grant, but I thought you would want to know."

"Know what?" Regis said.

"Here it is." He extracted a wrinkled page. "You paid some Lopez heirs up in Taos for their share in the grant, right?"

"Three sisters and a brother. What of it? I paid Lopezes all over the territory to get that grant."

"Yes, but these particular Lopezes had no real claim to the grant."

"They had the last will and testament of their great-grandfather," Regis argued.

"You mean this?" He handed the will to Regis. "It's a forgery."

The speculator studied the leaf of parchment. "How do you know?"

"It's written with a steel pen."

"So what?"

"It's dated 1769, and the steel-point pen wasn't even invented until the 1790s. I'm afraid they took you, Vernon."

Fincher broke into a laugh. "Hoodwinked by ignorant Mexicans!"

Regis held his composure, but the forgery burned his fingers like hot coals. He could not tolerate being made a fool of.

"It's an excellent forgery, except for the steel pen they used," Bart said. "After I noticed it, I did some checking, and it seems this great-grandfather who supposedly wrote this will never even existed."

An ugly, rambling grin stretched across Regis's face.

"Good work, Bart." He looked at Fincher, who was still chuckling. "Oh, shut up, R. T."

Regis offered to help Bart carry the documents back to the archives. Leaving the surveyor general's office, they turned toward the plaza, bowing their heads to the snow whipping down the street on a north wind.

"You're getting awful proficient at this archive business," the speculator said. "Not even I caught that forgery, and I've seen dozens of them. I'll remember that thing about the steel pen."

Bart stiffened with pride. "Antonio got me to thinking about that. He remembers using quill pens when he was a boy."

Regis sensed the opening he had been awaiting for months. "Speaking of Don Antonio . . ." he began. His unwieldy shoes left long streaks in the snow as he shuffled out on to the Plaza. "I probably shouldn't be telling you this. . . ."

"What?" Bart asked.

"Some of my colleagues would consider it treasonous, letting you in on their plans, but, dammit, they've gone too far this time. They're going to give us all a bad name if somebody doesn't do something about it."

"What are you talking about?"

"I heard a rumor. Some lawyers are going to challenge Antonio's claim to his grant."

Bart laughed. "The Montoya grant is the most well-documented grant in the archives. Who would be fool enough to challenge it?"

"The challenge is just a trick to get Antonio into court," Regis said. "He'll need a lawyer. So, some lawyer who is in on the scheme will come out to his hacienda and offer to fight the challenge for him. But only if Antonio pays in land. They'll probably demand a third of his grant. That's the going rate. The same scam has been played on other grants in the territory."

Bart stomped the snow from his boots under the shed porch of the Palace of the Governors. "He won't fall for that. He'll just hire his own lawyer."

"That's the problem," Regis said. "Any lawyer who represents Antonio will incur the disfavor of the Santa Fe ring."

"I thought that whole business about the Santa Fe ring was a myth," the archivist said, leading Regis into the building.

"It's nothing organized, but it works. It's hard to explain. The more connections you have, and the more favors you can call in, the deeper you are in the ring. If somebody went against the ring on the Montoya grant, he would find legal roadblocks everywhere he went for months, maybe years. It would take somebody of high caliber to pull it off."

Bart stopped at the door to his office and struggled to get a hand on the knob. "Somebody like you?"

Regis put on his best look of surprise. "Don't drag me into it. I'm only telling you this because I think it's criminal what some of these speculators are getting away with these days."

"That's why you're just the man to fight it," Bart replied, finally putting his burden down on his desk. "You have the influence to survive the Santa Fe ring."

Regis appeared nervous as he put his load next to Bart's. "Now, don't jump the gun. If they really challenge Antonio's claim, tell me; then we'll decide what to do about it. Hell, it's probably just a wild rumor, anyway. I wouldn't worry about it. I thought you might want to warn Antonio, though. Just don't tell anybody you heard it from me."

"I won't," Bart promised.

"Now I have to get back to the office and deal with these Lopezes in Taos who defrauded me with that forgery you discovered."

"All right," Bart said. "Thanks for the help with these documents. Say, before you go, I've got one more for you."

"One more what?"

"How many eggs could the giant, Goliath, eat on an empty stomach?"

Regis sighed and feigned his look of concentration. These riddles were beginning to irk him, and he was still boiling mad over those Taos Lopezes. He couldn't wait to get back to his office where he could kick something.

TEN

The fire in the back room of the Paisano Club roared up the chimney, and Domingo Archiveque sat with his feet propped on the hearth. A hole in his boot had let in the slush from the Santa Fe streets, and the heat pricked his toes as they thawed.

He was alone, his back to the darkened room. Only the firelight moved in his emotionless eyes. It flickered across his spotty beard and the ugly knife scar that started at the nostril and ended at the earlobe. He wore his grease-stained sheepskin coat draped over his shoulders like a cape, and under it he had his hand on his pistol grip.

There was nothing fancy about the old Colt—it had seen decades of service in many hands. But none was as ready to use it as Domingo's.

When he heard the door latch move, he turned sideways in his chair, making certain the Colt would slip from the holster if he needed it. The door opened, and Vernon Regis stood silhouetted by the light in the saloon, waiting for his eyes to adjust to the darkness.

"Is that you?" he said.

Domingo grunted.

Regis grabbed a coal-oil lamp off the wall of the saloon and filled the back room with its light. He put a bottle of tequila on the table as he sat. Domingo moved like a cat to the bottle and poured a glass.

"How did things go down at Torreon?"

"There are still three who will not sell their farms," Domingo said.

"Did you threaten them like I told you?"

He nodded.

"You'll have to go back and get rough, then."

Domingo said nothing, but his lips formed a smile as he touched them with his tequila glass.

"I have another job for you to take care of, first, though." The speculator removed a piece of paper and several gold coins from his pocket. "These are the names of four Lopezes who live up in Taos. Three sisters and a brother. They cheated me out of some money. Make them sorry for it."

Archiveque held the paper between his fingers for a moment, then threw it in the fire.

"Don't kill them," Regis said. "They only took me for fifty dollars a head. I don't suppose that's worth their lives. But make sure they know I sent you."

Archiveque nodded as he picked up the gold coins.

The speculator rose from the table. "Want me to leave the lamp?" he asked.

The Mexican shook his head.

"No, I don't suppose you were ever afraid of the dark, were you?"

"Once, I was," Domingo said. "I was afraid the old man I lived with would start beating me if I went to sleep. But then I killed him."

Regis was never sure whether or not to believe Archiveque's many boasts of murder. "How old are you, Domingo?"

"Almost twenty."

Regis laughed as he grabbed the lamp. "You must have

killed a man a month from the stories you tell." He stopped at the door and turned back to the gunman. "One of those Lopez sisters in Taos is damned good to look at," he said. "You'll know the one I mean when you see her. Give her one of those so she'll remember what she did to me." He traced his long gaunt finger from nostril to earlobe.

Archiveque nodded and smiled again as he was left in darkness.

ELEVEN

One?" Bitora said, wrinkling her nose under the flat brim of her riding hat. "Goliath was a giant."

"But he could only eat one egg on an empty stomach," Bart explained, "because after that his stomach wouldn't be empty any more."

"How was I supposed to guess that?"

"I guessed it the first time I heard it."

"You are lying!"

They argued as they wound down the trail, returning from their Saturday ride in the mountains. When they came within earshot of the hacienda, an angry shout interrupted them.

"That's my father's voice," Bitora said, spurring her mount to a gallop.

Bart's horse kicked rocks from the rough trail as he pursued her. He caught her just before they entered the corrals at the rear of the hacienda, but Bitora pressed her horse right into the courtyard, ducking under the archway. Bart came to her side again as they heard the old *rico* shout over the rattle of hooves on the stone walkways.

"He's out front," Bart said. "Wonder what he's so mad about?"

They raced their horses through the front archway and

found Antonio shouting at a Santa Fe lawyer named Lefty Harless who was scrambling into a buggy. Tomasa and Gregoria stood agog, watching. Francisco and Vicente looked on with satisfaction as their father berated the Anglo in Spanish. Sebastiana was there, too, standing apart from the others.

It had been weeks since Vernon Regis's warning about the challenge to the Montoya grant. Bart had almost dismissed it as rumor. But now Lefty Harless, one of the least ethical land speculators in the territory, had set foot on the Montoya grant. Bart could tell by Don Antonio's threats what had brought Harless out: Somebody had challenged the authenticity of the Montoya grant in district court, and Harless had offered to defend the case if Antonio would pay with a third of the grant.

After the lawyer's buggy bounced away toward Santa Fe, Antonio turned to Bart. "It is just as your friend warned, Bartolome. We must go to Santa Fe immediately and find out what we can do."

Vicente and Francisco glared at Bart with jealousy for knowing more than they about the problem.

They saddled four fresh horses and galloped into the territorial capital, passing Lefty Harless on the outskirts of town. Bart led the Montoyas to Vernon Regis's rambling adobe house on the Santa Fe River and asked the scar-faced guard at the gate to take a message to the speculator. They let the spring sunshine take the chill off the brisk ride from their faces as they waited.

In a few minutes Regis appeared at the front gate to ask what was wrong. When Bart told him, he frowned and nodded. "So, the rumor was true. I was afraid it might be."

"What do you recommend that I do?" Antonio asked.

"Get a lawyer, of course," Regis replied.

"Will you take the case, Vernon?" Bart asked.

Regis chuckled. "You don't want me, Bart. I've got too

many irons in the fire. But I'll refer you to some decent attorneys who might help."

Bart and the Montoya men spent the rest of the day tracking down the lawyers Regis had recommended. None of them had the time to fight the challenge.

"Why won't they help me, Bartolome? I have the money to pay them."

"The Santa Fe ring is behind it. They're all afraid of being blacklisted."

"I will have to get a lawyer from the States," the *rico* suggested.

"He wouldn't know anything about Spanish land grants. Let's go see Regis again. This time we won't take no for an answer."

Regis flatly refused at first, but Bart argued until it was pitch black, and Regis finally gave in.

"Oh, all right, Bart," he said. "It'll be the end of my career in Santa Fe, but I'll do it. I guess you're right. The ring has gone too far this time, and if I don't fight it, I might as well be part of it. It will take time, though, and I don't work cheap."

"I can pay your fee," Antonio assured him.

"It might go higher than you ever dreamed, Antonio. The plaintiffs will drag this thing out as long as they can, and they'll have the judges on their side. They'll get postponements and cause delays for months in order to wear us out. They'll want to make an example of you for having the audacity to fight the ring."

"And I will make an example of them!" Antonio said with fire in his voice. "There is not a Mexicano in Santa Fe who will not spit at that little coward who came to my hacienda today! His servants will leave him! The cafés will not feed him! Not even the whores will take his money!"

Regis chuckled to think of Lefty Harless being turned away from his favorite whorehouse. "That's the spirit, An-

tonio. That's the only way to deal with these greedy bastards. Hit them where it hurts."

As Regis had warned, the proceedings dragged on for
months. Bart testified several times, explaining to the court
in great detail the validity of the Montoya grant, using the
old papers from the archive to bolster his position and
pointing out that Congress had confirmed the grant several years before.

As the trial dragged on through the summer, public sentiment began to favor Antonio Montoya. The newspapers
mocked the tactics of the land-grabbing plaintiffs. Vernon
Regis grew into something of a crusader.

Through it all, Bart was more excited than concerned
by the trial. He felt as if he were bringing about changes
of great importance in the territory, in addition to protecting the Montoya grant, which he had begun to think might
someday be his if he were to actually marry Bitora. He
wrote letters about the trial to Randy Hendricks, who had
passed the bar and was now working on the staff of a Louisiana congressman in Washington, D.C. He even wrote
to his father in Houston, for the first time since coming to
New Mexico. He thought the old man would be impressed
with his involvement in legal matters. George Young, however, failed to write back.

Only one thing truly concerned Bart about the entire
affair. Regis had started spending weekends at the Montoya hacienda to report to Don Antonio on the case and
discuss strategy. Bitora noticed before he did that Sebastiana had cast her spurious eyes on the speculator. Bitora
said her stepmother was sneaking out of her room at night
to spend time with her father's lawyer.

Bart was stunned. He had never thought of Regis as a
lady's man. "Are you sure?" he asked Bitora that night in

the courtyard as Sebastiana played the guitar and sang. "He's not all that handsome."

"He's ugly," she answered. "Look at how big his head is on his neck. He has hands like a skeleton. But that doesn't matter to her. She would go to bed with a leper."

The case dragged on until leaves began to fall from the cottonwoods on the Plaza. When the plaintiffs had exhausted every attempt to prolong the proceedings, Regis finally succeeded in getting the suit against Antonio dismissed. He and Antonio walked arm-in-arm from the courtroom as citizens slapped their backs and hailed them as great reformers.

They settled accounts that weekend at the hacienda. The first hard freeze had come down from the mountains, and the house servants had stoked a crackling fire in Antonio's office. The lawyer, the hacendado, the two brothers, and Bart cradled brandy snifters in their palms around Antonio's huge hand-carved desk.

Antonio paid the victorious lawyer in cash, and his sons frowned when they saw how high Regis's fees had mounted. But Bart and Antonio smiled with gratitude. The grant was safe, more secure than ever. They cared little for the money. The title to the land was solid.

Regis, on the other hand, seemed rather solemn. He stacked the money several ways as the men conversed, but seemed reluctant to put his earnings in his pockets.

Finally he sighed and said, "Antonio, I have a proposition for you. One that I think will benefit us all. If you accept, I can leave this money right here on your desk."

The Montoya brothers raised their eyebrows and turned their ears.

"But you have earned every penny," Antonio said.

"Yes, I know, but coming out here so often over the past several months has given me an idea."

Antonio was intrigued. "What is your proposition?"

"Let's say I take this much of my legal fees," he said, setting aside a stack of cash on the desk, "and buy your livestock—cattle, sheep, and goats. Not the horses, because I know you're partial to them. Then I take the remainder of my fees and lease your grazing lands for a year. That way you get to keep all this money, and I get a herd of livestock."

"But, my friend, what do you want with all those animals? You are no ranchero."

"No, I'm not," Regis agreed. "But for years I have wished I had ready access to livestock when I needed it. I buy and sell a lot of land, and some buyers want livestock included when they buy a spread. Why, just a couple of months ago, I had a deal fall through on a large tract of land across the mountains because I couldn't find a herd for sale to throw in as part of the deal. Now, if I had my own herd, right here on your place, and could lease your lands to graze them on, I would never have to worry about finding livestock when I needed it."

"But you have ranchland all over the territory," Bart said. "Why not stock one of your own places with a herd?" He felt suddenly as if Regis were trying to horn in on his domain.

"Then I'd just have to hire cowboys and goat herders to look after them. Too damn much trouble. I might as well go into the ranching business if I did that. Antonio, on the other hand, already has vaqueros and herders right here. They would go on tending the animals as if he still owned them."

Vicente nodded and looked at the two stacks of money on the desk. "It is a good idea."

"A very good idea," Francisco agreed.

"Yes, but there is one problem," Antonio said. "Not all of the animals belong to me. And, more importantly, not all of the land belongs to me. You forget, Vernon, that this is still a community grant. The common lands belong not to me, but equally to everyone who owns a share in the grant. They, as well as I, would have to agree to lease the land to you."

Regis's head nodded for several seconds as if his skinny neck were too weak to stop it. "That complicates things a little. But if you speak to all the shareholders, and convince them to sell their animals and lease the common lands, we could try it for one year to see how it works out. Then we could renew every year as long as things remain profitable for all of us."

"Think of it, Papa," Vicente urged. "For once, we would know exactly how much the land and herds would bring us for the year."

"Yes, regardless of the weather or the markets," Francisco said.

Antonio sloshed his brandy in his snifter for a moment, then admired its color against the fire.

"I'll tell you what," the speculator said. "I'll leave that money right there on your desk until tomorrow. That will give you an opportunity to talk to the other shareholders and try to convince them to lease to me."

Bart found it difficult to keep his mouth shut, but it was really none of his business. The Montoya grant was not his, and wouldn't be unless he married Bitora.

Vicente and Francisco, on the other hand, belabored their father with their advice. They cared nothing for cattle and sheep. Their interest was in the trading business in Santa Fe—and the fortune in the family vault. They saw it growing annually with predictable lease revenues.

That afternoon, Antonio went down to the fields to talk to the farmers. All agreed to lease. Vernon Regis had saved the Montoya grant, hadn't he? So why not lease it to him?

Antonio came to Bart almost apologetically that evening.

He could tell his young friend had reservations about the proposed transaction. "It is only for a year, Bartolome," he said. "We will see how it works out."

Regis promised he would draw up the appropriate papers and bring them for signing at the fiesta in two weeks.

That night as Bart lay awake, he saw Sebastiana's lantern light through his keyhole. She passed his door, and he heard her enter Regis's room down the hall. First Sebastiana, then the Montoya herds. What would Vernon want next?

TWELVE

Bitora dusted her face with a powder made of ground deer antlers before she came down to the courtyard. The fiesta had already begun, but its revelers made a collective pause when she appeared. Even Bart scarcely recognized her in the flowing silk gown and lace rebozo, her hair and face done up as he had never seen.

Some of Regis's lease money had been applied to the fiesta, making it the biggest one on the Montoya grant in years. Antonio had chosen a husband for Gregoria, and they were to be married before Christmas. It was a marriage Bart approved of, though he had no say in it, of course. The groom was a successful restaurateur in Santa Fe—not the sort Antonio would deed land to. Now if only he could get Tomasa married off to some merchant or other city dweller, then marry Bitora himself . . . But he was thinking too far ahead again.

"She looks beautiful tonight, doesn't she, Bartolome?" Antonio said, retrieving Bart from his fantasies of the future.

"Yes, sir. She sure does."

"Where is Vernon?"

"I don't know."

"Will you find him, *por favor,* and tell him we are ready to sign the lease papers in my office?"

"Sure," Bart said. He worked his way around the courtyard, looking for the speculator. He passed a group of young men, including Gregoria's fiancé. Across the courtyard, at that moment, Gregoria and Tomasa were engaged in a squabble and the fiancé's friends were ribbing him terribly about having to put up with such behavior once he made Gregoria his wife.

When he came near Bitora, Bart detoured to speak to her. "You look lovely tonight."

"Tonight?" she said, looking at him scornfully.

"Well, I mean always, but especially tonight."

Bitora was fuming about something, but she thanked Bart anyway. Her anger did not make her any less attractive. It was energy, and that was what he liked about her.

"Have you seen Vernon?" he asked.

"Yes," she said. "He is over there in the shadows with that *puta.*"

Bart followed her eyes and saw Sebastiana standing too close to Regis behind one of the archways. "This is getting out of hand. I'll have to talk with him."

Bart pulled Regis away from Sebastiana and led him down a lantern-lit adobe corridor to Antonio's office. "Don Antonio's wife is a beauty, isn't she?" he said as they walked.

Regis grunted, shrugging his narrow shoulders.

Bart stopped in the corridor and held the speculator back by the elbow before they reached the office. "He'd kill any man he caught fooling around with her."

Regis stared straight-faced at him. Though the lawyer did not say a word, Bart got an idea—for the first time—of how well he could lie.

"I suppose he might," Regis finally said. "These old

ricos live by a different code. I thought you said we were going to sign the lease. What are we waiting for?"

"Nothing," Bart replied. He smiled and proceeded down the hallway with the land speculator, confident that he had made his point.

When they entered the office, Bart found Antonio putting his signature at the bottom of the lease contract. Eight farmers were lined up at the desk, ready to put their marks under his.

"Bartolome," the hacendado said, "you will sign with me as a witness when these men make their X. If that is agreeable with Vernon."

"Oh, sure," the speculator said, folding up like a collapsing trestle as he sat in a cowhide chair. "This is all just formality, anyway."

Bart witnessed the marks of the illiterate farmers, then handed the pen to Regis, who put his signature in the appropriate spaces.

"Now, let's get back to that fiesta," Regis said, folding his copies into his coat pocket. He shook hands with Antonio and each of the farmers, then led the way back to the courtyard, his huge feet slapping against the tiles.

Bart stayed behind as Antonio prepared to lock the contract away in the iron safe. "I suppose you found the terms satisfactory," he said.

Antonio shrugged. "I did not read it all, but discussed it with Vernon earlier today."

Bart felt a tinge of panic. "Antonio, you're not supposed to sign something you haven't even read."

The *rico* chuckled. "Relax, amigo. What is wrong with you tonight? Vernon saved this grant, did he not? He has proven that we can trust him."

"I want to read that contract," he insisted. "You go on back to your guests if you want, but I'd like to find out exactly what I just witnessed."

Don Antonio scoffed, but handed the contract to Bart.

"All right, Bartolome. But, you are forgetting that he was the one who told you to warn me in the first place about the challenge."

Bart sat down by the fire as Antonio left. To his relief, he found the contract exactly as Regis had represented it. One year. Grazing rights only. Hunting and timber rights reserved for shareholders of the grant. Antonio Montoya had control of stocking rates and all other matters concerning livestock.

He put the document on Antonio's desk and stared into the fire. He felt at home here. He was getting territorial, and the place did not even belong to him yet. He propped his feet on Don Antonio's ornate desk. Forty-eight thousand acres. Bitora by his side day and night. Mountains and adobes. He could see his future taking shape. He loved New Mexico. She had no banks or railroads, but her civilization was ancient and deeply rooted. He loved her native tongue. He was speaking it well now. He found he could readily say things in Spanish that would have sounded ridiculously sappy in English.

He was where he belonged. It would all be his someday. He had been lucky. Randy Hendricks had made a mistake staying in law school, then going to Washington. He was missing everything.

Suddenly he flinched as if snake bit, and jumped up from his chair. Bitora was waiting to dance with him in the courtyard.

THIRTEEN

But, honey, I'm on my knees," Bart said.

Bitora tore her hand from his grasp. "Not good enough," she answered. "You must propose the way my father did to my mother. I will have it no other way."

"But it's not the same with us," he said, dusting his knees of gravel as he got up.

"That is the only way I will marry you."

He sighed and rolled his eyes to the high walls of the courtyard. "It's ridiculous. I'm inside the hacienda right now."

"My father let you in. I want you to come back on Wednesday when he is not expecting you and the gates are bolted. My father proposed to my mother on a Wednesday night."

She had remained adamant for weeks, since the night he first bent his knee and asked for her hand. She was nineteen now, beautiful beyond comparison and the object of every bachelor's desire for miles around. Even so, Bart knew he had no competition to fear. She wanted him. Antonio approved. He was going to marry her and gain control of the Montoya grant, its lands and hacienda. Everything would have been fine if not for this ridiculous insistence of Bitora's that she relive her late mother's romance.

"Why should I have to scale two walls and climb up to your room in the dead of night, when your father will let me in here any day of the week?"

"I insist," she said, stalking away. She glanced back once, a seductive glint in her eyes that suggested he might earn a reward for fulfilling her wishes.

For a moment, Bart wondered if Antonio's visit to Bitora's mother, many years ago, had included more than a proposal.

Antonio had found his bride in Chihuahua. Her father, a wealthy ranchero, had refused to let her marry a poor freighter. Antonio would not be turned away, however. He had invaded the ranchero's hacienda, snuck into his daughter's room, and proposed marriage. They eloped a few nights later.

Now Bitora demanded the same romantic exploits of

Bart. They wouldn't have to elope, of course, but she wanted him to prove he loved her as much as her father had loved her mother. There was more to it than mere formality. There was some real risk involved. Bart had lately gotten on the wrong side of Antonio with a harmless practical joke.

The hacendado had invited him to hunt deer in the mountains, taking a whole party of guides and servants. Carlos, a young cook whom Antonio had recently hired, conspired with Bart to pull one over on the old *rico*. They caught one of Vernon Regis's Merino rams, sheared it, rolled it in dirt to approximate the color of a deer, sawed its horns off short, and tied antlers to the stubs with wet rawhide. They staked the doomed sheep in a clearing and led Antonio there the next day. The hacendado made a perfect kill from two hundred yards. Arriving at the trophy, Bart and Carlos broke into fits of laughter, but Antonio was unamused.

There had been a time when his eyes would no more have mistaken a sheep for a deer than a house cat for a grizzly bear. The prank had made him feel old, and he had hardly said a civil word to Bart since, though he continued to receive him at the hacienda.

Bart didn't care to deepen the hole he had dug for himself on the hunt by getting caught sneaking over the hacienda walls to propose to Bitora. He would have to be careful. It wasn't Antonio's vigilance that concerned him, for he knew how much of a sound sleeper the old *rico* was. It was Sebastiana that had him worried. He might well bump into her tip-toeing around the hacienda at night. If she caught him, Lord knows what she would demand to keep the secret from Antonio.

But Bitora was adamant. He was going to have to scale the walls in the middle of the night like a thief.

* * *

When Wednesday night came, Bart found himself approaching the Montoya hacienda at midnight. He wore the most outlandishly dashing cowboy gear he could find in Santa Fe. He only wanted to do this once. He was sure his horse was making enough noise to wake the whole village of farmers below the hacienda, but no one challenged his right to pass. When he got to the outer wall, he found Carlos had failed him. The gates were locked.

There was nothing to do but climb over. He rode his horse up next to the wall, making the animal stand as close as possible. Gingerly, he raised himself up in the saddle until he was standing precariously on the highest ridge of the cantle. Just as he got one elbow on the top of the wall, the horse shifted its weight from one hip to the other. The smooth soles of Bart's boots slipped on the slick saddle leather. He kicked; the horse flinched. Rocks jabbed him and tore at his skin as his mount jumped out from under him, but he held on. Grunting, he managed to pull himself to the top.

He sat in the moonlight awhile, panting, checking his skinned palms. Descending would probably prove no more amusing.

He walked the wall like an acrobat, arms outstretched, until he came to a tree branch that reached over the rock barrier. Its girth did not satisfy him, but it had green leaves, so at least it wasn't rotten. This was ridiculous, he thought, as he grabbed hold of the limb. Fun, though. It was like pulling off a daring jest on somebody. And that look Bitora had given him kept playing before his eyes in the moonlight. What reward awaited him in her room?

The cracking of green wood brought him back to his senses. He swung apelike, hand over hand, as fast as he could, but before he reached the thicker base of the limb, it gave way. Luckily, the limb did not break completely away, but held by a splinter, slamming him against the tree trunk as it swung downward.

He nursed his scratches as he watched for movement from the hacienda. When he was sure he had woken no one, he got up, found his hat, and limped to the large gate at the front of the hacienda. This, too, he found bolted, and he cursed Carlos under his breath for not keeping his promise. He ran as quietly as he could to the back of the hacienda, climbed over the stable fences, and checked the rear gate—also secured.

But Bart had planned for the worst. Under the straw in one of the stalls he found the crude ladder he had built for emergency use. He leaned it against the adobe wall of the house and began climbing. He had made it barely tall enough. From the top rung he still had to scramble to get on the roof. The rest would be easy, he told himself as he lay on his back, catching his breath. Maybe Bitora was right to demand this. He would certainly remember it. It would make a good story someday. He opened the collar of his riding jacket and let the starry New Mexico night cool the sweat around his neck.

In the corner of the courtyard opposite the well, an old grapevine clung to a trellis mounted to the adobe wall. Bart had tested it a few days before. It would hold his weight. After creeping across the flat roof, he sat on the edge of the high courtyard wall and lowered himself on the vine. It was thick as his arms and firmly placed after decades of cultivation.

Halfway down, however, he felt the trellis coming loose from the adobes. Desperately, he reached for the younger, thinner vine. It held, but slipped through his soft archivist's hands, burning them. He stripped leaves faster than a herd of goats. The fall through the grapevine must have sounded like a bull in a rose hedge fence, and he was amazed that the entire hacienda hadn't been awakened. It was going to hurt to hold Bitora with those chafed palms.

He had to watch out for Sebastiana now, especially as he passed the wing that led to the servants quarters. Carlos said she had been taking turns with the housemen, threatening to blackmail any who refused her. Bart saw no sign of her, though, and tip-toed to the well, which stood under Bitora's corner of the courtyard.

The most logical route would have been up the stairs and in through Bitora's bedroom door. But she had ruled that out. He must climb the balcony as her father had done to win her mother, a generation ago.

With his sore hands and his battered shins, he crawled onto the little shingled roof that covered the well. Locking his boot heels over the peak of the roof, he stood precariously upright and looked with dread toward Bitora's balcony. He would have to leap to reach it. It looked much farther away in the dark than it had last weekend in the daylight. It was his final test.

He drew several deep breaths, searching for courage in the night air. Finally he gathered himself in a crouch and vaulted. His hands barely caught the bottom rail of the balcony. After kicking at thin air for a minute, he managed to pull himself up, pausing triumphantly to look down on the courtyard.

He caught his breath, then tested Bitora's balcony door, finding it unlocked. She had kept her word better than Carlos. She had even oiled the hinges as she promised. He whispered her name in the darkness of her room. He could hear her breathing deeply. He couldn't believe she had fallen asleep. He would have thought she'd be too excited. He had never visited her room before. The layout was a mystery to him, but he spied the bright value of linen in the dark, and eased toward her bed on the floor.

He knelt beside her and put his hand on her soft face. Her warmth at once soothed his injuries. He felt her stir, then heard her speak.

"Bartolome?" she said.

"Expecting somebody else?"

"You came."

"Of course. Now, for heaven's sake, will you finally agree to marry me?"

"Yes," she whispered, slipping her arm around his neck. "I was going to marry you even if you did not come."

"*What?*" he said, pulling back from her bed.

She held on to him. "But, because you have proven yourself, now you will have your reward."

Bart weakened as she pulled him onto her mattress. He had judged well that look she had given him in the courtyard. There was more to this test than a proposal. He could read her thoughts like poetry.

Then, like a sudden avalanche, the world seemed to cave in. Bart gasped with such a start that he almost sucked Bitora's upper lip from her face. He rolled off of her as light flooded the room, and he saw Antonio, wearing night clothes and a visage of murder, carrying a lamp and a sawed-off shotgun.

"Bartolome! You?"

"It's not what you think!" Bart said, scrambling to his feet. "Bitora, tell him!"

The hacendado shot a fierce glance at his daughter. She only screamed and pulled the covers over her head.

Antonio cocked both hammers of the double-barrel. "And to you I gave my trust," he growled. "Now you will pay for this insult."

"I can explain!" Bart said. "Bitora, tell him how it is!" He saw her peeking out from under her blanket.

"Enough!" the father cried. He backed Bart into a corner and put the twin muzzles against his chest. "Do you have any idea how I am going to make you pay for this invasion?"

"But . . . but . . ."

"I am going to make you . . ."—Antonio paused and grinned victoriously—"marry my daughter."

Bart gulped, then squinted. He couldn't quite gather what had happened. He heard Antonio laughing and saw the shotgun lowered from his chest. He heard Bitora shrieking and saw her throw back her blankets. She was lying fully dressed in bed. Gradually, the realization sank in, and he slapped his tender palm against his forehead in relief and embarrassment.

People began to flood into the room. Sebastiana was among the first. She did not laugh, but she glared at Bart with a look of contempt and satisfaction. The house servants came in after her. Many of them had suffered Bart's minor pranks over the past three years, and now they had their collective revenge.

"You, too, Carlos?" Bart asked as the cook entered.

"Who do you think bolted the gates?" Antonio said, "and sawed halfway through the limb of that tree, and loosened the trellis?"

Bart shook his head and gritted his teeth in a forced grin. "I could have broken my neck!"

Antonio put his arm around Bart's shoulder. "Perhaps you will think of that the next time you bind the antlers of a deer to the head of a ram!"

Howls of laughter rang in Bitora's room as she came to Bart's side to soothe his bruised pride. He had scaled the walls. Now he had his reward. He would marry Bitora. He let his own laughter join that of his tricksters.

FOURTEEN

To satisfy Antonio's traditional streak, Bart had to accomplish the formalities of betrothal. First he wrote a letter of proposal, describing his genealogy and his personal financial circumstances. This letter he sent to Antonio, who answered it fifteen days later, approving the proposal.

Bart then wrote to his father in Houston, whom he had

not heard from in over three years. He also wrote to Randy
Hendricks in Washington, D.C., who had been appointed
third assistant to the under secretary of Interior. George
Young made no reply to his son's wedding announcement,
but Randy Hendricks sent his kindest regards and best
wishes.

The wedding was scheduled for the spring, soon after
Bitora turned twenty. Following the honeymoon, Bart
would resign his position at the Territorial Archives, move
to the hacienda, and take over the operations of the
Montoya grant's eleven square leagues.

In the meantime, the official betrothal ceremony, the *prendario,* would come in conjunction with the hacienda's
annual fall fiesta. Since Vernon Regis had purchased the
Montoya herds and begun leasing the grazing lands, the
fiestas had grown yearly in size and revelry. The speculator seemed to enjoy them more than anyone, and even invested some of his own money in food and drink for the
festivities.

To Bart's relief, Regis had ceased his frequent visits to
the hacienda that had been common during the court case
against the Montoya grant. It seemed the subtle warning
Bart had given him in the corridor the night of the first
lease signing had taken its desired effect. Even when he
came to *fiestas,* Regis kept his distance from Sebastiana.
Bart remained quite friendly with the speculator.

Bitora's *prendario* took place before the fiesta celebra-
tion could begin. First, she made her appearance before
Bart, dressed stunningly in her finest gown. The onlookers gasped at her grace and beauty as she performed the
traditional curtsy for her intended. Tomasa and Gregoria,
both married to Santa Fe men now, appeared rather jealous
of their younger sister's beauty, and the brothers, Francisco
and Vicente, seethed throughout the entire *prendario.* Bart
was the first Anglo to marry into the Montoya family, and
they considered it a scandal.

As required by custom, Bart presented Bitora with her *donas*—her wedding dress, plus all the rebozos, silks, and linens he could afford. His offering was so meager that Francisco hissed audibly.

Then Antonio presented Bart with Bitora's dowry—two of his finest saddle horses, a stallion and a mare. With them, the couple would begin their own fine line of mounts.

After many toasts and much wine, Antonio gestured toward the musicians. But before Bart and Bitora could dance, he ushered them down an empty corridor and into his office, commanding them to sit before his desk.

"Perhaps you are thinking that I have been less than generous with the dowry, Bartolome."

"To the contrary. The horses are more than I expected. The main thing is that I'll have Bitora as my wife." He actually meant it. The land and livestock, the hacienda, the horses—all paled in comparison to the prospect of having Bitora by his side forever.

"Ahh!" Antonio said, swatting at Bart as if he were a fly. "You young people do not understand the importance of an advantageous marriage. I like you, Bartolome, but if I thought for one second that you would fail to provide for my daughter, I would never allow you to marry her."

"But I have no money," Bart said. "You could have married her off to a lot of *ricos.*"

"Of money I have enough to last myself and my children a lifetime. I give you my blessing for a better reason, Bartolome. You have something this family needs dearly."

"What's that?" Bart asked. "A sense of humor?"

"No, *idiota!*" The old man chuckled. "Bitora and I have enough of that to make up for the others. But what you have, Bartolome, is a love for the land. I have watched your eyes when we ride together. I have seen you pull weeds and treat wounded trees and plunge your face into our springs. Tomasa and Gregoria married men of the city. Francisco and Vicente think only of money and business. But you, Bartolome. You are my hope that the Montoya grant will remain indivisible for generations to come."

Bart looked at Bitora. She shrugged. Neither knew exactly what Antonio was getting at.

"I would not say it in front of my other children, for they would ruin this evening for us all, but Bitora's dowry includes more than just a couple of horses, amigo. I have rewritten my will. The older children will divide equally among them all the money I leave, the buildings in Santa Fe, the trading houses, and the freight lines. Bitora will receive the land and the hacienda. And you, as her husband, will become master of it."

Bart felt a surge of glory, followed by panic. Forty-eight thousand acres! How would he manage it all? Then Bitora took his hand, calming him. And he realized that Don Antonio would be there to help him for years yet. The old man enjoyed vigorous health.

"I have already discussed it with Vernon," Antonio continued. "The latest lease you helped me to witness this afternoon is valid only until you and Bitora are married in the spring. At that time, I will purchase the livestock back from him, and you will have your work cut out for you."

The panic welled up in Bart again. "The lease! Did you read it this year? I didn't think about it!"

Antonio laughed. "Relax, amigo. You are taking your new responsibility too seriously. I glanced at the lease. It looked like the same one I signed last year, and the year before. Nothing is going to happen to your new rancho, Bartolome. You have the land you came to New Mexico for. You have my blessing to marry my daughter, and you have your life before you. What more could you ask?"

Bart smiled and sighed. "I won't let you down."

"Of course not, my friend. Now, let us go back to the fiesta, before Bitora's brothers and sisters guess that we are conspiring against them." He shook Bart's hand, kissed his daughter, and led them back to the party.

When Bart Young stepped out into the courtyard—*his* courtyard—the music and dancing almost dizzied him. He filled his lungs with cool October air as he put his arm around Bitora's waist. He found his eyes sweeping the courtyard, searching.

He located Tomasa, Gregoria, Vicente, Francisco, and all their spouses. Still, his eyes searched. He did not quite know why. He found Sebastiana, whispering in the ear of the guitar player. His eyes pulled away from her, too.

There was Carlos, the cook, carving the beef, a smile on his face. And Hilario, the agreeable young man who had recently taken the job as Don Antonio's valet and coachman.

Still, there was someone missing. Bart continued to search the crowd. Suddenly he realized that his ears were straining to separate from the music and conversation the voice of the land speculator, Vernon Regis. He didn't really know why, but he wanted to see the lawyer. His eyes probed every shadow and alcove. It was useless. Regis was nowhere to be found.

FIFTEEN

B art had only been asleep a couple of hours when the shouts woke him. Someone was calling Antonio's name loudly from the courtyard. He rubbed his eyes, got out of bed, and squinted against the morning glare as he opened the balcony doors.

Below, he saw Vernon Regis and four armed men wearing badges. "A little early, isn't it?" he grumbled.

Regis shot a glance up at the balcony. "Where's Antonio?"

"Asleep. The fiesta went dang near till dawn. Where were you last night? We missed you."

"Just wake the old man up."

"Can't it wait?"

"Wake him up!"

"Something wrong?"

"Dammit, Young, I said wake the old man up and get him out here. Now!"

He woke Antonio, and they wondered together what had the speculator so riled. They went to the courtyard and found a crowd of groggy farmers and servants gathering. Regis was waiting with two U.S. marshals, and two deputy sheriffs.

"Amigo," Antonio said, "what brings you here so early?

"You knew our agreement. You're to be out of here today, so you'd better get started packing your things."

Antonio stared in confusion. "What is this?"

The speculator snapped his finger at one of the marshals, who stepped forward and put a court order in Antonio's hand. Bart looked over the hacendado's shoulder as they read it. It required the Montoya family to be out of the hacienda by midnight.

"This is madness!" Antonio cried. "Who orders me from my own home?"

"You mean *my* home," Regis replied.

"Vernon, what is this all about?" Bart demanded.

"You know what it's about, Young. You witnessed the contract yourself. I bought the Montoya grant last night."

A flood of worry came down on the hacendados. They suddenly saw beyond the court challenge of two years before, Regis's false friendship, the mutually beneficial lease agreement. They had been drawn stupidly into a snare that was now tightening around their necks.

Suddenly, Francisco was charging from the crowd, and

Bart thought the younger Montoya would attack Regis. But, instead, he turned on his own father.

"You stupid old fool!" he shouted. "You have given away our land for nothing!"

"Shut up," Bart said, shoving Francisco in the chest. "As I recall, it was you who advised your father to lease to this son of a bitch in the first place."

"You brought this Anglo lawyer here yourself!" Francisco shouted. "You are with him in this!"

Bart felt so instantly insulted that he belted Francisco in the eye. The two of them traded punches and pulled at each other's jackets until Antonio came between them.

"Stop it!" he cried.

Regis was chuckling.

Bart saw a swift movement from the crowd, and knew it was Bitora, rushing forward to scratch the eyes out of the man who had taken her land. But before she could reach Regis, one of the deputies caught her around the waist and lifted her from the ground.

Bart sprang again, this time on the deputy who had grabbed Bitora. The three other lawmen wrestled Bart to the ground, one of them drawing a revolver and putting it against his head.

"Easy, son," said one of the marshals, a big blond-haired man. He looked up at Antonio. "Regis has a court order, Señor Montoya. We've got no choice but to escort you out of here. There's no use in fighting it this way."

The speculator's chuckle became an outright laugh.

"Bartolome!" Antonio said. "Stop kicking and get up from the ground! You, too, Bitora! Behave yourself! Hilario, saddle the horses! We are going to Santa Fe. Vicente, you will see the governor. Francisco, you will speak to the judge who gave this order. Bartolome and I will find a lawyer to fight this foolishness in court."

Regis's guffaws echoed throughout the courtyard. "You

should have thought of that before you signed the contract and took my money. Now, get out. Everybody!" He lunged at the confused farmers, making hideous faces at them, laughing.

Antonio gave the orders in Spanish, and the crowd began to disperse. Bart moved with the Montoya men toward the stables, taking Bitora by the arm as he passed her. They had just reached the edge of the courtyard, when the astonished gasps of the farmers' wives turned their heads.

Sebastiana was embracing Vernon Regis right in the middle of the courtyard. The grotesque head bent on its toothpick neck over her comely face. Bart reached for Antonio's vest, not knowing whether the hacendado would try to murder them now, or wait until later. He felt the old man trembling, and turned to see his face contorted with ire. Antonio pointed a gnarled finger at the obscene couple in his courtyard, but could not conjure words. He turned into the stables, his eyes blazing with more hatred than Bart had ever seen any man display.

Every avenue they tested closed before them. Regis's case was sound. He claimed he had purchased the Montoya grant from Antonio fairly. Antonio's signature, after all, was on the paper that listed, explicitly, the terms of the sale.

Antonio argued that it had been drawn up to resemble the lease agreement with the same number of pages and paragraphs, signatures in the same places, and that he had been duped into believing it was the same lease agreement he had signed twice before.

To win their home back, however, the Montoyas would have to prove Regis guilty of conspiracy, and not a lawyer in town would face him in court.

The *rico* came to Bart's boardinghouse room after dark with his mattress rolled under his arm. "May I stay with you?" he said.

"Of course," Bart replied, opening the door wide. "But, I thought—"

"Francisco turned me away. Vicente's wife would not let him take me in, either. Tomasa agreed to let Bitora stay at her house, but she was too angry at me. Gregoria said that I have lost the home of her childhood, and I deserve no other. I was too ashamed to go to a hotel. Everyone in Santa Fe knows what a fool I am."

Bart pulled his old friend into his room. "Did you have any supper?"

"I have no appetite." He spread his mattress on the floor. "I am going to sleep. That will give me some peace until I wake."

Bart sat on his own bed as Antonio lay down. The old man's eyes stayed closed for a long time, and Bart thought he was asleep. He dimmed the lantern and thought about turning in himself.

"Do you still want to marry my daughter?" the small voice said from the floor.

Bart stared for a long moment. "Don't insult me, Antonio. It was you who taught me the value of an advantageous marriage. I would marry Bitora if you were dirt poor. There are some advantages you don't measure in square leagues or silver."

The eyes did not open, but the face on the floor smiled.

Bart wrote a letter to Randy Hendricks, asking for assistance and counsel. He even wrote to his father in Houston. Perhaps George Young would come to his aid in this time of need. The reply from Houston arrived first. George Young had died weeks ago. He had told no one where his son could be found. Not until the letter from Santa Fe had arrived could Bart be notified.

Bart had once envisioned coaxing his father to Santa Fe—maybe even tricking him there. When the old lawyer saw how well his son had done, he would forgive Bart for not finishing law school to join the family firm. But now that dream had flown like dust.

The letter from Randy Hendricks proved almost as bad. Yes, he would like to help an old friend, but as counsel for Department of the Interior, he was advising the General Land Office not to get involved in any investigation. That would not be politically expedient at this time. It was a matter for the Justice Department. Let the courts handle it. He was sure Bart would understand.

But Bart did not understand. He knew all about Randy's ambition, but a friend was a friend. He wondered what men learned in that last year of law school that made them abandon their loyalties and ethics.

He kept assuring Antonio that they would find a way to fight back, but his hopes were dwindling.

With the first snowfall to blanket Santa Fe, Bart found himself brooding in his office in the archives. A box arrived from the surveyor general's office. R. T. Fincher needed a routine title search accomplished before he could approve the sale of a tract of public domain to a speculator. Bart dove into the case, almost relieved to have some task to take his mind off Vernon Regis.

But the speculator's name was the first thing that leaped out at him from the land office documents. The second thing was the location: the Sacramento Mountains.

Regis was moving his operations into fresh country. He was buying canyons where he would establish cattle ranches, mountain slopes that he would strip of timber, gullies where traces of gold and silver had been discovered. It was almost as if the speculator had chosen the site to further humiliate Antonio. Hadn't Nepomeceno Montoya, Antonio's great-grandfather, won honors as a Spanish officer in the Sacramentos? Antonio had claims there that went back three generations. The idea of Vernon Regis moving in almost made Bart's stomach turn.

He virtually ransacked his own archives, searching desperately for the document that would deny Regis a claim in the Sacramentos. A lost grant. A forgotten pueblo or rancho. A title that preceded any Regis could ever buy.

There was nothing. The place was a virtual wilderness, never before settled by men who used plat maps. He would have done anything to find a paper claim to the mountains where Nepomeceno had saved the life of Comandante Hugo O'Conor. He would have coughed one up if he were able. He would have sweated one in blood. He would have forged one, were he so desperate.

Bart left his office in the middle of the afternoon. He could hardly think straight. He saw himself as an old man, trudging back and forth between the archives and the boardinghouse, day after day, never claiming his mountain domain.

The Montoya grant had been his overnight.

He wanted to see Antonio's face. He needed to talk to the old man. What could be done now? How would they right the wrong Regis had dealt them? When would the meek inherit the earth?

As he opened the door to his room, he found Antonio sitting on his bed with a revolver in his hand. He stared, shocked. "What are you doing with that gun?"

"Do not try to stop me."

"Stop you from what?"

Antonio pointed the muzzle to a newspaper on the bed beside him. "Did you see?" He picked the paper up and shook it at Bart, almost weeping as he spoke. "They have sold my grant! They call it the Regis grant now, and they have sold it!"

"Who's sold it?"

"Vernon Regis, R. T. Fincher, Lefty Harless, Alfred Nichols . . . They were all in it together, Bartolome. They have sold it all except for the hacienda, and that still belongs to Vernon Regis. He is going to *live* there."

Bart took a step forward. "Give me that Colt, Antonio."

"Go back to your archives. I have work to do with this pistol. I am going to kill Regis first. Then, if I get away, I am going to my old hacienda to kill that whore who called herself my wife."

"Then what?" Bart said. "You'll rot in jail if they don't hang you."

Antonio shook his head. "It is the only way, amigo. Now, leave me!"

"It's not the only way, it's just the stupid way. I just had a thought over at the archives. It seemed a little loco at first, but now I can see it working. We haven't been thinking big enough, Antonio. We've only been thinking of getting even with Regis. We should have been planning all along to go him one better."

"What are you talking about?" Antonio demanded.

Bart sat on the bed and put his arm around the old man's shoulders. "How would you like to play a little trick on Vernon Regis?" he said. "No, not a little trick. A big one. Maybe the biggest ever."

"What do you mean? How big?"

Bart grinned. "Let's say"—he looked blankly at the ceiling—"a million acres worth."

PART TWO

SIXTEEN

The crate weighed a good twenty-five pounds, but Bart carried it almost without effort. The warm breath of spring was whispering across the Santa Fe plaza, the cottonwoods sprouting tender leaves. A butterfly perched on one of them, sunning its wings. Bart felt a hundred fluttering in his stomach.

Ulysses S. Grant was out of the White House, Rutherford B. Hayes was in, and with him had come a new contingent of political appointees all the way down to the Office of the Surveyor General of New Mexico.

R. T. Fincher had gone back East with his spoils, and one Rudolph Raspberry had taken his place. Raspberry knew perhaps six words of Spanish. His background in land title litigation did not exist. Of surveying he knew zero. A compass to Raspberry was something to draw circles with. Yet, he possessed unimpeachable integrity. Charges of corruption in the surveyor general's office had reached Washington. Raspberry was the only honest man available to clean the place up.

Today was Raspberry's first full day in office, and Bart had made one of the first appointments to meet with him. It was the perfect opportunity to launch his little prank on Vernon Regis. When he entered the office, he found Raspberry familiarizing himself with his new surroundings.

"Hello, Bart," said Raspberry's secretary, George Baird. Baird had served under Fincher and was helping his new boss get settled in.

Bart nodded and dropped his crate on Raspberry's desk. "Howdy, George. And you must be Rudolph Raspberry," he added, extending his hand. "Bart Young."

"Bart administers the Territorial Archives over at the Palace of the Governors," George explained. "He's one of our foremost experts on Spanish land grants."

"Pleased to meet you, Mr. Young," Raspberry said. "What brings you here today?"

Without waiting for an invitation, Bart sat down, crossing his legs casually in the uncomfortable chair. "I've a little story to tell you."

"You'll excuse me, then," George said. "I've heard enough of Bart's stories."

"No," Bart insisted. "Stay. This tale will fascinate you."

Raspberry shrugged and motioned for George to take a seat.

The archivist put his palms together in front of his lips, and stared at the ceiling. "Where shall I begin?" He paused for a long moment, building suspense.

"Fifteen years ago, my father came to New Mexico as a volunteer in General Sibley's brigade during the Civil War. He was badly wounded in the fighting at Glorieta Pass, and spent months convalescing at the rancho of Don Antonio Montoya, in the hacienda east of town that now belongs to Vernon Regis.

"During his recovery, my father became very friendly with Don Antonio. Because my father was a lawyer, Antonio shared a family secret with him. It seems that for generations, there had been a legend in the Montoya family about a lost Spanish land grant—one that would entitle the Montoyas to great expanses of valuable property. Antonio was unfamiliar with United States courts, and he wanted my father to find out what it would take to prove the existence of such a grant."

"Wait a minute," George said. "Antonio already had eleven square leagues at that time."

"I'm not talking about the Montoya grant here in Santa Fe County," Bart said, "lately referred to as the Regis grant. I'm talking about an entirely different grant—one that was rumored to have been granted to one of Antonio's ancestors by the king of Spain, a hundred years ago."

The new surveyor general was in a stupor, watching the conversation bounce between his secretary and the archivist.

"Anyway," Bart continued, "when my father returned to Texas after the war, his health never permitted him to pursue Antonio's request for help. But he confided in me, and I found the story so intriguing that I came to New Mexico myself to help Antonio. I managed to get the job in the archives, and there I searched for years, until finally, with Antonio's help, I began to piece together the fascinating tale of the lost Montoya grant."

Rudolph Raspberry looked at his secretary, then back at Bart. "This is all new to me, Mr. Young. I'll have to ask you what your point is, and why it should concern this office."

"That's what I've come to explain," Bart said. "In the past, this office has been so plagued with corruption that I didn't dare risk bringing this story forward. But your reputation for honesty precedes you, and I am going to put my trust in you."

"Please do," Raspberry said.

"I would like to take you back over a century, to 1775. That year, Hugo O'Conor, Comandante Inspector of New Spain's Northern Frontier, campaigned against the Apache Indians in the Sacramento Mountains, located in what is now southern New Mexico Territory. A garrison captain named Nepomeceno Montoya saved O'Conor's life during the bloodiest battle of the campaign. In return, O'Conor recommended that the king of Spain grant a large tract of land to Nepomeceno, in those very mountains where he had fought so valiantly. The recommendation went up the ranks, through the viceroy of New Spain, and across the ocean to the king.

"In 1777, exactly one hundred years ago, gentlemen, King Carlos the Third signed the royal *cedula* granting Nepomeceno Montoya virtually all of the Sacramento Mountains. This grant of land was referred to as a barony, and thus Nepomeceno became the first baron of the Sacramentos. In addition, His Majesty had bestowed upon Nepomeceno the Star of the Order of Carlos the Third, and made him a Knight of the Golden Fleece and a member of the Military Order of Montesa."

The surveyor general and his secretary stared speechlessly. George raised one eyebrow in warning.

"I know that look, George," Bart said. "You're thinking that this is one of my jokes. You couldn't be more mistaken. I'm dead serious."

"Mr. Young," Raspberry said. "Once and for all, how does this fanciful legend concern this office?"

"Because it's not just a legend. Our investigations over the past seven years have proven the legend to be truthful in fact. Nepomeceno Montoya, the first baron of the Sacramentos, was Antonio's great-grandfather. That makes Antonio the fourth baron. And I—because I married Antonio's daughter Bitora, and because Spanish custom allows a husband to assume his wife's hereditary titles—will be the fifth baron of the Sacramentos.

He turned to George. "Actually, Bitora's older brothers and sisters got first crack at the title, but none of them cared to move into the wilderness to take possession of the barony." He shrugged and turned back to Raspberry. "So, you're looking at the future fifth baron of the Sacramentos. But I'm getting ahead of myself. Let me return to Nepomeceno Montoya, the first baron."

"If you must," Raspberry said, smirking incredulously.

"Nepomeceno was a bit eccentric. He was consumed

with paranoia, convinced that his enemies—jealous army officers—were plotting to destroy his title to the barony. So he scattered the grant documents throughout New Spain and New Mexico, hiding them in obscure files in old missions, forts, and archives. These documents included Hugh O'Conor's original petition to the viceroy, the viceroy's letter to the king, the king's *cedula,* reports and orders from every level of government. Together, they proved Nepomeceno's title to his barony.

"It seems the first baron didn't even trust his own children with his barony. At least not all of them. He told only one son about the grant. This son, Miguel Montoya, became the second baron of the Sacramentos, and inherited the barony by means of a secret codicil. The second baron passed it on to his son, the third baron, Estanislado Montoya. Estanislado passed the barony down to his favorite son, Antonio, again by means of a secret codicil."

"Let me see if I understand correctly," the surveyor general said, interrupting. "Your father-in-law, Antonio Montoya, claims to be the fourth baron of the Sacramentos, yet cannot prove it because the old documents establishing his title have been lost? Scattered across the Territory of New Mexico and the Republic of Old Mexico?"

"That," Bart said, snapping his fingers, "is where the situation stood when I came to New Mexico, seven years ago, and agreed to help Antonio find the lost documents. For years, our search proved fruitless. I wrote to archivists and records keepers all over Mexico, and found nothing. It seemed Nepomeceno had hidden the documents so effectively that they couldn't be traced in any way. Until—"

"Until what?" George Baird demanded. "Get to the point, Bart!"

Bart grinned. He had his listeners right where he wanted them. "I wrote a letter to the National Library of Mexico, desperate for information on Nepomeceno. To my surprise, the head librarian wrote back, informing me that he had in his collection a handwritten manuscript authored by Nepomeceno Montoya himself. A book of riddles!"

"Riddles!" Raspberry put his hands on his head. "Sir, this entire story has become a riddle!"

"A real-life riddle," Bart replied, "which I will solve for you in a moment. You see, Antonio went to Mexico City to copy his great-grandfather's book of riddles. He brought the copy back here to Santa Fe where we could study it. It consisted of puzzles, conundrums, mathematical brain teasers—riddles of every description. At first we thought it just another example of Nepomeceno's eccentricity. Then, we began to see its genius.

"After deciphering all the riddles, my wife, Bitora, noticed a pattern. Often, the answer to a riddle would be the name of a Mexican city. Such a riddle was always followed by three mathematical problems. I'll give you an example:

"One riddle was of the sort commonly used to vex school children. It said that the Viceroy of New Spain was leaving the city of Mexico, traveling north, in a coach that would travel at a certain speed. If it traveled at that speed for a certain amount of time, would the Viceroy reach Durango, Chihuahua, or Santa Fe? The answer was Santa Fe.

"Now, after this riddle, we found three mathematical puzzles. The answers to these three problems were sixty-two, seven, and thirty-one. The moment I saw those three numbers after the name of Santa Fe, it struck a familiar chord with me. You see, in the archives, we still organize our documents by the old Spanish system: in numbered cases, drawers, and files. Any document can be located by its three numbers. Nepomeceno's book of riddles was trying to tell me something: Santa Fe archives, case sixty-two, drawer seven, file thirty-one!

"Antonio and I rushed to the archives and looked in the

appropriate file. There, mixed in with the documents that were supposed to be there—I believe they were militia rosters, or some such thing—we found several documents pertaining to the barony of the Sacramentos. One was a sketch map drawn by an alcalde in 1781 that outlined the boundaries of the barony!"

"The book of riddles was a book of codes?" Raspberry asked.

"Exactly!" Bart said. "We wrote down all the answers to the riddles on a piece of paper. We came up with combinations like Guadalajara, seventeen, ninety-three, fifty-two. Or Mexico City, eighty-nine, ten, forty. Antonio had to go to Mexico, Texas, Arizona, and California in order to find all the documents, but they were all just where Nepomeceno had hidden them, a hundred years ago. He found them all: The *cedula* signed by King Carlos the Third: the Act of Possession conducted by the alcalde on the actual soil of the barony of the Sacramentos; everything! Where he couldn't talk the archivists out of the documents, he had official copies made and notarized."

Bart stood and covered the distance to Raspberry's desk in one stride of his gangly legs. "And, here, gentlemen," he said, patting the top of the crate he had carried in, "are the documents that will prove to this office, and to the Congress of the United States of America, that the Most Excellent Señor Don Antonio Geronimo Montoya de Cordoba y Chaves de Oca, fourth baron of the Sacramentos, knight of the Golden Fleece, caballero of the Chamber of His Majesty, member of the Military Order of Montesa, is the true and rightful owner of some one million acres situated in and around the Sacramento Mountains in southern New Mexico!" He grasped his lapels and stood in triumph before his listeners, defying his knees to tremble.

"You can't be serious," George said. "Do you mean to say that you are submitting to this office a lost Spanish land grant?"

Bart laughed. "How would such a thing be possible, George? This grant is not lost, it has been found! Open the crate and see the documents for yourself."

George looked at Raspberry and shrugged.

The new surveyor general stood excitedly and fumbled with the brass latches on the crate. He lifted the lid, flipping it back. Reaching into the crate, he removed a weathered leaf of parchment, handling it delicately. "What the devil is this?" he asked, baffled by the old pen script.

"This," Bart declared, "is the royal *cedula,* signed by King Carlos the Third one hundred years ago, entitling Nepomeceno Montoya to two hundred fifty square leagues in the Sacramento Mountains." He removed another wrinkled sheet from the crate. "And this is an order by the royal supreme court, directing the governor of New Mexico to make the grant." Another sheet of old paper fell on top of the first two. "Here we have the alcalde's report stating that no existing claims conflict with the proposed grant. And this one is the codicil to the will of the first baron of the Sacramentos, giving his son exclusive title to the barony. Now, here's an interesting document. . . ."

As Bart piled the sheaves of parchment higher, Raspberry stared with wonder, at a loss as to what he should make of it all. Finally he turned to his secretary. "Am I to take this matter seriously, George?"

Baird blew the dust from an old directive. "I don't think I've ever seen a grant so well documented," he said. "These papers are definitely genuine. A lost Spanish grant. Leave it to Bart Young."

"Handle those with care," Bart warned. "They're a hundred years old, you know."

SEVENTEEN

Bart came up the street at a trot, his eyes fixed on the adobe at the end of the row. The little house had insufficient space for the four people who lived there—Antonio, Bart, Bitora, and the baby, Nepomeceno—but it was only temporary.

"What are you doing here at this hour?" Bitora asked when he burst in.

He found her lying on a mattress on the floor, holding her giggling baby above her. He took the child away from her and pretended to gnaw at its ear like a hungry dog. The baby laughed with surprise and joy to see his father.

"Raspberry wants to see me and Antonio," Bart said, dangling his son upside down by the heels. "No, not you, Nepo, just me and Grandpa. Honey, have you realized that Nepo will be the sixth baron of the Sacramentos?"

Antonio was reading his paper at the window. "What does Raspberry want?"

"He's had the grant papers a week now. I suspect he's going to tell us he'll recommend confirmation to Congress." He handed little Nepo back to Bitora.

Antonio folded his newspaper. "Then we must not keep him waiting. I am anxious to settle my barony." He rose with the air of a grandee and reached for his sombrero.

Bart kissed his wife and baby and left with his father-in-law. When they were safely away from the house, they looked at each other uncertainly.

"What does it really mean?" Antonio said.

"I don't know. But, remember. If they challenge our title, you have the right to get madder than hell. You are baron of the Sacramentos, Knight of the Golden Fleece, Caballero of—"

"I know," Antonio said. "Caballero of the Chamber of

His Majesty, Member of the Military Order of Montesa."
He smiled. "I know it well." He had recited his hereditary
titles a thousand times over the past three years.

It began after Bart's honeymoon with Bitora. By that time,
he and Antonio had been secretly plotting for months.
They would not even let Bitora in on their scheme, for
doing so would make her an accessory to fraud.

When their plans were complete, to the last detail, Antonio had called the family together at Vicente's house and
told them the legend of the barony of the Sacramentos,
adding that Bartolome would now help him locate the
long-lost grant papers. Vicente and Francisco scoffed. Tomasa and Gregoria hung their heads in shame, believing
their father had lost his mind.

Bitora, on the other hand, joined in the search. She went
to the archives every night with Bart and Antonio, making it impossible for them to produce any forgeries.

"You must give me a grandchild," Antonio finally told
Bart. "That will give Bitora something else to worry about
and allow us to get on with our work."

"I've been trying," Bart said resolutely.

After she got pregnant, Bart refused to let Bitora come
to the archives, insisting she must get her rest while carrying his child. That gave him and Antonio the privacy they
needed to practice the art of forgery.

First, they had to find parchment that would resemble
the ancient documents. Antonio turned up some likely
material in the back of one of his warehouses, but there
was not enough. They finally had to buy new stock from
various Santa Fe trading houses, intending to antique it
after applying the forgeries.

Next, they had to figure out how to fade the ink to the
proper value, and make it soak through the paper as in
some older documents. They diluted it with water and al-

cohol, exposed it to sunlight, painted it with acids, finally arriving at a combination of techniques that would make it appear a century old.

Bart used an old quill pen to apply the ink, working for months at matching the flourishes of long-dead Spanish scribes. He forged the signatures of alcaldes, governors, viceroys, and kings. He spent nights working on a single page, and when he got home, Bitora would chide him for spending so much time away.

"When I have the baby, I know where you are going to be," she complained. "In those cursed archives!"

While Bart fabricated documents, Antonio traveled from Texas to California, Santa Fe to Mexico City. He charmed archivists and records keepers everywhere with his tales of the lost grant. In Mexico City, he found the actual will of his great-grandfather Nepomeceno. The will, of course, said nothing about the barony. That was why Bart had struck upon the idea of the secret codicils— additions to the wills.

Antonio smuggled Nepomeceno's will out of the Mexican archives so Bart could learn the first "baron's" signature and place it on the forged codicil. Months later, he went back to Mexico City and returned the will without it having been missed.

After twenty-one months, the forgeries were completed. The next several weeks were spent staining them with various vegetable juices, drying them in the sun, folding and pressing them between heavy books, fading them with acids, packing them in dust.

Bart fabricated wax seals for some of the forgeries. He made plaster casts of authentic seals he found in the archives, then damaged the originals so that his copies could not be traced to them. He had to mix the wax by hand to achieve the correct hues: the king's blue, and the Inquisition's red.

They had decided that the king of Spain would grant

Nepomeceno two-hundred fifty square leagues. But the problem in fixing the boundaries was that there were not going to be any old Spanish survey markers around the Sacramentos, since the barony never really existed. To solve this problem, they decided to use one natural landmark as a corner of the barony, and figure the boundaries from that corner.

Studying the few available maps of the area, they chose the confluence of the Rio Bonito and the Rio Ruidoso as the northeastern corner of the barony. From this corner the boundary ran twenty leagues to the southeastern corner, whence it turned westward and ran twelve and a half leagues to the southwestern corner, whence it turned northward and ran twenty leagues to the northwestern corner, whence it turned eastward and returned to the confluence of the two rivers.

The huge rectangle closed in every peak and virtually every foothill associated with the Sacramento Range. When Bart converted the old Spanish dimensions, he found the barony measuring about thirty-three miles east and west by fifty-three miles north and south—over seventeen hundred square miles.

Finally, one late night in the archives, the tricksters spread the documents on the floor to look at them. They included scores of orders, reports, wills, codicils, land patents, petitions, maps, and royal edicts. Bart knew what the surveyor general required of a grant to recommend approval to Congress. His perfect forgeries would leave no doubt. Every line and flourish had been calculated to convince. The Spanish was flawless, checked and rechecked by Antonio.

After admiring and scrutinizing the documents, the forgers gathered them and stashed them in a locked drawer in Bart's office—except for the book of riddles. This all-important forgery would have to be planted in Mexico.

Antonio departed for Mexico City, the book of riddles

hidden in his bag. Arriving, he disguised himself as an old peasant and donated the book of riddles to the national library, saying his father had given it to him as a boy.

Weeks later, Bart wrote the Mexican library, requesting information on Nepomeceno, and was informed about the book of riddles. Antonio then made another trip south to copy the book, though he knew very well what it contained.

Bitora found the book of riddles absorbing, as Bart had hoped she would. She tore through the mathematical problems like lightning, and soon noticed that they came in sets of three. Bart and Antonio shrugged when she first told them. Then, several days later, Bitora realized that each set of three was preceded by a riddle answered by the name of a Mexican city.

"By golly!" Bart said. "I think you've stumbled onto something!"

That was when Bart and Antonio ran to the archives in the middle of the night and returned with the first set of documents pertaining to the lost barony of the Sacramentos.

Bitora was ecstatic. The fact that she had discovered the code in the book of riddles made her as much a part of the barony as her father or her husband. If she hadn't had an infant to take care of, she would have gone with Antonio to Mexico, Texas, Arizona, and California, to find the other documents referred to in the book of riddles. But Antonio had to accomplish that task on his own since he was not, of course, going to find documents, but to plant them.

In Guadalajara he planted three of the most important documents—the royal *cedula,* the alcalde's act of possession, and the viceroy's directive to the governor—in case number seventeen, drawer number ninety-three, and file number fifty-two, slipping them in with some obscure probate proceedings. When he brought these documents to the attention of the archivist, whom he had befriended during earlier visits, the man swallowed his story about the coded book of riddles without hesitation and let Antonio borrow the documents from the archives, requiring only his signature as security.

After a few months of traveling, Antonio returned to Santa Fe in triumph with his documents. Bitora wanted to present the evidence immediately to the surveyor general. But Bart cautioned her against telling anyone, explaining they would wait another several months to see if New Mexico would get a new surveyor general after the elections. He had reservations about handing the material over to R. T. Fincher, seeing as how Fincher and Vernon Regis were such good friends.

When he heard that Fincher was out, and a new man—Rudolph Raspberry—was coming in, Bart knew the time had arrived to launch the grand jest on Regis.

Now he was walking to the Office of the Surveyor General with his partner and father-in-law, hoping against hope that he hadn't made some silly mistake or failed to take some detail into account. He didn't see himself taking very well to prison life. But the risk was worth it. This was the only way to keep Antonio from hanging for the murders of Regis and Sebastiana. Besides, he was going to gain quite an expanse of land if it worked, to the detriment of no one but Vernon Regis.

". . . Grandee of Spain," Antonio mumbled, as they strode down the street, "bearer of the Cross of the Order of Carlos the Third, fourth baron of the Sacramentos . . ."

George Baird greeted them with a smile when they reached the Office of the Surveyor General. "Welcome, Baron," he said to Antonio.

Bart knew immediately that all was well.

"Please sit down, gentlemen," Raspberry said as the

men entered his office. "I've presented your documents to several experts, and all agree that they are of the most genuine nature. Not that I doubted you, of course, but these things must be investigated fairly."

"Then I assume that you will be recommending approval to Congress," Bart said.

Raspberry frowned and stroked his chin. "It's not quite that simple. Congress is becoming more reluctant to approve these large grants. Changes are in order. That's why I was sent here. Congress now requires a survey before considering any new grant, to determine exactly how large the thing is beforehand. And in your particular case, there are other disturbing considerations."

"Like what?" Bart asked.

"George," Raspberry said, nodding at his secretary.

Baird unrolled a plat map on Raspberry's desk and put his finger on the Sacramento Mountains. "According to the boundary descriptions on the old act of possession, your barony encompasses the whole of the Sacramento Mountain Range. The biggest problem with that is that the government ceded about half that area to the Mescalero Indians four years ago."

"Congress is very unlikely to confirm a grant that takes land away from the Indians," Raspberry added. "Especially the Mescaleros. They are just now settling down to reservation life."

"We've already thought of that," Bart said. "We'll honor the government's cession of land to the Mescaleros and issue them a quit-claim deed to their reservation."

George's mouth dropped open. "But, that will amount to about half of your barony. Roughly half a million acres."

Antonio shrugged. "As Señor Raspberry has said, Congress will not confirm my grant if I take land from the Indians. Will I have half of my barony, or none of it?"

"Besides," Bart said, "we believe the Indians will benefit

us. We'll be in a perfect position to win the government contracts to supply their rations of beef and grain. Lucien Maxwell made a lot of money off the Indians who lived on his grant, and as you know, both Antonio and I were good friends of Maxwell before he died."

"He never should have sold his grant," Antonio interrupted, shaking his head. "He survived only five years without it."

Bart put his hand on his father-in-law's shoulder. "Maxwell also used the Indians as guardsmen on his grant. The Mescaleros could serve us in the same capacity."

Raspberry exchanged a look with Baird. "So much for that problem," the surveyor general said. "But there are others." He gestured toward his secretary.

George continued: "There are several claims already taken up in the Sacramento Mountains. Congress is going to be reluctant to displace settlers."

"We don't intend to deprive anyone of home or livelihood," Bart replied. "There are only a few farms down there along the rivers. We'll quit-claim them all. They can't amount to more than a few thousand acres."

"Actually," George said, "it adds up to quite a bit more than that if you figure in Vernon Regis's holdings. He's been buying ranch, timber, and mining claims down there for the past several years. He owns quite a lot of valuable property in the Sacramentos."

"We will deal as fairly with Señor Regis as he has dealt with us in the past," Antonio said, poker-faced.

"Gossip places Mr. Regis's fairness in question," Raspberry said. "I understand the two of you had a disagreement over a piece of land a few years ago."

Antonio waved the suggestion away. "That was exaggerated in the newspapers. We had a contract. What could be more fair?"

"So, you'll quit-claim Vernon's land in the Sacramentos?" Baird asked.

Bart smiled. "We'll give him the opportunity to lease from us at fair prices. That's more than we're required to do, given the obvious validity of our title."

Raspberry grunted his approval. "Very well, gentlemen. I will include the intelligence from this interview in my report to Congress. I thank you for stopping by."

Bart rose with Antonio. "One more thing you might want to mention in that report," he said. "Neither Antonio nor I speculates in land. We're not going to sell the barony. We intend to reside permanently on it and colonize it with good, honest, hard-working settlers. Now that Antonio has finally obtained his legendary lost grant to the Sacramentos, he would no sooner give it up than he would surrender his hereditary titles."

"Titles?" George asked.

"Baron of the Sacramentos," Antonio began, jutting his chin, "Grandee of Spain, Knight of the Golden Fleece, Caballero of the Chamber of His Majesty . . ."

Baird walked the two men to the door of the office, and Bart took him by the arm and pulled him out into the street.

"George, does Regis know about our grant yet?"

"Word's getting around. I suspect he'll know soon if he doesn't already."

"Where are you keeping our documents?"

George jutted his thumb toward his office. "In our files."

"One burning lantern thrown through your window would destroy everything Antonio and I have worked for. Some of those documents are irreplaceable originals."

Baird smirked. "You're overdramatizing a little, aren't you?"

"Maybe. But you know how Vernon works. I'd feel better if those documents were stashed somewhere else for safekeeping. Hide them in the archives. He'd have to burn down the whole Palace of the Governors to get at them there. I know it's extra trouble, but I'll compensate you for it. And, for your own safety, I won't mention to anybody that you know where the documents are being held."

George laughed. "Now you're really overdoing it!"

"Am I? Do you know who Domingo Archiveque is? Rumor among the Spanish-speaking population has it that he cuts people up for Vernon." He stabbed the secretary with an imaginary knife.

Baird grew wide-eyed.

"It's best to take precautions, George. I'll pay you fifty dollars a week to guard the documents for us."

George swallowed hard. "If you insist."

Bart and Antonio shook hands with George, and headed up the street.

"What now?" Antonio asked as they walked back toward the plaza.

Bart interlaced his fingers and bent them backward, cracking his knuckles. He tipped his hat back and took in the blue New Mexico sky, inhaling a breath so fresh and dry that it almost made him dizzy. "First, I quit my job at the archives. Then, I suggest we take up residence on our barony."

"So soon? What about our confirmation from Congress?"

Bart hissed. "The more settled we are on our grant, the more likely they are to take us seriously. Besides, did Lucien Maxwell wait for Congressional approval before settling his grant in 'forty-eight?"

"No, he did not," said the fourth baron of the Sacramentos.

"Then neither will we," replied the fifth.

EIGHTEEN

I wish I could go," Francisco said, "but I must stay in Santa Fe to look after the freighting and the trading houses."

"And for me it is the legislature," Vicente added.

Bart shook the hand of each brother-in-law. "I understand. And thank you both for relinquishing the title of baron. As the older brothers, you were in line before me to inherit it."

Francisco put his hand on Bart's shoulder and tried to mask the ridicule in his voice. "You make a much more convincing baron, Bartolome."

Bart assumed a posture of high nobility, but in fact, he knew Francisco was embarrassed by the entire idea of the barony and doubted his father would ever gain legal title to the land. Vicente held the same view, as did the husbands of Tomasa and Gregoria. None intended to move to the Sacramento Mountains and risk losing his scalp to Apaches just for the dubious honor of styling himself a baron. The only members of the Montoya family to make the move would be Antonio, Bart, Bitora, and little Nepo.

It was June when the grandees began loading their wagons. Antonio had recruited two hundred farmers, shepherds, vaqueros, masons, carpenters, and general laborers, many of them from the old Montoya grant. He had promised them homes and farms on the barony. He had purchased herds of goats, sheep, cattle, and horses with which to stock his grazing lands.

Every adult male in the party had been armed with a Winchester rifle. There was the possibility of trouble with Indians—and the near certainty of reprisal from Regis.

As Bart and Antonio supervised the loading of the last wagon in front of Francisco's house, a buggy approached with a pair of passengers. Bart saw the oversized head bobbing on its shrunken neck with every bump in the road. He had been expecting Vernon Regis. Sebastiana's presence, on the other hand, took him off guard.

The speculator stopped his buggy horse with a jerk of the reins and unfolded his stork's legs as he got out. Sebastiana turned sideways on the black-leather seat and crossed her legs casually, revealing quite a length of hosiery.

Regis chuckled as he watched the men load the last wagon. "Look who we have here—the baron of Bad Jokes, and the lord of Lord-Knows-What. I can't believe you're actually going through with this scam."

Bart answered without looking at him. "You'll believe it when you get our first bill for lease payments, which, by the way, are already overdue."

A dry laugh rattled from Regis's throat. "You're out of your mind if you think you and that old man can extort one cent from me."

Bart turned his palms to the bright blue sky. "You have your choice. Pay us for the use of our land, or we'll chase you off of it with your tail between your legs. And if you choose to lease from us, this time *my* lawyer will draw up the papers."

"Go to hell, Young. You don't know what you're up against."

"If you wait until after we get Congressional confirmation, the lease fees will double," Bart warned.

Regis shook his head slowly as a grin stretched across his face. "You've got guts, Young. It's just a shame you don't have the brains to go with them." He turned back to his buggy. "I hope that pretty little wife and that baby of yours get to the Sacramentos all right. I'd hate to see something happen to them."

Bart smiled. "Do you know what our settlers call you, Vernon? *Cabeza de Calabaza.* It means 'pumpkin head.' I don't think you're that smart, though."

Regis turned to Antonio, who had been glaring silently and listening to the conversation. "By the way, Montoya. Sebastiana sends her warmest regards." He gestured toward the buggy.

Antonio spit on the ground as the speculator left, laughing. Bitora came from the house, carrying Nepo, to watch the buggy turn in the street. She had been listening at the gate. "Why did that ugly devil have to be the one to take up our land before us? It is like a curse. Everywhere we turn, he is there."

Bart glanced at Antonio. "It is some coincidence, isn't it? Serves him right, though. Now we can get back at him for taking the Montoya grant. Funny how things work out, isn't it?"

Wicked laughter growled from Antonio's throat.

"What do you find so amusing?" Bitora asked. "Didn't you hear him threaten your grandson?"

"I am thinking about how he will curse us when he gets back to the hacienda he stole from me to find it empty. When he sees that every servant in the house is coming with us today, he will probably order Sebastiana to cook his dinner, then beat her when he finds that she does not know how."

After Regis left, Bart inspected the string of thirteen *carretas* in the back of the immigrant train. Each cart was made solely of wooden members mortised together and bound with rawhide. The wheels were huge disks carved from big cottonwoods, sometimes one piece, sometimes three pieces doweled together. When in motion, they moaned and howled around the heavy cottonwood axles for want of grease. A long beam served as a tongue, an ox yoke lashed crossways to its end. The yoke itself was little more than a hand-hewn cottonwood beam, devoid of oxbows. It was lashed with rawhide to the horns of the beasts. Some of the *carretas* carried as many spare axles and wheels as cargo, and Bart assumed breakdowns would be frequent.

In addition to the *carretas,* the train included eleven American freight wagons and two strings of burros, not to mention the herds of cattle, sheep, and goats. The immigrants carried food for two months and every kind of tool necessary for building a new colony.

After siesta, the drivers cracked their whips over the backs of mules and oxen, and the train took its first lurch toward the Sacramentos. The music of the *carretas* filled the streets of Santa Fe like gobbling turkeys, yodeling ghosts, and screaming stallions breeding hollering nightmares.

The would-be barons rode at the head of the column on their finest mounts as the train passed the Santa Fe plaza. Bart saw a reporter taking notes, and sat a little straighter in the saddle. He had taken to styling himself "Don Bartolome Cedric Montoya-Young," often followed by one or more of his heraldic titles. He relished every word of publicity the barony had brought him.

Bitora and Nepo rode on the tailgate of the lead wagon. The baroness swung her feet and played with her son as the cumbersome vehicle bounced under her. Santa Fe's adobes shrank away in the distance as the wagons rolled down the valley toward Albuquerque.

Bart held his horse back on the last swell that gave a view of the venerable city. He let Bitora's wagon come up beside him. "Take a last look at old Santa Fe, honey. Don't know when we'll get back up this way."

He was looking over his shoulder, twisting in the saddle, when he heard a pop in the canvas cover of the wagon beside his head. Glancing, he saw a hole in the material. An instant later he heard gunfire. Three more bullets peppered the wagon sheet, slamming into the articles inside.

Bitora rolled like an acrobat into the wagon, protecting Nepo in the cradle of her arms.

"There!" Antonio shouted. The old *rico* pointed and charged toward a ridge some two hundred yards away.

Bart spurred his own mount and followed his father-in-law. He drew the Winchester from the saddle scabbard and gave his horse rein to run its fastest over the rocky ground. Mounting the hill, he smelled the faint odor of black powder smoke and knew Antonio must have seen the muzzle blasts. Then he spotted a lone horseman galloping across the arroyo to the east.

Both barons fired from the saddle, though the target was a hundred yards out of range. Bart gritted his teeth, trying to wish his bullets home, but the rider crossed the arroyo unscathed and vanished along the outskirts of a village.

Bart panted. It had felt good to return the fire of the ambusher, but the attack still had him rattled. "Damn," he said. "That could have hit Bitora. Or Nepo." He looked uncertainly back toward the wagon train.

Antonio seized him by the elbow and shook him. "What did you think it would be like? Another joke? When you take land, it is always a war. When I settled the Montoya grant, more than forty years ago, it was war with the Apaches. Now it is war with Vernon Regis. And it will be war for a long time. Are you prepared for it?"

Bart yanked his arm away. "Does a cactus have stickers?" he said, glaring at his father-in-law. "I've been waiting years for this."

Antonio smiled and stroked his whiskers into place. "*Sí*, amigo. You are ready." He swept his arm grandiloquently toward his son-in-law. "You are Don Bartolome Montoya-Young, baron of Bad Jokes. Come, we must get back to the wagons."

Bart reached for a cartridge from his belt and began reloading the rifle. He glanced once more toward the arroyo where the attacker had disappeared. "After you, Sir Lord of Lord-Knows-What."

NINETEEN

The cottonwood axles groaned like braying mules as the wagon train pulled up near the Mescalero village on the Rio Bonito. The *carretas* had long since lost their charm for Bart Young. A day had seldom gone by that didn't require stopping the train to change a wheel or an axle.

Men went to work tending the animals while the women set up the camps. The weeks had taken much out of the immigrants, but now there was a new energy up and down the train. The barony was only a couple of days distant. Bart could see the summit of Sierra Blanca up the valley to the southwest. It stood like a boundary marker to his barony, for his forgeries had placed it just inside the northern borderline.

Bart and Antonio marched to the Indian village strung out along the Rio Bonito. Over the trees that flanked the streets, they could see the flagpole of Fort Stanton, but they had no business with the army. In Spanish, they asked a Mescalero boy to fetch the chief. They got two chiefs instead of one. The young one introduced himself as Estrella. The old one was called Ojo Blanco.

They wore shirts, pants, vests, moccasins, earrings, necklaces of elk teeth and bear claws. Estrella had a sash around his waist; Ojo Blanco wore a peculiar headpiece with no brim that looked like a Turkish fez with a feather on top instead of a tassle.

Bart made the introductions in Spanish. "We have come to negotiate a treaty with you," he said.

The chiefs looked at each other. "Come to my lodge and smoke with us, then," Estrella finally replied. "We have no food to share, but I have some tobacco."

"We have food," Antonio said. "I invite you to a feast at our camp tonight."

"First," Estrella said, "you will smoke with us." He walked to a nearby tepee, leading the older chief and the two visitors past a tripod made of lances hung with a painted shield and bows cased in deerskin.

They sat on holey blankets inside the hide tent, watching in silence as the chief's young wife fanned a fire. When the woman had gone, Estrella filled a pipe with tobacco, lit it, drew a breath through it, and passed it to Bart.

"Who are you to make a treaty with the Mescalero?" he asked suspiciously.

"We are the owners of your reservation," Antonio replied.

Bart almost choked on the tobacco smoke as he passed the pipe to Ojo Blanco. He considered Antonio's approach a little too bold for comfort. The Mescaleros had lived more or less peaceably on their reservation for the past few years, but many braves in camp still felt their battle scars.

"The United States had no right to give this land to you," Antonio continued, taking the pipe from Ojo Blanco. He pulled a measure of smoke through it, and passed it to Estrella. Breaking a twig from a chunk of firewood, he peeled back the corner of the blanket he was sitting on and began drawing in the dirt with his twig.

"The Sacramento Mountains lie here," he explained, drawing in several peaks. He traced a rectangle around the mountain range. "All this land belongs to me." At the northern end of the barony, he drew a square. "This is your reservation. As you see, it belongs to me."

"We have papers," Estrella said, the scowl deepening on his face.

"So do we," Antonio answered. "And our papers are much older than yours, and signed by a king."

The chief held his pipe and glowered at Antonio for several seconds in silence. "You say you come here to make a treaty. Instead, you tell us you own our reservation."

"We have a deal for you," Bart said, removing a folded

sheet of paper from his pocket, handing it to Chief Estrella.
"With this deed we will give you the land the government
says is your reservation. We will also grant you hunting
rights on our land to the south. These things we will give
you, if you will do something for us in return."

Each chief looked at the deed for a long moment,
though neither of them could read—Ojo Blanco held it upside down. They were skeptical, and wary of tricks, but
Bart's offer to double their hunting territory obviously
intrigued them.

"What do you want from us?" Estrella finally said.

"We need your braves to help us guard our boundaries,"
Bart explained. "Our enemies will try to take our land
from us. They've already shot at us three times during our
trip here. If you will help us, we will work and hunt together, like good neighbors."

The chiefs sat in silence and passed the pipe until
Estrella replied, "We will come to your camp tonight and
tell you what we have decided."

Antonio nodded. "Come when you smell the meat
cooking."

Before he could rise, Ojo Blanco put his hand on Antonio's shoulder. "I know you," he said. "You have come to
our mountains before."

Antonio smiled and nodded.

"I told you then that if you came back here, I would kill
you."

"That was long ago," Antonio said. "Much has changed.
Now I can make things better for you and your people—
and for myself."

Bart was squinting at the old chief. He recalled now that
Antonio had told him about a young Indian brave named
Ojo Blanco with whom he had had a Mexican standoff in
the Sacramentos, decades before. How the chief had recognized Antonio after all the years passed, he could only
guess.

As the men rose from their blankets, Ojo Blanco smiled, revealing his only three teeth. "It is too late to kill you now, anyway," he said to Antonio. "We have already smoked the pipe together. It would be the same as killing a brother."

The flap of the tepee suddenly flew open. An army uniform stepped in, followed by another. Two corporals pointed their army carbines at the visitors and ordered them out of the lodge.

When Bart stepped into the twilight, he spotted the familiar face of a cavalry captain standing outside. The officer wore an almost invisible yellow mustache and stood with his hands on his hips, scowling.

"What are you men doing here with my Indians?" the captain said. He had both brims of his campaign hat buttoned up against the sides of its crown, as if he were wearing a wedge on his head.

"Delton!" Bart replied, spreading his arms as if to embrace the captain. "I see you've made rank since we last met." He smelled a touch of whiskey on the officer's breath. The face was still fair, but the youthful blush of Semple's cheeks had weathered away.

Semple pushed Bart from him. "Who are you? Why didn't you report to me? I'm the Indian agent here. You have to get my permission to meet with the Indians."

"Delton, don't you remember me? We fought Comanches together on the stage to Maxwell's Ranch."

Semple's eyes shifted. "Young," he said, with a note of disgust in his voice. "I've read about your scheme to take over these mountains. I can't believe you're actually going to try to get away with it."

"I can't believe your scalp isn't dangling from a Mescalero lance by now. How have you been?"

"Never mind. Just leave these Indians alone. They don't need your influence."

"What they need is a quit-claim deed to this reservation.

Antonio and I have just given them one. We're making a treaty with them."

"What treaty?" Semple shouted. "What deed? Let me see it!" He took the deed from Estrella. "My God, it's in Spanish!" He tore the document into four pieces and let them flutter away on the breeze. "You have no authority here. Get out!"

Antonio stepped in front of Semple as he tried to walk away. "*You* have no authority to give me orders, Captain. I suggest that you do not destroy any more of my deeds."

"Corporal," Semple said, trying to step around Antonio, "seize this man."

Both corporals postured uncertainly with their carbines, pointing them at their own captain as well as at Antonio.

The *rico* finally stepped out of Semple's way. In Spanish, he repeated his invitation to the Indians to eat at his camp that night. Then he left, gesturing at Bart to follow.

"What did you say to them?" Semple demanded. "Come back here!"

The two barons would not obey.

Semple looked across the parade ground from the front door of his quarters on officers' row. The morning sun was striking the trees along the Rio Bonito and the grassy hills beyond. As he sipped his coffee, he tried to figure out why something seemed to be missing. He burned his lips when the answer struck him. He could no longer see the tops of tepees over the trees.

He shouted at the first two enlisted men he saw and marched them toward the Indian village. Where the evening before some eight-hundred Mescaleros had languished, he now found nothing but ashes from cook fires. Every man, woman, child, horse, mule, burro, and dog had vanished overnight.

The captain then marched for the wagon train camped

upstream. He found Bart saddling his horse as the immigrants doused their own cook fires and hitched draft animals. "Young!" he shouted. "Where have my Indians gone?"

"They're not your Indians, Delton. You're not God."

"Where are they?"

"I invited them to go hunting on our barony. I suppose they accepted my invitation."

"Damn you, Young. They're supposed to be confined to the reservation. They're not allowed to hunt on the public domain."

"They're not hunting public domain. They're hunting private domain. Mine and Antonio's. They said they'd be back by next ration day."

Semple fumed. "I don't want them hunting. I want them farming."

"You can't make a bird dog out of a burro, Lieutenant."

"That's captain," Semple said, pointing to his bars. "And if they get hungry enough, they'll learn to farm."

"They might. Then again, they might fall back on something they already know how to do. Like scalping soldiers or raiding settlements. A man's got to eat."

"They get plenty to eat on ration day."

"You'd never know it by the way they stuffed themselves at our camp last night."

"That's because they haven't learned discipline yet. They eat everything I issue them in two days, then starve until the next ration day."

"Well, then, why don't you issue them more? Damn, Delton. Don't you have a lick of common sense? You don't want them to hunt, but then you won't give them enough food to get by on without hunting. You want them to farm, but you won't show them how. How in the world did you ever become an Indian agent?"

"Not by choice. I'd rather fight them, but I have my orders, and I'll carry them out to the best of my ability—

and that does not involve fattening the heathens on government rations. The last agent here—a civilian—did just that, and couldn't get a lick of work out of them."

"From the looks of things, nothing's changed since you took over, except now they're skinny. If you want them to work, give them something they like to do."

"Such as?"

"Hell, I don't know, Del. I just met them yesterday."

"Exactly. You don't know what you're talking about. These people are savages. It's my job to civilize them. I have to crush their barbaric customs, and you're making my job more difficult."

"What customs do they have that could possibly be more barbaric then the United States Army's?"

Semple's pale lips twisted. "When I came here they were brewing a drink called *tulapai* that they made by chewing maize kernels, then spitting them into a pot to cook and ferment. And they would get stinking drunk from it."

"I smelled whiskey on your breath last night, Captain. Does that make you a savage?"

"A few years ago, they burned one of their own women at the stake as a witch! Tell me *that* isn't barbaric!"

"Our own people did the same thing in Salem, less than two hundred years ago. We're not that far ahead of them."

Semple's fists clenched in frustration. "Their customs and taboos are ridiculous."

"What taboos?" Bart said.

The captain's mouth writhed in an attempt to form words. "They go to extravagant lengths to avoid their mother-in-laws!" he finally blurted.

"Then they're more civilized than we are. We generally have to put up with ours. And, by the way, Lieutenant, the plural is mothers-in-law, not mother-in-laws."

"Captain!" Semple shouted, tapping his bars again.

As Bart continued to aggravate the officer, Antonio rode

to the head of the wagon train. "The wagons are ready, Bartolome," he said.

"Good," Bart said, springing into his saddle. "Adios, Captain. I have a million acres to remove from the public domain today. Come see us when we get settled in. Bring your mother-in-law!"

Semple glared at the train of freight wagons and ox carts as it began to move. "Stay away from my Indians, Young! I'm warning you!"

The laughter of the so-called baron brought a fever to the soldier's skin.

TWENTY

Domingo Archiveque arrived at Dog Canyon an hour after nightfall on a lathered horse. He left the animal hitched in front of the ranch house gallery, not even bothering to loosen the saddle cinch. His spurs rang like tambourines as they raked the wooden steps, and the meaty bottom of his fist pounded on the door.

"Who's there?" Vernon Regis called from inside.

"Domingo."

"Come in."

Archiveque entered, the pale light of the pink lantern globe confusing his senses for a moment. Then he saw Sebastiana wrapped around Regis, the sheen of her satin dressing gown clashing with the floral pattern of the sofa.

Regis pushed her aside for the moment, and pointed to the bar. "It's about time you got here. Pour yourself a drink."

The gunman splashed the finest brandy he could find into a shot glass.

"Did they scare?" Regis asked, reaching for Sebastiana's thigh.

"No," Archiveque said, avoiding the woman's eyes. He knew she would be looking at him. "I fired at them from three different places south of Santa Fe, but they kept going. They camped near Fort Stanton last night."

The speculator shrugged. "It's just as well. Let them get way the hell out in the hills where nobody will ever know what hit them. Can you hire men around here?"

Archiveque nodded. "I can find maybe ten men in Socorro and El Paso."

Regis nodded. "You can stay out in the guest house tonight. There's some beef in the kitchen. Help yourself."

Archiveque threw back the brandy, allowing himself to glance at Sebastiana. Her lashes languished over her eyes, but he saw her dark pupils staring back. He took the bottle of brandy with him, his spurs ringing as he walked behind the sofa, through the dining room, and into the kitchen.

As he ate the beef and buttered bread, he could hear Regis grunting in the parlor and knew Sebastiana was pleasuring him with a few of her many wiles. He put his hand over his right spur, to keep it from jingling, and unbuckled it. He raked his fork across his plate a few times to make it sound as if he were still eating, then unbuckled the left spur. He slurped his brandy and clinked the glass against the plate as he got up. Moving silently through the dark dining room, he went to the parlor door, and peered through the crack he had left on purpose.

In the pink light he saw the back of Regis's head above the sofa back. Sebastiana was on top of him, facing him, holding him by the ears, rising and falling as if riding a rough horse at a trot. The speculator's breath rattled from his lungs in short gasps.

Sebastiana saw Domingo watching from the kitchen and smiled at him. She licked her lips. She reined her horse in from its trot, and settled low in the seat. Pushing herself away from Regis's face at arm's length, she looked blankly

into the speculator's eyes as she reached for the belt of her
dressing gown. Untying it, she let the satin fall away from
her shoulders. She grabbed the ears again and plunged the
ugly face between her breasts.

She rode on at a trot, returning Archiveque's stare from
the kitchen. Domingo gestured toward the guest house
with his head, and she nodded. When she put her tongue
in the speculator's ear, he almost bucked her over the back
of the couch like a bronc.

Domingo went back to the kitchen table, clinked the
dishes a few times, and put his spurs on silently. Grabbing
the bottle of brandy, he clopped loudly across the kitchen
floor and slammed the door as he went outside.

Regis felt her leave his bed and waited to hear the back
door click. He sighed. It was a shame Sebastiana couldn't
be satisfied with one man. He would probably never find
another whore to pleasure him like she could. But he had
already warned her, even going so far as to blacken her
eyes the night before they had left Santa Fe, when he
had caught her with one of the servants.

Domingo should have known better, too. He was the one
who had carved a large S, for Sebastiana, on the back of
the offending servant, a permanent reminder for a night's
indiscretion.

Regis got out of bed and dressed in the dark. He did not
hurry. He had plenty of time. Sebastiana liked to make it
last. He found his gun belt on the bureau and strapped it on,
feeling the chambers for cartridges. He put a cigar and a
few matches in his pocket before he left his room.

Taking an unlit lantern from the kitchen, he slipped
silently through the back door and walked down the steps.
He heard a bull bellowing a challenge somewhere up Dog
Canyon, and stopped to listen to the night.

The precipitous western face of the Sacramentos loomed

above his ranch house, a black veil over the eastern stars. He knew that somewhere across the mountains, where gentler slopes rose to the summit, Bart Young and Antonio Montoya were camped with their wagon train. The thought threw a crick into his neck.

He was just now getting established in this mountain country, after three years of development. He had bought Dog Canyon as his ranch headquarters, built his rambling frame ranch house, and hired cowboys to work his herds. He had bought timberland in the mountains, brought in lumberjacks to cut the trees, and bullwhackers to haul them. He had begun building his sawmill on the Tularosa River. Most importantly, he had blasted wagon roads up to his gold mine in La Luz Canyon, hauled in his stamp mill, and was now getting ore out at an encouraging pace.

He had counted on taking his first profits from the Sacramentos in three years—until Bart Young and old man Montoya had filed their ridiculous claim with the Office of the Surveyor General.

It was so outlandish that he almost had to admire them for it. The book of riddles was the most irksome part. He knew Young liked riddles. But the new surveyor general wouldn't know any better. Nor would Congress. Already, the population at large was fascinated with the story of the lost barony. But Regis didn't give a damn about public sentiment. He was going to wipe his shoes on Bart Young.

The guest house was dark, but he knew Sebastiana was in there. His anger made him strangely giddy. From the first night she had slipped into his room at the Montoya hacienda six years ago, he had known it would come to this. She was an odd woman.

He stepped quietly onto the guest house porch and lit the lantern. The board and batten walls were thin. He could hear the bed springs squeaking. Turning the lantern wick up, he kicked the door in and pulled his revolver from the holster as he rushed in.

Sebastiana gasped. Archiveque leaped out of bed and tried to grab his gun belt.

"I wouldn't, Domingo!" the speculator said, cocking his pistol.

The Mexican gunman stopped short of his weapons. Regis walked into the bedroom and put the lantern on a chest of drawers, its light bathing the two naked bodies. Sebastiana got out of bed and reached for her dressing gown, but Regis pulled it away from her. He grabbed her by the hair and shoved her into Archiveque.

"No need to dress for me," the speculator said. "Domingo will deal with you in a minute. But, first, I'll deal with him." The pointed nails on the ends of his spindly fingers scratched at the stubble on his chin. "Let me think. What will it be?"

Sebastiana glanced at Archiveque and began to shiver.

"I know," Regis said. "Domingo, get your knife." He waved the revolver recklessly. "Go ahead, get it!"

Archiveque obeyed, drawing the knife carefully from his gun belt. Unlike Sebastiana, he remained in perfect control of his faculties. He did not attempt to cover himself with his arms, the way she did. He knew how Regis fed on fear.

"Now, Domingo, what do I usually have you do when I want you to warn somebody?"

Archiveque turned the knife handle in his hand. "Cut them."

"That's right. Now, I want you to warn yourself against fooling around with my women. So, take off an ear."

Archiveque stared blankly. "Señor?" he said.

"You heard me. Cut off your ear. And feel lucky I'm not making you cut off something you're more partial to."

Sebastiana's knees buckled, and she staggered back and fell onto the bed.

The speculator took a menacing step toward his hench-man with the revolver. "The one at the end of your scar. Do it!"

Domingo took the ear in one hand, and put the knife blade on top of it. The cold steel made him flinch. It was honed like a razor. He found a new grip on the knife han-dle. He heard Sebastiana start to cry. He felt himself be-gin to shudder, but then gritted his teeth and got control of himself.

Slowly, he took the knife away from his face and glared down the barrel of his boss's revolver. He lowered the blade to his side. He had almost forgotten who this Anglo was. He had no stomach for killing. Why else would he hire it done? And Regis had forgotten who Domingo Archiveque was. He was not afraid. He parted his lips in a smile as his grip relaxed on the knife. "You will not shoot me," he said, almost daring the speculator with the tone of his voice.

"No?" Regis replied. He changed the angle of his weapon and fired a shot that hit Sebastiana in the temple, bathing the headboard with gore and fragments of her skull. Her body jerked once, then slithered off the bed to the floor.

Archiveque was looking back down the muzzle of the revolver before he realized the woman was dead. A warm drop of blood had splattered against his naked side and cooled, prompting him to wipe it away with his palm. The smell of powder twisted his stomach.

"The ear," Regis offered.

Domingo felt numb as he put the knife back in place. He distanced himself, feeling as if he were watching through Regis's eyes. The scorching pain and the sound of the blade cutting the skin and cartilage so near his ear-drum brought his senses back to the horrible reality. He averted his eyes from the hot river of blood he felt flowing down his chest.

"Drop the knife," Regis said, his eyes bulging. He picked up Sebastiana's robe and threw it at the Mexican. "Here. You don't want to bleed to death."

Archiveque dropped the knife—and his ear—and held the robe to his wound as he sank onto the bed. He heard the brandy bottle rattle against the shot glass.

"Drink!" Regis said, grinning down at the gunman. He shoved the glass at Domingo, continuing to cover him with the revolver. "I said drink, dammit."

Archiveque felt dizzy and ill as he put the glass to his mouth. Then a cigar poked him between the lips.

"Smoke!" Regis ordered, lighting a match on the cross-hatched steel of the pistol hammer.

The cigar smoke stuck in Archiveque's throat like a clod.

"You can use my liquor," Regis said. "You can use my tobacco. You can use my very home. But, by God, don't you *ever* use my women!"

The Mexican trembled so that brandy sloshed on to his fist.

Finally, Regis put the revolver in its holster. "I want that whore buried by dawn, and this place cleaned up. Understand?"

As Archiveque nodded, each movement of his head pumped the clod of tobacco smoke higher in his throat. He looked down and saw his own ear lying on a blood-speckled floor. He spit the cigar out, stumbled through the door Regis had kicked in, and vomited off the porch.

The speculator's sledlike shoes scuffed the steps as he walked casually past the prostrate gunman. "Now, see what you've done, Domingo?" he said. "What a waste of good beefsteak."

TWENTY - ONE

The road led southeast from Fort Stanton, then turned into the Sacramentos. The two barons at the head of the emigrant train wanted to follow the road up into the cool elevations of their domain, but they had to establish a stronghold in the lowlands before riding through the tall timber in the high country.

They turned off the road and continued along the eastern foothills of their mountains, with only trails to guide them. What Bart found strange was that he couldn't see his mountains. He had expected to see them raking the sky when he was this near. But on the eastern slope the mountains rose so gradually that they seemed nonexistent. Each hill hid a slightly larger hill to the west of it, but nowhere did he see his mountains jutting as in his dreams. It was a little disconcerting, but he trusted Antonio when he said they were there, and higher than he could imagine.

By the middle of the second day out of Fort Stanton, Bart knew he must have crossed the Mescalero reservation onto his own land. He had taken possession of his barony at last.

At sundown, they struck the Penasco River, and the next day he and Antonio explored upstream, finding a few remote farms where settlers—Mexicans for the most part—raised irrigated crops. Antonio told the story of the lost barony and handed out quit-claim deeds, winning instant friends.

The Penasco Valley wound among the foothills of the Sacramentos, narrowing between canyon bluffs in places, widening into expansive stretches of bottomland elsewhere. The barons decided to establish their headquarters at a place where the valley broadened out enough to make room for a village, fields, and pastures.

Bart led a timber expedition into the mountains to cut pines. He even swung an axe himself a couple of hours a day for the exercise. The trail from Santa Fe had toughened him, but he knew he was going to have to get tougher yet if he wanted to hold on to his barony.

The pines he found weren't really very tall, and they were spaced far apart. Still, it was good land for stock, and he continued to believe in Antonio's description of the thick forests higher up. He wanted badly to ride to the summit of the Sacramentos, but there was too much work to do now.

Oxen hauled the harvested pines down to the town site, where Antonio had established a regular factory for adobe bricks. His people would need tens of thousands of them to build their homes and the presidio.

"What are we going to call the place?" Bart asked as they laid out the settlement.

"The town we will call Montoya, New Mexico," the fourth baron said. "The presidio we will call Fort Young."

Chief Estrella stopped by on his return to Fort Stanton for ration day. He thanked Bart and Antonio for letting his braves hunt on the barony. He also performed his first function as chief of the baronial guards by reporting on the activities around Regis's gold mine in La Luz Canyon on the western slope. Several Mexican gunmen had arrived at the high mining camp, their leader a tough-looking man with a scar on one side of his face, and a bandaged ear.

Bart thanked the chief, lent him a fresh horse, and asked him to keep his guards circulating throughout the mountains. "One more thing," Bart said as the chief mounted. "I'd like you to carry a letter to Fort Stanton for me and post it."

Estrella agreed, and left with the envelope addressed to Randy Hendricks tucked into the balloon sleeve of his Mexican-style shirt.

Randy had disappointed Bart a few years before, when he refused to help take the Montoya grant away from Vernon Regis. But Bart was willing to give his old friend another chance. Besides, he knew no one else in Washington, and he needed a lobbyist to help push his confirmation through Congress. He was offering thousands of dollars, plus a bonus to be paid after confirmation. If Randy accepted, he was to come to Santa Fe, all expenses paid by the Montoya family, to review the grant documents. Then he would tour the barony before returning to Washington.

The walls of the presidio climbed daily with new layers of adobe brick. It was to be part palace, part fort. The parapets would stand four feet thick. The ceiling beams would be whole timbers, peeled of bark. Two stories would surround a central plaza. It would be large enough to afford protection for the entire village in case of attack by Regis men, hostile Indians, outlaws, or border renegades.

Antonio and Bart had worked for days on the plans for the presidio, sketching them on paper. Then Bitora had come behind them and changed everything. Her designs were practical, however, so they had let most of her changes stand. Their fort would include a kitchen to feed an army, a huge dining hall, two parlors, a music room, bedrooms, guest rooms, servants' quarters, barracks, blacksmith and carpenter shops, a powder magazine, a laundry, a trading post, stables, and a billiards hall. Like the old Montoya hacienda in Santa Fe County, it would have no windows to the outside, and two gates would secure it from the world.

The walls were ten bricks high when Chief Estrella rode into the valley with urgent intelligence. "They are coming," he told Antonio and Bart. "From the mine."

"How many?" Antonio asked.

The young chief held up his ten fingers.

"Guns?"

The chief nodded. "They are coming for a fight. The one with the big scar on his face is leading them."

"How far away?"

"They will be here tonight."

"Maybe we should plan a reception," Bart said.

"A wonderful idea, Bartolome. A surprise reception."

Bitora led the evacuation of the village site between sundown and moonrise, taking the women and children in groups of twenty to their hiding place in the piñon brakes over the hill. Crying babies caused her biggest problems. Otherwise, she accomplished the evacuation with little trouble. Her noncombatants were settled in among the piñons an hour before the moon rose.

Antonio sent ten men to guard the women and children, then positioned the rest around the rim of the valley, overlooking the village site. He and Bart took up stations flanking the trail they expected Archiveque to ride in on. They waited an hour for the moon to rise, then waited two hours more.

Bart began wondering if the attack would come tonight or at dawn. Or at all. He was well hidden in a clump of alligator juniper, his Winchester repeater across his knees. He was getting drowsy when he heard stones rattle on the trail above him.

Moonlight made the attackers look almost friendly as they rode down toward the village among the scrubby evergreens. Bart tried hard to watch their every move through the branches of the juniper he hid in. He eased his rifle slowly to his shoulder, his heart pounding as though he were trying to find a big bull elk in his sights.

The half moon caught the scar line on Archiveque's cheek. Bart counted as his thumb pulled the hammer back. Ten men, just as Estrella had reported. He held the trigger until the hammer was all the way back, then eased his finger off the trigger, preventing any part of the gunlock from clicking.

His left eye closed as the hooves became louder. He was looking down his rifle sights, waiting for Archiveque's men to ride by. They were going to pass not more than ten yards from his position.

His pulse throbbed in his ears as the attackers approached, but his hands were steady. Archiveque stood in his stirrups as he approached the overlook. The moment he rode in line with Bart's rifle sights, he stopped, raising a hand to his men. Bart found the ugly scar in his irons.

Unless he wanted to count the Comanche who had fallen under the stagecoach that had brought him to New Mexico, Bart could not say he had killed a man. Domingo Archiveque, however, was a good place to start. He felt his trigger finger curl a little as he held his bead. He heard the henchman's voice, followed by the sound of ten guns sliding from their scabbards. Three men soaked rag-wrapped torches with coal oil. Another struck a match.

One squeeze would drop Archiveque from the saddle right here and now. Bart felt a surge of excitement, and thought he heard a sound like distant thunder in the back of his head. He decided for a mere moment that he would do it. Then he remembered Antonio's plan, and his grip eased on the trigger. There would be nine others after Archiveque. It was better to wait.

"Vamanos!" Archiveque said, his voice striking through the moonlit night like a hammer on an anvil. He led his mob in the plunge down the valley slope, and rent the air with the first of the Indian yelps.

The torches shrank into the distance as Bart repositioned himself for the new angle of fire. He heard the bleating of terrified animals as two riders veered into a goat herd. The first gunshot punctured the darkness, and a wagon sheet in the valley took flame from a torch, helping to illuminate the attackers.

When Archiveque's men realized the village had been evacuated, their yells died and they turned their mounts back to the hills. Antonio chose that moment to fire the first shot of the surprise reception.

A ring of riflemen hurled a hundred slugs down at the ten invaders. Two of the torch carriers fell from their saddles, and the third threw his flaming branch aside. The other invaders scattered in confusion or fired ineffectually at the hills.

Archiveque attempted to lead two charges out of the valley, but lost another three men to hidden rifles. In desperation, he turned toward the walls of the unfinished presidio for cover. As he led his men into the plaza, a dozen farmers rose from their hiding places and raked the hired guns with deadly accuracy. Three men dropped. One of them screamed in pain in the presidio plaza, until another bullet silenced him.

Archiveque escaped the fort with only one of his men, and the two invaders retreated on the same trail that had led them into disaster. As they rode toward him, Bart located the scar-faced gunman in his sights, and squeezed his trigger. The muzzle blast blinded him for an instant; then he saw Archiveque rolling from his fallen horse.

Bart tried to aim for a second shot, but his initial blasts had speckled everything he looked at with spots. He shook his head and blinked hard, trying to clear his vision. He could make out only enough in the moonlight to see Archiveque climbing on behind the other surviving raider.

Bart ducked a smoking cartridge that flew from the chamber of his Winchester as the pair of raiders rode double toward him. He waited as the dancing spots melted away. He would let the raiders get closer. Then, if someone hadn't picked them off already, he would put a bullet through Archiveque himself.

A few shots were still ringing across the valley, but it seemed most of the riflemen had paused to reload. As he paced the two raiders with his rifle barrel, he tried to remember how many rounds he had fired. Certainly not enough to empty his magazine. They were within a hundred yards now, whipping the winded horse out of the valley. Then a lull came in the firing, and Bart saw the man in front of Archiveque fall inexplicably from his horse. The lone survivor shifted into the saddle, bent to catch a dangling bridle rein, and gouged the pony with his spurs.

Bart's finger drew the trigger back, but the hammer dropped on nothing, like a dead man falling into a bottomless grave. Archiveque was going to make it. As the mob leader reached the overlook, Bart saw his face turn back to the valley. The moon caught his smile.

Before he knew what was happening, Bart felt himself leaping from his cover. He sprinted for the trail to intercept Archiveque. The raider's head turned toward him as he leaped. He felt like an eagle as he vaulted, spreading his arms. He saw Archiveque reach for his sidearm, then slammed into the Mexican as the horse ran out from under them both. Archiveque took the impact from the waiting ground, and Bart wrestled the pistol from his grip. Archiveque lay on the ground gasping for wind. Bart cocked the old Colt, knelt, and put the barrel against the scarred face.

Antonio and a few village farmers scrambled to his side.

"Kill him," Antonio said.

Bart heard stray shots in the valley and knew the farmers were finishing off the wounded raiders. Archiveque turned his head and looked beyond the pistol barrel with complete detachment in his eyes.

"My Lord, Domingo!" Bart said. "What happened to your ear?"

"Kill him," Antonio repeated.

Bart shifted the revolver in his grasp. "No, I don't believe I will," he said. He pulled the panting gunman to his feet, keeping the cocked pistol against his throat. "Domingo, I want you to take a message back to Dog Canyon for me. Tell Regis we intend to seize his ranch and timber interests for payments past due. Tell him he can keep the gold mine, as long as he starts paying us royalties on it. If he doesn't, we'll close the roads and take over the mine ourselves. Tell him he's just a filthy trespasser to us, and we'd just as soon gut shoot him and leave him lay. You got all that?"

Archiveque nodded.

"Well, don't just stand there, boy. Go catch your horse and get the hell off of our barony."

Archiveque turned away.

"And, Domingo," Bart said, stopping the hired gun. "Next time, I'll take Antonio's advice."

They heard his spurs jingle into the darkness. Antonio ordered the farmers who had gathered around to escort the women and children back to the village site. When they had gone, he turned to Bart.

"I was worried about you," he said. "You can never predict how a man is going to act in a fight. I think you lost your senses, leaping on Archiveque like that, but it was a courageous thing to watch, and the men are already talking about it."

Bart shrugged with modesty.

"However . . ." Antonio motioned for Bart to follow him down the slope, toward the dead man who had rescued Archiveque. "The only reason Archiveque did not stick you with his knife is because he left it here." He nudged the corpse with his boot.

In the moonlight, Bart saw the knife handle jutting from rib cage of the dead man. "He killed the fellow who rescued him?"

"Of course he did. The horse was running too slow. I have heard that he killed his own mother. Why, then, would he spare this man? Promise me something, Bartolome. The next time you have Domingo Archiveque in your sights, kill him."

Bart studied the glistening current of blood trailing from the knife wound of the dead man. "By golly, I believe I will," he said.

TWENTY - TWO

B y October, the settlers had almost finished building Fort Young. The women were coating the walls with a mixture of mud and straw when Chief Estrella delivered the first mail from Fort Stanton.

Two important dispatches required Bart to make a hasty trip back to Santa Fe. One was from Vernon Regis. He wanted to negotiate. The other was from Vicente, concerning Randy Hendricks. The redheaded lawyer was on his way to New Mexico.

Bart hated leaving just as his fort was about to become habitable, but the future of the barony rested with the powers in Santa Fe and Washington. He saddled a good horse to ride over the mountains to La Luz, where he could catch the Mesilla-to-Las Vegas stage.

He took Hilario and a guard of five Mescaleros, but he wasn't expecting any trouble. It was his first trip over the summit of the Sacramentos, and he was enthralled to at last find the dense forests Antonio had told him of.

Every bend in the trail filled him with wonder. He spooked a herd of elk from one meadow, and found two bear cubs hiding in a tree near the Sacramento Divide. He couldn't believe he owned it all. It had started as a prank, a way to get even with Regis. But now there was much more to it.

Nothing to feel guilty about, he thought. *You've deprived*

*no one but Regis of anything. You handed out quit-claim
deeds to the farmers who came here before you and doubled the hunting territory of the Mescaleros. You must
serve these mountains. Then you will be a true baron.*

Suddenly, Bart jumped from his horse and marched out
into a small trailside clearing. Chief Estrella watched in
shock as the baron began pulling at weeds and throwing
rocks into the forest.

"Long live the king, and may God preserve him!" Bart
shouted. "Long live the king, and may God preserve him!
Long live the king and may God preserve him!"

"Don Bartolome!" Hilario scolded. "What is wrong
with you? You are making the Indians nervous."

Bart came back to his mount, grinning and panting. "It's
the ancient Spanish Act of Possession. You're supposed
to do that when you take possession of your grant."

"I thought you were going crazy. Look at Estrella. He
is still not sure."

"Sorry, Chief," Bart said, returning to his saddle, "but I
always wanted to do that." He sighed and looked around
him. "We're like *conquistadores,* Hilario. You and me,
conquering these mountains for God and king."

"I am jut a servant," Hilario insisted. "And I have no
king."

The party continued on and reached a pass along the
divide before sundown. As Bart admired the newly revealed scenery to the west, a large flock of band-tailed
pigeons chose his pass to cross the range. Their wings
whistled just a few feet over his head for a second; then
they were gone, flying over Fort Young and the village
of Montoya before he could catch his breath.

Before dark, he led a side trip to the nearest peak. It
sloped gently to a crest wooded heavily with evergreens.
A labyrinth of small interconnected clearings, fringed with
white-trunked aspens, led to the top where wildflowers
dotted a field of knee-high grass. From the summit he saw

the sun sink beyond the next range of mountains, far to the west. He remained there, gazing out over his domain, until the first star came out. He named the peak Star Mountain, and Chief Estrella was highly pleased, thinking it had been named for him.

The night was cold, but Bart found the clime invigorating after the long summer below. He decided he would build a grand lodge on Star Mountain. Maybe next year. It would be his summer retreat and autumn hunting lodge.

The next morning, Bart, Hilario, and the Mescaleros struck the old La Luz-to-Fort Stanton Road that ran northeast across the Sacramentos. It had been there over twenty years, since the establishment of Fort Stanton in 1855. It would lead them to the little Mexican town of La Luz, where Bart could catch the stage. But when they reached the mining road Regis had blasted into La Luz Canyon, Bart decided to investigate.

He came to a collection of ramshackle buildings on a bluff, and heard a muffled blast from the mine. The town had one crooked street of rocks and mud. The shacks were built of bark-covered planks the sawmill blades had cut from the big pines when squaring the timbers for lumber production.

Bart and Hilario decided to visit a shanty labeled "Regisville Saloon," but the Indians refused to go in. They wouldn't even dismount and seemed extremely uneasy in the village.

Inside the saloon, Bart found five dirty men bandaged with blood-soaked linens lying on cots. "Good Lord!" he said to the bartender. "What on earth happened here?"

The bartender leaned on his broom. "Not *on* earth, stranger. Within it. A shaft caved in two days ago. Three men killed. These boys hurt bad enough to lay up." He looked at Hilario. "Your man will have to go. We don't allow Mexicans or Indians in this camp, unless they work for Mr. Regis."

Bart felt his baronial ire flare. "You'd better get used to it, mister. I own these mountains, and I have many friends among Mexicans and Indians. If you'll look out your front door, you'll see five Mescaleros waiting for me outside."

The bartender cracked the door to look. He gasped, shutting the door again. "Who the hell are you?" he asked, examining the revolver on Bart's hip.

"Don Bartolome Cedric Montoya-Young, fifth baron of the Sacramentos."

One of the injured men chuckled. "You're that bullshit baron that's supposed to own these mountains."

"There's no supposition about it. My father-in-law and I are currently in possession of this range."

"Is it true you've got a fort on the Penasco?" the bartender said. "We heard there was a battle there."

Bart nodded. "With our militia and our Mescalero Guard, we all but wiped out a band of hired renegades." He drew his revolver and put it on the bar. "Now, my friend and I will have a whiskey."

Hilario grinned as the bartender poured the drinks.

"Why are these men quartered here?" Bart asked, taking his glass. "Doesn't this sorry excuse for a town have an infirmary?"

"This is it," the bartender said, shrugging.

Bart turned to the injured men. "How did the cave-in happen?"

"The shafts ain't shored up right," said a man with a broken leg. "Regis don't put enough timber in 'em."

Bart shook his head. "That will change. How much do you men get paid to lay up here?"

They looked at each other. The man with a broken leg started laughing. "What do you mean, Baron? Men don't earn nothin' layin' up."

"Our relief fund feeds them," the bartender said. "This 'sorry excuse for a town' takes care of its own."

Bart threw back his whiskey, then said, "Take your time mending, gentlemen. When I get back from Santa Fe, I'll have your wages in full for your time spent convalescing."

The bartender laughed as he took up his broom again. "If you manage that, Baron, we'll name this town after you."

"Bullshit, New Mexico," an injured man suggested, wheezing.

Bart frowned. "Come on, Hilario," he said. "We'd better get going."

He rode back to the La Luz Road and headed downhill with his Indian guard. As they neared the lower reaches of the pine forests, the deep shade suddenly gave way to stark sunlight. The scene reminded him of a photograph he had once seen of a Civil War battlefield. A clear-cut one mile wide flanked the road, exposing the sun-scorched forest floor. Thousands of the stumps jutted like poorly placed gravestones. Eroding soil had left dead roots bare. Bart heard the sounds of axes coming from over a ridge.

"Hilario," he said, "remind me to ask Randy Hendricks about hiring a forester from back East. I don't like what this does to my mountains."

The Mescaleros refused to ride any closer to La Luz, so Bart and Hilario went on alone. They made their guns ready, but found no Regis men to deal with. Bart was beginning to think that Regis was sincere about negotiating.

The Mesilla-to-Las Vegas stage arrived in the afternoon. Three men and a woman were in the coach when Bart and Hilario climbed in.

"Howdy," he said. "Allow me to introduce myself. I am Bartolome Cedric Montoya-Young, fifth baron of the Sacramentos, knight of the Golden Fleece, caballero of the Chamber of His Majesty . . ."

TWENTY - THREE

Is Randy here yet?" Bart asked Francisco over a late breakfast. He had arrived in the night, and slept well into the morning.

"He should be here this week. Have you heard about the surveyor general's office?"

"No, what about it?"

"It burned about two weeks ago, in the middle of the night. Raspberry told me the papers for the barony were out of the office when it caught fire."

"I planned it that way," Bart mumbled, his mouth full of tortillas and eggs and hot peppers. "I'll bet anything Vernon Regis is behind the fire."

Francisco shrugged. "When will we start seeing profits from the barony?"

"Maybe today," Bart said. "Regis wants to negotiate terms." He reached for his jacket hanging on the back of his chair, and pulled a letter from its pocket. "Here's your father's list of supplies for the fall. We need more cash, too."

"Chihuahua!" Francisco said, banging his fist on the table. "That damn barony is supposed to be making us money, not taking it."

"We have to make a few improvements. We'll be the richest men in the territory when the investments start to come together."

Grudgingly, Francisco took the letter and began reading his father's demands. He didn't speak to Bart again all morning.

When Bart rode to the Santa Fe plaza before noon, he noticed a few people pointing at him. Celebrity agreed with him. He even went so far as to hitch his coat tail behind the grip of his side arm for show. He tied his horse at

Regis's office, and the speculator's assistant announced him immediately.

"Come in, Bart," Regis said, an illegible expression on his oversized face.

Bart wasted no time with small talk. "Let's start with your ranch in Dog Canyon," he said, plopping into a chair. "I want you out of there immediately, and I'm going to take over your ranch house and herds for payments past due."

"I've already abandoned the ranch," Regis said. "As for the house, and the herds, you can't have them."

"I will have them," Bart said. "They are on my land."

"I'm afraid they're not negotiable. You see, a band of rustlers attacked my ranch, burned my ranch house, and stole all of my cattle." He smiled.

Bart shook his head with disgust. "As long as you're out of Dog Canyon."

"I am. At least for now."

"And forever, if you enjoy what little good health you have."

Regis laughed at the ceiling. "Threats sound ridiculous coming from a jester like you. I suggest you abandon them."

Bart stood and started pacing. "You will also cease your timbering operations. I don't like the way you're stripping my mountains."

The speculator sighed with disinterest. "The market's no good, anyway. You'll find out there's little profit in timbering. My interest is in the mines." He opened his desk drawer. "I have a little something drawn up for you."

Bart yanked his revolver from its holster as Regis reached into the open drawer.

"Easy, Bart," the speculator said, shaking with laughter. "Damn, you've gotten antagonistic."

"As anyone is apt to when they're shot at. Get your hand out of that drawer."

"You don't mind if I remove your royalty check while I'm at it, do you?"

"My what?"

"Your mining royalties projected through the end of the year." He eased the check from the drawer, placed it on the desk in front of Bart, and closed the drawer.

Bart slipped his Colt into the holster and picked up the check. "Ten thousand," he grunted. He sat back down and pondered the amount. "This isn't like you, Vernon. What's your plan?"

"To ruin you, of course."

"By paying me royalties? I can abide that kind of ruination."

"I figure it won't be long until somebody reveals your entire scheme as a monumental hoax. Then, I'm going to stretch your guts clear across New Mexico for extorting money from me, and people will call me a hero for doing it. But for now, paying the royalties is cheaper than hiring the guns to take on your so-called militia and your Indian guard."

Bart folded the check into his pocket. "You'll pay more next year, but this will do for now, provided you agree to a few concessions."

"Like what?"

"Hire another shift of men at the mine and put them on eight hours a day instead of twelve. Hire a qualified mining engineer to improve the safety standards of that death trap you call a mine. Pay the men you've already injured their wages while they convalesce, and provide the wives of the dead ones with pensions."

Regis lost his temper in an instant and swatted a stack of papers from his desk. "What do you care about those goddamn miners?"

The outburst amused Bart. "I want them on my side, just like the Indians and the settlers down there. Do you agree, or will I have to blockade your ore wagons?"

Regis gritted his teeth and got control of himself. "You're costing me a fortune, Bart."

"Pen the orders to your mine boss right now. I'll deliver them myself." He gloated. "They're going to name the mining village after me. How does Youngstown sound to you? Much better ring to it than Regisville, don't you think?"

TWENTY - FOUR

Three days after he deposited the mining royalties in the Bank of New Mexico, Bart greeted Randy Hendricks at the stagecoach station on the plaza. He was wearing his most baronial costume: pants tucked into polished stovepipe boots, shiny gold watch chain swaying from his vest pocket, broad felt hat, its brim flapping on the cool norther.

"Randy! By God, it's good to see you!"

The lawyer stepped from the stagecoach scratching his head of red hair. "I haven't been called Randy since law school. I go by Jay Randolph Hendricks now." Grudgingly, he shook his former classmate's hand.

"And I go by Baron Bartolome Cedric Montoya-Young, but you can still call me Bart. I haven't outgrown my britches." He slapped the dust from Randy's back and helped him with his bags.

Randy grunted and rubbed his rear end. "Whatever possessed you to take up residence in this godforsaken country? When I found out the railroads don't even come to New Mexico, I almost turned around and went home."

"The railroads are coming," Bart assured him, "probably next year. The next trip you make will be in the comfort of a Pullman coach."

The old classmates headed directly for the archives so Randy could see the grant papers.

"Shouldn't the papers be filed with the surveyor general?" the lawyer asked.

"Normally. But I'm paying Raspberry's secretary to hide the documents in the archives. Good thing, too. Somebody already tried to destroy them by burning down the surveyor general's office."

"I can't make heads or tails of these documents," Hendricks complained after examining a few files. "You know I don't read Spanish."

"I just wanted you to see them, so you'd know they're authentic. I'll introduce you to some land grant experts who can attest to their authenticity."

Bart spent several days setting up interviews between Randy and the local title experts, who all swore they had never seen a Spanish land grant so well documented. The story of the barony had them transfixed, and Randy had to hear the details of it several times.

Francisco and Vicente complained about the amount of money Bart spent showing his old law school chum around Santa Fe—feeding him in the most expensive restaurants, buying him drinks in every influential saloon, purchasing souvenir moccasins and hats and weapons in the trading posts.

After the last land grant expert had been consulted, Bart took Randy to the Paisano Club for drinks and free lunch. They sat at a table in the middle of the barroom to consume their beers and sandwiches.

"Tomorrow we'll take the stage down to La Luz," Bart said, "and you can see the barony first hand. Meet Antonio and Bitora. Stay a month or so. I'll take you hunting. Wait till you see my fort, Randy. You've never seen the likes of it."

"Why do I need to do all that?"

"You want to see that the barony actually exists, don't you?" He reached across the table as Randy took a bite. "Here, let me help you hold on to that sandwich," he said, as he squeezed his lobbyist's fingers through the bread and into the mustard and meat.

"Dammit, Bart," the lawyer said, spraying bread crumbs from his mouth. "When are you going to grow out of these stupid pranks?"

Some men nearby were laughing. They had been eyeing Bart since he came in, hoping to see him pull one of the little jokes he was famous for.

"I can't help myself," Bart said, tipping his hat to the men in the saloon. "I'm the baron of Bad Jokes. It's a hereditary title."

"Well, I'm sick and tired of your bad jokes. And I'm sick and tired of the Territory of New Mexico. The only stagecoach I want to ride is the one that takes me back to civilization."

"What about the barony?"

"I don't need to see it," Randy said, wiping his fingers on his napkin. "What matters to Congress is paper title. Which reminds me, you'll need a survey of your so-called barony. The Lands Committee won't even consider any of these Spanish land grants anymore unless they know exactly how big the parcels are."

"What do you mean, 'so-called barony'?" Bart demanded.

The lawyer smirked. "I knew you before you came out here, remember? You're no more a baron than I am."

"Spanish custom allows a husband to assume his wife's hereditary titles. My father-in-law is a baron and a grandee of Spain, and so am I."

"Titular precepts in Spain are no different than they are elsewhere. So if you really knew anything about Spanish custom, Bart, you'd know that you can't inherit your father-in-law's title until he's dead."

Bart flicked the idea aside like a crumb from the bar-room table. "You're talking like a lawyer again. Those technicalities don't carry much weight out here in the ter-ritories. Antonio has assured me that I will be the fifth baron. It's already in his will. So I figured I might as well go ahead and get used to calling myself Baron Bartolome."

Randy just shook his head. "What about the survey?"

Bart tried not to show his consternation. Randy had become a real pain. "I've already contracted the survey-ors," he said. "They're going with me back to the barony. Although it baffles me why the size of the grant should make any difference to Congress. If we have legal titles to the land, it should make no difference how much land."

"Politics," Randy replied. "Those congressmen have to answer to the folks back home. They don't understand how one man can claim a million acres of public domain. Pub-lic sentiment has a lot to do with it."

"That's exactly my point! There's more to it than paper title, Randy. There's public sentiment. And I have the pub-lic on my side. I'm a hero—a Robin Hood passing out quit-claim deeds to my new neighbors when I could be running them out of their homes. The public is fascinated with the barony of the Sacramentos. It's like buried trea-sure, or a lost mine. Use it!"

"All right, I see your argument. Just don't push my fin-gers through my sandwich again."

"Why would I do that? It wouldn't be funny a second time."

As Randy drank from his mug, Bart reached across the table and lifted the bottom of the glass, sloshing beer up his old friend's nostrils. The saloon erupted with laughter at Jay Randolph Hendricks's expense.

TWENTY - FIVE

Randy had waited for three hours to see Senator Miles Armour, Republican from Pennsylvania, chairman of the Senate Lands Committee. Finally, the senator's aide called him in.

"Jay Randolph Hendricks," the lobbyist said, reaching over Armour's desk for a handshake.

The senator looked through his wire-rimmed spectacles at his docket. "Oh, yes," he said, his tired eyelids lifting. "The Montoya-Young grant in New Mexico. I read your dossier on the matter, Mr. Hendricks. What a fascinating tale."

"Yes, sir."

"And you represent these modern-day barons who claim this ancient grant entitles them to a million acres?"

"According to the survey, which Mr. Young orchestrated himself, the barony now encloses roughly six hundred thousand acres," Randy said. "They deeded about half of the grant to the Mescaleros after I suggested that taking tribal lands might be an impediment to Congressional approval."

"Wise counsel," Armour said. "Well, there's no need for you to take up any more of my time. I suspect you're going to try to convince me to get the grant approved."

"Not necessarily," Randy said.

The senator looked over the top of his lenses. "You are the lobbyist for this Bart Young, aren't you?"

"Yes, sir," Randy said. "And in that capacity I feel obligated to tell you that I have seen the many documents pertaining to the grant with my own eyes, and they do appear to be quite genuine. I have also met with several impartial experts on Spanish land grants, all of whom insist that the barony is valid. And, as you know, Rudolph

Raspberry, surveyor general of the Territory of New Mexico, is recommending approval, and he is a gentleman of unquestionable integrity, and a good Republican. However . . ."

Armour removed his spectacles and put an earpiece in his mouth. "Yes?"

"As a citizen, and a member of the Republican party, I feel obligated to report to you on some other aspects of the case."

"Please do," the senator suggested.

"The night before I left Santa Fe, I had a secret meeting with a man named Vernon Regis, a very influential land speculator in the Territory of New Mexico, a former Union officer from Missouri, a Republican, and a good contact in the West."

The senator nodded. "What was the nature of this secret meeting?"

Randy pulled his chair a little closer to Armour's desk and spoke in a hushed tone. "Regis believes Young manufactured the documents giving him claim to his barony."

Armour pinched the bridge of his nose and squinted. "Mr. Hendricks, you are the most confusing lobbyist I have had in my office in a long time. Are you suggesting that your own client may be a fraud?"

"There's no solid evidence of any such thing," Randy insisted. "Only Regis's word. But as I mentioned, he carries a great deal of influence. And, I did some checking into Mr. Young's background, and I found some rather disturbing things. He once attended Tulane University, though he didn't graduate. He was known as a habitual prankster who talked a great deal about Spanish land grants. He was also remembered for a certain facility he had with a pen. Some of his former classmates recalled that he forged signatures of their professors or their parents for them to get them out of awkward situations."

Slowly, Miles Armour put his glasses back on. "Mr.

Hendricks, are you working for Vernon Regis as well as Bart Young?"

"Regis offered, but I refused. That would be an obvious conflict of interest."

"But you seem to be painting your own client as a fraud. Do you suspect that the documents for this barony of Young's may have been forged?"

"No, sir. Their appearance is quite genuine, and the experts have accepted them without question. However, if this news about Young's college forgeries gets out, your committee might stand quite a bit of ridicule if it recommended confirmation of the grant to the Senate."

"Do I take it, then, that you are advising the Senate *not* to confirm this barony of the Sacramentos as a valid land grant?"

Randy chuckled and scratched his scalp. "I wouldn't be much of a lobbyist if I suggested that, sir. Besides, Young has the public sentiment right now. I understand the *New York Times* has dispatched a reporter to New Mexico to interview him. You wouldn't make yourself popular if you ruined him."

"Then just what the devil *are* you suggesting?"

"That you delay action."

The senator slumped over his desk and glared at Randy. "Young man, I am a member of the United States Senate. I have to work within the multifarious manifestations of the federal government. *Of course* I am going to delay action! I delay action on *everything*! What kind of advice is that?"

"I mean, to delay indefinitely. If Vernon Regis loses his influence in New Mexico, or turns out to be nothing more than a disgruntled land speculator, then recommend confirmation of Young's grant. If, on the other hand, this news about Young's career as an amateur forger gets out, you can advise Congress against confirmation, or dismiss the case altogether, without embarrassment."

Armour turned in his swivel chair and stared through his window at the Capitol grounds, cloaked in pure-white snow. "That seems to make sense, except for one thing. Just where does it all leave you?" He laced his fingers together and propped his feet on a windowsill.

"Young will continue to develop his grant, with or without confirmation. That's the way they do it out there in the territories. I've done my duty as a lobbyist, and my duty as a member of the Republican Party. After all, I don't plan to make a career of lobbying. I prefer public service."

Armour turned back to his guest and stared into the pale-green eyes. "You have been most enlightening, Mr. Hendricks. Your counsel is appreciated."

Randy rose, bid the senator a good day, and left with a grin on his face. Armour's aide stepped into his office to announce the next appointment.

"All right, Richard, send him in," Armour said. "And, Richard, send a note to Secretary Schurz over at Interior. There's a position for a legal researcher open at the Land Office. Recommend that Hendricks fellow who just left."

TWENTY - SIX

Bart felt himself trapped in the dream—the same dream that came to visit him every couple of moons. He knew what was going to happen, but he couldn't stop it. He saw himself putting the final touches on the forgeries: the comandante's petition, the alcalde's report, the Viceroy's order. Then came the royal *cedula,* and, though he tried to fight it, his hand signed the name of Bart Young instead of His Royal Majesty, King Carlos the Third.

He woke with a start and sat up in bed.

"What is it?" Bitora said, she was sitting in front of her mirror, brushing her long, shiny hair, the pale light of dawn reaching in for her from Fort Young's plaza. "Bartolome, was it the dream again?" She came to his side of the bed.

He saw his familiar room and felt relief engulf him. "Yes," he said. "It was terrible. Archiveque had a hundred men this time. And a howitzer cannon!"

Bitora caressed his face as she crawled onto the bed next to him. He put his arms around her and buried his face against her warm neck. He held her for a long time; then his hands began to wander.

"Not now," Bitora warned, pushing herself away with a reproachful smile. "I have to go feed the baby. You know she will sleep all day and cry all night if I don't wake her up."

Grudgingly, he let her go.

After she left, he got out of bed and looked at himself in the mirror. His thinning hair was standing on end. Back-lighted by the glare from the plaza, the top of his head looked something like a clear-cut. Well, at least his mountains weren't losing timber as fast as he was losing hair. Not since he had hired the forester from New England to establish a sensible harvest regime.

As he trimmed his beard, then dressed himself, he wondered what Carlos would have cooking down in the kitchen. He stepped onto the balcony overlooking the plaza and filled his nostrils. A cool snap was in the air, bracing him with anticipation of hunts in the snow, and cold nights by the fire with Bitora.

As he descended the stair steps made of halved logs, a chorus of familiar yelps reached him. The Mescalero guards were coming, and they were excited about some-thing. He looked toward the western watchtower.

"Don Bartolome!" the man on watch duty shouted. "The Indians have captured somebody!"

"Open the gates!" Bart shouted.

Antonio stepped from the kitchen with a cup of coffee as two of the fort's workmen threw the heavy squared-timber bar from the west entrance and swung the gates open. Chief Estrella and four Mescalero braves rode into the fort, holding an old man in buckskins at gunpoint. The prisoner's hands were bound tightly behind him, his ankles lashed to his stirrups. His face consisted of the oldest looking batch of human skin Bart had ever seen, webbed with creases. Hair trailed in greasy gray strands from the back of his hat. He twisted relentlessly in the saddle, trying to loosen his bindings, his eyes raking the Indians with hatred as he used up every cuss word Bart had ever heard.

"Capitan," Estrella said. "We caught him hunting."

Bart looked at Antonio, who, leaning casually against a pine post, made a gesture indicating that he wanted nothing to do with the problem. "Stranger," Bart said to the old man, "I'll have them cut you loose if you'll settle down."

The prisoner forced himself to cease his struggles but sat quivering with rage in the saddle. Bart gave the order, and one of the Indians cut the rawhide bindings, jumping clear in case the old man intended to kick.

"Who are you?" Bart asked.

"Tolliver. They called me Uncle Dan, back to Tennessee."

Bart noticed, as the old man rubbed his wrists, that he was still hunched over unnaturally, as if being tied up had permanently disfigured him. "Why can't you straighten up?" he asked.

Through the folds of wrinkled flesh, the beady eyes shifted. "Fell down a mountain when I was young. Broke both shoulders."

"How long have you been hunting in my mountains?"

"Your mountains grow in hell. Anyway, I don't track years much."

"Years? Were you here before we built Fort Young?"

"Before the army built Fort Stanton."

"That would be more than twenty years ago. Why didn't

you come down and introduce yourself if you were here before us?"

"Because I don't give a damn for you, that's why. Now, tell your Indians to stand aside before I show fight."

"Wait a minute," Bart said, squinting at the old man. "You're not the one the Mescaleros call *El Cimarron*—the wild one." He looked at the Indian guard and found them nodding. "Son of a gun! I thought you were just a legend. I've listened to tall tales about you in their tepees."

"Tell 'em I want my rifle back," Uncle Dan insisted.

"They say you can fly away like an eagle when you're cornered."

"Ignorant bastards. I kick like a mule, and bite like a bear, but ain't a man alive flies." He looked up and saw Bitora on the balcony with her baby. He didn't look again, but removed his hat in honor of her presence. He hadn't seen a woman in civilized dress in decades.

"What's wrong, Uncle Dan? Don't you like being a legend?"

"I like bein' alone. Tell that red buck if he drops ol' Kaintuck, I'll wear his scalp."

Bart saw Estrella holding an old Kentucky rifle, its heavy octagonal barrel mounted in a stock of tiger-stripe maple. "Chief, give him his weapon back. Where's your cabin, Uncle Dan?"

"I sleep on the ground," he said, yanking "Kaintuck" from Estrella's grasp.

"Tell you what. I'll build you a cabin and give you a deed to any place you want to settle in the mountains. You don't bother the Indians, and I'll see that they don't bother you."

Uncle Dan put his hat on and reined his horse toward the open gate. "See that *you* don't bother me, either, or ol' Kaintuck'll do you like a Indian."

"Where do you want your cabin built?" Bart asked as the old man rode out.

"I don't."

"How about over Five Springs up Bear Canyon?"

"Suit yourself," the mountain man answered, nudging his horse to a lope.

When the old man had gone, Bart noticed something different about the Indians. "Why'd you boys cut your hair?"

Estrella looked downward, almost in shame. "Semple said he would cut our rations if we did not cut our hair. So, we cut our hair, and then he cut our rations anyway."

Bart looked at Antonio. The old *rico* raised his coffee cup as if toasting his son-in-law. "You are doing well, Bartolome. Why do you look at me?" He turned into the kitchen laughing.

Bart sighed. "Chief, how many problems are you going to bring me this morning?" He stared at the stone-faced Mescaleros for a few seconds. "Well, if Semple cut your rations, I guess you boys are hungry. Come on in the kitchen and fill yourselves while I think of a way to get you a new Indian agent."

The Mescaleros leaped from their ponies and left them loose in the plaza. Carlos had to split more wood before they were through with breakfast.

"I think I've got it figured out," Bart finally said as the Indians lounged in the kitchen, rubbing their full stomachs. "Now, the first thing you do, Chief, is go down the river and steal about twenty head of my cattle."

The two barons rode down to their Penasco Ranch with the Indians and showed them which steers to steal. Estrella and his men went at it as if it were really a raid, riding hard, practicing their battle cries, looking over their shoulders for pursuers. They herded the beeves upstream, past Fort Young, into a secluded bend of Penasco Canyon.

While Estrella rode to his reservation to bring back the

tribe for the feast, Bart retired to his office and started writing letters. He wrote first to Captain Semple's commanding officer at Fort Stanton, Colonel Hampton, telling him that Semple's policies as Indian agent were starving the Mescaleros and driving them to thievery. He also requested a troop of cavalry soldiers to protect Fort Young.

Next he wrote to the Bureau of Indian Affairs, demanding compensation for the stolen cattle and lambasting Semple's lack of compassion. Finally, he demanded that the bureau remove Semple as agent and appoint a civilian to replace him.

"Why did you ask Colonel Hampton to send troops for our protection?" Antonio asked, the letter in his hand. "We are in no danger."

"First, it will give this Indian crisis a facade of authenticity. Secondly, it will give us a chance to personally harangue Colonel Hampton about Captain Semple's incompetence as an agent. And third, I can sell the army a fortune in food for the troops and grain for the horses while they quarter here."

Antonio nodded approvingly, shuffling to the Bureau of Indian Affairs letter. "I will write a letter to the bureau, too," he promised. "And I will include the signatures of the chiefs on my letter."

"And if that doesn't work, we'll get Randy Hendricks to lobby the bureau for us. That will get some action."

The Montoya villagers attended the Mescalero feast in Penasco Canyon and contributed more food—mutton, *cabrito,* corn, beans, tortillas, honey, and *leche quemada.* Antonio spent most of his time swapping old stories with Chief Ojo Blanco.

For days, the Mescaleros feasted and dried the excess beef for future use. When a rider announced the approach of the cavalry, the Indians scattered across the mountains.

As Bart had predicted, Colonel Hampton had left Semple at Fort Stanton while he came to Montoya to investigate the reported Mescalero raid. The barons insisted that the blame was Semple's more than the Mescaleros'. Even Indians had to eat. Hampton listened without response. He was an old veteran of the Mexican War, the Civil War, and numerous Indian campaigns—a tough warrior, but an honest and fair-minded man.

"Semple's a good soldier," he finally said. "He follows orders. But I would just as soon remove the Mescalero agency from Fort Stanton. It would prevent them from prostituting their squaws to my men."

Bart felt near victory. "When they have enough to eat, and some dignified work to earn their own keep, they won't have to prostitute their squaws."

As Bart had predicted, the barons procured government vouchers from Hampton before he left Fort Young. They would make a nice profit on grain for cavalry horses and grub for the soldiers.

"Gentlemen, I'm going to request that Captain Semple be relieved of his duties—with honors—as Indian agent," the colonel said as he climbed into his cavalry saddle. He looked at Antonio. "I have just the man in mind to recommend as his replacement. Maybe it's time for a civilian agent." He tipped his hat and waved his troops toward Fort Stanton.

TWENTY - SEVEN

One evening in June 1879, Chief Estrella and two braves galloped into Fort Young with the mail from Fort Stanton, including a letter from the commissioner of Indian Affairs.

Bart was riding Nepo around the courtyard on his

shoulders and carrying his baby daughter, Maria, in his arms when the Indians arrived. "Get down and stay awhile, Chief," he said. "This may be good news for you." He tore eagerly into the letter from Indian Affairs. He had been waiting months for the reply.

Estrella shook his head. "I am going back to the reservation. We have trouble there."

"What kind of trouble?"

"Victorio has come."

"Who?"

"Chief of the Mimbres Apaches."

"What's he doing here?"

"He doesn't want to stay on his reservation at San Carlos."

"Well, he can't stay on *your* reservation."

"He doesn't want to stay on any reservation at all."

Bart looked at the blank faces of the three Indians. "Antonio!" he shouted. "You better get out here!" He tucked the rest of the mail under his arm and unfolded the letter from Indian Affairs. "At least stay until I read this letter. It probably concerns you more than me." He scanned the first couple of paragraphs as he heard Antonio's boots striding across the plaza.

"What is it, Bartolome?" the old baron said.

Bart glanced up from his letter. "Some Mimbres Apaches under Chief Victorio have jumped their reservation and moved into the Sacramentos."

"How many?" Antonio said.

"Only thirteen," Estrella said, "but Victorio is trying to get Mescalero braves to follow him. Raiding."

"Did you hear that, Bartolome? We will have to send riders to the Penasco Ranch, and across the mountains to the Dog Canyon Ranch, as well. We have some sheepherders on the Sacramento River this summer, don't we? They will be easy targets if we don't warn them. Bartolome, are you listening?"

Bart was staring at the letter in his hands, his mouth hanging open, his eyes showing rare surprise. "They made *me* the new Indian agent," he said.

"Of course they did," Antonio said. "I recommended you. So did Colonel Hampton and Ojo Blanco."

"Didn't you think about asking me?"

"I know how tricky you are. You might have talked your way out of it."

"But, why would I want the job?"

"For your friends the Mescaleros. And for the barony. If the Mescaleros are happy, the barony is safe."

Bart's arms went limp and the letter hung in his grasp at his side. "Why now? There's an Indian war brewing. What am I supposed to do about it?"

"The army will go after Victorio," Antonio said. "Captain Semple will kill any Indian not camped at the agency. I suggest you establish your agency here, at Fort Young, and tell all the Mescaleros to come here for protection if they do not want to be mistaken for Mimbres."

Bart looked at Estrella.

"I will bring everyone from my camp," the chief said. "But Ojo Blanco has maybe a hundred others at Fort Stanton."

"Start for here at dawn," Bart said. "I'll ride to Fort Stanton and bring Ojo Blanco's band back myself."

The chief jerked his reins and thundered out of the fort's plaza, his two braves on his heels.

"I will go with you to Fort Stanton," Antonio said. "Ojo Blanco will listen to me."

"I don't know why in hell they didn't make *you* Indian agent," Bart said. "I wish I'd have thought of recommending you before you recommended me."

Antonio chuckled and held out his hand. "Congratulations. You are going to be a good agent."

* * *

They started for Fort Stanton the next morning before dawn, riding the longest-winded mustangs they had in the stables. It was fifty miles to the fort, and they intended to make the ride in one day.

At noon, they saw a faint dust plume in the distance, and knew Estrella's people were on the move. They veered from their trail to meet the chief, who was riding at the head of a large band. The scene struck Bart with dread: Horses, mules, and burros dragged travois; women carried papooses on their backs; dogs and children ran everywhere. He could not imagine moving everything he owned overnight. How was he going to administer to these people, so different from himself?

"Victorio left our camp last night when we started taking the lodges down," Estrella reported. "Seven of my warriors rode with him. I told them you are going to be our new agent, Capitan, but they said it is too late. They want to go raiding again, like in the old days."

"I can only help the ones who camp at Fort Young," Bart said.

The barons swapped their tired mounts for two Indian ponies, and continued toward Fort Stanton at a gallop. For two hours they rode through a mountain thunderstorm, then finally broke free of it.

They were crossing a meadow, less than an hour from the army post, when they saw half a dozen Indians approaching from the tree line.

"Recognize them?" Bart said, reining his mustang back to a walk. The horse blew like a bellows.

Antonio squinted and shook his head. "I cannot see their faces from here. But that pinto pony in the middle is one I have seen in Ojo Blanco's camp."

The rains had been plentiful on the Mescalero that summer. Grass was knee-high in the meadow, and green as new aspen leaves. A huge ponderosa pine stood alone in the middle of the meadow, and Bart rode into its shade to wait for the Indians. He sat casually in the saddle, trying to find a familiar face among the six warriors who loped toward him.

Then, without explanation, one of the braves flew from the back of his horse, his moccasined feet cartwheeling over his head. Bart heard the shot and the dull thud of a heavy rifle ball hitting flesh. He reached for his Winchester even before he understood what had happened.

The Indians milled around their fallen friend long enough for Antonio to find the black puff of smoke at the edge of the meadow. As Bart looked toward the place, he saw the unmistakable figure of Uncle Dan Tolliver galloping toward the lone pine, his long rifle in his hand.

The war cry from the five braves leaped into Bart's ears and crawled up and down his spine on scorpion legs. He drew his rifle, not certain what he would do with it, and levered a cartridge into the chamber. Two of the Indians charged Uncle Dan. The other three came directly toward him and Antonio.

Bart rode into the sunlight, holding his rifle over his head. "Whoa, boys!" he shouted. "Don't shoot!" He looked toward Uncle Dan. The old man was still coming, but had dropped to the off side of his saddle, clinging there like a Comanche raider, his horse shielding him from bullets.

Bart heard the grass hiss around him and heard the rifle reports. A pine branch split above him.

"Behind the tree, Bartolome!" Antonio shouted. "Take cover! They are trying to kill us!"

Bart wheeled his pony behind the pine and hit the ground with one rein in his hand. The tree trunk was wide, but not wide enough. "Why are they shooting at us?" he yelled. "They must think we're with that old bastard!" He looked toward Uncle Dan in time to see the long Kentucky rifle belch smoke over the saddle seat. Another brave twisted from his pony, and the old man kept coming.

"I don't know," Antonio said. "But I am going to show

them I can shoot back." He leaned around the tree and let a few rounds go over the heads of the attacking braves.

Bart stepped into the open and added to the barrage. The three warriors parted, held their horses back, and returned the fire. Bart jumped back behind the cover of the lone pine as Uncle Dan arrived, leaping from his horse, holding his rifle in one hand, reaching for his powder horn with the other.

"What the hell is wrong with you, old man?" Bart shouted. "The Mescaleros aren't hostile!"

The old man smiled as he took a greased patch from the box on Kaintuck's stock. "Damn fool. You don't know coons from ringtail cats. Them ain't Mescalero, they's Mimbres."

Bart checked the four Indians for position and found them regrouping two hundred yards away, contemplating another attack. "How do you know?"

"I know," the mountain man said, ramming the patched ball down the muzzle. He leaned his ramrod against the tree.

"But those are Mescalero ponies."

"Ponies is swappable. You're ridin' a Mescalero horse yourself."

The shrill cry came across the meadow again, and bullets started tearing into the lone pine. If those were Mimbres Apaches, Bart figured he had good reason to shoot for the kill. Victorio's renegades had no business here causing trouble among his Mescaleros. He braced his Winchester against the tree and worked the action as fast as it would go, taking little time to aim. Antonio fired more deliberately. Uncle Dan was merely aiming, awaiting the perfect shot.

As the four Apaches rode by, firing their repeating rifles, Bart wheeled and shot from the hip, hitting an Indian pony in the neck. As the horse collapsed, the Indian flew through the air and disappeared in the tall grass.

Old Kaintuck roared, and Bart turned to see another empty Apache saddle.

"Get any?" Tolliver asked.

Antonio shook his head as he pushed rounds into the loading port of his rifle.

"I unhorsed one," Bart said, pointing.

The old mountain man leaned his long rifle against the tree, handed his bridle reins to Bart, and skulked into the grass. Dropping to his stomach, he vanished, the grass in front of him falling like wheat before a mowing machine, revealing his progress as he scrambled toward the dead horse.

"What's he going to do without a gun?" Bart asked.

"*Quién sabe?*" Antonio replied. "Let him kill himself if he wants to."

One of the Apaches caught a loose horse and charged back toward the downed warrior, leading the extra mount. Bart tried to find him in his sights, but the Indian was riding fast and Bart's nerves were wound. His shots went wild. When the rescuer came near enough, the warrior Bart had unhorsed jumped up from the grass and ran for the extra horse. He vaulted into the empty saddle just as a shot from Antonio's rifle took the horse out from under him.

The Indians tried to mount double, but Dan Tolliver rose from the grass, not thirty feet away. A flash of reflected sunlight glinted from his hand, then flickered through the air like ball lightning. The steel blade hit the mounted Indian high in the shoulder and almost knocked him from the horse.

The Apache on the ground wheeled and pointed his rifle at Uncle Dan, but no report came. As the mountain man rushed the two Apaches with bare hands, the one on the ground jumped behind his rescuer, holding the knifed man in the saddle. He urged the pony on, but Dan Tolliver was there, clawing at the bridle with one hand and the Indians with the other.

"He's trying to get his knife so he can stab the poor bastard again!" Bart said, looking over his rifle sights for a clear shot.

The Indian riding double brought his rifle down on Dan's head like a club, then rode away with the knifed man in front of him. Bart followed them in his irons, and twice lined up a shot, but he couldn't see killing either man after they had shown such courage in rescuing each other.

Antonio had been watching the other mounted Indian catch the last loose horse. When the three surviving Apaches were all mounted separately, they sent a last barrage of shots toward the lone pine, then disappeared into the woods, the knifed man riding between the other two.

The two barons mounted and rode to check on Uncle Dan. They found him on his hands and knees, shaking his head.

"You all right?" Bart asked, dropping from the saddle to lift the old man to his feet.

"Did you get my knife?" he asked.

"Hell, no, I didn't get your knife. You left it stuck in that Apache."

"Damnation," he said, rubbing a bloody spot in his long gray hair. "My old Green River knife."

"What are you doing on the reservation, anyway?" Bart asked. "You don't have authorization to be here."

"You'd be dead if I wasn't here. Been followin' that bunch of Victorio's boys for two days, waitin' for a chance to get their scalps. You two spoilt it for me."

Bart shook his head in disgust and handed the old man his reins. "I want you to stay clear of the Mescalero from now on, you hear?"

"Go to hell. I was here before the damn reservation. Who are you to tell me where I go?"

"I'm the new Indian agent. You'll do as I say or I'll have the Indian police arrest you."

"What Indian police?"

"The ones I'm going to form to take care of trespassers like you. Why don't you stay up at that cabin I built for you at Bear Canyon?"

"Been usin' it."

"Good." Bart got back on his horse.

"Tore the damn floor out of it, dug me a fire pit, and used it for a smokehouse."

Antonio broke into laughter in spite of the glare Bart gave him.

"Just stay off this reservation," Bart warned, reining away.

"Wait, dammit!" Uncle Dan shouted. "I need a loan of a knife."

"What for?"

"Take them Mimbres scalps."

"Forget it," Bart said. He spurred his mustang, and headed for Fort Stanton, Antonio laughing behind him as they began to gallop.

TWENTY - EIGHT

Five minutes from Fort Stanton, Bart sensed the sky rumbling over the thundering of hooves. His pony slid on its hocks as he yanked back on the reins. Echos of gunfire were leapfrogging around the valley of the Rio Bonito.

The barons looked at each other. They heard stray shots now, piercing the air from the direction of the fort. The reports did not come with the regularity of a rifle drill. Bart and Antonio spurred their exhausted mounts on as the sun sank behind the western hills.

At Fort Stanton they found a couple of hundred soldiers herding Indians like cattle. The bugle blew mixed signals. The muzzle of a Mountain howitzer trailed smoke. They rode on, and at the edge of the village on the Rio Bonito, Bart saw the bodies—men, women, and children. A mother wailed as she dragged her wounded son, begging the soldiers for help, leaving a trail of blood.

Flecks of foam dropped from Bart's horse as he rode to the woman and jumped from the saddle beside the wounded boy. He wrapped his bandana around the shattered leg to stanch the flow of blood. In Spanish, he told the mother to lay the boy in the shade until the post surgeon could help.

"All Indians in the corral!" a private shouted. "Baron, you'd better get the hell out of the way. We're rounding up Indians."

"You're not rounding this one up. He's got a busted leg."

"Orders, baron. That squaw will have to drag him."

Bart drew his Colt and pointed it at the private. "Tell Colonel Hampton I want him here *now*."

"Colonel Hampton's at Fort Union."

"Where's the major?"

"Sick in bed."

Bart trembled with rage. "Captain Semple's in command?"

"Yes, sir," the private said, staring down the barrel of the Colt.

"Get him."

As the private galloped away, Bart carried the wounded boy to the shade and calmed his mother. He looked for Antonio, and saw him kneeling over a body on the riverbank. Ojo Blanco. Antonio crossed the old chief's arms over his chest. His eyes met Bart's, a fury in them such as Bart had seen only once before, in the courtyard of the old Montoya hacienda, the day Regis took Sebastiana in his arms.

Captain Semple rode back with the private. "Young! This is army business. Stand aside, or you'll be arrested."

"This is the business of the Mescalero Indian agent. And

that's me." He handed the letter from Indian Affairs to the officer.

"You?" Semple said, glancing down the letter. "I was told a civilian was coming. "But *you?*"

"What happened here?"

Semple handed the letter back to Bart. "Victorio killed two prospectors on Eagle Creek this morning. I had reason to believe some of his men were in Ojo Blanco's camp. When I ordered the Indians to turn over their weapons, some of them tried to sneak away up the river, so I had my men open fire."

Bart saw Antonio stalking toward the captain and knew trouble was coming.

"You stupid son of a bitch. You don't know coons from ringtail cats!"

"What?"

"Can't you tell the difference between a Mimbres and a Mescalero Apache?"

Semple's pale lips curled under his wispy yellow mustache. "I can tell a good Apache from a bad one." He pointed at the body of Ojo Blanco. "There lies a good one now."

Antonio grabbed the silver bars on the officer's collar and pulled him down from the saddle. Bart just watched as the *rico* pummeled Semple with his fist, his knees, and his boots once the captain had fallen.

"Private!" Semple called as he collapsed. "Arrest him!"

The private spurred his horse forward, grabbed Antonio by the arm, and pulled him away. Jumping from his mount, he pinned Antonio to the ground, putting the muzzle of his carbine against the old baron's chest.

As Semple struggled to find his feet, Bart drew his Colt, grabbed a handful of yellow hair, and held his gun barrel against the captain's head. "Tell that private to drop his carbine."

The officer and the enlisted man looked at each other.

"Tell him, or you'll leave your brains in this Indian camp," Bart warned, shaking the captain.

"Do as he says, private."

Reluctantly, the private dropped his carbine and stepped away from Antonio. The *rico* was slow getting up, and Bart knew he was getting too old for this sort of scuffle.

He shook the captain again, unable to check his anger. "This is what's going to happen, Semple," he said. "You're going to order an ambulance brought here to the village, and you're going to take every wounded Indian back to the infirmary where the post surgeon can work on them. Then you're going to order a burial detail to put these massacred citizens in the ground, one to a grave, each with a marker and the name of the person buried there on it. Finally, you're going to release the rest of those citizens from your damn stinking corrals and turn them over to me. I'm taking them to Fort Young. Do you think you can remember those orders to the letter?"

Semple nodded as Bart shoved him toward his horse. "Come on, private," the captain said, picking up his campaign hat. He mounted, but looked down at Bart before riding to the fort. "You've never seen what an Apache on the warpath can do to a good man in uniform, Young. This private here has seen it, haven't you, private?"

"Yes, sir. I've seen the guts of my friends stretched across the desert to cook in the sun."

The soldiers rode away, leaving the barons to hunt for survivors among the dead.

Bart saw the body of a dead Mescalero woman draped through the entrance hole of her tepee. "I wonder why, Captain," he muttered to himself.

TWENTY - NINE

L ittle Nepo rode just in front of the pack mule that carried the antlers of the buck his father had killed. He had to look back at the trophy every few steps. He believed his father was the best hunter in the world, not even excepting Indians or mountain men. And, why not? His father had told him so, and his father was the fifth baron of the Sacramentos. Someday Nepo would be the sixth.

Nepo was eight, and on his first big hunt. His mother had tried to keep him from going, but his father had insisted. He was ready to get home to Fort Young—his toys were there, and it was warm—but he had enjoyed the hunt. The horses stepped high through the fresh snow. They knew their stables were near.

"Hey, Nepo!" his father shouted. "Come here. I want to show you something."

The boy reined his mount out of the pack line and joined his father under a small pine sapling.

"You see all the snow on these pine branches?" Bart said, when his son came to his side.

The boy looked up into the gray sky. "Yes, sir," he said.

"I want to show you what you can do with it. Call Carlos over here."

Nepo scanned the pack line for the cook. "Carlos!" he cried, squinting his eyes. "Come here!"

"Qué pasa?" Carlos said, riding under the branches of the small pine.

"Look what we found up in this tree, Carlos," Bart said. When the cook looked up, Bart shook the trunk of the sapling, bringing a cloud of frozen powder down on Carlos's face.

Nepo kicked in his stirrups as he laughed.

"You are going to teach that boy all of your bad habits!" Carlos scolded, shaking the snow from his face.

When they arrived back at Fort Young, Bitora was waiting in the plaza with Maria and Lucia. "You have a visitor," she said, handing her daughters to Bart one at a time so he could hug them. "In the saloon with Papa." She kissed him, then helped Nepo down from the saddle.

"Who is it?"

"That deputy sheriff. Yarborough."

Bart found Antonio entertaining Linden Yarborough over a game of billiards.

"How'd the hunt go, baron?" the deputy asked.

"Damn good," Bart said, shaking Yarborough's thick hand. He saw the lawman maybe twice a year and didn't know him well, but he had no reason to dislike him. Yarborough stood a few inches short of six feet, and was built stoutly. His broad face grew the thickest, curliest mat of whiskers in the county. Bart considered him a rather simple man, but he was hell on criminals. He had ridden with Sheriff Pat Garrett in the Lincoln County War and had helped capture Billy the Kid at Stinking Springs.

"What brings you to Fort Young?" Bart asked. "Chasing outlaws?"

"You might say so. I came to lay down the law to your Mexicans. I'm going to be the new justice of the peace for this precinct, and I intend to clean this place up and Americanize it. I was just telling Antonio that he's the only good Mexican in the county, as far as I'm concerned. Every other one I've ever known was either a thief or a killer."

Bart sauntered around behind the bar and poured himself a glass of whiskey. "Deputy, you live in Lincoln, right?"

Yarborough nodded as he rammed the cue ball with his stick.

"I don't suppose you live on the Mexican side of town."

"Hell, no."

"Got any Mexican deputies working with you?"

"Wouldn't have 'em."

"Mexican friends?"

The sheriff smirked.

"That explains it. You've got honest Mexican citizens everywhere around you, but the only ones you associate with are those you track down to haul into jail. Your opinion's slanted."

"You don't know what the hell you're talkin' about," Yarborough said. "You don't have to keep the law in this county."

"I maintain perfect order on this barony, and I do it with the help of the Mexican citizens in Montoya."

Yarborough straightened slowly and put his cue stick on the table in the middle of the game. "You never got congressional approval for this grant did you, Young?"

Bart shrugged. "Congress works slow."

"As far as I'm concerned, your so-called grant ought to be opened up to settlement by Americans. I'm on my way up, Young. I don't plan to be a deputy forever. I've got connections in Santa Fe. If you don't want me to open your grant up to settlement, you better not stand in the way of me cleaning out that den of thieves you call Montoya."

Bart chortled in disbelief. "We haven't had a serious crime since we established the village."

"You've exported your share. I'll be holding court in Montoya the first Friday of every month," he said, taking his hat from a set of antlers on the wall. "Of course, I'll still be deputy sheriff as well as justice of the peace. I can arrest 'em and try 'em all in one breath if I want to. Too many Mexicans on your side of the county, Young. Time to get some of them out and get some Americans in."

"Just when did you become justice of the peace?" Bart demanded. "I didn't hear anything about it."

"The commissioners' court is going to appoint me at its next meeting. It's all arranged." He put on his coat and headed for the door. "I won't have Mexicans taking over this county. If you want to hold on to this grant of yours, I suggest you remember that."

Bart stood with his mouth open for several seconds after Yarborough walked out. He looked at Antonio, still standing across the pool table and holding his cue stick in both hands, scowling.

"Antonio," Bart said suddenly, "put that pool stick down." He walked around the table and tugged on the bottom of his father-in-law's vest.

"What are you doing, *idiota?*"

Bart stepped back, put his hand on his chin, and studied Antonio. "Go stand behind the bar."

"What?"

"Go on, do as I say." He led the old grandee around the end of the bar by the arm. "Slick your hair back on the right side."

"Stop acting like a fool. What are we going to do about that deputy?"

"Hmm . . ." Bart said, observing Antonio. "I don't know. I just don't know. It might work."

"What might work?"

"Stay right there. Don't move a hair." Bart ran out of the saloon, down the stairs, and across the plaza to the carpenter's shop. He found a heavy wooden mallet with a head the size of a peach can.

"What do you have that thing for?" Antonio said when Bart came back with the mallet. "Are you going to knock some sense into yourself?"

"Here, hold it," Bart said, handing the mallet to Antonio. He backed away to behold his old amigo across the billiards table. "Now, pound that thing on the bar three times, and shout, 'Order! Order! Order in the court!' "

THIRTY

A heavy snow made traveling difficult, but the barons got every healthy man in Montoya over the rolling plains to Lincoln for the next meeting of the commissioners' court. The Mexican population in Lincoln had been alerted, too, and met the procession from Montoya as it came in from the south. Other Mexican citizens streamed in from all over the county to join the movement.

They gathered outside the courthouse, and harangued the Anglo commissioners as they went to convene. When the meeting was called to order, Bart led in as many of his followers as would fit the cramped quarters.

"Mr. Young," the county judge stated, pounding his gavel. "This court is well aware of your penchant for practical jokes, but this disturbance is beyond decorum. Why have you brought this rabble here?"

"Why, to show our support for this august body, Your Honor," Bart said.

"Your support is noted. Now, please clear this room."

"And to get these citizens registered to vote," Bart continued. "And to inform this court that if it appoints Deputy Sheriff Linden Yarborough justice of the peace in my precinct—or any other precinct, for that matter—not a single Mexican in the county will vote for Your Honor or any of the commissioners come next election!"

A cheer rose from the Mexican contingent, and the judge banged his gavel ineffectually until Bart quieted the crowd.

"However," he continued, "if this court were to exercise its infinite wisdom by appointing the venerable Don Antonio Geronimo Montoya de Cordoba y Chaves de Oca justice of the peace instead of Linden Yarborough, Your Honor would be virtually assured of re-election!"

The judge pounded his gavel again until the voices died down. "Where is Deputy Yarborough? Why isn't he here to speak up for himself?"

"Strangely enough, Your Honor, he had to investigate an alleged shooting over at my Penasco River ranch—an incident that I fear may have been greatly exaggerated. But, you know Lin. He had to see for himself. He'd make a damn good sheriff!"

Again the county judge had to pound his gavel until Bart quieted the crowd. "This court is going into executive session to consider this matter," the judge declared. "I want all citizens and newspaper reporters out!"

Bart was unable to attend Antonio's first session of court at Fort Young. Pressing matters required his attention elsewhere on the barony. The graders for the Sacramento Railroad had reached the Regis mine and would work through the winter to get to Star Mountain, where Bart had wanted for years to build his grand log lodge house. With the money the railroad would bring him, he would be able to appoint it in high luxury.

It was his railroad. He had gone to Santa Fe to recruit investors, but he was president of the company and the largest stockholder. The narrow gauge spur from El Paso would enable him to better get his timber to market. Regis would also pay dividends getting his ore out of his mine.

When he got to Youngstown, where the railroad construction crews were quartering, a fancy coach in front of the Youngstown saloon caught Bart's eye. When he entered the saloon, he saw Vernon Regis sitting at the bar, his long, paper-skinned fingers wrapped around a jigger of whiskey.

"Hello, Baron," the speculator said.

As he glanced quickly around the barroom for Domingo

Archiveque, Bart opened his coat so he could get to his side arm.

"He came alone, Bart," the bartender said.

Regis laughed. "You're a little nervous, aren't you . . . Baron?"

Bart hung his sheepskin coat on a hook. "I underestimated you once, Vernon. Never again." He felt like a regular mountain man when he compared his red-flannel shirt and hunting moccasins to the speculator's patent leather shoes and boiled collar. "What are you doing here?"

"Damn miners are threatening to go on strike again."

The old woodstove stood in a box of sand that had caught many a hot coal. Bart hooked his heel over the rim of the box as he warmed his hands. A gust whistled through the cracks between the warped pine boards.

"Doesn't surprise me. I encouraged them to strike months ago." He moved to the bar and sat two stools away from Regis. The bartender had a jigger of bourbon waiting for him. "Did you see the trestle my railroad engineer started across La Luz Canyon?"

"Yes. That's going to be quite some feat of engineering. Too bad you'll have to give it to the government."

"What's that supposed to mean?"

"It means you never did get your congressional confirmation."

"Congress works slow." Bart rubbed his cold hands together before picking up the shot glass. "I've got my lobbyist in Washington working on it."

"You mean that redheaded Hendricks fellow? Last time he reported to me, he said the debate over your claim would never get out of committee. I know as well as you do that he's working for the Land Office now. He doesn't have time to lobby for you."

This was a shock. Randy reporting to Regis? No, that was just a bluff. But, Randy *had* been neglecting the question of confirmation for the past couple of years. It was time to renew the campaign. "Randy Hendricks is not the only lobbyist in Washington," he said, scrambling to cover himself.

"He's the only one you ever hired."

Both men went back to drinking their whiskey.

"Where's old Antonio?" Regis asked.

"He's holding court across the mountains."

"I heard about that stunt you pulled with the county commissioners." Regis took a swallow. "You two bullshit barons are building your own little dynasty down there. What I can't figure out is why you ever agreed to serve as Indian agent. Can't be the salary."

"As long as I keep the Indians happy, they'll help me look after my barony."

"Happy? I heard you got fourteen of them massacred your first day as agent."

"That was also Delton Semple's last day as agent. He's the one that shot them down."

"*The* Delton Semple?" Regis said, craning his frail neck to look at Bart. "The Indian fighter? I don't remember him getting reprimanded for any massacre."

"The army promoted him to major and sent him out after Victorio."

Regis laughed and pounded his fist on the bar. "Now he's a bigger hero than you!"

Bart winced. "I was just happy to get shed of him. We haven't lost a single Indian to disease or murder since Semple left. I got the Bureau of Indian Affairs to increase rations, and nobody's been able to put in a lower bid than me to supply them. The Mescaleros and I have a great partnership.

"Chief Estrella has ten officers in his Indian police now. His band is building cabins on the reservation. I've got five braves learning how to farm over at Montoya, two learning the cow business at my Dog Canyon ranch—you remember the place, Vernon—and three more at my Penasco River ranch. One brave is working in that old sawmill you built on the Tularosa River, another three are earning wages in the grist mill we just built at Fort Young, about half a dozen are learning how to tend sheep on the reservation, and nine or ten have entered into the freighting business."

"If they'll work cheaper than these Irishmen, I'll hire them as scab workers in the mine," Regis said.

"Indians don't like working underground. And I wouldn't let them work for you, anyway. I wouldn't want to lose their trust."

Regis poured himself another drink and stared at the wall. A gust howled through the cracks and sounded as if it would tear the roof off of the saloon. Bart threw his whiskey back, slid from his barstool, and fetched his coat from its hook.

"I noticed your railroad crew is grading above town," Regis said. "How high's the road going to go?"

"All the way to the summit of Star Mountain. I'm going to build a lodge up there, and I want all my influential friends to be able to ride in style right to my front gate. It's going to be quite a mansion, Vernon. A summer retreat. Up there the dog days run about seventy-five degrees." He slipped his coat on and put his hand on the door handle.

"When you get it built, I hope you'll invite me to come see," Regis said.

Bart chuckled as he held the door open to let the frigid mountain air in. "Sure," he said. "The day you get frostbit in hell."

PART THREE

THIRTY - ONE

Bart heard the *Conquistador's* steam whistle from the music suite of his Star Mountain Lodge. He usually went to the window to watch it chug up the tracks, belching smoke and spewing steam, but this morning he had other matters on his hands.

"I know you don't want to go, son," he said, "but you're going to be the sixth baron of the Sacramentos, and you have to finish your education."

"Why can't I just go to the Indian school at Montoya this year?" Nepo pleaded. He was fifteen now, and hated leaving the adventures and luxuries of the barony to go to school.

"Son, you know the reverend doesn't teach those Indians anything but reading, writing, and ciphering. No Latin, no Shakespeare, no history. Even the Indians have to go away to Carlisle if they want to learn more."

"But, Papa, I learn more here with you than I do at school."

The baron grinned appreciatively. "Nice try, Nepo, but you're going back to school. You need a city education if you want to get into a good college. Anyway, Albuquerque's not so bad, and you'll be back for the holidays."

Nepo clenched his fists and bunched his lips, but he knew it was useless. His father had always been strict about his education. He stalked out of the music room and stomped up the log stairway to his bedroom.

The Star Mountain lodge had turned out grander than

even the baron had imagined: two stories high, covering an acre of ground, looking more like a hotel than a home. Bart claimed it was the largest log structure in the world, though he wasn't at all sure about that.

Bitora rose from the piano bench and marched to the door to watch her son go up the stairs. "He has been seeing some girl at Montoya," she said, her voice rasping her disapproval. "That's why he doesn't want to go back to school."

"Really? Mexican or Indian?"

"Indian?" Bitora hissed. "My son had better not be fooling around with any squaws!"

Bart sipped his morning coffee casually. "Why not? Why shouldn't the seventh baron be half Mescalero?"

"Because I am his mother, and I say he is not going to fool around with any Indian girls."

Bart chuckled. "Well, honey, he's going back to school, anyway, so I wouldn't worry about it. Just sit down there and play some more of that Beethoven you've been working on."

Reluctantly, Bitora returned to her piano bench.

Hilario entered the room with a bundle of envelopes. "Don Bartolome, the mail has come up with the *Conquistador*."

Bart put his cup on the coffee table. "Hand it over, and let's see what's new." He untied the string binding the envelopes together.

"Mas café, Don Bartolome?" Carlos asked, carrying the coffee pot into the room as the piano started playing.

"Por favor, Carlos," the baron said, nodding at his cup. He shuffled through a few envelopes, opened one, read the contents, then said, "Francisco wants to know why the mill earnings are down this year. Doesn't he realize there's a drought on?" Bart tossed the letter on the sofa and shuffled more envelopes, flipping them aside like a card dealer,

until one caught his interest. "Here's something from George Baird."

"Who?" Bitora said, pausing between chords on the piano.

"He used to work in the office of the surveyor general. He hid the grant papers for us, remember?" The baron read in silence for several seconds. "I'll be switched! Looks like we're finally going to get our grant confirmed. George says Congress has established a Court of Private Land Claims to settle the question of all the old Spanish and Mexican land titles. They're going to have headquarters in Santa Fe."

"What kind of court is that?" she asked suspiciously, turning away from the ivory keys.

"Says it's like no other court ever invented. Five justices will decide each case. He's got their names listed here. A bunch of fellows I've never heard of. All of them from the States. Says the court will include a government lawyer to argue against each claimant. The lawyer's name is—" Bart's mouth dropped open, and he stared at the letter in silence.

"Who?" Bitora demanded.

"Jay Randolph Hendricks." His eyes drifted across the room.

"What does that mean?" she asked.

"What does it mean? My Lord, woman, what a stroke of luck for us! It means Randy's going to be arguing the government's case against us in the Court of Private Land Claims, but just how hard do you think he'll argue against his old pal?"

The boyish look on her husband's face made Bitora smile. "That's wonderful."

"Where's Antonio? He'll jump through the roof when I tell him."

"He's probably still in bed," Bitora said. "He's getting lazier every day."

"Well, he's old, honey. He's earned it. I'll go wake him up and tell him the good news."

He sprang from the sofa and bounded out of the room. Taking three stairs in each stride, he ascended to the second floor and trotted down the long hall to Antonio's wing, where the old don's bedroom, library, and office overlooked the slopes.

He knocked on the door as he opened it. "Antonio," he said, peering into the room. The velvet drapes were open, and the sun was beaming in on the old man's head, pressed neatly into the pillow. "Good news, Antonio," he said, walking to the bed. "We're finally going to get our grant confirmed." He sat on the mattress and felt Antonio's weight shift loosely toward him. "Antonio?" he said, putting his hand on his father-in-law's shoulder.

The old baron's body was as cool as a chunk of granite in a shady canyon. Bart shook him but knew Antonio would never wake again. The letter he had brought with him dropped unnoticed to the floor. He sighed and looked down at the lifeless face.

He had always known this moment would come, but somehow it seemed impossible. On their last ride together, just a week ago, the old man had pointed out the meadow on the mountain peak where he wanted to be buried.

"All right, I promise," Bart had said, "*if* I outlive you." But Antonio had seen the end of the road.

He could not think of going downstairs to tell Bitora. He would wait here. She would suspect something after awhile, and come up to investigate. For now he would have a few last minutes alone with the old man.

If he suffered tortures the rest of his days, he would still die wealthy for having known Antonio Montoya. Together, they had accomplished what perhaps no other men could have: pulled off the world's greatest hoax. A million acres of historic jest. It had been good for a few laughs.

"Ol' Antonio . . ." he said, pulling the covers up on his

father-in-law's chest, as if to warm him. "Now you're going to miss it. We've finally got a chance to get our grant confirmed." He didn't really feel very sad. That would come later. "But, don't worry. I'll get it done by myself. I'll put our barony on the map."

THIRTY - TWO

Bart produced a whiskey bottle from the bar in Fort Young's billiards parlor. He poured three shot glasses, giving one to Jay Randolph Hendricks and another to his lawyer, Clarence Tankersly of Denver.

"You've seen the barony now, Randy. You've seen the documents. You've talked to the land-grant experts. How long do you think it will take to get me a trial date with the Court of Private Land Claims, and to get my patent?"

Randy nodded. "It's about time we got down to talking business."

For seven days, the men had toured the barony from Dog Canyon to Fort Young, from Star Mountain to the Mescalero. At Fort Stanton, the new commander, Colonel Delton Semple, had let them use the guest quarters.

"I'd do anything to help the government take Young's land away from him," Semple had said to Hendricks.

"Why?" Tankersly had asked.

"He's turned the entire Mescalero nation into his own private army. The man's dangerous."

"For an army, they sure get a lot of farming, stock raising, timber cutting, and freighting done," Tankersly had argued.

Now they were back at Fort Young, and Randy was ready to negotiate. He turned his back to the baron to confer with Tankersly. "I've worked up a proposal. If you would agree to give up all but, say, a hundred thousand acres, we could reduce the amount of the claim, restore most of it to the public domain, and still leave your client with a sizeable piece of property."

"Absolutely not," Tankersly said. A brilliant court lawyer, he was a handsome young man with long waves of hair.

"You tell him, Clarence," Bart said. "That's the lamest idea I ever heard."

"I've got a better idea," Tankersly said. "The original grant was for roughly a million acres, right? But the baron deeded about half of it to the Mescaleros. So, why not have the court reduce the grant by half, and take away the Indian reservation and that little bit of land around it that Bart hardly uses anyway. That would look good on paper for you, and still leave the baron with almost everything he's using right now."

"Now, wait a minute, Clarence," Bart said. "I don't plan to give up one acre—"

"Not good enough," Randy said, interrupting the baron. "The cession of land to the Indians has received too much publicity. I'll have to reduce the grant by more than half. I won't let your client get away with any more than a quarter of a million acres."

"*You* won't let me get away with it?" Bart said, his anger building. But the lawyers ignored him, and continued to negotiate.

"Hendricks, you don't want to argue this case before the public. The baron's documents are too complete. You're better off taking the Indian reservation, and maybe another fifty thousand acres as a token of my client's willingness to deal with the court, but that's all you'll get."

Bart picked up the half-full whiskey bottle and hurled it across the room, shattering it on the adobe wall. "Damn you two arrogant little lawyers!" he bellowed. "Who in the hell do you think you are, trying this case in my saloon?

"Randy, I will not cede so much as a square inch of my barony to the government without a fight! I have killed men in defense of this property, and damn near been killed myself! You can argue yourself blue in the face, but you won't get an acre!

"And as for you, Clarence. How dare you negotiate away even an acre of my domain without consulting me first? If I didn't like you so much, I'd terminate your services right here and now for such a stunt! Now, brace yourself for a fight, and get me every clod of dirt I'm entitled to—and the Court of Private Land Claims can be damned!"

Tankersly stood and took Bart by the arm. "Excuse us," he said to Randy as he pulled the baron to the far end of the saloon. "I can get you an excellent deal tonight," the young lawyer whispered. "You'd hardly miss fifty thousand acres on a place as big as this. Your legal expenses would be minimal, and you could have your patent before spring."

"I'd miss fifty thousand acres like I'd miss my front teeth," Bart growled. "I won't give up one rock or blade of grass."

"Baron, I'm talking about getting a cinch on this case tonight. This Court of Private Land Claims is the strangest body the United States has ever created. We don't know what it's going to do. The justices are going to favor the side of the government that hired them for this court. They'll want to make an example out of you. You can't fight them."

"Clarence, you don't know what I can and cannot fight," Bart said, loud enough for Randy to hear. "Let me tell you one more time. The legal expenses are immaterial. The time is of no importance. The justices can make an example of somebody else. The barony is *everything!* Every square foot of it. Every rock, tree, cactus, and lizard will remain under my dominion. If you're not up to that, I'll get another lawyer. We're going to fight!"

"I wouldn't do that, Bart," Randy said, grinning at the other end of the saloon.

"And just why not?" the baron said stalking toward his old friend.

"I can tell you why not," Tankersly said, following his client. "You may not like this, Baron, but you hired me to give you legal advice, and, by God, that's what I'm going to do. If you fight this case in court, Hendricks will drag it out as long as he can. He'll use every delaying tactic in the book. He'll disrupt your family life and your ability to do business. He'll cost you a fortune. And then, who knows whether or not you'll win your case."

Bart looked at Randy and found the redhead nodding, grinning smugly. He sat down at the table with his old classmate. "Randy, we go back over twenty years. Why in hell are you doing this to me now?"

The lawyer scratched his crown convulsively, shaking his red curls like loose springs. "You never understood the legal system, did you, Bart? I am counsel for the United States government. I have to argue against you with everything I've got. *Especially* because you and I were once friends. I won't be accused of favoring you. To you, the barony is everything. To me, the law is everything."

"The law can go to hell. What about justice?"

"To ensure justice for the government, I have to take an adversarial point of view to your claim. The whole thing is your fault, Bart. If you hadn't brought me out here to lobby for your barony in the first place, then I wouldn't know a thing about Spanish land grants, I wouldn't have been appointed to this court, and I wouldn't have to live in this godforsaken country for the next several years of my life."

"If you don't want to live in New Mexico, you should have turned the appointment down. You don't think straight anymore. You don't understand what's right or wrong. You've only said one thing tonight that makes sense."

"What's that?"

"You and I were once friends. Once, but no more. I want you on the next train that leaves the Star Mountain depot; then you can go back to Santa Fe and prepare yourself for the fight of your life in court."

Randy shrugged and pushed his whiskey glass away. "I'll get an early start in the morning." He rose and left the saloon without even saying good night.

"Now, you," Bart said, turning to his lawyer. "Are you ready to argue my case in court?"

Tankersly picked up his whiskey glass and poured its contents down his throat. "I'm advising you against it, but if that's what you want, I'll fight the Court of Private Land Claims until I'm as old as its damned justices are now."

THIRTY - THREE

The baron provided his former friend with a hearty breakfast the next morning while his men hitched the carriage to take Randy from Fort Young to the Star Mountain depot. Bart and Tankersly stood in the plaza as Randy came from the dining room to get in the coach.

The crisp smell of the New Mexico morning grabbed Bart by the nose and put a smile on his face. He was shoving loads into the open cylinder of a Smith and Wesson revolver as Randy threw his bags into the coach.

"Is that for me?" the lawyer asked.

"Not the way I'd like to give it to you." He snapped the breech shut and put the loaded pistol in Randy's hand.

"What do I need that for?"

"Indian trouble. A radical bunch of ghost shirts have gone on the warpath. They've been stirred up ever since they heard about the Battle of Wounded Knee up north. A scout came in last night and warned me that they would be looking for scalps today."

"I don't even know how to use this thing," Randy complained.

"Double action. Just point it and pull the trigger."

"Your driver is armed. Why do I need a gun?"

"Just take it," Bart said. "Now, get in the coach and keep your head low."

Randy frowned as he climbed inside.

"And remember the code of the west, Randy."

"What code?"

"Save the last bullet for yourself."

"What for?"

"You'd rather die quick by your own hand than suffer slow in their's." He nodded at Hilario in the driver's seat, and the horses snapped tension into the rigging.

The carriage had just passed Burnt House Canyon when Randy heard the yelps. He thought geese were honking until the first gunshot rang out. A pang of fear leaped from his heart, and he glanced at the revolver on the seat across from him.

Sticking his head out the window, he saw a dozen Apaches giving chase. They were close enough for him to see their gaudy Mexican and American dress, accented with beads and feathers. He heard the driver whistle and shout Spanish at the horses.

Falling back into the coach, he stared at the Smith and Wesson. He hated New Mexico. He remembered what Bart had said as he picked the revolver up. Point it and pull the trigger. The war cries of the Apaches had already engulfed the coach, grating on Randy's nerves like a rasp. He sank as far back into the seat as he could and waited.

Suddenly, a dark face and a tomahawk appeared in the window. Randy closed his eyes, pointed the pistol, and fired. When he looked again, the face was gone. His hopes mounted. Maybe the others would go away, now that he had shot one.

But the hideous squalls only mounted, and a shot splintered the ceiling of the coach. When the next rider appeared at the window to the right, Randy jerked the trigger of his weapon again and saw the Indian roll from his mount. Glancing to the left, he saw more braves. He shoved the muzzle of the revolver through the window and fired. Another warrior fell from his horse, but others came to take his place.

Save the last bullet for yourself, he remembered. Certainly it wouldn't come to that. Surely this wasn't really happening.

He killed a fourth Indian, but several others reached the team and slowed the coach. Randy heard the driver's shotgun erupt and saw two more dead bodies pass by his window, but the carriage continued to slow.

As the coach came to a stop, the lawyer pointed his revolver at the war party and fired his fifth round. To his surprise, two warriors fell to the ground. He could hear Indians crawling all over the coach. A movement outside caught his attention, and he saw two warriors dragging the struggling driver into the trees. A long, horrible yell came from the shadows where they had disappeared, and Randy felt a core of nausea grip his stomach.

Sinking to the floor of the coach, he wondered what he would do. Jump from the coach and catch a loose Indian pony? No chance. Maybe rescue would come. Certainly it would. Where was the army? Where were the good Indians, the Mescalero guard Bart had told him about? The tortured scream of agony came from the forest again.

Randy put the muzzle of the pistol to his chest. The coach was rocking with Indians. He tried to make his finger tighten around the trigger, but it wouldn't. He didn't know if it was courage or cowardice that prevented him from using the last bullet on himself, but he couldn't do it. That was too final. There had to be some hope of rescue.

He gritted his teeth and cursed Bart Young for bringing him here. He took the revolver in one hand and waited for the next savage to try him. Maybe he could kill one in the coach, steal the dead man's weapon, and keep fighting.

The door flew open, revealing a young brave in the white cotton of a Mexican peasant, a red sash tied around his waist, and a knife in his hand. Randy leveled the pistol, almost point blank, and fired.

The brave looked down at a black spot that appeared on his white shirt, then looked back at Randy. "Are you Mr. Hendricks?" he asked, speaking perfect English as he tucked his knife into the red sash. It was John Seven Stars, a bright young brave whom Bart had sent to the Indian school at Carlisle, Pennsylvania.

Randy could find no words to answer.

"I have a message for you," John Seven Stars said, pulling a piece of paper from his sash. "From the baron." He tossed the folded missive down on the lawyer and vanished from the doorway.

Randy heard the wild yelps again, and saw riders passing by outside. Relieved, but infuriated, he clutched the message with shaking hands, and unfolded it.

Randy,
Did you save the last bullet for yourself? It's just tallow and charcoal mixed together, with hardly enough powder behind it to send it down the barrel. Ha, ha.

Disrespectfully,
Don Bartolome Cedric Montoya-Young, baron of the Sacramentos, caballero of His Majesty's Chamber, knight of the Golden Fleece, etc., etc.

His rage and embarrassment mounted until he saw the face of his coach driver appear over the top of the letter.

"Did you like all that screaming?" Hilario asked. He rolled his eyes back in his head and filled the coach with another gurgling yodel. "I bet you thought they were cutting my guts out or something like that, huh?" He jumped down from the coach step and climbed up to his driver's seat, laughing harder with every step.

THIRTY - FOUR

I t's the dangedest court you ever heard of," Clarence Tankersly said. He had just arrived at the Dog Canyon ranch from Mexico City, where the court had gone to gather testimony.

"So I've heard," the baron said, "but just what makes it so all-fired peculiar?"

The young lawyer threw his coat on a chair back and sank into the seat. "The government won't spend money to bring witnesses to the courtroom, so it sends the courtroom to the witnesses. One of the five justices will go wherever Randy Hendricks wants to gather testimony, and takes along an interpreter, a translator, a stenographer, and a photographer. It's a traveling courtroom. Of course, I have to go along, too, if I want to cross-examine the witnesses."

"Where all has Randy dragged you?" Bart asked as he adjusted the flue in the stovepipe.

"We were at the old San Xavier Mission in Tucson before we went to Mexico City. Before that it was Texas to California."

"Retracing Antonio's trail?"

Tankersly nodded. "Going to all the archives where your

father-in-law found documents hidden, interrogating the archivists. He's trying to make them suggest that Antonio could have planted the documents instead of actually finding them there, but I've been able to head off any damaging testimony through my cross-examinations."

"Planting documents?" Bart said. The suggestion truly shocked him, though that was exactly what Antonio had done, with great success. "Why would Randy insinuate such a thing?"

"He's trying to make you look like a master forger, Baron. He's going to try to get your entire grant rejected. It's personal with him now."

"A forger!" The baron kicked a billet of stove wood, sending it rattling across the wooden floor of the ranch house parlor. "This is not a criminal case!"

"He doesn't have the evidence to get you arrested for forgery, of course, but he's trying to plant a seed of doubt in the minds of the justices. He won't get your barony away from you—I can almost guarantee you that—but if he can raise enough doubts, he might get the justices to reduce the acreage on some technicality."

"Reduce it! Can they do that?"

"I'm not sure what they can do, Baron. Yours is the first case to come to trial before this court. All Hendricks needs is a quorum. He has to convince three of the five justices that your grant is somehow irregular. The problem is, I don't know what all he has on you. In addition to his own investigation, the Secret Service of the Treasury Department has loaned him two detectives, and they're working for him."

Bart sank into a bentwood rocker and stretched his stocking feet toward the stove. The big toe on his right foot was throbbing where he had kicked the stove wood, but he didn't let on. "When do I get to testify?" he said.

"The court will convene April first in Santa Fe. The justices will review the ambulatory testimony first; then

Hendricks and I will call and cross-examine additional witnesses. You'll be my star witness, of course. I'll save you till last."

The baron smiled, looking forward to making a fool of Randy Hendricks in court. It wouldn't be difficult. Randy had always been an easy target. "Clarence," he said, "Randy Hendricks, the Secret Service, and the Court of Private Land Claims can all be damned. This trial is going to make me a legend."

THIRTY - FIVE

The halls of the Court of Private Land Claims filled with Santa Fe citizens an hour before the court convened. When Bartolome Cedric Montoya-Young strode in with his lawyer, a cheer rose from the ranks. Rumor had it that the secret mission of the court was to take land away from native New Mexicans and that baron Bart Young, true champion of the people, was spending his fortune fighting the court.

Bart strode to his table wearing spurs and a huge Mexican sombrero. Clarence Tankersly came in behind him, dressed in conservative courtroom attire. Behind Clarence came a dozen servants carrying small boxes, each containing papers of the fabled Montoya-Young Grant—the *cedula* with the signature of King Carlos the Third, the book of riddles written by Nepomeceno Montoya, orders, reports, wills, and the secret codicils.

The chief justice almost broke his gavel quieting the crowd, but finally the trial got under way. Bart had trouble staying awake the first couple of days, as Jay Randolph Hendricks and Clarence Tankersly presented their ambulatory testimony to the justices.

"In summation," Randy suggested, at the end of the

third day, "not one of the archivists anywhere in Texas, New Mexico, Arizona, California, or the Republic of Mexico could recall seeing any document pertaining to the alleged barony of the Sacramentos before Antonio Montoya showed up and produced them. The government intends to prove that the documents didn't even exist until Antonio Montoya planted them in the various archives. And where did the late Mr. Montoya procure these documents?" He swept his finger across the courtroom and pointed at Bart. "The government will prove beyond the shadow of a doubt that this man forged them! This man who calls himself baron of the Sacramentos! This fraud sitting here!"

The court spectators roared with indignation and rose to their feet. The chief justice pounded his gavel, but the rabble grew even more unruly and began pushing against the railings.

Finally, Bart rose, turned to the crowd, and held his hands in the air, imploring the spectators to return to their seats. When they had quieted themselves, he pointed at Randy. "Counsel seems to have missed his calling in the theater," he said.

When the laughter died, Clarence Tankersly summarized the ambulatory testimony for the claimant:

"Not one of the archivists so vigorously interrogated by counsel for the government even remotely suggested that the documents of the barony had been planted in their files. The reason the grant papers had never been discovered before Señor Montoya found them was because they had been so expertly hidden by Nepomeceno Montoya, first baron of the Sacramentos."

Tankersly put his fists on Randy Hendricks's table and glared down at the redheaded lawyer. "The fact that counsel for the government cannot grasp this genius should come as little surprise to the court."

The courtroom roared with laughter, and Randy's face turned red as his hair.

"Order!" the chief justice shouted, banging his gavel. "This court will now recess until the fifteenth. When we reconvene, counsel for the claimant will refrain from insulting the personal intelligence of counsel for the government!"

Live witnesses took the stand when the court came back in session. Francisco and Vincente Montoya were among the first. Randy made them both admit that before Bart Young came to New Mexico, they had never heard of the barony of the Sacramentos.

Randy shook his head as his fingernails circled through his curly red locks. Addressing Francisco, he asked, "Mr. Montoya, don't you think it rather odd that your father did not deed this valuable tract of land equally among his heirs, instead of giving it all to your youngest sister and her husband?"

"No," Francisco answered. "It was part of Nepomeceno's plan to deed the barony through the codicils to only one family member of each generation to prevent the barony from being divided. Its value to the entire family is much greater as a whole. My brother, my sisters, and I relinquished our rights to the inheritance because none of us cared to move into the mountains to take possession of the grant. Besides, we all agreed that our brother-in-law would, by his passion for the land, manage the barony far better than either I or my brother ever could."

The Montoya brothers had two things going for them. First, they honestly believed in the authenticity of the barony. Secondly, Tankersly had laboriously rehearsed their testimony with them.

When Bitora took the stand, Randy thought he could

badger some kind of damaging testimony out of her. He
knew her only as the demure hostess of the Star Mountain lodge, not as the young mother who had braved
assaults by hired assassins to take possession of her inheritance.

"Mrs. Young," he said, "what was your role in this fraud
against the state?"

"Objection!" Tankersly shouted, springing to his feet.

"Sustained."

Randy bowed his head before the court and scratched
it. "I'll rephrase the question, Your Honor. What was your
role in producing the documents to the alleged land grant?"

"I was the first to suggest that the book of riddles may
have contained a code."

"Of course you were," Randy said. "Wouldn't it have
looked much too convenient if Bart Young himself, or your
father, had discovered the code?"

"Objection!" Tankersly shouted.

"I'll withdraw the question, Your Honor," Randy said.
He strode to the table holding the documentary evidence, and picked up Nepomeceno's book. "The book of
riddles!" he shouted, smirking and waving the volume
about carelessly. "Isn't it true, Mrs. Young, that your husband has always been rather fond of riddles?"

"Yes, I suppose so," she said.

"In fact, isn't it true that before you ever laid eyes on
this book, your husband had recited some of the self-same
riddles to you in person?"

Bitora looked away from the lawyer. "Only one or two.
They are probably very old riddles. . . ."

"No further questions!"

The court recessed again for an Easter holiday and reconvened the first Monday in May. Clarence Tankersly brought
an impressive parade of character witnesses from the bar-

ony to testify on Bart's behalf. Bart's railroad engineer, Youngstown's mining engineer, Dog Canyon's ranch foreman, the baronial forester, farmers, shepherds, and even Chief Estrella came to praise the baron's accomplishments.

"Mr. Young's actions are not those of some document-forging land-grabber," Tankersly insisted. "These are the responsible deeds of a true and rightful steward of the earth."

Next, the lawyer called in a string of land title experts, and each testified that the Montoya-Young grant was the most highly-authenticated he had ever seen. Paper, ink, style of writing, and Spanish grammar were all flawless. Signatures of individual Spanish officials stood up against the harshest scrutiny.

Randy Hendricks chose to cross-examine just one of these witnesses: George Baird.

"You were present at the original unveiling of the baronial documents in the office of the surveyor general, were you not?" he began.

"Yes," George said. "I was secretary to the surveyor general at the time."

"Did you file the documents in accordance with standard procedures of that office?"

"No. I hid them in the territorial archives."

"Why?"

"Bart asked me to. He said certain parties might try to destroy them. And in fact, the office of the surveyor general later caught fire in a very suspicious—"

"Just answer the question before you, Mr. Baird. How much did you receive for this service of hiding the documents?"

"Objection!" Tankersly shouted, leaping from his chair. "Your Honor, whether the documents were hidden or not has nothing whatever to do with their authenticity."

"Your Honor," Randy argued, "I intend to exhibit to this court that at least one of Mr. Young's so-called experts received payment from him for services relating to this case."

The justices whispered among themselves for a few seconds. "The court will allow the question," the chief justice finally said.

"Well, Mr. Baird . . ." Randy said, looking down his nose at the witness.

George sighed, and glanced at Bart. "The amount was so trivial that I don't even recall how much it was."

"But isn't it a fact that Mr. Young paid you cash money for hiding the grant documents in the territorial archives? Answer yes or no."

"Yes."

"Might we also assume, then, that he paid you or the other experts for your endorsement of the grant papers?"

"Objection!" Tankersly shouted.

"Never mind," Randy said, grinning. "No further questions."

After the land grant experts had been examined and cross-examined, Randy called his star witness to the stand, one Vernon Regis. The old speculator hobbled grotesquely toward the bench. His health had been declining in recent years. Arthritis had struck his knees and he had a bad back, to say nothing of his stomach trouble.

"Mr. Regis," Randy said after the swearing-in, "how did Mr. Young get his job as custodian of the territorial archives?"

"He came to my office looking for work. I knew the position in the archives was about to vacate, so I recommended him."

"Did he specifically request the archivist job?"

"No, he did not. He didn't even know about it."

"But Mr. Young has long maintained that he came to New Mexico with explicit intentions of landing a job in the archives where he could search for the lost barony documents his father had told him about."

"Mr. Young is a liar."

The courtroom erupted with laughter and angry shouts from opposing factions. The chief justice had to threaten to clear the courtroom before the crowd would contain itself.

After the disturbance, Regis told his version of the sale of the old Montoya grant. He said Bart and Antonio, when they realized they had made a bad deal, had decided to get even by forging the papers for the barony that would displace Regis from the Sacramentos.

"When did you first suspect that the documents were forged?" Randy asked.

"When I procured a copy of the book of riddles from the surveyor general."

"Were you aware of Mr. Young's affinity for riddles?"

"I'll say I was. In fact, there isn't one riddle in that book that I didn't hear spoken from Young's own lips *before* he supposedly found the book in Mexico. He forged the entire thing himself!"

The baron backers rocked the courtroom with their jeers, and the justices took turns with the gavel.

"After the claimant took up residence on his so-called barony," Randy continued, "what happened to your land holdings in the Sacramento Mountains?"

"Young's gang of thugs chased me off of my ranch and my timber claims."

"What about your gold mine?" Randy asked.

"He let me keep that, but extorted mining royalties from me at gunpoint."

Bart found the testimony so absurd that the judges had to caution him for guffawing.

That afternoon, Tankersly called Regis back to the stand for cross-examination. He glared at the speculator for several seconds, then picked up the famous book of riddles from the exhibits.

"I have just one question to ask you, Mr. Regis," the young lawyer said. He thumbed through several tattered pages, scanning them in silence. "Ah, here's a good one. How many eggs could the giant, Goliath, eat on an empty stomach?"

Regis stared, dumbfounded.

"I object!" Randy cried. "That's not a question. It's a riddle!"

"Your Honor," Tankersly insisted, "Mr. Regis testified this morning that he has both heard and read every one of the riddles in this book. If that is so, he should remember them. I simply wish to confirm the value of his testimony."

The chief justice rubbed his chin. "You may proceed," he said.

"Again, Mr. Regis. How many eggs—"

"I don't remember the riddles individually," Regis blurted.

"But you testified just a few hours ago that you heard Bart Young tell every one of these riddles *before* he found the book in Mexico City. Is there something wrong with your memory? Do you want me to try another riddle?"

"No."

"Then we'll try this one again. How many eggs could the giant, Goliath—"

"Are you deaf?" the speculator bellowed. "I've told you I don't know the answer to that damned riddle!"

"Why not?"

"I don't remember it!"

"Might we assume, then, that your memory also fails you in regards to the way Mr. Young got his job in the territorial archives?"

"No."

"Or the way he allegedly chased you off of your ranch and timber claims?"

"No."

"Or the way he allegedly extorted mining royalties from you at gunpoint?"

"No! No! No!"

"Mr. Regis, how many eggs could the giant, Goliath, eat on an empty stomach?"

"I don't know!"

"Why not?"

"Because I don't remember!"

"No further questions, Your Honor."

As the speculator's face writhed with indignation, the judges huddled, whispering, for almost a minute. Finally, the chief justice looked toward the witness stand. "You may step down," he said to Regis. "Mr. Tankersly," he added, "it would please the court to know the answer to that riddle."

THIRTY - SIX

B art recognized a familiar face as he approached the courtroom. He tipped his sombrero to Linden Yarborough and noticed the U.S. marshal badge pinned to the weathered jacket.

"Well, if it ain't the baron of bullshit," Yarborough said. Since losing the appointment as justice-of-the-peace to Antonio, Yarborough's political ambitions had slid into oblivion. He had, however, become noted for his efficiency as a U.S. marshal, and carried what grudge he still held with hardened grace. Linden Yarborough was still hell on the criminal population, and had accepted the apprehension or obliteration of that element as his lot.

"Howdy, Lin," the baron replied, stopping to shake hands with the lawman. "You come to see the show?"

"No. I heard you were wrapping up your testimony today."

"So what?"

"That lawyer, Hendricks, says he'll prove you a fraud today. If he does, I'll have to put you under arrest."

Bart smiled. "You'll have the day off, then. In fact, meet me at the Paisano Club after court, and I'll stand treat for drinks." He slapped Yarborough on the shoulder and entered the courtroom.

The onlookers rose to applaud when Bart appeared. He doffed his sombrero as he strode confidently to his seat, then made a pistol of his right hand and fired a playful round at the newspaper reporters on the front row. Their columns had become megaphones for Bart's voice, and they had made great sport of Randy Hendricks's head-scratching antics.

Since destroying Regis's testimony, two weeks before, Tankersly had been brilliant, finding every chink in Randy's case. Randy had stooped to bringing the marshals to court in a show of false confidence.

The spectators did not hiss when Randy came in. They simply laughed. He marched sheepishly to his table, avoiding the eyes of Bart and Tankersly.

When the judges had taken their places and called the court to order, Randy called his former classmate to the stand for cross-examination.

"Mr. Young," he began. "For the past few days you have kept the spectators and newspaper reporters in these chambers spellbound with your fanciful stories of lost land grants, secret codicils, hidden documents, and coded books of riddles."

"Thank you," the baron said, "You know, I've always considered myself something of a elocutionist—"

"However!" Randy interrupted, "you seem to have omitted two important aspects of your story."

"If that is true," Bart said, "I will beg the court's pardon."

"Isn't it true, Mr. Young, that you are quite a practical joker?"

"I have been dubbed the baron of Bad Jokes, the count of Humbuggery, and the duke of Tomfoolery."

"Isn't it also true that you are a practiced forger?"

Bart bunched his eyebrows for a second. "Isn't it true that you always ask your questions in the negative because it is an old lawyer's trick designed to elicit a confused response?"

"I object," Randy blurted, stomping his foot as he turned to the black robes.

The chief justice covered his smile with his hand. "Counsel, you have the floor. You are in no position to object. However, I will advise Mr. Young to answer counsel's questions, even if they are phrased negatively."

"In that case," the baron said, "absolutely yes, I am not a forger."

Randy stood transfixed for several seconds, then seemed to gather himself. He straightened his lapels, pulled his sweaty collar from his neck, and threw a new bearing into his posture. Slowly, he turned on Bart Young.

"Mr. Young," he said quietly, "Isn't it true that you and I were classmates at Tulane University?"

Bart saw Tankersly about to object, but pinned the lawyer in his seat with a glare. "Yes, it isn't altogether untrue," he said, his eyelids sagging as he looked back at Randy.

"And isn't it true that you once forged documents for me?" Randy began ferociously scratching his favorite place above his right ear.

The courtroom murmured with confusion.

"As I recall, I signed your father's name on a check because you had spent your allowance on a harlot. Whose honor do you intend to impeach here? Mine or your own?"

The chief justice fired a warning shot with his gavel, but the crowd continued to hum.

Randy's fingernails had worked their way up to his crown. "Isn't it true," he shouted, "that you also forged diplomas and transcripts that you used in an attempt to lure me to New Mexico to help you with this preposterous scheme of yours?"

"Objection!" Tankersly yelled.

"Your honor, I intend to prove once and for all, despite the personal embarrassment to myself, that Mr. Young has a long history of forging documents to meet his every whim." His fingers were at his left temple now, his arm virtually wrapped around the back of his head.

"Objection overruled," the chief justice said, turning his ear to the witness stand.

"Well, isn't it true?" Randy demanded.

Bart looked with awe at the vibrating mop of red hair. "You know, Randy, I could recommend a really good brand of sheep-dip for that itch of yours." He paused to let the laughter roar through the chambers. "Why, I would even volunteer to help you soak your head in it!"

Laughter regenerated itself in orbits around the outer walls, twisting Randy's thoughts until he forgot his question. When the judges finally regained control and admonished Bart against personal remarks, Randy Hendricks made one last attempt to proceed.

"Isn't it true," he said, his voice quavering, "that this case is nothing more than a historic practical joke to you?" His voice rose. "That the barony of the Sacramentos never existed, and"—he drew a breath meant for shouting—"that your entire case—every leaf of every codicil, *cedula,* report, and order—is nothing but a monumental fraud!" He pounded his fists on the baronial documents like a madman.

Bart watched Randy with satisfaction as the lawyer stood wild-eyed and panting. When the murmurs died in the courtroom, he put his elbows on the railing of the witness stand to lean into the glare of his adversary. "Counsel," he said, "the only fraud that has been presented to this court is your case against me."

THIRTY - SEVEN

A week later, Randy Hendricks still hadn't figured a dignified way out of the embarrassing defeat that was sure to visit him when the court reconvened. The justices had called for an adjournment of two weeks to let things settle down and allow the lawyers to prepare their closing statements. Bart and Bitora had gone back to their barony, trusting Clarence Tankersly to wrap the case up.

Counsel for the government sat like a drunk in his office chair, staring at the baronial documents. They were scattered all over the desk and the floor as if a whirlwind had passed through. Bart Young was no fraud and he knew it. Why had he ever taken that tack? Imagine a man forging all these documents so perfectly. Ridiculous.

He had treated this case as a personal score he had to settle, and it was the mistake of his career. One that would follow him everywhere. There were suspicious coincidences involved with the case—like the book of riddles conveniently turning up in Mexico City about the time Bart and Antonio needed to find it—but there was no proof of forgery. Never had been. Vernon Regis was a liar. Bart Young was a baron.

Randy had come up with a new argument yesterday. He could claim that the barony was illegitimate since the documents had been improperly filed with the Spanish and Mexican authorities, hidden as they were. Why hadn't he thought of it before? That was a tricky angle, and the courts loved technicalities.

But it was too late for a new strategy now. His closing statement was next week. He needed more than an idea. He needed proof of forgery, and that proof didn't exist. He had let Bart beat him at his own game of law.

Jay Randolph Hendricks hated New Mexico.

As he sulked in his chair, his office door opened and Sam Kincheloe, Secret Service detective, came in with a bolt of blinding sunlight. "Morning, Mr. Hendricks," he said.

Randy squinted. "Morning, Kincheloe. I don't suppose you've turned up anything new on the Young case."

Kincheloe shook his head. "I heard about what happened in court. Too bad."

Randy sighed and rose from his chair. "What's that?"

"Something I thought would cheer you up. You may have lost the Montoya-Young trial, but your next case is a cinch." The detective waved Randy to the window. "This is one of the documents from the Smith-Gutierrez grant. Take a look at it."

Randy studied the document, but his mind was too worn out to find anything unusual. It was an old Spanish deed, much like the one pertaining to Bart's barony. Randy had no idea what it said without his translator at his elbow. "I don't see anything suspicious," he confessed.

"Neither did I, at first," Kincheloe said. "Then I started thinking: If we want to find out whether or not this document is counterfeit, why not examine it the way we examine counterfeit bills at the Treasury Department?"

"How's that?"

"Hold it up to the light."

Randy put the leaf of parchment against the window and felt the warm morning sun on his palm. "So what?" he said, the parchment glowing in a rich amber hue above him, like a pane of stained glass.

"Look right there," Kincheloe said, putting a manicured finger on the paper. "Do you see that light area in the grain?"

Randy's eyes widened. "It looks like the letter W."

"It's the watermark of a paper mill in Wisconsin. This document is supposed to be over a hundred years old, and yet the mill that produced this parchment has only been in operation eleven years." Kincheloe stood beaming with pride, his finger still pointing out the character in the paper.

Randy's mouth dropped open, and his mind started feeding on new ideas. He looked down on the Montoya-Young papers scattered all over his office. He backhanded Kincheloe hard on the shoulder. "Why didn't you tell me about this before?"

The detective retreated, letting the counterfeit document flutter down from the window. "It just occurred to me yesterday," he said, holding his shoulder where Randy had stung him. "What difference does it make? The Smith-Gutierrez case hasn't even gone to trial yet."

"Yes, but the Montoya-Young case has!" Randy shouted. He started gathering Bart's documents from the floor.

"But, those papers are genuine. You won't find any watermarks on them."

"You don't know that!" Randy said.

Kincheloe stared for a moment, then picked up a few old sheets of parchment at his feet.

"Give me those," Randy snapped. "I'll conduct the examinations. You go find one of the justices."

"What for?"

"If I find a watermark on one of Bart's documents, I want an immediate warrant for his arrest!"

It was almost midnight when Bart heard the whistle of the *Conquistador* blow somewhere down Star Mountain. He sat up in bed and listened, straining to hear. Finally the steam blast came again, and he knew something unusual was happening. The *Conquistador* had never approached the lodge in the middle of the night.

He slipped out of bed without waking Bitora, got dressed, and ran downstairs. Pulling on his coat by the door, he left the log mansion and trotted to the depot to meet the *Conquistador*. He heard it chugging up the

mountain, saw its headlamp casting fragmented rays among
the tree trunks.

As the engine neared the depot, Bart saw Clarence
Tankersly jump from a passenger car. The young lawyer
trotted to him in the moonlight and leaped onto the depot
platform.

"Clarence, what have you done? Bought the railroad
with all the legal fees I've been paying you?"

Tankersly shook his head as he caught enough breath
to speak with. "Trouble's coming, Baron."

"What trouble?" he shouted over the hissing of the steam
engine.

"A warrant has been issued for your arrest. Conspiracy
to defraud the government. A U.S. marshal named Yarborough and a Secret Service detective named Kincheloe
are coming with Randy Hendricks to get you tomorrow."

Bart felt a knot in his throat. "How can that be?"

Tankersly gritted his teeth and looked up at the moon's
silver light on the pine needles. "Hendricks held one of
your documents up to the light and found a watermark."

"A what?"

"He found the mark of an American paper mill on one
of your old Spanish documents."

A pang of nausea hit Bart in the stomach. "Which one?
Which document?" he demanded.

"I don't know. I didn't get a chance to see it, but it convinced the justices of the court that you are a fraud. You
have some explaining to do, Bart. What does it mean?"

A watermark! Bart's mind race back to Santa Fe, fifteen
years ago. The paper. Where had he gotten the stock for
the forgeries? Some of it had been old, authentic parchment
Antonio had found in the back of one of his warehouses.
But there hadn't been enough. They had purchased some.
Bought it at a Santa Fe trading house. Where had that stock
come from? Missouri, probably. Of all the stupid mistakes!
A watermark! The one thing he had failed to look for.

"Baron!" Clarence said. "What does it mean?"

Bart felt the sick tide of guilt rise in his stomach, but he glowered at his lawyer with a look of false anger. "It means Randy Hendricks is a lying little fart. You better get back to Santa Fe and have a look at this supposed watermark."

"I don't think so," Clarence said. "I'd better be here when the officers arrest you."

"You don't understand, Clarence. All hell's going to break loose in these mountains when word gets out that I'm wanted. I'll be lucky if Marshal Yarborough gets to me before Vernon Regis's gang of regulators—or the U.S. Army."

"The army?"

"Colonel Semple's been dying for an excuse to campaign against my Mescalero guard, and this is it. He'll say they're rising up to protect me, and he'll come to slaughter them and me both." He grabbed Tankersly by the arm and led him to the passenger car door that had pulled up to the depot. "Now, get back on that train, and get to the bottom of this watermark business." He shook his lawyer's hand and slapped him on the shoulder. "I have until dawn to prepare my barony for invasion!"

The baron left Tankersly bewildered on the platform.

Somewhere between the depot and the lodge, the sickening feeling of remorse passed, replaced by the smell of pines and the bite of the cold wind on his cheeks. How many men could claim their own barony? He thought of Antonio. The *rico* owed his last fifteen years of happiness to Bart's pen. Hadn't it been worth it? He had to remind himself that they were invading *his* barony. They would have to play by his rules now. He would plan his escape to Mexico, and his family's. Then, if it killed him, he was going to have some fun.

THIRTY - EIGHT

Bart saw smoke as he rode nearer to the top of the rise. The wind had stretched it to a faint haze, but he had learned to look for such sign in the sky. Then the stone chimneys rose over the hill, and the shingled roofline, the peeled timbers of the huge log lodge house, and the manicured gardens surrounding it.

Leaning over the saddle horn, he gave the stallion his head, and galloped down the slope. As he jumped the second rail fence of the great pasture, he saw Bitora coming from the doorway at a trot. He watched her carefully. This would be their last hour as baron and baroness of the Sacramentos.

"Bartolome!" she scolded. "Where have you been? Nobody will tell me anything, but I know something has gone wrong!"

"Nothing's wrong," the baron said. "I just came home for dinner."

"Don't lie!" she ordered. "I heard one of the servants say that they are coming to take us from the mountains."

"Who is?" Bart demanded, looking over his shoulders as if he would see some invaders.

"That is what I am asking you! They say the papers for the Montoya-Young grant are fake, that you forged them!"

Bart shook his head and laughed. "It's just more of Randy Hendricks's danged rumormongering."

"Look at me," she said, grabbing him tightly by the arm and turning him to face her. "I can always tell when you are lying. Now, tell me the truth. Do these mountains belong to us, or not?"

The baron tipped his hat back and looked her straight in the eyes. "As sure as you belong to me, and I belong to you. By everything that is holy and fair, these mountains were your father's, and now they are ours. And damn any soul who should ever try to take them from us."

She sighed with relief and hugged him, pressing her face against his chest. "You are telling the truth, aren't you?"

"What do you think I am, a liar?"

"I know you are a big liar when you are trying to play a trick on someone."

"Let's go eat dinner. I'm starving." He handed his reins to Hilario, who had sauntered out to take the stallion to the stables. "Have the coach hitched and waiting for us after dinner," he said to the servant.

"Where are we going?" Bitora asked.

"We'll go down and stay at Fort Young tonight, then we'll take a nice trip to Santa Fe and straighten out this latest nonsense about forged documents. Have the girls been fed?"

"Yes, but if we are going to Santa Fe, why don't we ride the train?"

"There's some kind of trouble on the tracks. The *Conquistador* can't get up. That's where I've been this morning. Taking care of business."

They walked beneath the mammoth pine transom and entered the lodge. Bart tossed his hat onto a brass hat tree as they passed through the front room with its mounted heads of deer, elk, and bighorn sheep hanging over the fireplace, its bearskin rugs on the floor.

After dinner, Bart went outside to find Hilario standing beside the coach, the team of four hitched.

"Did you empty the safe?" the baron asked.

"*Sí.*"

"How much was in it?"

"About twenty thousand dollars, I think."

"Where is it now?"

"Hidden in the luggage boot, where you told me to put it."

"Good man."

When Bitora finally came out with the girls, Carlos took her baggage from her and loaded it in the boot. Bart held the door open for Bitora and helped his daughters in. As soon as they were settled into their seats, he closed them inside, jumped onto the step and shouted at Hilario to whip the horses.

"What are you doing, you fool?" Bitora said, as the vehicle lurched forward. "Get in the coach. You are not going to ride out there."

"Kiss me," he said, clinging to the outside of the vehicle, and sticking his head through the window opening.

The girls giggled.

"What?" demanded Bitora.

"Kiss me, or I won't do a thing you say."

She pressed her lips together in frustration, but then put them on his, knowing she must humor him. Bart grabbed the back of her neck and held her lips on his until a bump in the road shook them apart. Bitora reeled back into the coach, against her daughters, staring at her husband in amazement. "*Idiota*," she said, panting. "Get in the coach with us—now. And tell Hilario he is going the wrong way."

"No, he's not," the baron said. "We're not going to Fort Young, or to Santa Fe. I'm sending you on that trip you've been wanting to take to Mexico City. I'll meet you there and explain everything."

"What are you talking about?"

Bart looked back and saw Carlos riding from the lodge house, leading a fresh horse. "*Vaya con Dios, querida,*" he said to his wife. "*Mi corazón vaya contigo.*" He jumped from the coach step, thinking how corny that would have sounded in English: *My heart goes with you.* He ran a few steps as he hit the ground, then stood to watch the coach drive away between the rows of firs and spruces.

Bitora was hanging out the window, shouting hysterically at Hilario to stop, but the coachman obeyed his orders from the baron. He wouldn't stop the horses until he changed teams at Caballero Canyon.

Carlos led the fresh mount to his employer. "I wish you wouldn't have made them leave like that, Don Bartolome." He took a gun belt holstered with a Colt revolver from his shoulder and handed it to Bart. "I don't like it."

"I didn't have a choice, Carlos," Bart replied, buckling the belt around his waist. He drew the weapon to check the loads. "You know Bitora wouldn't have left me behind of her own free will if she knew what was going on. I can't drag them along where I'm going. Hilario will get them across the border."

"*Sí,* but your wife is going to be very mad at you, señor."

"I'll smooth the whole thing out with her in Mexico City." He took the Marlin repeating rifle the cook handed to him and opened the breech to find brass in the chamber. "Carlos," he said, looking back at his huge lodge house, "I want you to get everybody out of the lodge. You and the other servants can take anything you want from it. Then I want you to burn it to the ground."

"Con permiso?"

The conifers lining the road framed the log mansion beautifully, the spruces draped with strands of greenish moss. "You heard me. I won't have Colonel Semple and Vernon Regis and Randy Hendricks sitting around my fireplace drinking toasts to my downfall with my liquor."

"But, Don Bartolome . . ."

Bart slid the Marlin into his saddle scabbard. "I don't like it any better than you do, Carlos. I might as well be burning what little hair I have left right off my head." He raised his hat to run his hand over his nearly slick crown. "But it has to be done. I've already sent men to blow up Fort Young, too. I didn't build it to quarter Colonel Semple's troops so they could invade my domain."

Carlos sighed heavily and looked back at the grand log lodge. "If you order it, Don Bartolome, I will do it."

"I do and you will." The baron took the reins of the horse from Carlos and climbed into the saddle. He urged his mount next to Carlos's. "I don't know when I'll see you again, amigo." He grasped the cook's hand and shook it. "Maybe a long time."

Bart smiled, cast a final gaze at the log palace on the mountaintop, and spurred his horse onto a trail branching off of the Caballero Canyon Road.

THIRTY - NINE

Dan Tolliver's cabin stood cold and dark, while an open fire blazed nearby. Uncle Dan never used the cabin, except maybe as a place to hang game where bears and wolves couldn't get it, or to shelter his horses when the weather turned stormy.

Bart reined his mount in at the edge of the clearing and cupped his hands around his mouth. "Uncle Dan!" he yelled. A man had to be careful riding into Dan's camp. "It's Bart!"

"What do you want?"

The voice came quietly, but it made both Bart and his horse flinch. He turned around to see old Dan rise from a clump of scrub oak beside the trail, holding his ancient Kentucky rifle. "How'd you sneak up behind me so quiet?"

"Didn't have to. You rode right by me. Didn't you notice your horse smellin' me?"

"No," Bart admitted. "How'd you know I was coming?"

"Seen you comin' a hour back. Knowed when you'd git here. Kilt a deer and waited for you. What do you want here?"

Bart noticed the dried blood of the deer on Dan's knuckles and remembered hearing the rifle shot. "I was wondering if I might stay in your cabin tonight."

"Won't crowd me. I sleep on the ground." The old man stalked out of the bushes and onto the trail. He looked beyond Bart to the southwest. "Your little gals got off the mountain," he said.

The baron's heart ached to think of his family heading for Mexico without him. "Did you see them?"

"No, but I seen some lawmen what told me they let 'em go. Didn't have a warrant for 'em. Just you." His eyes narrowed. "I always knowed they'd come to get you. Be glad when you go. Get the hell off my mountain."

"What kind of lawmen were they?"

"That Marshal Yarborough, and some other feller I never heard tell of. Rode like he was saddle sore."

"Detective Kincheloe of the Secret Service," Bart said. "Any others?"

"They had that redheaded lawyer with 'em."

His insides went cold as an anvil when he thought of Randy Hendricks invading his mountains. "Where did you see them?"

"Caballero Canyon Road."

"They'll probably camp on Alamo Peak tonight, and split up to find me in the morning."

"That marshal'll likely git you. Might git out if you go down the Sacramento River, over to Shakehand Springs, then run for the Guadalupes."

The old man was reading his mind. Uncle Dan was the only white man who knew his barony better than he did. Bart patted the flap of his saddlebag. "I brought you some coffee and whiskey."

Uncle Dan marched toward his camp, hunching so far forward that he looked as if he would fall on his face.

Bart brewed the coffee and laced it heavily with bourbon. Dan fried venison in bear fat, boiled some beans, and roasted a few ears of corn over the coals.

The stars came out as they ate, and the darkness from the forest crept into the meadow until it enveloped them like a cocoon. The mountain man took his time eating. He had an annoying habit of sniffing his food for several seconds before every bite, like a wolf smelling a carcass for poison.

They were picking their teeth with wood splinters when they sensed a distant rumble, first from the mountain, then through the air. Uncle Dan dropped his toothpick from his mouth, reached habitually for his old musket, and clutched the breast of his deerskins, blackened where he so often wiped the grease from his fingers.

"Easy, Uncle Dan," Bart said. He had never seen the likes of fear in the old man's eyes. "That'll be Fort Young. I had the men blow it up so the army couldn't quarter there."

Uncle Dan panted and put his rifle aside. "And may God damn you to hell for doin' it! I thought the world was shakin' again."

"Huh?"

"Back to Tennessee, when I was a pup. Damnedest shake-up ever you felt. Knocked down trees. Cracked the ground. Made lakes where weren't none there before. They told me the Mississippi run back'ards and blowed water spouts up in the air like the Yellowstone country. Scared me so bad I went to soilin' my britches again, right when my ma thought she had me broke of it. Ain't nothin' come worse enough to scare me since."

"The New Madrid earthquake," Bart said, more to himself than to Dan. "That was in 1811, wasn't it?"

"Hell, I don't know."

"How old are you, Uncle Dan?"

The mountain man shrugged. "Old."

"If you remember the New Madrid earthquake, you'd have to be . . . over eighty."

"Feels like a hunnerd."

"When did you come West?"

"Never tracked years much. I was married four years when I left Tennessee. I 'member that much."

"You had a wife?"

"What else would a man marry?"

"What happened to her?"

Dan spit in the fire and listened with satisfaction to the sizzle. "I like to hunt. Come in one mornin' with some meat—been after it a few days—and she went to naggin' about me never workin' none. Told me if I liked huntin' so much, I'd shoot that chicken hawk that was killin' her settin' hens. I picked up ol' Kaintuck again, and went out after that hawk." He slurped his coffee and stared into the darkness as if he saw something there.

"And what happened?" Bart asked, following the old man's gaze.

Uncle Dan put his coffee cup aside and wrapped his gnarled fingers around the breech of his rifle. "That hawk flew west." He stood suddenly and kicked the wood from the fire, scattering embers.

"What are you doing?" Bart said, dodging coals.

"Man's a damn fool to set by a fire at night in Indian country." He stomped out the last flames.

"The Mescaleros aren't hostile."

"They'll have your scalp one day. Them reds'll rise back up some half moon and kill every white man breathin'. Them ghost shirts are bulletproof. You mind what I say."

Bart began to feel uneasy about staying with Uncle Dan overnight.

"Yeah, that hawk flew west," said the voice in the dark. "I come out here with it and found me these young mountains."

"Nice of you to name them in my honor," Bart said. "Young Mountains. Has a nice ring to it."

"I wouldn't name a clod after you. When I say young, I

mean not old. Them mountains back to Tennessee, them was old mountains. Now, these ones out here is still young."

"I didn't realize you knew anything about geology," Bart said.

"To hell with all them -ologies. Man's a fool can't tell a old mountain from a young one just lookin'. Them old ones back to Tennessee, they're all slump shouldered and beat down—carved up by the weather, like me. Mist cloudin' around 'em like a old man's breath in the cold.

"Now, these here mountains, they stand straight and up-right, like I was when I first found 'em. Young, high, and mighty. Give a damn about fire and blizzard. Shoulders like somebody chiseled 'em fresh." He sniffed and spit in the dark. "Hell, they'll be young yet when I'm a thousand years dead."

Bart remained silent. He knew the old hermit was talking mostly to himself. As he warmed his fingers around his coffee cup, he realized that something about the night was making him feel uneasy. He listened, and his eyes swept the tree-tops against the stars until he located the strange flicker of orange far up the mountain to the north. Carlos had followed his orders. The Star Mountain lodge was burning.

This was no way to spend his last evening on his barony—with a man who had never wanted him here in the first place. For all he knew, Uncle Dan might shoot him in the dark to collect the bounty. *Whoa, Bart,* he thought. *Don't let the old codger rattle you. He's more talk than anything else.*

A sorrowful moan suddenly rose from the darkness nearby, and Bart heard Uncle Dan scramble in the dark.

"Goddamn Indian wolf call," he whispered hoarsely.

Bart heard the percussion lock catch on ol' Kaintuck. "That'll be Chief Estrella. I told him to meet me here."

"You brung a Indian to my camp?"

The wolf call wailed from the darkness again and Bart started collecting wood to stoke the fire.

"Don't light the fire!"

"It's just Estrella. I've been expecting him." He fanned the coals with his hat until a tiny flame leaped onto the kindling.

Old Dan cussed and hid in Bart's shadow, ready to shoulder his long rifle.

"*Venga,* Estrella," Bart shouted, waving the chief into camp.

The chief materialized from the dark carrying a Winchester rifle decorated with brass tacks hammered into the stock and feathers tied to the barrel. The ends of the woman's *rebozo* he wore like a sash around his waist hung to his moccasins.

"What have the scouts found out, Chief?"

Estrella squatted by the fire and put his rifle butt on the ground, but remained vigilant of Uncle Dan. "Colonel Semple is riding to Fort Young with a column of hand-picked soldiers."

"You'd better keep your people out of his way, or he's liable to slaughter you."

"I will. You must ride south, Baron."

"That's what I had in mind. Anybody else coming after me?"

"Red Hair is camped on Alamo Peak with two officers."

Bart turned to Uncle Dan. "What did I tell you, Dan? Randy's predictable as sunrise. I guess Vernon Regis and ol' scar face haven't showed up yet."

"No sign of them," Estrella said.

"If I know Vernon, they'll be coming on the *Conquistador* tomorrow. He never was one to ride. Want some coffee, Chief?"

Estrella shook his head and rose. The mountain man rose with him like an image in a mirror. Estrella backed away from the fire a few steps, then looked at Bart and tossed his head as a parting gesture.

"*Adios*," the baron said, watching the chief back away into the darkness. Another friend he would never see again.

Just as the night swallowed Estrella, Bart saw him turn his back to the camp. At the same instant, he caught a glimpse of ol' Kaintuck's long barrel swinging upward. He lunged for the muzzle, swatting it aside as it erupted inches from his face.

The powder flash took his sight momentarily, and the ringing in his ears muffled all sound, but he didn't let on to the mountain man that he was deaf and blind. "Damn it, Uncle Dan! What the hell do you mean?"

"You fouled my bead!" the old man growled, as if it were an indiscretion beyond sin.

Bart turned to the darkness where Estrella had disappeared and raised his hands. "Don't shoot, Chief. Just ride." He heard no answer. "Chief? You all right?" The wolf call moaned from the darkness, followed by the pounding of hooves on the trail.

He turned to Uncle Dan, who was pouring black powder from his horn down Kaintuck's muzzle. "What makes you hate Indians so damn much?" he demanded.

The old eyes rose and glared at him as the knotty fingers opened the brass lid of the patch box carved into Kaintuck's maple stock. "I hate you, too." He walked away from the fire and disappeared.

Bart knew about how long it would take Dan to finish reloading the long rifle in the dark, and he was in the cabin, with the door bolted, before the time elapsed. He was able to calm his nerves inside and spread his blankets on the floor. As he lay his head back and stared at the darkness, he cursed Dan Tolliver for ruining his last night on his barony.

* * *

When he stepped out of the cabin before dawn, he found Uncle Dan waiting for him. The mountain man had put Bart's saddle on one of his own horses.

"Take Peso," Dan said. "He's got bottom, and he's rested. Meet me at Shakehand Springs before sundown and I'll have another fresh mount waitin' for you. You can make a run for the Guadalupes." He handed the reins to Bart.

"Why would you do that for me? You just told me last night that you hated me."

"I hate everybody. This here's the best way to git you and all them damn lawmen off my mountains. It'll be nice and quiet when they chase you south to Mexico. I don't reckon you'll be comin' back."

"No," Bart said. He slipped his boot into the stirrup and mounted Peso. "I don't reckon I will."

FORTY

What the hell have we stopped for?" Vernon Regis bellowed from his Pullman car. He was sitting on a velour settee, his waxy white fingers interlaced like stripped willow branches woven into a basket. "Domingo, go see what's wrong!"

The Mexican gunman stared at Regis blankly for several seconds. His five hired guns wouldn't respect him much for hopping to orders like a servant boy. Finally, he stepped from the Pullman, leaving the door open.

"Goddammit!" Regis yelled. "The damn smoke's coming in! Close the door!"

Archiveque's five gunmen stared at the old Anglo without concern.

"La puerta, la puerta!" the land speculator shouted, squinting against the cinders floating into the coach. He

could hear the boiler letting off steam as one of the gun-men got up slowly to close the door.

Archiveque returned, letting a last puff of smoke into the car as he entered. "The engine fell off the tracks," he said.

"What do you mean, fell off?"

"That's what they said." Archiveque shrugged and sat down.

Regis had to get up then, no matter how badly it hurt his stove-up knees and back. He paced to the rear of the car, his arms and legs swinging like those of a misguided marionette. He knew exactly what the delay meant. Bart Young had chosen this site well. The canyon was so steep here that Domingo and his cutthroats couldn't unload their horses from the stock cars. They would have to back the stock cars down to a place where the horses could jump out. Then Archiveque and his gunmen would have to ride into the mountains to find Bart. He would resist them, of course, and they would have to kill him. Regis wasn't about to let the courts have the baron. He had waited years for this.

"Domingo!" he shouted. "Come with me!" His stomach was burning like fire as it always did at times of stress. He lowered himself laboriously down the iron steps on his bad knees, and hobbled toward the steam engine, which was hissing like a monster ahead in the mouth of the Devil's Canyon tunnel.

The engineer and his fireman were walking back to Regis's Pullman car from the mouth of the tunnel, feeling the morning sun on their backs.

"What's the problem?" Regis shouted.

"Somebody lifted the tracks inside the tunnel where we couldn't see," the engineer replied. "Lucky the grade is steep here, and we weren't going very fast. The engine just drove off the end of the rails and sat there."

"Young," the speculator growled. "How long will it take to get going again?"

"Mr. Regis, we aren't going anywhere. We'll have to hike up to Youngstown and get a repair crew down here. Lord knows how we'll get the engine back on the track."

"You hike anywhere you want. We don't need the damn engine to coast downhill. We'll just uncouple the cars and coast down the grade until we find a place where we can let the horses off."

"Suit yourself," the engineer said.

"Domingo, get up there and ride the brake."

Archiveque climbed the rungs on the back of the stock car with amazing agility for a man of his spread—he was over forty now, and rather fat. The shaft of the brake wheel ran up the rear end of the car, next to the ladder rungs, and the wheel itself came to the gunman's waist when he stood on top.

One of the Mexicans uncoupled the forward stock car. When the three loose cars started rolling, Archiveque had to put all his weight and strength into the wheel to lock the brakes.

"All right, get back in the Pullman," Regis said. *"Venga, venga!"* he prodded, waving at the gunmen, who had stepped out to see what was going on. "You sons of bitches don't understand a word I say, do you?"

Bart looked at his watch. Everything was on schedule. His railroad crew had been ordered to blow up the La Luz Canyon trestle in fifteen minutes.

The explosion would serve two purposes. First, it would strand Vernon on the tracks between the derailed engine and the demolished bridge. Vernon would have to ride out, and that would dang near kill him. There wasn't even a road within five miles where he could order his coach to meet him.

Secondly, Regis would have to build his own trestle if he wanted to continue using the narrow gauge to work his mine. Bart wasn't about to leave behind anything his enemies could profit from.

From around the bend, he watched the Pullman and the two stock cars coast down to the mouth of Devil's Canyon. Domingo and his men found a place to let their horses out there, and rode into the mountains. Vernon would wait for them in the Pullman.

Bart chuckled as he mounted Peso. He tried to rein the stallion toward Shakehand Springs, but couldn't do it. He just had to see the look on Vernon's face. The speculator was going to be mad as hell.

He made sure Archiveque's men were well up La Luz Canyon before approaching the stranded railroad cars. Just as he was ready to ride out of the trees for a social call, he heard the door of the Pullman open.

Regis laboriously lowered himself down the steps, both hands on the rail. He hobbled toward the lead stock car, paused to piss beside the tracks, then began trying to climb the rungs that led to the brake wheel on top of the first car.

Bart had underestimated Regis again. The speculator was going to stand on top of the car, ease the brake off, and coast the three cars down the mountain, riding the brake all the way. He never dreamed the old stove-up bastard would try such a stunt.

He couldn't let him do it, of course. The railroad crew was going to blow the La Luz Canyon trestle to splinters any minute now, and Regis would plunge to his death if he didn't get the brake clamped down in time.

As the speculator reached the second rung of the ladder, Bart came up with a great idea. He left Peso tied at the edge of the trees and sneaked down to the front of the first stock car as Regis was climbing up the back.

He climbed quietly up the side of the car, stepping in the spaces between the boards left to give the animals fresh air. He slung one arm over the top of the car and pulled himself up. He could hear Regis heaving on the ladder at the other end, damn near killing himself just climbing a few rungs. Bart rolled onto the top of the car as he saw the long clammy fingers of his old rival reach over the far edge of the stock car roof.

When the speculator climbed high enough to see over the top of the car, he looked up in midgrunt and saw the unexpected image of a man sitting cross-legged on top of the car, facing him. His heart surged, and his reflexes almost jolted him off the ladder.

"Howdy, Vernon," Bart said, listening to the echoes of his own laughter bounce across La Luz Canyon.

Regis wrapped his left arm around the shaft leading up to the brake wheel. He rested his forehead against the top of the car, and panted. His free hand reached into his coat. "Goddamn you, Young," he said.

"What are you doing?"

The speculator found the grip of his pistol in his shoulder holster. "Getting the hell off of this godforsaken mountain."

"I wouldn't do that if I was you," the baron replied. "You're stuck here. I sent a crew to . . ."

He saw gunmetal rise above the car in Regis's hand and reached for his own Colt, but it was too late. The blast covered him with darkness, and he felt himself rolling backward, then falling. A painful blow to the shoulder revived him, and a crosstie slammed into his back, taking his wind. Gasping, his eyes focused on the coupling that had hit him in the shoulder, the sky beyond it. He reached for his revolver, expecting Regis to start shooting down on him from the top of the car at any second.

He managed to get his Colt drawn and cocked. He put his hand on top of his balding head and found the warm, slick feel of blood where Regis's bullet had creased him. As he tried to catch his breath, sit up, and watch the top of the car all at once, a screech of metal on metal gripped his nerves and gave him strength.

Bart heard footsteps on the roof as the stock car rolled

slowly away. A gun barrel appeared over the top edge of the car, followed by the watermelon head of the speculator. The baron flinched as he pulled his trigger. His eyes opened just in time to see Regis's revolver hit the steel rail beside him, its grip spattered with blood. He heard the speculator scrambling on top of the car.

Bart managed to stand up. He was getting air to his lungs now, but he couldn't find enough of it to shout. He stumbled to the side of the tracks until he could see the speculator crawling awkwardly on top of the car, holding his bleeding right hand under his left arm. Bart fired a shot in the air to get Vernon's attention, but the speculator only shrank down on the roof as the cars sped away downhill.

Heaving for oxygen, the baron sprinted to the tree line to get his horse. Just as he unwrapped the reins from the pine branch, a clap of thunder shook the whole mountain. The stallion reared and jerked him from his feet, but he held one rein. Above the echoes of the dynamite blast, he could hear the creaking timbers of the trestle falling into La Luz Canyon.

He leaped into the saddle, jabbed his spurs into horseflesh. Old Uncle Dan was right. Peso could run. He galloped like a racehorse on the downhill grade, closing the distance to the runaway cars.

When Regis heard the blast, he figured out what Bart had been trying to tell him just before he shot. He gripped the brake wheel with his good hand and pulled himself uncertainly to his feet, the car lurching dangerously under him, building speed. Putting both hands on the iron rim of the wheel, he tried to turn it, but the right hand had been shattered by Bart's bullet and was useless. It had taken all his strength with both hands to loosen the brake in the first place. His left hand alone could not move the wheel, though his hooklike fingers pulled with everything he had.

Ahead, a cloud of dust was rising from the blast and the collapsing bridge. Regis looked over the side of the car.

The gravel roadbed rushed by in a blur. He would bust himself to pieces if he had to jump. A movement pulled his eyes backward. Young was coming. The damn fool was going to try to rescue him.

Bart knew the stretch of road well. Once around the next curve, there was still a quarter mile to the trestle. Plenty of time to catch the car, climb aboard, and apply the brakes. The stallion seemed to sense a race, stretching every stride as he gained on the car.

The stock car was just two lengths ahead, but still building speed as it rounded the curve. Bart glanced at the dust cloud from the trestle, then threw his concentration back to the three-car run-away. Still time. He could almost number the crossties. He would stop the cars a hundred yards shy of the gulch. He hadn't killed anybody yet. If he let Regis go over the edge, it would just make things worse for him.

The side boards of the car were almost within his grasp. He began to lean left, settling his weight in one stirrup for the leap. Three feet, two feet . . . He gathered himself for the jump.

The sky shook again, louder than before, and the stallion shied from the car, planting his hooves. Bart saw timbers sailing end-over-end across the gulch as he fell forward onto the neck of the horse and grabbed a handful of mane. Again, he held his rein as he hit the ground.

"Jump! Vernon, jump!" he yelled as he sprang back into the saddle. He saw the speculator peer over the edge of the rushing car. The speed was too great. Regis could not find the courage. His broad white face turned back to Bart as he rushed away, and the bloody fingers reached for nothing, like the splayed tines of a deer antler.

Bart was fifty yards from the gulch when the cars left the crippled trestle and plunged downward. He saw the outline of the speculator drift away from the stock car, one arm flailing like a broken wing. He heard the scream. Then

another blast, and a new cloud of dust grew to the size of a
thunderhead in a second, engulfing the railroad cars and
the speculator in midair.

Flinders fell around him as he felt the pain in his shoulder where the stock car coupling had broken his fall. He
raked his shirtsleeve over the top of his head to sop the
blood from the bullet wound. One thing for sure. Regis
would be mad as hell when he hit bottom. He never could
take a joke.

FORTY - ONE

Now the baron knew he had trouble. The explosions
alone may not have attracted much attention—his
enemies surely knew by now that he was destroying
his baronial monuments—but the gunfire before the explosions would make them wonder. Bart knew Domingo
Archiveque, Randy Hendricks, and the two federal officers had all been within earshot of the shootout.

He spurred Peso back up the railroad grade and mounted
a steep trail that would lead him over Star Mountain. If
he happened to pick up any pursuers on his way southeast
to Shakehand Springs, he had a trail of surprises planned
for them.

He came to the edge of a clearing, and was about to
swing down from the saddle and loosen the cinch so Peso
could breathe, when a rifle shot ripped through the tree
limbs behind him. He spurred the stallion across the
meadow, riding low over the saddle horn, looking for
the source of the shot. He heard more muzzle blasts and
saw the six Mexicans riding hard to catch him as he made
it safely into the trees.

Archiveque's men wouldn't be easy to outrun, but Bart
knew the terrain, and they didn't. If he could just get over

the summit and past the lodge house before them, he could beat them.

He put Uncle Dan's stallion to the test, and the animal answered, covering ground like a thoroughbred, thundering onto a long stretch of straight trail. Bart looked back to see the Mexicans holding their ground, maybe gaining. He drew his Colt and slung a couple of shots their way to slow them down.

When he came over the last high roll before the summit, the sight of the smoking logs reeled him. They had taken everything from him. Never again would he sit in his parlor and listen to Bitora play her piano as he sipped his brandy and watched the sun set beyond the San Andres Range. It was over, and he was being hunted like an animal on his own barony. Maybe he should have skipped the social call on Vernon Regis. He could have been halfway to Shakehand Springs by now.

He scolded himself: *Now, Baron, you're not whipped yet. Pull yourself together.*

He thundered past the charred remains of his little passenger depot at the end of the tracks, and rode through the smoke of his own lodge house. He paused, looking over his shoulder. He wanted to make sure Domingo followed him on the right trail. When the gunman appeared, Bart got his attention with a pistol shot, then reined Peso down the trail, into the forest.

He could hear the rumble of pursuing hooves as he anticipated every turn in the trail he had memorized yesterday. About a mile from the lodge house, he rounded a crook and saw the place he had been looking for—a bright spot in the forest where the sun shone down through a stand of young aspens, spaced far enough apart that he could see through them easily. With rehearsed precision, he reined his mount off the trail, running between the two trees he had marked so certainly in his memory. He slowed the stallion, then stopped at the edge of the dense evergreens, turning to watch. A thousand aspen leaves fluttered as if in warning.

Only three rounds in the revolver, he reminded himself, but the rifle magazine was full. Within seconds, Archiveque appeared on the trail with his five gunmen. The Mexican saw Bart waiting, pistol drawn, and jerked his reins back. But the horse suddenly dropped from under him, sending him flying through the trees.

Bart's spirits leaped as he saw the first four horses trip and fall over each other. Two other riders tried to avoid the pile, reining their mounts off the trail, but they stopped in midair, their saddles running out from under them. The ropes stretched across the trail at ankle level had brought the horses down exactly as Bart had planned. And the ones suspended at chest level had unhorsed the other riders better than he could have dreamed.

He fired his three pistol rounds into the woods to scatter the frightened animals, then watched Domingo roll to his feet as he holstered his pistol and reached for the Marlin. He could have ridden safely for cover, but he knew he had Domingo beat. His rifle came up as the Mexican reached for his hip. He saw the scarred face over his irons and remembered Antonio's advice: The next time you see Domingo Archiveque in your sights . . .

The blast jerked the one-eared head back on its thick neck. Then Bart was gone, listening with satisfaction to the scattered horses of the gang crashing downhill through the pines.

The shootout with Archiveque would bring more trouble, of course. He might as well have been telegraphing his location all over the mountains with all the shooting he had been doing.

His instincts were telling him to ride now for everything he was worth to Shakehand Springs. But for now he had to stop. The pony would die running at this rate. He came to a rise in the trail, jumped down, and loosened the cinch.

Peso was puffing like a locomotive. He began to reload his weapons.

He wasn't worried about Semple's army. Troops moved too slowly in formation. The investigator from the Secret Service concerned him even less. Mountain trailing was not his specialty.

Marshal Yarborough worried him, though. What he lacked in brains, he made up for in trail savvy. This was going to be the narrowest escape in the history of the old Southwest.

FORTY - TWO

It had been less than forty-eight hours since Clarence Tankersly had come to warn him, and now the fifth baron of the Sacramentos was trying to think like a U.S. marshal, riding hard for Shakehand Springs. He hadn't seen Yarborough, but he knew the lawman would be closing in.

His strategy had to be apparent to them: Run for the Guadalupes and follow the mountains through Texas and into Old Mexico. What the marshal didn't know was that Bart had a fresh mount waiting at Shakehand Springs, courtesy of Uncle Dan Tolliver. That would put some distance between him and his pursuers. He would be halfway to Mexico by the time they got to a telegraph office.

He was riding near the east rim of the Sacramento River valley, staying off the ridges where he would be easily seen. He would have to cross the ridge soon to get to Shakehand Springs, and he knew just the place to do it.

About a mile ahead, the dirt trail turned to rock for a long stretch. When he hit the rock, he would rein his stallion up and over the ridge. Yarborough would lose his trail on the rocks, and that would slow him down.

This southern extreme of his barony was the least familiar to Bart, but he had been here just a year ago, thinking
about establishing a new ranch on the Sacramento River.
He had visited Shakehand Springs then. It was the only
water hole he knew of between here and the Guadalupes.

He stopped when Peso's hooves first rattled on stone, and
looked at the mountain slopes over his shoulder, looming
above him now. He was leaving forever. Already he had
left the firs and spruces. Here the ponderosa pines were not
quite so tall, not nearly as thick, and interspersed with
scrubby piñons. His barony was slipping away from him.

He saw nothing of Yarborough in the trees above, so he
spurred Peso up the steep rock slope, toward the ridge. He
wasted no time getting over the divide and back into cover,
but he did glimpse the Organ Mountains, far to the southwest, and the Guadalupes to the southeast. He remembered
his trip here last year. He had looked south from this ridge
in the night and had seen the lights of El Paso, seventy
miles away.

Four miles to Shakehand Springs.

As he loped the exhausted buckskin around a rocky
point, a uniformed man on horseback suddenly appeared
a hundred yards ahead of him. He jerked his reins, and the
stallion's hooves clattered against the rocky ground. The
soldier looked up from the trail he had been studying.

For several moments they stared. Each man had surprised the daylights out of the other. The baron risked no
move until he saw the soldier clawing at his holster.

Nothing to do now but charge. Gouging the stallion hard
with his spurs, Bart drew his revolver and began firing over
the head of the soldier. He gave the Mescalero war cry so
well that the soldier's horse shied from the trail. The baron
used every round in his Colt, and was near enough with
the last shot to see fear in the soldier's eyes.

The bluff had worked; the scout ran for cover. Would
he follow? No, too scared. He would go back for help. Sol-

diers fought in bodies. But who was he? Probably a scout Semple had sent out. How far away was Semple? Near enough to have heard the shots? Yarborough had certainly heard—and now had a new bearing. The gunshots would draw him like a homing pigeon.

Looking back to make sure the scout wasn't following, a flash of metal up the canyon caught Bart's eye. He had to rein the stallion in to make it out. Not one, but two—no, several glints of sunlight on metal. He squinted the dust from his eyes. A whole column of cavalry rode single file down the slope at a trot, coming to save its scout.

Semple must have guessed that Shakehand Springs was the place to cut the deposed baron's trail to freedom. Still, his lead was five minutes. Maybe six or seven. Enough time to switch his saddle to a new horse and run for the Guadalupes. He could see them, almost due east from here, dark mounds of timbered land rising above the desert, twenty or thirty miles away. It was going to be a punishing ride.

The sun remained just high enough to cast its light on Shakehand Springs when the baron first caught sight of the water near the base of the bluff. It was a small, clear pool on a rock-and-sand bed, surrounded by a few trees. And there was Uncle Dan, straddling a horse at the edge of the piñon brakes! The spare mount? In the shade, probably. The old man knew how to keep a horse fresh for a hard ride.

Peso was frothing. Since dawn, he had covered more ground than any horse should have to in a day. He was too tired to even drink when he carried the baron up next to the old mountain man.

"Where's the horse?" Bart asked, peering into the piñons and alligator junipers growing near the springs. "The cavalry and Marshal Yarborough are biting my tail!" The only answer he heard was the sound of the old musket's lock catching. When he turned back to Uncle Dan, he was looking down the long octagonal barrel.

"Don't try your luck, Baron, or ol' Kaintuck'll take a hunk out of you."

"What the hell is this, old man? You were supposed to bring me a fresh horse! Son of a bitch, you brought Semple, didn't you?"

Uncle Dan merely smirked as he turned his face toward the piñon brakes, keeping his eyes locked on the baron. "Lawyer!" he shouted, his voice full of gravel.

Faintly, Bart could hear the weaponry of the horse soldiers rattling not far enough up the canyon. Then he saw the shock of red hair coming down from the piñons above the springs.

"I brung you a fresh hoss, all right," Dan Tolliver drawled. "Didn't say who'd be ridin' it."

Bart's breath caught on a heartbeat and came up his throat hot as chimney smoke. Uncle Dan had sold him out. He thought about the revolver. He had spent all six rounds on the scout up the canyon. He would have to reach for the Marlin rifle in the saddle scabbard, but ol' Kaintuck had him covered, just five feet away.

"Bart," Randy said, pausing to look up the canyon, "we'd better talk."

"Like hell," Bart replied. He could already feel the checkered grip of the rifle against his right palm. He leaned to the off side of his horse as he drew the Marlin, but ol' Kaintuck followed.

The rifle ball hit his left shoulder like the blunt end of an axe, twisting him in the saddle. The stars he saw parted in time to reveal Uncle Dan wielding his long rifle overhead. The right hand worked alone with the Marlin, cocking the hammer, raising the muzzle, pulling the trigger.

He barely clung to the saddle as Peso lurched away from the other two horses. Uncle Dan and Randy hit the ground at the same time. The mountain man dead, the lawyer merely thrown. That was Randy yelling. Two horses were running.

He collected his wits and looked down at a bloody left sleeve. The arm wouldn't work. He managed to get his saddle squarely back under him, but couldn't find the reins. He remembered: Uncle Dan trained his mounts like buffalo horses, to respond to knee signals. He turned Peso to face the lawyer.

Locking his fingers in the loop of the rifle's lever, the baron slung its muzzle downward, pivoting the action open with one hand, sending a fresh round to the chamber. A wisp of gun smoke stung his nostrils like smelling salts. He glimpsed blue uniforms moving in the canyon above him, three minutes away.

Randy had clawed his way to the body of the dead mountain man. He looked up at his former friend, disbelief in his eyes. "My God, Bart, what have you done? What in God's name are you doing this for?"

"What did you think I would do? Go to prison without a fight?" He lifted the rifle and tried to find the lawyer in the wavering sights.

"My God, don't shoot me, Bart!" Randy yelled, jumping to his feet. "It was just a joke! For Christ's sake, Bart, it was only a joke!"

Bart narrowed his eyes and lowered the rifle. "What?" he said, wincing against the pain in his shoulder.

"The watermark was on a document from some other case. I just told the judge it was one of yours. He didn't know the difference. He can't read Spanish. It was a joke. I was going to have the marshal bring you to Santa Fe in leg irons and handcuffs; then I was going to tell the judge I had accidentally mixed up the papers. I was going to recommend that your grant be confirmed. We were going to have a big laugh over it, Bart."

"A laugh?" the baron growled. "We were going to have a *laugh?*" He could hear the colonel shouting orders now, forming the men into a skirmish line.

Randy smirked and shrugged. "I had to get you back for

that Indian attack you pulled on me. I had to save face in Santa Fe somehow. As God is my witness, I never dreamed the army and Regis's gang of thugs would come after you. I never dreamed you'd blow up your fort and your railroad and burn down your home."

"A laugh?" Bart said. He felt his anger and hatred settle. A snicker was coming on. "A laugh? Randy, you son of a bitch." His shoulders bounced on a couple of chuckles, racking the left one with pain. "Just a joke!"

"Yes, I swear, it was just a joke," Randy cried, sniggering uncertainly.

It was ludicrous! Bart laughed straight up at the skies of his barony. "*Just* a joke, your hide! It was the joke of all jokes, Randy! By golly, you got me with this one!"

They enjoyed a strange moment of camaraderie, shaking their heads, blinking tears of joy from their eyes. Then the smile wilted on Randy's face as he looked down at Dan Tolliver's corpse.

"You did it, didn't you, Bart? You really did forge those papers."

Bart heard the order given to advance, and he looked up the canyon. A wounded man on a tired horse would get nowhere. He had nothing left. "You told me once, Randy, that one of these practical jokes was going to get me in trouble." Resting the butt of the Marlin on his hip, he nudged his stallion back up the canyon. "I guess you were right. Adios."

He left Randy at Shakehand Springs with the dead mountain man. He would find the cavalry waiting for him around the bluff. When he glanced back, Randy was shaking his head, and scratching it.

"Hold it, Young!" a voice ordered, just before the baron prepared to charge the soldiers.

Looking up to the west, he saw Lin Yarborough against the glow of the evening sky. The sun was setting on his barony. He raked his spurs along the stallion's ribs, whirled the rifle from his hip, and blasted the sky over the head of the lawmen.

Yarborough was hell on fugitives. Bart felt two hammer blows hit him between the shoulders and the hips as he flailed the rifle on its lever again, working a fresh shell into the chamber. The line of horse soldiers appeared before him as a marshal's bullet sang against a rock. He loosed a round over the troops and one-handed the Marlin's action as he charged.

Every sense he had groped for life. He smelled the sharp fragrance of evergreens, saw tree-broken rays of sun streaking dust above the cavalry, felt the powerful surge of the good horse under him. He tasted his own blood. He heard Colonel Semple's saber ring from its scabbard, found its glint against the mountain.

He fired another round, but couldn't find the strength to sling the rifle's action open again. His left arm was flopping loosely at his side. He smiled up at the Lost Barony of the Sacramentos. The colonel's saber fell, and the whole line of rifles saluted him in unison.

In the instant it took for the bullets to reach him, Don Bartolome sensed a presence, and turned slowly to see Antonio loping beside him, grinning wide. The fourth baron joined the fifth. Then came the third baron from the trees, and the second from the sky. Then Nepomeceno himself appeared, with a silver-studded saddle and a white sombrero. They rode five abreast through the fusillade, and up the mountainside. They drew rein on the summit, looked over their barony, and swapped riddles until the thunder drove them home.

Forge

Award-winning authors
Compelling stories

· ·

Please join us at the website
below for more information
about this author and other great
Forge selections, and to sign up for
our monthly newsletter!

· · · · · **www.tor-forge.com** · · · ·